"I'll live the rest of my life wondering what it would have been like...."

Her arm swept toward the shaded, grassy lawn. "I almost wish I hadn't stopped you," she whispered.

"Would you stop me now?" So softly she could barely hear the words, he whispered temptation in her ear. Leaning forward, ignoring the hand she thrust against his chest, he bent to her, his breath warm against her face.

She shivered, beguiled by the thought of his hands against her skin, lured by the dark splendor of his scarred face, enticed by the image of their coming together. And then she thought of the emptiness she would face, once she'd known the joy of loving Shay, only to have him walk away. It stretched before her, and she closed her eyes against the pain.

"Could you do that? Take everything I've offered you—and then walk away from me?"

Praise for Carolyn Davidson's recent works

The Midwife
"…an earthy, emotional love story,
peopled with unforgettable characters."
—*Affaire de Coeur*

The Tender Stranger
"Davidson wonderfully captures gentleness
in the midst of heart-wrenching challenges,
portraying the extraordinary possibilities
that exist within ordinary marital love."
—*Publishers Weekly*

The Wedding Promise
"…a tense, involving love story…a beautiful,
old-fashioned romance with a charmingly sensuous touch."
—*Romantic Times Magazine*

The Seduction of Shay Devereaux
Harlequin Historical #556—April 2001

THE SEDUCTION OF SHAY DEVEREAUX

Carolyn Davidson

HARLEQUIN®

TORONTO • NEW YORK • LONDON
AMSTERDAM • PARIS • SYDNEY • HAMBURG
STOCKHOLM • ATHENS • TOKYO • MILAN • MADRID
PRAGUE • WARSAW • BUDAPEST • AUCKLAND

ISBN 0-373-29156-6

THE SEDUCTION OF SHAY DEVEREAUX

Copyright © 2001 by Carolyn Davidson

Printed in U.S.A.

Please address questions and book requests to:
Harlequin Reader Service
U.S.: 3010 Walden Ave., P.O. Box 1325, Buffalo, NY 14269
Canadian: P.O. Box 609, Fort Erie, Ont. L2A 5X3

Because you read whatever I hand you,
and give me your unbiased opinion...
Because you clean up my messes when
I'm running behind schedule...
Because you cook for my family
when I invite you for dinner...
Because we share a love of books
and discuss them by the hour...
Because you call me "friend"...
This book is dedicated to you, Betty Barrs

And to the man who tells me
he loves me every single day...
I love you, too, Mr. Ed

Prologue

The hand reached for him. Cold, skeletal fingers wrapped around his wrist with unbelievable strength. Shrinking from the grasp, Shay groaned aloud, and the sound of his own voice wakened him. He sat upright on the narrow bed, his eyes searching the darkness, his breathing harsh and rapid.

A dream…another nightmare. The second this week. And yet, more than a dream, for the memories evoked by that groping hand were all too valid. All too painfully real.

Rolling from his bed, he stalked to the open window, looking out upon the thick greenery hedging his hideaway. Moss hung from oak trees, silver in the moonlight, and the grass held glistening drops of moisture, where dew lay heavy on each blade. It must be nearly dawn, he decided, resting one hand on the wide window frame.

He watched as an owl spread wide wings, swooping soundlessly across the span of sky between barn and trees. Dangling prey hung from sharp talons, and Shay felt a strange affinity for the hapless creature. His low chuckle was without amusement, holding instead dark shreds of bitter remembrance. He knew only too well the feeling of being captured, of the torment endured as soul and body were torn asunder, until all that remained was a shell of manhood, its essence swept up in hours and days of misery. He closed his eyes and saw another glimpse of that place called *Elmira.*

Another name for Hell.

Men with little to live for had been freed at the end of the conflict. He counted himself among that number. Some, with wives and children awaiting their return, had been buried beneath the northern soil. One of them, Carl Pennington, had been his friend, his commanding officer. During the time they served together, they'd discovered their families lived less than a hundred miles apart. Taken prisoners during the same battle, Shay had survived. Carl had not lived to be released.

He'd given Shay his last bits of food, aware that his own life was fast ebbing, yet grimly determined that Shay should survive. And survive he had, kept alive by another man's sacrifice.

"Promise me, Gaeton." Death molded Carl's features, yet he'd struggled to breathe. The same fever had killed many, perhaps hundreds, in this camp. But Carl's strength lay in his love for the wife and child he'd left behind.

"Promise me, Gaeton." Again he'd demanded the pledge, and Shay's heart plunged within him as he recalled the answer he'd given.

"Gaeton Devereaux died the day he walked into this prison," he'd muttered. "I'm not sure there's enough of him left to *make* a promise."

"Take care of them." Carl had gasped the words with his last breath, and Shay's hand had closed the staring eyes. Shay looked out upon the darkness, reliving once more that hellish day. Remembering the promise he'd refused to make. It had haunted him for four years. As had the man who'd trusted him.

"Damn you, Carl." The curse breathed softly upon the humid air and Shay bent his head in surrender.

For four years he'd sought peace, making his way from one town to another, one ranch to the next, regretting the words he'd swallowed, the promise he'd refused to give. He'd managed to win more hands of poker than any man had a right to claim, and found his ease with less than a handful of women. And all the wandering had brought him back to where he'd begun. Louisiana...where his family lived and worked the home place. Louisana...where Carl Pennington's wife and child lived from hand to mouth, or so he'd heard only yesterday.

Here where Shay's name had been Gaeton Devereaux.

The curse he'd spoken was beyond recall. Ahead of him waited the task he would undertake, the promise he would finally speak aloud, and honor.

"Rest in peace, Carl," he whispered. "I promise you. I'll do what I can."

Chapter One

March, 1869

Four years. She'd given herself four years, measuring the days since the letter had come, telling her of Carl's death. At first, when his horse had carried him away, she'd been hopeful. Sure he would return, the battle won. Soon, he'd come back to her and the long days and nights would be in the past.

Her laughter was bitter as she recalled her youthful optimism. For close to six years now, she'd struggled. Struggled against impossible odds, enough to scatter every lovely dream to the four winds. At first, in those early days, she'd been optimistic, vowing to put her shoulder to the wheel, as her father used to say, and make a success of the plantation. And then the awful letter had come, and that day she'd stiffened her spine and vowed to give herself four more years to make a profit and gain a foothold on that elusive thing called success.

No more. She'd run out of time. Jenny Pennington lifted a hand to her brow, her gaze seeking the horizon. The field before her was the brilliant green of early hay, ready for reaping. Three men worked in tandem, swinging scythes in a rhythm that seemed to depend on the song they sang, a mournful tune that tugged at her emotions.

She turned away, her strides long as she headed for the wagon, anxious to flee from the harmony, that minor key that spoke of betrayal and sorrow. Her skirt caught on the wagon wheel and she muttered a word beneath her breath as she tugged it free.

"That's one of those words you told me not to say, Mama." From behind the wagon seat, the voice of her son admonished her.

"You'll get soap on your tongue if you try it," she warned him. "I won't have you using vile language, Marshall Pennington."

"Yes, ma'am," he murmured agreeably.

Jenny picked up the reins and glanced over her shoulder. He was tall for a boy just a few months past his fifth birthday, and his grin met her gaze. "I won't say it again, either," she told the boy. The leathers cracked over the broad backs of her team and the wagon jolted into motion.

Behind her the sound faded, muffled by the trees surrounding her, carried by the breeze toward the east. "Are we gonna eat dinner pretty soon?" Marshall asked. On his knees now, he leaned against the back of the wagon seat, one hand clutching her shoulder.

"As soon as we get back to the house," she told him. "Isabelle will have it ready for us." And for that she could be grateful. Three men and one woman remained of the workers that had kept the Pennington Plantation in order.

No wonder the crops shrank every year, the house sat empty, but for the four rooms they used. The entire top floor was vacant, the furniture long since sold at auction, and for a pittance at that. Bare spots on the wallpaper bore silent witness to pieces of art she'd sacrificed for seed and wages. Using what little of value she had available, she'd bartered and bargained, until this spring, when her favorite portrait had purchased cotton seed for planting, and food staples enough to last through the summer.

She'd cried that night, sobbed into her pillow, stifling the sound so that Isabelle would not hear. For too long, she'd struggled. For too many days she'd worked in the fields. For too many nights she'd held Carl's pillow against her barren body, yearning for the warmth of his embrace.

And for what? Her long years of work and sacrifice had earned her but a respite from the inevitable end. For whatever it was worth, Pennington Plantation would be sold. Once the crops were harvested this year, once the cotton was weighed and sold, the plantation house and the acres surrounding it would be put up for auction to the highest bidder.

I'm sorry, Carl. She'd whispered those words more times than she could count. And now, for the last time, she repeated them aloud. "I'm sorry, Carl."

"Are you talkin' to my papa?" Marshall asked in her ear.

A smile teased at Jenny's lips. "You'll think your mama is daft, sweetheart. And yes, I was talkin' to your papa."

"What are you sorry for, Mama?" The boy climbed over the wagon seat, teetering precariously atop the backboard until he gained his balance and plopped beside his mother.

"You wouldn't understand," she told him. "Matter of fact, I don't understand it myself." And wasn't that the truth. It seemed that hard work should somehow be rewarded in this life, but thus far, she hadn't found the end of her particular rainbow. Maybe her reward was to be in the rearing of this small boy, the best part of her inheritance.

The house loomed before them, windows gleaming in the sunlight. Isabelle was a great believer in cleanliness. Windows and floors got a weekly going-over, and one expense Jenny was not allowed to scrimp on was the purchase of vinegar for window washing and the preserving of pickles, and thick bars of soap for laundry and cleaning. Strange that her household should be run by the dictates of a former slave, Jenny thought. Former slave and best friend, she amended silently. Almost her only friend, actually. A woman alone was not welcomed in polite company, and a widow living hand-to-mouth was not often included on what few guest lists existed these days.

Marshall jumped from the wagon as she drew it to a halt near the house. "I'll carry in the basket, Mama," he said, running to the rear of the wagon bed.

Jenny climbed down quickly, lest Marshall should tug at the basket and send it flying to the ground. Always eager to help, he tended to rush headlong into things, and she was hard put sometimes to harness his energy. Today was no exception, and he danced impatiently as she rounded the back of the wagon.

"Hurry, Mama. Isabelle promised me a treat when we got back from takin' dinner out to the men." He reached for the handle and Jenny delivered it up to him, watching as he carried it to the house. "I'm here, Isabelle," he called out. "Open the door for me."

Jenny turned away, leading the mules to the barn, leaving Marshall in capable hands. She blinked in the shadows as the team halted just inside the wide doorway, and then she set to work unbuckling the harness. Sliding halters in place, she led the pair through the barn to the corral where she spent long minutes wiping them down. They gleamed in the sunlight, and she bent to examine their hooves, plucking a stray bit of stone from where it had lodged in one shoe.

"I don't need you to go lame on me, Pretty Boy," she murmured, rubbing at the bigger mule's flank. He turned his head and nudged her shoulder. "I don't have anything for you, sweetheart," she told him, stepping to his head.

"The carrots are about gone, and Isabelle wants what's left for cooking."

From behind her a horse nickered, announcing its arrival, and her team answered in unison. Jenny turned quickly, leaning back against the jack, looking up in surprise. Company was rare, and since the end of the war, what few men meandered by were not always kindly. She'd learned to carry a gun with her, or at least have one close at hand, but right now the nearest thing to a weapon was in the tack room.

A man sat astride a black horse, bending his head to move beneath the open doorway. His shirtsleeves were rolled up to his elbows, a large pistol was holstered against his thigh. To the left side of his saddle, just touching his hip, a scabbard held a long gun, probably a rifle, she thought. And yet he was relaxed in the saddle, both hands visible, fingers curved against the pommel of his saddle.

"Jenny Pennington?" he asked. His gaze was penetrating, his eyes shaded by the brim of his hat, and his voice deep, almost rasping. No trace of a drawl softened his words, and no smile curved those wide lips.

"Yes," she answered curtly. "I'm Mrs. Pennington." And if he wanted to take her mules, or the lone horse that grazed in the pasture, or rummage through the house for whatever booty he might find, she would forever curse her lack of caution today.

"Was your husband named Carl?" At her nod, he glanced behind him, through the barn, toward the house. As if he were determined to be in the right place, he mentioned the facts that made up the boundaries of her life. "And is the boy yours?"

She nodded. "What do you want with me?" Her voice came out sharper than she'd intended. The mention of Carl's name did that to her, put her on the defensive and brought resentment to the surface. As much as she'd loved him, and loved him still, she reminded herself. The fact that he'd gone to war and left her to cope with impossible odds was enough to make her angry whenever she thought about it. And lately, she'd thought about it a lot.

He slid from the horse's back in an easy motion that did little to reassure her, dropping the reins to the ground. His horse stood, immobile but for an ear that flicked, and then was still. Before her, the man was sleek and agile, garbed in dark clothing. He looked...*threatening*. It was the only word she could think of to describe him.

There was about him an almost tangible sense of menace, a glimpse of danger in the depths of dark eyes visible beneath a wide-brimmed hat. It shadowed his face, but could not conceal the scar that slashed one cheek from jawbone to temple. White against deeply tanned skin, it proclaimed a message of danger, of battles fought, and apparently won, since the man wearing it was alive. And, she'd warrant, there were those who'd died at his hand.

His gaze raked her, measuring and weighing, and she stiffened, squaring her shoulders. "What do you want?" she repeated. "There's not much left here if you're looking for a handout."

She thought one corner of his mouth lifted, a faint sign of amusement, and then he shook his head. "Carl sent me."

A rush of heat rose to envelop her, and she drew in a trembling breath. "What are you talking about? Carl is dead. He died in the north, in a prison camp."

Her visitor nodded. "I know. I was with him."

"You knew him? You were there when he died?" The words sounded fragile, as if they might disappear on a breath of wind, and she gasped for air, filling her lungs.

He stepped closer and strong fingers gripped her elbow, steering her into the barn. She tottered, her legs barely holding her erect. A heavy piece of tree stump sat upright against the wall, providing a seat, and Jenny sank onto its surface, grateful that her trembling limbs needn't carry her farther.

He crouched in front of her, one long finger nudging at his hat brim. Silent, unmoving, he watched her, and she drew in deep breaths, thankful for this short respite before Carl's name would once more be spoken between them. A chill took her unaware, and her arms wrapped protectively around her waist as she bowed her head.

Closing her eyes, she blotted out his image, the black shirt, the gleaming dark hair, and the ragged scar. "Who are you?" The whisper was faint, but he responded with a single word.

"Shay."

"Is that your last name?" she asked, looking up from beneath her lashes, aware suddenly that tears blurred her vision. She folded her hands atop her knees and straightened her shoulders, attempting to gain some small measure of control.

He shook his head. "No, but it doesn't matter for now."

"Tell me about him," she said, embarrassed that her voice trembled.

"All right," Shay began, his words a sigh, his voice bleak. "He had the fever, ma'am. A lot of men died from it. I only got sick with it, and lived to tell it. I was lucky." And at those words he laughed, a rusty sound that held no humor. "I guess *lucky* isn't the word for it."

His fingers touched the back of her hand, barely moving against her skin. "You were married to a good man, Mrs. Pennington. When he died, his last thoughts were of you and your child."

"My *child*? He never knew I'd had a boy? I wrote," she said. "I sent letters after Marshall was born," Her lips compressed and she struggled for control. "I never heard back from him."

"We didn't get much mail from home. He didn't know if it was a boy or girl."

Jenny looked up, aware now that tears fell without ceasing, yet unable to halt their flow. His fingers enveloped hers and she leaned toward the warmth, as though the hand that had touched Carl might yet carry some faint trace of the man she'd loved. Her indrawn breath caught a scent of leather and wood smoke from his clothing, an aroma of soap that lingered on his skin. A male essence that spoke to a part of her she'd thought long since dead.

"I'm sorry," Jenny breathed, tugging her fingers from his grip. "I don't usually fall apart this way. In fact," she murmured, her breath trembling, "I thought I was all done with the mourning and the carrying-on."

A shadow fell in the front entrance of the barn, and she looked up, catching a glimpse of a figure in the doorway. A shotgun held firmly before her, Isabelle watched in silence. Jenny shook her head, waving a hand reassuringly. "It's all right," she said, aware that the other woman feared for her well-being.

In one swift movement Shay rose and spun to face the threat, his hand falling to the butt of his revolver. One knee bent, he surveyed the dark-skinned woman, unmoving as Isabelle's sharp gaze took stock. "You want to turn that barrel in another direction, ma'am?" he asked quietly.

Isabelle hesitated, then at another nod from Jenny, she turned the long gun, cradling it in her arms. "I didn't know what was goin' on out here, Jenny. Marshall come runnin' in and said a man was in the barn with you." She walked a few steps closer. "You been cryin'?"

Jenny shook her head. "No, not really." Carefully she stood, willing her legs not to buckle. "Mr. Shay has come here with a message from…my husband."

Isabelle snorted unbelievingly. "Mr. Carl's been dead a

long time, Jenny. If this fella's got word for you, what took him so long to bring it?''

"I don't know." Jenny took a step, steadying herself, one hand touching the wall beside her. "We hadn't even gotten to the message part."

She turned to Shay. "Do you want to put your horse up and stay for a bite to eat? We're about to have our noon meal. I'm sure Isabelle has enough for you to join us."

He nodded. "Thank you, ma'am."

Jenny walked past him. "We'll talk in the house." Her mind spinning, she followed Isabelle from the barn, trudging across the yard, aware of the curiosity that hung between them.

Isabelle opened the door and Jenny walked past her into the kitchen. "What you s'pose he wants with you?" Isabelle asked, reaching high to place the gun over the door. Two pegs held it in place and Isabelle, satisfied that it was secure, stepped back. "I never seen a man so hard lookin', Miss Jenny. There's no give to him, not one little bit, is there?" She slanted a look from dark eyes, and Jenny caught a glimpse of fear within their soft depths.

"I'm not afraid of him," she said quietly. She found another plate and placed it on the table, then reached for silverware from the drawer. "I think he's ridden a long way to get here, probably had other things to see to before he set out to find me."

"I'd think carryin' a message from a dead man to his wife would rate pretty high up on the scale," Isabelle said darkly. "You think he's tellin' the truth?"

The sound of boots on the porch caught Jenny's ear and she shook her head at Isabelle. "Later," she whispered, stepping to the kitchen cupboard to draw forth cups for coffee.

A pot sat on the back of the stove, and Isabelle lifted it, a folded dish towel protecting her hand from the hot handle.

"Let's see how strong this is, first off," she said, pouring the dark liquid slowly.

"A little cream will do wonders," Jenny told her.

"There's a whole pitcherful already rose to the top from this morning's milking," Isabelle said. "I'll pour it off and set some aside for your coffee. Thought I'd make rice pudding for supper. We got eggs aplenty."

Jenny turned to the door, where Shay waited admission. "Come in, Mr.—"

"Just Shay," he reminded her, opening the screen door and stepping into the kitchen. One hand lifted his hat, then held it, as he glanced around the room.

"You can hang it on a hook next to the pantry, if you like," Jenny said. She watched as he crossed the room, met his gaze as he turned back to face her. "Coffee?" she asked, motioning to the table where two cups stood, steam rising.

He nodded, pulling out a chair. "Y'all help yourselves to fresh bread," Isabelle said, her dark eyes intent on the visitor. From beneath a dish towel, she produced a plate, placing it between Jenny and their visitor. A small bowl containing butter was beside it, and a knife lay across the edge of the dish.

Jenny nodded at Shay. "Go ahead."

He glanced at the sink in the corner. "You mind if I wash up?" At Jenny's nod of agreement, he rose, then stepped to the drain board where a bucket of water rested, pouring a small amount into the wash pan. Isabelle provided a bowl of soft soap and a towel, and in moments, Shay was back at the table. "Thanks," he murmured, picking up the knife and spreading butter across a slice of bread.

"Isabelle baked this morning," Jenny told him, pouring cream in her coffee, then adding a heaping teaspoon of sugar. A bowl of stew appeared in the middle of the table and Jenny reached for the serving ladle. Shay nodded as she cast him an inquiring glance, and she served a generous portion on his plate.

The steam rose and he inhaled it, then spoke his satisfaction. "This is much appreciated, ma'm. I haven't had a hot meal in a couple of days." Picking up his fork, he stabbed a bite of potato and began eating. His gaze scanned the room, settling on Isabelle, who watched from near the stove. "You've already eaten?" he asked.

"When I fed Marshall." Her answer was curt, but he seemed uncaring, returning to his food, picking up his cup to drink. After a few moments, his first hunger apparently appeased, he leaned back in his chair. "You're alone here?" he asked.

Isabelle glanced up at the shotgun over the door and Jenny shook her head, then brushed her mouth with a linen napkin. "No, there's Isabelle's husband and their two sons. They're working in the hayfield. And you've seen my son."

He nodded, chewing long and hard on the crust of bread he'd chosen, then bent to his dinner once more.

"Do you think my boy looks like Carl?" she asked after a moment. "His folks are gone, over three years now, but his mama said Marshall was the image of his daddy."

"Hard to say," Shay temporized.

"Carl had the same brown eyes. But then you know that. Having seen him more recently than I. Mine are blue." She paused for a moment, but the words would not be halted, falling from her lips as if she must somehow reinforce Carl's memory through the small child he'd left behind. "Marshall's hair is streaked from the sunshine now, I know. But you should see it in the winter. It darkens up, without a trace of red in it like—" Jenny hesitated, aware of rambling on. She lifted her cup and sipped at the bitter stuff. Her heart was stuttering in her chest, and she felt her throat close as she asked the question she'd held within her heart for the past half hour.

"How did he die?" Her hands fluttered, then settled in her lap. "Did he suffer long? Was there a doctor in the camp?" She looked up at him and winced at the forbidding look he wore. "Please, Mr. Shay."

The woman was trembling, her mouth twitching at the corner, her chin wobbling. Damn, she was about to cry again, and he didn't know if he could stand it. Enough that he'd put this visit in limbo for so long, now he had to dredge up all the memories and break her heart all over again.

"There were a couple of doctors in camp, but we tried not to let the Union army know who they were. They'd have been taken out and put to work in the army hospital for the northern troops." He shrugged, curling long fingers around his cup. "There wasn't any medicine anyway, ma'am. We all just did the best we could."

"You said you were with him?" she asked, biting at her lip. "He spoke of us?"

"Yes, ma'am. I told you he sent his love, to both you and the child." That hadn't been exactly how it happened, but instinct told him she would be soothed by the words. Her eyes filled with tears and they overflowed, dampening the bodice of her dress as they fell. His gaze rested there.

"Mr. Shay?" Her hand lay on the table now, reaching for him, yet even as he watched, her fingers curled into a fist. "Did he say anything else?"

He shook his head. *Take care of them.* The words that haunted his dreams had brought him here, on a roundabout route, to be sure. But here he was, and here he'd stay until he was sure she was safe, had enough to eat, and that the boy was taken care of, had some sort of future in the offing.

"Have you got any crops in, ma'am?" he asked. "Is there any livestock in the pastures?"

"The kitchen garden's planted, of course, and it's almost time to plant corn, maybe next week or the week after.

After the hay gets put up. We've a cow in the barn, and a good flock of chickens. There's three hens setting on nests. We'll have chicks soon, and fryers in a couple of months."

"Horses?" he asked.

"A team of mules. They're in the corral, waiting for me to take them back to the hay field later on. And a mare to pull the buggy."

"Nothing to ride?"

"No, the Yanks took most of the horseflesh hereabouts with them when they passed through. We were lucky to keep what we did. Noah and the boys hid the animals in the woods. We penned up the chickens in the root cellar and put a washtub over the door when the army came through. I thought they were going to burn the place, but—" She hesitated and glanced at Isabelle, whose mouth shut reprovingly.

"They left us alone, and went on without torching the house and barn." Beneath the freckles dotting her cheeks, Jenny's face was pale and her gaze focused steadily on the tabletop between them.

His instincts told him she'd left much unsaid. Her hired help, or whatever relationship the woman had to Jenny, was keeping secrets, as was the girl across the table from him. She wasn't much more than a girl, yet she'd borne up beneath the load she'd been called to carry, and borne up well. Her dress was ill-fitting, tight across the bodice, as if it had fit a younger, more slender female. Well-worn, and washed until the faint pattern of flowers had submitted their color to soap and water, it looked on the verge of being fit for the ragbag.

Yet, she wore it well, and he had a fleeting glimpse of what it must have looked like, years ago when both dress and woman had been untouched by the desolation of the war.

Jenny looked up at him, her dignity once more in place,

only damp spots on her dress remaining of the tears she'd shed for the memory of her husband. "Will you stay the night?" she asked politely.

"I can sleep in the barn." He glanced out the window to where the shabby outbuildings were drenched in sunshine. "I have a bedroll, ma'am. Is there hay left in the loft?"

"No, but there will be in a couple of days, once it dries in the field. The men are out there cutting it now."

"Can I give them a hand? I've done my share of swinging a scythe in my day."

"And where was that?" she asked, her eyes lighting with interest.

"I was born and raised here in the south, ma'am." And that would be enough for now, he decided, rising and reaching for his hat. "I'll just ride my horse out to where the men are, and put in a few hours' work. Maybe I'll do enough to earn my supper."

"Wait," Jenny said quickly. "I'll take you out in the wagon. Noah won't know who you are."

"I'll tell him," Shay said politely. "Don't worry. It'll be fine."

And it was. Coming upon the three men, their heads covered with straw hats, their arms swinging in unison to the mournful notes they sang, he'd sat astride his stallion for long minutes. One of the younger men had noticed him first, glancing up, and then halting midswing. The older man, Noah probably, turned to face him, taking his hat off and nodding slowly.

"Sir?" The tone was polite, yet wary, and Shay slid from his horse. A hundred feet or so separated them, and his steps were unhurried as he watched the three men.

"I'm here to help," he said. "Carl Pennington sent me."

A visible shiver went through the shortest of the three

men, and he turned quickly to the eldest of the group. "Pa?"

Noah stepped forward. "You knew Mr. Carl? In the army?"

Shay nodded. "I was with him when he died."

Noah looked him over well, his shoulders straightening, his head erect. "Took you long enough to get here, I'd say, mister."

Shay nodded his agreement. There was no arguing that point. "I'm here now."

"You wanta use the scythe or start rakin'?" Noah asked.

Shay held out his hand. "I'll give you a break. You can rake, if that's all right."

Hand outstretched, he waited as the older man scrutinized him, and then, with a nod at his two helpers, walked the few steps it took to face Shay.

"These here are my boys, Caleb and Joseph. Miss Isabelle's my woman." He held out the scythe and Shay took it from the callused hand.

"I'll just tie my horse," he said. A glade of trees edged the hayfield on three sides, telling wordlessly how the field had been wrenched from the woods surrounding it. Shay led his horse into the shade and slid the bridle from his mouth and over his head, then reached into his saddlebag for a halter. He put it in place, adding a long lead line before he loosened the saddle cinch.

"You can work at keepin' the grass mowed," he murmured to his stallion, leaving the animal knee-deep in lush greenery. The scythe fit his hand as if he'd only yesterday laid it down, and in moments he was adjusting his swing to the momentum of the other men. The sun beat down through his dark shirt and sweat beaded his brow, burning his eyes as it dripped from his forehead. Tying his kerchief around his brow relieved that situation, and he moved forward, enjoying the flex of muscles unused to the physical labor of harvest.

For a while the singing stopped, and then Noah took it up again, timing his rake to the rhythm he set, his sons following suit. The scythe sliced hay smoothly, and Shay silently thanked whoever had spent long moments with a stone, sharpening its blade. The men surrounding him worked as a team, apparently accepting his presence.

Shay thought of those he'd known, worked with, played poker with, then ridden away from during the past years. All the while heading back to where he'd lived as a boy. The ranch in Kansas had been the latest stopping place. Until circumstances had sent him on his way, and he was once more traveling. Finally with purpose.

It was time, he'd decided. Time to face the past, time to find the woman and child Carl Pennington had spoken of. Maybe time to finally heed Carl's plea. He'd never agreed to his friend's request, but those dying words had haunted him for too long.

Now, whatever he could do to help Carl's wife, whether it be by the sweat of his brow, or the gold in his pocket, he'd do his best. The thought of Jenny, copper hair shimmering in the sunlight, brown eyes soft against his scarred face, was enough to make him eager for suppertime to arrive. And that thought caught him up short.

He was here to help Carl's widow, not take advantage of her. It would be easy to look on her as an available woman. Honesty nudged him to admit he already had. She might be available, but not to a man like Shay. He'd soiled his hands beyond redemption, and touching Jenny Pennington... His body hardened at the thought, and he swung the scythe with a jerk, spoiling the rhythm he'd set. It hit the ground and vibrated in his hand, and he halted, lifting his face to the sun, closing his eyes against the radiance.

She was there, burned into his memory, waving locks of

hair tempting his fingers, gentle eyes melting his defenses. And scattered across the fabric of her dress, luring his gaze to the curves defining her breasts, were tears she'd shed for Carl Pennington.

Chapter Two

Giving the man run of her house was not wise. Even as Jenny heard his boots on the curving staircase, she knew she'd probably made a mistake. True, his chosen room was on the second floor, and her own was the old library near the front door. Also true was the fact he'd offered to sleep in the barn.

To which she'd demurred. It was not proper to send a gentleman to sleep in the hayloft when perfectly good rooms were standing empty in the house. Even if those rooms were stripped bare of furnishings and cold during the short months of winter. He wouldn't be here that long anyway, she comforted herself.

Standing at the foot of the curved staircase, she cocked her head to listen as his footsteps moved on down the uncarpeted hallway upstairs, and stopped. Not the master suite, she decided, with a sitting room attached. She backed up a bit, peering past the balcony, seeking a glimpse of his tall figure. The only rooms that far down the corridor were the smaller bedchambers, designed for children, yet it seemed he'd chosen one of them for his own.

"Miss Jenny? What're you doing?" Isabelle's soft voice

from behind her had Jenny rounding about quickly, her
cheeks flaming.

"Just looking after our guest," she muttered.

"Looking *at* him, is more like it," Isabelle said, her own
gaze following the path Jenny's had taken. "And ain't he
a fine one to watch."

"He's chosen to stay in one of the smaller rooms, I believe. I can't think that he'll be comfortable with just a
bedroll, but he insisted."

"There's a couple of mattresses in the attic, if you want
Noah to bring one down for him," Isabelle offered. "He'd
might as well be as comfortable as we can make him."

Jenny nodded, walking toward the back of the house.
The kitchen was warm, the stove throwing off an abundance of heat, and she opened the back door, allowing air
to flow through the room. "For someone who didn't take
to him…" Her words slowed, and then she turned to face
her friend. "I thought you didn't like him," she said quietly.

"Haven't decided about that yet," Isabelle told her.
"But I decreed right off the bat he was a prime specimen."

"He looks a bit the worse for wear, I think," Jenny said,
her words mumbled into the apron she pulled over her head.
"And he probably won't be here long enough for me to
change my mind."

Isabelle nodded wisely. "We'll see." She handed Jenny
plates and silverware, then turned back to the stove. "Noah
says the man's a hard worker."

Finished with setting the table, Jenny walked to the back
door. Her hands lifted to her forehead, brushing back tendrils of hair that defied her best efforts at tidiness. "He'll
soon tire of working long hours and getting nothing in return."

"Beg your pardon, ma'am. I didn't mean to eavesdrop,
but I think you've got it all wrong." From behind her,

Shay's deep tones denied her theory, and she spun to face him, one hand rising to cover her mouth.

"I didn't hear you, sir. You startled me." It seemed the man called Shay could move silently when the mood struck him.

He was quiet for a moment, watching her from beneath lowered brows. "Maybe I should have knocked. But then, the door wasn't shut," he said finally. "As to what I overheard, I beg to differ with you." His hands folded into fists, then rose to rest against his hips. "I'm here to fulfill an obligation to a friend. Receiving a reward doesn't enter into it."

"It's a good thing," Jenny returned starkly. "A floor to sleep on and three meals a day will be the limit of your pay." Her words sounded harsh to her ears and she bit at her lip, ashamed of herself.

"Miss Jenny, don't forget the mattress," Isabelle reminded helpfully.

Jenny cast her a grateful look, softening her tone. "I'll have Noah help you bring a mattress out of the attic for your room," she said. "Isabelle reminded me that we put a couple of them up there."

Shay nodded, relaxing his stance, one hand sliding into his pocket, the other flexing open against his thigh. "I'll take care of it later on. For now, I'll just need a container for water, so I can wash in the morning, ma'am."

Buckets were in short supply, the two in best condition being used for milking the cow. Jenny thought of the rough wooden ones in the barn and dismissed the idea. There was no choice, she decided. A guest must receive preference.

"I'll give you the pitcher from my room," she told him. "There's a basin with it."

"I won't take yours," he said sharply. "Surely you have a kettle I can use."

She shook her head. "Most everything is gone, sold

piece by piece. We only have enough to cook in, nothing extra.''

His eyes narrowed, taking in her dress, the scuffed toes of her shoes and the worn apron she'd slipped into only moments past. ''You haven't spent much on yourself, have you?''

A flush climbed her cheeks and she felt her jaw tauten as he took inventory of her clothing. ''I'm not complaining. We're getting along.''

''For how long?'' he asked bluntly. ''You need something besides a field of corn and a couple of cuttings of hay to get you through the year. Where's your cash crop?''

''They're still buying cotton,'' she told him proudly. ''And ours has always been some of the best in the parish. We'll be planting ten acres pretty soon.''

''Not enough of it to support you,'' he said, and the truth of his judgment pierced her to the quick.

''There's no sense in planting more than we can harvest,'' she told him. ''And with only the five of us to pick…''

''There'll be four men this year, and the boy can help out,'' he told her, amending her words.

Jenny's lips compressed, holding back words better unspoken, given her tendency to allow her temper full rein. Marshall was a baby, not fit yet for field work. And the son of a gentleman, to boot.

''He's not too young to carry sacks out to us and help dump them in the wagon,'' Shay told her, his words gentle, as if he sensed her thoughts. ''He shouldn't stand by and watch his mother work. He'll learn to do his share, and probably feel better for it.''

''You haven't the right,'' she said, her words stiff with anger.

''Carl gave me the right. He asked me to come here, and

part of my duty to him is to teach his son how to deal with whatever life sends his way.''

There was no rebuttal to that argument, Jenny decided, for if Shay told the truth, Carl had indeed bestowed upon him that duty. And Shay gave every indication of being a gentleman, no matter his appearance. His speech, his bearing, even the tilt of his head and the calm arrogance of his manner, gave testimony to his claim. Whoever his family, they had reared him well.

''I can't turn down your help. I can't afford to be proud,'' she said quietly. ''If Carl sent you, I'll give you leave to do as he asked.''

Shay bowed his head, a movement she sensed signified his acknowledgment of her words. She'd accepted his help. Now to learn compliance. For six years she'd been in charge, controlled the work done on Pennington Plantation. A sense of relief washed over her as she looked at the man who'd offered—perhaps insisted—on taking that control from her.

For the life of him Shay didn't understand how she'd talked him out of sleeping in the hayloft. Yet, here he was, in the house this morning. He stirred, then rolled over, thankful for the mattress he'd hauled from the attic by candlelight last night. It surely beat sleeping on the hard floor, and was a far cry from the burned-out house he'd slept in the past couple of days.

He rolled to his feet and listened to a rooster in the chicken yard. ''At least one of us has something to crow about,'' he muttered beneath his breath, pouring water from the flowered pitcher Jenny had pressed into his hands. He'd carried it, and the matching bowl up the stairs, unwillingly to be sure, but unable to deny her the right to do as she pleased in her own home. One way or another, he'd see to it that a bucket became available for his use today, and return the china to her bedroom, where it belonged.

In the meantime, he could enjoy the image floating through his mind, that of Jenny's hand pouring water for her use. Of Jenny's skin being cleansed by some floral scented soap. He lifted a towel to his face, inhaling the fresh aroma of sunshine clinging to its fibers. Maybe he'd settle for that, he decided. She didn't need some fancy milled bar to make her smell good. Whatever she used to wash with reminded him of meadow grass and spring flowers.

His mouth tightened as he sensed the direction of his thoughts. Water splashed over his hair as he doused himself in the china basin, and he closed his eyes against the blue flowers that reminded him of violets and forget-me-nots. It was time to fill his belly with food and get out to the barn. The men would be waiting and he wouldn't be deemed a laggard by anyone. Especially not three men whose cooperation he needed if he was to make any sort of a success of this venture.

They were waiting anyway, he discovered, stepping out onto the back porch. Isabelle had fed them earlier, before setting the table for Jenny and the boy. Whether he was to have eaten with the men or with Jenny, he didn't know. But, she'd offered him coffee and a full plate once he'd made his way down the stairs and into the kitchen. They weren't using the dining room these days, having turned it into a bedroom for the boy, and Jenny seemed to have taken over the smaller parlor as her own.

The furnishings in the big parlor were sparse, but comfortable, he'd noted yesterday. She'd obviously sold off most of her belongings. Probably to buy food and seed and whatever else they needed for survival.

Noah greeted him with a wave and led the way to the barn, where the mules were already harnessed and waiting.

"My boys'll rake up the hay and turn it so's it'll dry," he told Shay. "You and me'll finish the cuttin'." Placing two scythes on the wagon, he reached for rakes, then looked over at Shay. "Unless Miss Jenny wants it done different."

Shay shook his head. "Makes sense to me. We can't put it up till it's dry, and it can't get dry till it's cut. Let's get at it." He hopped on the back of the wagon, lifting one foot to the bed, and propping his arm across his knee. Noah's sons were crossing the yard as the wagon rolled from the big, double, barn doors and they eased their way onto the lumbering vehicle, one on either side of Shay.

His greeting was met by identical nods, and he grinned. Aside from the blisters he'd managed to gain yesterday from the unfamiliar motion of the scythe, he was pretty much on a par with the three men, able to work a full day in the sun. The blisters would doubtless be a different matter by day's end, he decided. Jenny might have some salve handy. He'd probably be ready for it.

What she had was a pair of gloves, old and worn, but welcome. Offering them to him at noon, she allowed a small smile to curve her lips. "I thought you might need these. I didn't know how long it'd been since you've done any haying."

"Not since last fall," he told her, slipping the gloves in place. They rubbed against a couple of raw places on his palms and he adjusted them carefully. "This will help."

"You've got blisters," she surmised, reaching to touch his wrist. "Let me see."

"No." He stepped back from her, uneasy with the men watching. "I'll let you take a look after we get done for the day." Her nod was reluctant, but the smile appeared again.

It was still in place when he entered the house just before supper time. Isabelle stood before the cookstove and Jenny turned to greet him from the pantry door. ''I'm glad you're a few minutes early,'' she said brightly. ''I'll just have time to take a look at your hands before we eat.''

Snatching up a box from the shelf behind her, she motioned at the table, and he obeyed her silent instructions, easing his weary body onto a chair. She sat close by, their knees almost touching as she reached for him.

Her skin was cool against his, her fingers slender, yet strong as she turned his hand over, then slid the glove from place. Her brow furrowed as she inspected the seeping blisters, surrounded by a reddened area, and she made a small noise with her tongue against the roof of her mouth. ''You should have told me about them this morning,'' she said reprovingly. ''I'd have brought the salve and bandages out to the field. It wouldn't be nearly this bad if we'd tended to it right away.''

His nape twitched as she bent to look closely at his hand, a stray lock of her hair resting against his wrist. One slender finger brushed lint from his palm and heat rose within him. Clenching his teeth, he closed his eyes against the demands of his body, aware of the evidence of his desire. An anguished groan rose in his throat and he swallowed it, anxious that she not hear the faint murmur escaping his lips.

''Did I hurt you?'' Jenny's voice was troubled, and she blew softly against his hand. ''There's lint stuck to your blisters from the gloves I gave you.''

Her breath was fresh, her skin dewed with perspiration, and the scent of woman rose to his nostrils. He'd endured much at the hands of the prison guards, had watched as flesh peeled from his feet in layers, been kicked and abused without cause. All of that faded into oblivion as he sank into the sweet torture of Jenny's gentle touch.

A soft cloth wiped carefully, cleansing his palm, then washing his hand both back and front. She dried the skin and then her fingers applied salve to the damaged flesh with feathered strokes. She murmured words beneath her breath, some of them scolding, more of them grateful, as she recounted the hours he'd spent in the hayfield. At last, the soft cloth was pressed tenderly against his oozing blisters and a wide strip of bandaging was wrapped around his hand.

He inhaled deeply, then opened his eyes. Her smile was teasing, her lips parted and, wonder of wonders, the woman was totally oblivious to his problem.

"You're almost as bad as Marshall," she said smugly. "I think all male creatures must be alike. They can cope with a broken nose easier than a blister."

He gained his breath. "And how would you know about broken noses, Miss Jenny?" he asked. Then watched as she stripped his other glove off with care.

"Carl had a shovel fall from the barn wall once. It caught him right across the bridge of his nose, and he bled like a stuck pig." Her hands repeated the cleaning process and he focused his thoughts on Carl's bleeding nose.

"What did you do for him?" The salve covered his palm now and his gaze swept her profile, noting the freckles across her nose, the sweep of eyelashes against her cheek.

"It was a cold winter that year, and I made an ice pack from the horse trough." Her hands stilled as she thought of that time, and a sad smile touched her full lips. "He wouldn't let me pamper him." Her eyes were bright as she blinked twice, then looked up at him.

I'd let you pamper me any day of the week. The woman was about as tempting as any female he'd ever met. No. More so, Shay decided as she rolled the remainder of her bandage, then pinned it carefully so that it would be tidy in the small box she held. Twists of paper, their contents marked with neatly printed labels filled one side. A cloth bag held an aromatic scent he could not place, though it seemed familiar. Probably herbs of one kind or another, he decided. A large tin of carbolic salve, a bottle of thick, creamy liquid and smaller bottles of camphorated oil and witch hazel made up the neat contents of her medical supplies.

"My mother used to have witch hazel," he said. "She used it for all our bruises and cuts." His mouth tightened, aware of Jenny's interest, her eyes lighting at his words. Her hands paused, holding the roll of bandage suspended.

"Where did you live?"

It was a simple question, one he should have answered readily, and yet some need for anonymity clutched at his throat and he shook his head. "It's not important."

Her eyes dimmed, the light vanquished by his terse reply, and she bent to her task, swiftly tidying the box, then rising to replace it in the pantry. He watched, aware of the hurt he'd inflicted, and his jaw tightened. It was just as well. He was becoming too attracted to her. *Attracted.* What a pale word to describe the desire that even now continued to find expression beneath the covering of the oilcloth that draped across his lap.

"We'll be eating in just a few minutes," Jenny said brightly. "You'd might as well sit there. Isabelle is ready to dish up, I think."

Murmuring agreeably, he glanced up to find Isabelle's eyes fixed on his face. Her hands busy with the kettle she held, she glanced away, but not before he'd gotten the message her gimlet gaze sent flying in his direction. She was only too aware of his reaction to Jenny Pennington. And if looks could kill, Shay would be stretched out on the floor, waiting for burial.

Isabelle saw too much, Shay decided. Her next move would no doubt be to warn her friend against him. For all that she was a woman full grown, there was an air of innocence about Jenny that inspired a protective instinct in those surrounding her. Even the men in the field had watched him closely today when she'd offered the gloves for his use. Hell, he was halfway to being her champion already and he'd only known her for a couple of days. He'd protect her gladly, against any and all comers.

He'd work for her, plow his hard cash into her farm, and help her survive through another growing season. He'd stick it out until he was sure she was on her feet, safe and secure. And then what? Leave and not look back?

Not very damn likely. He'd probably be looking over his shoulder for the rest of his life. Might as well add Jenny to the list of those he'd left behind. He had a notion she'd be haunting his dreams anyway. And then he realized something that caught him up short.

He hadn't dreamed of the prison camp in Elmira, or of Carl's death for the past two nights.

He'd worked, and worked hard, Jenny thought. There was no faulting the man's ambition. And she'd gotten used to his presence here over the past weeks.

The barn was filled with the scent of hay, bits of it floating to the floor as two men worked in the loft above. Jenny covered the pail of milk she'd just coaxed from the cow and rose from the three-legged stool. Shay said there was enough hay in the loft to feed for the better part of the year. Part of the second cutting, come August, would be sold to neighbors who needed more than they raised for themselves.

For the first time in months, she felt rich. Rich with the knowledge that her animals had good pasture to feed on, that there was an abundance of hay in the loft, and there was a field of corn ready to hoe. Shay was talking about a second crop. A late planting would take them through the winter, he said, and she'd agreed, after noting Noah's slight nod. In the meantime, the chickens were turned out to forage for themselves every morning. The pullets and young roosters were growing rapidly, and there were more hens wanting to nest, one of them determined to settle herself in the bushes near the house.

The sound of hammering caught her attention and she put the milking stool aside in haste. The man was up to something again, and it was barely past breakfast time. Sure as the world, he'd found another project to lay his hand to, and she hastened from the barn, following the noise of his labor. The remains of two old trellises lay on the back porch, Shay kneeling amid the fan-shaped designs, adding a strip of new wood. He caught sight of her and rose, watching as she walked toward him.

It made her quiver inside when he did that. Not that his perusal was intimidating or in any way worrisome. It was just that his gaze made her aware of herself. Aware of the way she walked, the way her hand dipped into her apron pocket, the way her hips swayed in rhythm with her steps. And he didn't miss a shred of it. His lips moved just a little, the bottom one twitching a bit, and his eyes darkened, if that were possible.

She hadn't been so studied, not ever in her life, as she had lately. Carl had paid attention to her, mostly in the bedroom, sometimes when he was feeling randy. But Shay was a different sort, more intense, more observant, and that intensity was focused on her, more often than not. As if each movement she made was unique, each word she spoke worth hearing.

It could be heady stuff, she decided, climbing the two steps to the back veranda, where he watched and waited. His hand reached for the milk pail and she gave it to him, unthinking. "I'll take it in to Isabelle," he said. "Wait here a minute. I want you to tell me where to put this trellis. There are roses blooming all over the ground on the east side of the house. They'd be better off with something to climb on."

Jenny nodded. His request was reasonable, no matter what Isabelle thought. A whispered warning early this morning had brought quick color to Jenny's cheeks. "You watch out for that man, Miss Jenny. He's a dark one, with thoughts about you he shouldn't be thinkin'." Isabelle's eyes were sparkling with indignation as she spoke. "He's lookin' at you like you're an available woman."

I am. Jenny closed her eyes as she remembered the words. *Available for marriage, anyway, though I doubt that's what Shay is thinking of.* The screen door slammed as he returned, and he lifted one finger as a signal.

"Just another couple of nails and this will be ready. Have a seat, ma'am." His words encouraged her to linger, and she perched on the edge of the veranda, arms wrapped around her knees as she watched him. Long fingers held the nail, and the hammer hit it twice, driving it firmly into the wood beneath. Another nail was pounded home and Shay set aside the hammer, lifting the trellis with him as he stood.

"I knew the roses were being neglected, but the wind kept blowing them down, and I didn't know how to fix..." Her voice trailed off as Shay carried the trellis past her, a nod of his head urging her to follow. She stood quickly, brushing her skirts down. A movement at the door caught her eye and she waved at Isabelle, flashing a smile as she trotted behind her new handyman.

Thorny branches, profuse with roses, lay beneath the library window. "I'll bet you can smell them at night," Shay said, leaning the trellis against the house. The sun was climbing rapidly into the morning sky and its warmth brought forth the scent of the flowers, rising from the ground to surround them with its aroma.

"Yes," she agreed, hands shoved into her apron pockets, watching as he lifted the heavy branches aside, making room for himself to stand. Curtains caught the breeze and billowed into the room as she watched, and past his bent form she caught sight of her bed. Covering the mattress was a pieced quilt, one her grandmother had made years ago, now the only memento she had of the elderly woman who lay in the churchyard. Her nightgown was tossed carelessly against the counterpane and Jenny wished fervently that it had been folded and put away in her chest of drawers.

Carl had told her more than once that she was always in too much of a hurry, anxious to move on to the next moment. Isabelle had called from the kitchen this morning as Jenny dressed and she'd hastened from her room, leaving an unmade bed and general disorder behind. Now it was exposed for anyone to see. For Shay to see.

"Here, hold this," he said over his shoulder, nodding with his head toward the place where he wanted her hands to rest. She did as he asked, standing beside him, stretching to grip the wooden frame. He knelt, one knee on the ground, the other bent, and dug with a small spade he'd carried along. The hole was narrow and deep enough to hold the bottom of the trellis, the earth piled up around it as he plied the spade.

"Let's drop it in," he told her, grasping the frame, allowing her to balance it above his hands. And then he lifted his head, looking inside her room, his hands unmoving as the curtains billowed, revealing the unmade bed and the white gown she'd left behind. He glanced up at her once more, his expression harsh. "Ready?"

She nodded, lowering the trellis, then held it steady as he packed dirt in the hole. He stood, brushing off his hands, stomping the loose earth to hold the latticework firmly in place. "I think I'll nail it in two places to the siding on the house," he told her. "That way the wind won't take it again."

She stepped back. "I thought you wanted me to tell you where to put it."

"You want it somewhere else?" His eyes glanced at her over his shoulder and her smile faltered. His mouth twitched. "I decided for you, ma'am. By the time I mend the other trellis and set it on the other side of the window, there won't be enough room for anyone to climb inside without getting stuck by the thorns. Thought it might be wise."

"Who'd want to climb in my window?" she asked incredulously. "There's only Noah and the boys and Marshall, and they can go right in the back door. Isabelle would never make it over the sill."

He was silent, that faint movement of his mouth turning into a slow grin. "And I'm upstairs. Reckon we don't need to worry about keeping you safe and sound, do we?"

"I've never worried for a minute," she said stoutly. "There's no one hereabouts to fear."

"Then why do you suppose Isabelle's been sleeping in front of your door? She was there again this morning when I got up early." He bent to pick up the hammer and spade and straightened to face her. His smile twisted the scar, lifting one side of his mouth, and her eyes were drawn there. With an oath that took her by surprise, he turned away.

"No. Don't do that," she whispered. "Don't turn from me. Please."

It was the addition of that small word that halted his retreat. She'd said *please,* and not for a moment could he deny her the courtesy of facing her again. "I know my face is beyond ugly, ma'am. I don't blame you for looking." His words became softer as he attempted to placate her with a touch of humor. "I've had babies cry, and women scream for mercy, just looking in my direction."

Jenny's eyes left his and moved again to that puckered

scar. As if she had reached to touch it, he felt a welcome warmth the length of its twisted ridge, and his own hand rose to tug at his hat brim, effectively hiding it from her sight.

"How did you get it?" she asked quietly. "It looks painful, but I suppose it's not, really."

"It's been a long time," he said. "You might say I stuck my nose in where it wasn't welcome." That he'd fought for a man's life in the prison camp in Elmira, fought and won, was something she didn't need to know. The Yankee guard had been buried quickly, and their captors had been too busy dealing with the water that overflowed the camp to make a fuss. They'd been in a deluge, wading in ankle-deep water in their simple shelter for three days. He'd shivered with cold and listened to men weep unashamedly.

"Was it in prison?" she asked, her eyes bleak as she probed for the answer.

"No," he lied. "In a saloon, before the war." He'd lied before, for lesser reasons, but this one stuck like wet feathers against the roof of his mouth. He'd lie again if he needed to protect her, he realized. And then he chuckled, a low humorless sound, to make certain she believed his tale.

"I'll finish up the other trellis now," he told her. "Guess my time could have been better spent on the cornfield, but my mama always liked her roses. I hated to see yours layin' in the dirt. I'll catch up with Noah and the boys a little later."

"Thank you for doing the repairs," she told him, walking beside him as they turned the corner to the back of the house. "My mama always said we all need beauty in our lives. I've missed seeing the roses climb the way they used to. Isabelle can find me a rag to tear up into strips, and I'll tie the branches up off the ground later."

She glanced up at him. "If you don't get the hoeing done

today, leave the part go that's closest to the house. I'll go out after supper and work at it a while, when the air's cooler.''

His nod was abrupt. ''You're the one in charge, ma'am.'' He bent to lift the tall framework he'd mended, carrying it from the porch. ''You going to help me with this?''

Jenny shook her head. ''You can handle it, I'm sure. I think I need to give Isabelle a hand in the house. Yesterday's cream is ready to churn.'' The door closed behind her and he retraced his steps to the library windows. She'd been embarrassed to have him see her gown on the bed. He'd sensed her squirming beside him, and deliberately taken long moments to gaze into the shadowed interior. It hadn't taken much imagination to visualize her inside that pale gown.

The hole was dug in moments and he dropped the trellis in place, holding it with one hand as he used his boot to shove the dirt in, firming it quickly. Stepping back, he eyed his work. She'd have the roses trained in no time. And every time she crawled into bed and inhaled the rich fragrance…

He turned away. Noah was heading for the field, a hoe across his shoulder. And if Shay knew what was good for him, he'd spend his energy on digging weeds instead of making monkeyshines with the boss.

Chapter Three

Dusk shadowed the graceful stalks of corn, yet still Jenny plied her hoe. To rest against its handle would only invite more of Shay's scrutiny, and she'd borne about all of that she could handle for one evening. His eyes rested on her between each movement of his hoe, ever observing, as if she might fade from sight if he didn't keep close track. Yet it did not detract from the rhythm he'd set, pushing himself to complete the task he'd taken on. It seemed the man would never say die, never cease his energetic removal of weeds from around each hill of corn. And who could argue with that?

Certainly not the woman who'd accepted his offer to work beside her in the cool of the evening. And then the mosquitos descended. To thwart the advance of the pesky critters she'd simply rolled her sleeves to her wrists, then buttoned them. Her bonnet kept them from her hair, and she waved away the few insects that buzzed near her face.

She cast sidelong glances in Shay's direction. The man could work. There was no getting around that fact. His hands and arms moved in a rhythm she could never hope to emulate. His own hat kept the bloodthirsty insects from his head, and he'd turned up his collar, somewhat protecting his neck from their bites. Shirtsleeves tightly fastened, he worked diligently. As if the crop of corn would be his to sell at harvest time, he chopped weeds with a vengeance.

Jenny moved between the rows at a slow but steady pace, noting that Shay uprooted the green predators in the row to her right before she could reach them, easing her workload by almost half. Leaving only the weeds to her left to the mercy of her hoe, he moved smoothly beside her, doubling her accomplishment, with no apparent effort on his part.

She paused, standing erect, her hand moving to the small of her back, and Shay glanced at her, his harsh features visible in the twilight. "Had enough for tonight?" he asked.

His words were low, drawled in a voice that made her think of cool sheets and moonlight streaming through her bedroom window. And where that thought had come from, she wasn't sure. She only knew that she hadn't traveled such paths since the day Carl rode his big buckskin stallion down the road, then turned to wave goodbye with a jaunty hand. That this dark, enigmatic stranger could elicit such pondering from her female mind was a fact she wasn't ready to cope with.

"Yes, I suppose so," she murmured, aware fully now of the aching muscles in her back, just below her waist. Hoeing corn had never been her favorite chore, yet she'd done it for the past four years or so without complaint. Mostly in the evening when Marshall was under Isabelle's care, bathing and readying for bed. Though the task was tedious, she enjoyed the stillness, when her only companion was a mockingbird in the hedgerow. When her thoughts could have free rein, and memories of past days and nights ran rampant through her mind.

None of those solitary evenings held a candle to this one, she decided, turning her hoe over to Shay's capable hands, watching as his broad palm encompassed both handles easily. Before them, rows of corn seemed to stretch endlessly into the field. At the horizon a pale moon appeared, rising in increments into the sky.

"You don't have to do this," she said, allowing her gaze to rest on the shadowed outline of his face. "You work hard all day long. I really don't mind coming out here alone in the evening."

"Do you think I'd let you work by yourself?" he asked. "Don't you do enough all day, let alone chopping weeds till dark?" He reached for her, gripping her hand firmly in his, and she followed his lead, a row of fragile, foot-high cornstalks between them as they walked. "Watch where you step," he told her. "I'll pick up the piles of weeds tomorrow."

"I can do that," she protested. "I'll bring a basket out in the morning." His hand was warm, his fingers enfolding hers with an easy clasp. She allowed the intimacy, relishing the brush of his callused hand against her own. In silence they reached the end of the rows and she turned to look back over her shoulder.

"Admiring your work?" he asked dryly.

"No," she answered, smothering a laugh. "Just being thankful for good weather, I guess. The corn's doing well."

He halted, drawing her across the few inches that separated them, where the tilled ground meshed with grass and tall weeds. "Listen, Miss Jenny," he whispered, cocking his head to one side. "You can almost hear it growing."

It was a whimsical notion and she smiled readily. "I've thought the same thing before," she told him, "when the heat of the day is gone and the night is quiet. My papa used to say that corn was the perfect crop for a man to plant."

Shay turned his head and she saw a flash of teeth as his lips parted in a smile. "I've never heard that theory before," he said. "I would have thought cotton would be on the top of his list."

Jenny lifted her shoulders in a small shrug. "Cotton is a moneymaker. But you have to have hands to harvest it. A poor man can only plant ten or fifteen acres. A man and his family can only tend to so much, if they're going to tend it well."

"Carl wasn't a poor man. He must have had plenty of field hands out there." His head nodded toward the far fields, where the land lay fallow.

"That was a long time ago," Jenny said quietly. "Things change. I've never forgotten the things my father told me though, when I was growing up. He didn't own a place like this. We weren't poor, but..."

"You were raised to be a lady," Shay said.

"Yes, I was. But I learned early on that life is uncertain, and tomorrow brings surprises."

"And so you've managed to take hold here and keep things going."

"I've done my best. For Carl's sake, and for Marshall. Yet, even now I think of all the things my father taught me, and they've proven to be true. He said that if we do the hard work, God will provide the rain and sun. Corn's the best crop we can raise to keep us from goin' hungry." She spread her hands in a gesture that encompassed the field. "You can't eat cotton. With corn we use the youngest, tenderest ears for our supper table, then when it's ready to shuck out, we feed it to our stock. The best ears we grind for cornmeal. We use the stalks for silage and plow the rest under to feed the land."

"You're quite eloquent, ma'am," he said soberly. "I suppose I hadn't thought of it that way before. I suspect your papa was an educated man."

She laughed, the sound husky in her ears. "He had some education, but mostly he read the Bible and a whole shelf full of books he brought with him from New Orleans.'' She tilted her head, the better to see beneath his hat brim, suspecting that his smile lingered at her expense. ''He used common sense, to tell the truth. I remember he told my mama that with a cow and a few chickens and a few acres of corn, a family could make out.''

''I suspect your father was rather more wealthy than that though, wasn't he?''

Jenny nodded. ''Yes, he had money. Not as much as Carl. I married 'up,' as the saying goes. Carl had the means to buy slaves, and these fields were white with cotton by summer's end.''

''And after the war, when the slaves were freed and released?'' Shay asked quietly. ''What happened then?''

''A good number walked away. I gave some of them land to work, and a few stayed on here.''

''Isabelle and Noah?'' His hand released hers and he turned her toward the barn, long fingers pressed against her spine, just above her waist.

She closed her eyes, then blinked away the rush of moisture that blurred her vision. That the warmth of a man's hand should touch some deep part of her was more than she could understand. And yet it had. Her spirit wept for the simple joy he brought her.

She relished the innocent pressure of his hand against her back, his fingers holding hers captive during the walk through the field. And now the weight of that same hand on her shoulder. Inhaling his essence, the musky scent he bore, she reveled for a moment in his protective shadow.

It was unexplainable, this tension that held her breath in abeyance. It was unbelievable, this sweetness that warmed her heart as he bent to speak her name.

''Jenny?'' His tone reminded her of the question he'd asked, and the answer she'd failed to give.

''Yes, Noah and Isabelle stayed on, with their sons. They

belong here, and this place belongs to them, almost as much as it does to me and my son.'' She held her breath a moment and then spoke the words that might draw a line between them. ''They're my family, Shay.''

His fingers squeezed hers gently and he murmured a sound of acquiescence. The barn door before them was open and even as they stood on the threshold, a light flickered, then took hold at the far end of the building. ''Noah,'' Shay said quietly. ''He must be finishing up for the night.''

A lantern was held high, its circle of light a beacon as they walked toward the man who was moving between the mules, and then into the stall where the mare stood, one foot lifted, her head drooping. His dark face glowed as he looked up and his smile was open and welcoming.

''I thought you was gonna sit out there all night watchin' the corn grow,'' he said with a soft chuckle. ''Y'all better be gettin' your sleep. Tomorrow's the day we plant cotton, Mr. Shay.''

Jenny glanced at Shay, his face illuminated by the lantern glow. ''Have you planted cotton before?''

He reached to hang the hoes against the barn wall, where nails protruded to hold tools in place. ''I've watched,'' he admitted. ''Never got down and did the deed myself.''

''First time for everything,'' Noah said smoothly, running his hand over the mare's flank. ''I suspect any man who can swing a scythe the way you do can poke holes in the dirt and plant some cotton seed in them.''

''This is the easy part,'' Jenny warned. ''Even Marshall can plant the stuff.''

''I'll be here to help pick it,'' Shay told her, even as his gaze met that of the man who watched him closely. ''Once I take on a job, I don't give up halfway through.''

''You want your stud brought inside?'' Noah asked. ''He's a mighty nice horse.''

''You have problems with raiders?'' Shay asked.

Noah shook his head. "No, but I think that big stallion might be a heap of temptation. My boys sleep in the tack room. They'd hear should someone come around."

"I'll get him," Shay said, turning toward the back of the barn. He opened the door that led to the corral and whistled, a low, soft sound that barely left his lips before the stallion was nudging his chest. He gripped the halter, then rubbed the stallion's long nose. Shay murmured words that appeared to please the animal, causing him to toss his head and swish his tail.

"How'd he get over the corral fence?" Jenny asked, peering past the horse to see if the gate had been left open.

"Jumped it," Shay said simply. "He's got power he's never used in those haunches." His tone was prideful, his eyes gleaming with pleasure as he led his horse into the nearest stall. "I'll give him some hay if you don't mind. He didn't graze much today."

Without pause, he poked a pitchfork into a stack of hay they'd left available near the barn door, then carried it into the stall. It filled the manger and his stallion bent his graceful head to eat. Shay backed from the stall, his hand lingering against the horse's side. Soft words soothed the animal and he whuffled, a smothered sound that made Jenny laugh aloud. Shay looked up.

"I suppose you think he doesn't understand what I'm saying to him." His mouth twitched and she was reminded of his reluctance to smile. Perhaps this was the best she'd ever have from him, this movement of his lips that signified his humor. It would be enough, she decided.

"Oh, I'm sure he does," she said agreeably, smiling broadly. "I think I'm just surprised that you spoil him. You don't strike me as the sort to pamper..." Her voice trailed off as his mouth became a thin line, lips compressed.

"You might be surprised, Miss Jenny," he murmured. And then with a final brush of his hand over his stallion's flank, he moved from the stall. "Come on, I'll walk you to the house," he offered.

"I'll send Isabelle out," Jenny told Noah and the man nodded.

"Night, Mr. Shay." He lifted the lantern to light their way from the barn.

Shay nodded and grasped Jenny's elbow, bending low to whisper against her bonnet. "I'll warrant she won't leave the house, Miss Jenny. She'll roll up in a quilt right outside your door, if I've got her figured right." His tone was amused and Jenny pulled from his grasp, irritated by his presumption.

"I've spoken to her about that. She knows I have nothing to fear from you, and I told her to sleep in her own bed from now on."

Shay's breath was warm against her neck as he whispered again. "She doesn't trust me, you know."

Jenny stalked ahead, irritation rising within her, that he should so mock himself. "I think Isabelle's a little over-protective, that's all. She's looked after me for years, and it's hard for her to stand back and let me fend for myself."

She climbed the single step to the back porch and glanced back to where he stood, one foot on the riser, the other still on the ground. "And you, Miss Jenny? Do you trust me?"

Did she? Could she cope with his masculine presence in her home? In the room almost directly over her own?

Did she trust him? Probably, she decided. Maybe even more than she trusted her own tangled emotions.

Her jaw firmed as she pondered his query, and with a shrug she turned away. Then she opened the screen door and entered the kitchen. Isabelle sat at the table, only a candle on the buffet casting a circle of light. "You can go on home to Noah," Jenny said, walking to the sink to wash her hands beneath the pump.

"I don't like leavin' you alone in the house," Isabelle said stubbornly. "I know you said you'd be just fine, but that man looks at you like he's been without water for six months and you've got the only water bucket for miles around."

Jenny laughed softly at Isabelle's words. "You have a big imagination, my friend. Shay is here to help Carl's wife and Carl's child. He'll stay long enough to be sure we're in good shape for the winter, and then he'll be gone, like a breeze blowing through the place." *And I'll be left alone...again.*

The cotton was planted, a task lasting almost two weeks, sandwiched in among the everyday chores. Between cooking and carrying meals to the field, Jenny found herself left out of the process, and wondered if that was Shay's intent. The sun was hot, early May bringing summer heat, and she toted quart jars of water several times a day to the laboring men. They left the jars in the shade, beneath tall trees at the edge of the fields, and it was near there that she waited at high noon, with thick slabs of buttered bread and slices of leftover ham from the night before.

The smokehouse was almost empty, last year's butchered hog having been rationed over the months when game was not plentiful. Noah and his sons brought down a deer several times through the colder weather and she'd managed to catch decent-size catfish in the river beyond the last of their tilled fields.

Cleaning fish was a simple matter these days, and she cringed when she remembered the reaction of her weak stomach the first time she'd peeled the tough skin from an ugly catfish. Jenny Pennington had done a heap of growing up over the past years, she decided. Swinging the bucket she'd carried from the house, she waited until the working men reached the end of the row they'd just planted, and then waved her free hand. The tallest of the four looked up, his gaze penetrating even from this distance.

Shay pushed back his hat and used his kerchief to wipe his forehead. She'd walked across the pasture, then down the hedgerow to the far end of the field where they toiled in the sun. His eyes had swerved in her direction between each hole he pushed into the soil. Her hair caught the sunlight, shimmering and drawing his gaze like a magnet. Even from a distance, he knew the exact shade of her eyes, knew the shape of her mouth, the tender slope of her bosom.

He cleared his throat as she deliberately caught his eye and waved, pleased at the small smile she made no effort to conceal. "Noah?" The man looked up and motioned toward Jenny, his sons following his lead. Their steps were eager as all four of them turned in her direction. Jenny settled her pail on the ground, spreading the small tablecloth she'd brought from the house. "Come and eat," she invited them, placing the platter she'd prepared in the center.

"Isabelle made cake." She lifted, lifting the lid from a tin box with a flourish. Inside, squares of golden pound cake awaited, a thin glaze coating each piece. "She said it was especially for you, Noah," she told him as he stood beside the food she'd arranged. "Sit down, won't you? I'll go and get your water."

Shay watched her walk away, to where they'd left the last of the water. Two jars remained of the four she'd brought earlier, and she carried them back, one in the fold of each arm. Her skirts brushed the grass and swayed with each step she took. Her sleeves were rolled to her elbows and the summer sun had left its signature behind, toasting her skin to a golden brown. He imagined the pale flesh above the rolled sleeves, and below the V of honeyed flesh at her throat. She was fair, if he was any judge, with that copper-colored hair. Where the sun had touched her face, she wore freckles, just a smattering across her nose and cheeks, and more of the same blended with the tan on her forearms.

Blue eyes found his and a rosy flush painted her cheeks. He'd warrant that the skin beneath her bodice held the same hue, and that thought released a rush of energy within him that stood no chance of being expelled. Not today, or tonight, or anytime soon.

She was a woman ripe for the taking, and he'd give his eye teeth and then some if he had any chance of snatching her for himself. Instead he could only watch, and try his level best to contain the desire she inspired.

She bent to the men, handing them the jars of water, and Noah gave the first to Shay. "Drink what you want," he said politely. "I'll share with you."

And not until I've had my fill, Shay thought, with a rueful nod of his head. Too many restrictions remained, even in the world where no man was a slave to another. Noah would not presume to take first place, and his easy acknowledgment of that fact of life as he knew it, made Shay cringe. He drank, long and deeply of the cool water, then handed it to the other man.

"Here you go," he said, "I'm fine." And then turned to his food.

"Are you sure, Mr. Shay? Take all you want," Noah offered, obviously unwilling that he should offend by drinking more than his share.

"There's plenty more, Noah," Jenny said quickly. "I have another jar in the basket." Obviously used to the traditions that would take long to die out after the years of rigid separation, she had come prepared, and Shay lifted his brow as she glanced at him.

The extra jar of water was nestled against the trunk of the tree and she settled herself in the grass beside it, watching the men devour the food she'd brought. Then as they stretched out on the grass, hats over their eyes, she piled the scant remains in her basket. Shay watched from beneath his hat brim, and his gaze traced the lines of her slender form, noting the shabby dress with a twinge of anger.

She deserved more, and yet, should he attempt to replace her worn clothing with new, she would be offended. Of that fact, he was certain. Jenny was used to making do; she was a magician at creating clothing for her child from Carl's castoffs, left in the attic. He'd found her sewing by candlelight one evening and scolded her for not using a lantern.

"It wastes kerosene," she'd told him, bending to stitch carefully at the small pair of trousers she was creating.

It wasn't his place to argue with her and so he'd pleased himself by moving the candle closer. Its light had shone in the tendrils of hair that fell against her jaw, glistened in the depths of her eyes as she glanced up at him, and he'd clenched his broad hands into fists lest he reach to brush the wayward lock from the fine line of her cheek.

Now she stood and lifted the basket, waving a hand at the four men, three of whom were dozing, obviously having learned at an early age to take cat naps where they could. Shay, on the other hand, found it difficult to close his eyes without the presence of walls around him, or at least a rocky ledge at his back. He watched through his lashes as her gaze lingered on him, noted the touch of her tongue against her upper lip and suppressed a shiver that threatened to translate into full-blown desire.

She turned away, and he sat up abruptly, jamming his hat atop his head. Less than two months here and he spent half his time teetering on the verge of snatching at her like a randy cowhand. He stood, gaining his feet in a fluid movement that caught Noah's attention. Scooping his hat from his face, Noah rose and Shay motioned at him with one hand.

"Rest awhile," he murmured. "You've been working hard all morning. Your boys can use a break, too. I just want to walk the length of the field and back. It looks a little swampy at the other end."

Noah's eyes flickered toward Jenny's retreating form and he allowed a grin to curl the corner of his mouth. "Miss Jenny surely is a nice lady," he said quietly. "My woman thinks you're taken with the girl, Mr. Shay."

"She's out of my class, Noah." And yet he could not resist another look in her direction. She'd halted by the pasture fence to talk to the mare, and her dress was hiked up, exposing slim ankles. How he knew they were slim from this distance was a mystery, yet Shay would have gambled his bank account on the fact. "She deserves a gentleman, someone worthy of her." If his words sounded harsh Noah paid no mind, but chuckled beneath his breath.

"She deserves more than that, Mr. Shay. But what she *needs* is a man to bring her to life, somebody who'll put a spark in her eye and roses in her cheeks." As if he'd said more than he intended, Noah lowered himself to the ground once more and shifted his hat over his eyes, his body visibly relaxing like a sleepy hound dog in the sun.

Jenny fanned herself with a hand-painted, pleated-paper specimen she'd found in the attic. "Do you think the corn is tall enough to cultivate?" she asked idly.

"Yeah, I'd say so," Shay answered. "Up past my knees already."

They sat on the porch, watching as Noah's boys carried dishes back to the house. Isabelle fed them nightly in the cabin she shared with her husband, and then the young men, whom Noah still considered his boys, brought the pots and dishes back to the house for washing. It was a complicated procedure, one Jenny had decried as a waste of time and energy, but Isabelle would not be dissuaded. And so the nightly procession continued, with Isabelle washing up after both tables were cleared.

Jenny ate, as usual, in the kitchen, with Marshall serving as a buffer between Shay and herself, his childish questions amusing Shay, and providing Jenny with time to enjoy her meals. She'd long since decided that a five-year-old child was the most inquisitive creature on earth, but Shay seemed to enjoy the boy. Their evening walk was a favorite time for Marshall, and today was no exception.

They'd marched down the lane between overhanging oaks, and Jenny had watched them go, her thoughts in turmoil as she saw Marshall offer his hand to the man who slowed his steps to a child's pace. Shay looked down at the outstretched fingers for a moment, his hesitation brief, then took the small hand in his own, strolling slowly as though his entire world was circumscribed by the realm of her child's universe.

What would happen to Marshall when his idol left? she wondered. For sure as the sun rose in the morning and set in the western sky every night, that day would come. Maybe not for a few months, but sooner or later, wanderlust would grip the dark, scarred man who had invaded their lives, and he would leave as he had come. The vision of that tall stallion galloping down her lane, with Shay in the saddle, was enough to bring tears to her eyes.

And that was ridiculous. He was here to help. He'd said he would lend a hand, get them on their feet. He'd talked about picking cotton, harvesting corn and cutting the second crop of hay sometime in August or September. Beyond that, he'd made no promises.

Beyond that, she saw only the bleak days of winter, chilly mornings, a Christmas without funds to buy gifts, save for a few handmade items she and Isabelle would put together. And yet, she could expect nothing more from the man than what he had promised he would give. *Carl sent me here...there'll be four men in the field.*

Her chin lifted and she gritted her teeth against the tears that overflowed her lashes, rolling down her cheeks and dampening her bodice. "He's not gone yet," she scolded herself quietly. "Land sakes, the man's only been here two months, and you're blubbering already about him leaving." She laughed, a rusty sound with no humor, and from the kitchen behind her Isabelle made a scoffing sound.

Jenny swung her head to find her friend at the door, visible through the screen. "You might's well dry those eyes," Isabelle said, her low voice grating out the words. "He's a man, with a man's ways, and he'll try to get past your bedroom door if you let him, Jen. He'll leave you with another young'un 'neath your apron if you don't take care."

"No." It was softly spoken, but held the steel of her mother's upbringing in the single syllable. "I'll not take a man in my bed without a marriage certificate hanging over the headboard, Isabelle. My mama taught me better than that."

"And that one—" Isabelle waved her hand in the direction of the two male creatures who meandered down the long lane "—that one'll sweet-talk you with promises and make you forget everything you ever learned about men. Mark my words, Jen, you're no match for a man like that."

Jenny turned away, pierced to the heart by the truth of Isabelle's predictions. "Maybe not," she admitted. "But wouldn't it be grand, even for a little while, to know that sort of loving?" She laughed aloud. "Listen to me, Isabelle. I'm spinning dreams out of shadows."

"Watch your step," Isabelle said glumly. "You can't say I didn't warn you, missy."

The two figures, one tall and straight, the other small and somehow vulnerable, even from this distance, turned and headed back to the house. Then they halted, and Shay bent low, picking up the boy and lifting him high, only to settle him on his wide shoulders. One arm raised in a broad wave and Marshall called out in a clear piping voice, "See me, Mama? I'm taller than anybody!"

The walk back was taken at a faster clip, with Shay trotting the last several yards, depositing Marshall on the porch with a flourish. "There you go, Marsh," he said, lifting his hand to smooth back his hair. Marshall had ruffled it, running his fingers through the dark length as he held tightly to his makeshift steed. Now, Shay's long fingers combed it into place, and Jenny watched each movement of his hand.

Marshall snuggled next to her on the edge of the porch and looked up with a grin that squinted his eyes and brought out the dimples in his cheeks. "Did you see me, Mama? Did you see me riding on Mr. Shay's shoulders?"

She nodded, wiping at a speck of dirt on his cheek, then allowed her hand to cup his nape. "I saw you, sweetheart. You were the tallest man on the place." She looked up at Shay and was lost in his gaze. "Thank you," she murmured. "Marshall has missed having a man around the place. He trots after Noah, but I'm afraid he gets in the way much of the time."

"He won't be in my way, Miss Jenny," Shay told her quietly. "Never."

She smiled and felt an unmistakable tremble in her lower lip. Lowering her head, she buried the telltale sign of emotion against Marshall's hair.

"Jenny?" Shay spoke her name, a questioning lilt in the syllables. And then he touched her, one hand reaching to press carefully on her shoulder. "I won't hurt you, Jenny."

She felt Marshall's head swivel, heard his indrawn breath, and closed her eyes as he spoke words that dropped from his lips like hot coals. "Don't you ever hurt my mama. That big man did, a long time ago, and he made my mama cry."

Jenny swallowed a gasp and lifted Marshall to his feet. "No one is going to hurt your mama, Marshall," she said firmly. "Now run in the house and let Isabelle get you ready for bed." Marshall's soft lips pressed a damp kiss against her cheek and he hugged her neck tightly.

"I love you, Mama." It was meant as a whisper, but his reedy tones vibrated in the silence, and she was hard put not to shed tears of thanksgiving for the tender heart of her child.

"I love you, too," she answered, turning him in the direction of the door. "I'll be up to hear your prayers in a few minutes."

And then she turned back to Shay.

Chapter Four

Shay's eyes were narrow slits, his mouth a thin line. He gestured toward the door behind Jenny, his hand slicing the air. "What man was Marshall talking about? Who was he?"

Jenny's heart sank. There were things she'd managed to tuck into a place marked as the past, things she chased from her mind when they poked their ugly heads into view. The subject Marshall had brought to Shay's attention with such childish innocence was one she'd determined to forget. And now it faced her head-on, brought to life again by a memory she'd thought long gone from her child's mind.

"It was a long time ago," she said, her voice trembling, her throat clogging with hateful tears. "I didn't know Marshall still remembered it. In fact, I'd thought him too young to understand."

"How old was he?" Shay asked, squatting before her, sweeping his hat from his head. Reaching forward, he placed it on the porch, next to where she sat. Her eyes followed his movements, focusing on the hand that hovered over his hat brim. And then she blinked as it moved, settling on her shoulder. His fingers squeezed lightly, and he repeated his query. "Jenny? How old was he?"

"A baby, not quite two. It was just before his second birthday." She allowed her gaze to lift from his hat, but could not meet the burning question in his eyes.

"It must have made a vivid impression," he allowed, softening his words, as if he would thereby coax her to his will. "What did he see, Jenny?"

Her eyes squeezed tightly shut, the vivid image of a blue-uniformed man appearing as if the sight were indelibly painted in her mind. And so it was, she realized. All of her trying could not erase the vision of terror she'd faced on that day. "It was after the war, long after I'd heard that Carl was dead. The army was still around, making its final raids, the soldiers heading back north." The image in her mind became more intense, the whiskered man's smile more coaxing, his rasping voice speaking words she'd never thought to hear.

You don't want your place burned now, do you?

"No! No!" She cried the reply aloud and her eyes flew open. Shay was before her, an emotion she could not fathom blazing in his eyes. Her fingers pressed against her lips, too late to silence the words she'd blurted aloud.

"What did he do to you?" His lips barely moved as the words were uttered, the rasping sound giving voice to his anger. "Tell me, Jenny."

Come on inside, honey. His teeth had been stained, his hands dirty, and the uniform stank of dried sweat and long days spent on horseback. Her stomach churned, as if those odors remained with her still, and she felt sour bile rise to her throat, gagging her with violent spasms.

"Damn!" Shay's curse was soft, but fervent, as he tugged her to her feet, lifting her into his arms. He carried her easily, as though she were featherlight, and her hand reached to clasp his neck, holding tight to the anchor he'd become. Pausing at the pump, he braced one foot on the watering trough. He lifted the handle, then pressed it down, allowing the water to gush forth. His hand snatched the kerchief from his throat and he held it beneath the flow, somehow balancing her weight on his knee.

"Put me down," she whispered. "I'm too heavy."

His glance was quelling and she bit her lip, motionless in his grip. The kerchief was squeezed in his wide palm and he shook it out, droplets shimmering in the setting sun. Folding it in upon itself, he wiped her face with the damp cloth, and she felt the nausea subside.

"Is she all right?" It was Isabelle behind them, and Jenny murmured words of reassurance.

"Get us a cup for water," Shay said curtly, and Isabelle responded with a breathless agreement. In moments she was back, and again water ran from the pitcher pump, this time filling a china mug from the kitchen. Shay held it to Jenny's lips and she drank, swallowing great gulps, until he tilted it away from her.

"Slow down, sweetheart," he whispered. "You'll be sick if you drink it too fast."

"I'm sick anyway," she muttered, her embarrassment rising as she took stock of her position. "Let me down now."

"In a bit," he told her. "Take the cup, Isabelle," he said firmly, and then, both arms encircling Jenny again, he lifted her high against his chest and walked to the barn. She glanced over his shoulder to see Isabelle near the watering trough, cup in hand, a look of fear bringing her soft features into bold detail.

"Where are we going?" His stride was long, his breathing deep, and Jenny felt apprehension nudging her. The man was beyond anger, way past the point of reasonable behavior, and she was being toted like a... Her mind was blank. His arms held her with care, firmly but without undue force. His face was drawn in lines of concern, but an underlying fury drove him beyond his normal conduct.

Shay was a man to be reckoned with, and she was about to face him, head-to-head. And in the barn, it seemed. He entered the wide doorway and halted, his head turning from one side to the other, as though he sought a place to conduct this conversation.

"This'll do," he said shortly, dropping her to her feet at the bottom of the ladder that led to the hay loft. "Climb," he told her.

She looked at him over her shoulder. "Climb? You want me to climb into the loft?"

He nodded. "I thought I was pretty clear on that."

The warmth of his body penetrated her clothing and she felt a flush warm her cheeks. "Can't we talk right here? Or back on the porch?"

"Climb." The single word left her no leeway, no room for argument, and she wondered at her own compliance as she obeyed his command. Jenny Pennington was not a pushover. She'd run a plantation, managed to keep her head above water and been a prideful woman for the past several years. Now she found herself bending to the will of a man who had literally scooped her up, mopped her face with a sopping wet kerchief, then ordered her to climb a ladder into the hayloft.

Her feet found the square rungs in rapid procession, and her wobbling legs propelled her over the edge into a deep pile of fresh hay. He was close behind, rising to his feet and glaring down at her as if she were a recalcitrant child.

"Everything all right up there?" Noah was below, peering upward and Shay growled a reply. "Yes, sir. I can see you got things under control, Mr. Shay." Noah's words faded as he left the barn, and Shay turned back to Jenny. His mouth twisted in an exasperated grimace, and he dropped down beside her.

"Damn, you sure know how to get me riled."

"Because I felt sick?" she asked. "Or because I didn't tell you my sad story?"

"Neither," he told her. "No, both, maybe. You were green around the gills, and I was afraid you'd faint dead away on me. And then I knew I'd have to fight to make you tell me what I need to know, and the porch wasn't the place for that kind of a battle."

She looked around the loft, only the open window allowing enough light for her to see him clearly. "And this is?"

"It'll do." He leaned beside her on one elbow. "Now, tell me what Marshall was talking about. He said a big man had hurt you."

The confusion of Shay's trip to the barn and the climbing to the loft had chased the images from her mind, and for that she was grateful. Perhaps, with Shay here, and surrounded by the safety of this private place, she could remember that day without falling prey to the heart-clenching horror she'd lived through.

And there was to be no retreat. Shay's grim features made that clear. Her mouth worked as she searched for the words, and her speech was halting.

"Yes, he saw a big man," she began, her gaze turning inward as she remembered Marshall's wide, terror-stricken eyes. "He watched a brute in a blue uniform take me inside the house, while he and Isabelle were kept in the yard. And later he saw me crying." She clenched her hands tightly, oblivious to the long fingers that untangled her own, and matched their palms in a warm embrace.

"What did he do to you?" His voice was low, rasping and she looked up to see darkness where so lately amusement and kindness had danced in the depths of his eyes.

Her words were careful, precise. "I don't think you want to know."

His dark head nodded slowly. "You may be right. But I *need* to know. I need to hear it from you." He bent closer.

"And maybe you need to tell me. Maybe speaking the words aloud will chase the memory from your mind."

The trembling began in her limbs, or perhaps it had never ceased, she thought, remembering the climb up the ladder. Shivers chased the length of her spine and gooseflesh turned her arms cold. She opened her mouth and felt the urge to scream, to let loose the shame, to shout her anger aloud. As if Shay were the culprit, she turned her fury in his direction.

"He made me strip and lay on the floor, right in the parlor. And then he used me like I suppose a man uses a whore...until I bled. He laughed at my tears, and told me I was lucky, that he'd saved up for weeks till he found a woman pretty enough to—" Her mouth could not speak the word, the ultimately filthy phrase he'd used to describe his act.

"And I was the *lucky* one he'd chosen." The bitterness she could no longer contain put a vile connotation on the word, and she bowed her head as grief manifested itself. The sobs were heart-rending, the tears profuse, and her wail of sorrow was muffled against his shirt. Shay lifted her on his lap, sitting upright against a post, and held her as he would a child, his arms offering comfort, his whispered words soothing her anguish.

She buried her face in the center of his chest, her fingers clutching the fabric of his shirt, and drew her knees up. Shay's warmth surrounded her, his face resting against her hair, his hands moving against her back, then rubbing her arm. He lifted his hand to her head, his fingers combing through the loosened locks of hair, and he buried his fist in the length of silken tresses.

"Jenny." That such soft, whispering comfort could come from the depths of a man like Shay was beyond her comprehension, and yet his whisper of her name conveyed an emotion too deep for words to express. Her name vibrated from the firm cushion of his chest, sounding against her ear as if it would enfold her in its syllables. He rocked her in his arms, swallowing her anger in his sorrow, smothering her fury with a blanket of tenderness. And mourning with her for the loss of her dignity, the trampling of her pride and the violation of her innocence.

Not that she'd been virginal, but that before that day she'd been treated with respect and love. Until the day she gave herself in trade for the safety of her family. Until she'd been called upon to purchase the plantation in a way she'd never imagined would be required of her.

The night grew cool, and the owl that made its nest in the rafters of the loft flew on wide wings to the window opening. Its mournful sound echoed as it took flight into the night air, and Jenny gathered herself, lifting her head, reaching for the handkerchief she kept in her apron pocket.

She'd cried copious tears, Shay's shirt soaking them up, and no doubt dampening his chest. He'd found her another kerchief in his pocket, and that, too, had been the recipient of more moisture than she'd thought possible. But blowing her nose was a private business, better done with her own white handkerchief. Sitting upright now on his thighs, she did so, aware of Shay's soft chuckle.

"Feel better?" he asked dryly.

"Does the word *cleansed* have any meaning right now?" she asked quietly, folding her hands in her lap and looking into his eyes.

His nod was barely visible and she sighed. "I've never talked about it before, not even to Isabelle. She knew, of course. And so did Noah, and the boys, I'm sure, but no one ever mentioned it. I suppose they understood that I wanted to forget that day." She touched his face, her fingers tracing the line of his scar.

"I don't suppose we ever really forget though, do we? When we're scarred beyond repair, I mean." She felt his jaw harden beneath her hand and she cupped his chin. "Do you blame me, Shay? Did I do the right thing? Or should I have watched while they burned my home and left the lot of us standing while they rode off?"

He was quiet, the muscles of his jaw clenching, and she felt his anger radiate from the depths of his being. Yet when he spoke, his words were soft, reasonable and soothing to her soul. "You did what you had to, Jenny. What we all do when the time comes to make a choice. Whether it causes pain or shame or sorrow, sometimes we're called on to make a sacrifice that scars the soul. And then we have to live with it."

"What happened soiled me," she murmured. "Made me not fit for a decent man. I doubt I'll ever feel..."

His hand covered her mouth, a rough, immediate response to her words that took her breath. "Don't speak such blasphemy," he growled. "You're a fine woman, a good woman. His actions didn't place a curse on you. But trust me sweetheart—the man will burn in hell for what he did that day. And if it were possible, I'd send him there myself."

She uttered a sound of disbelief. "I wouldn't want you to, Shay. Murder is never the right answer."

He was quiet, barely breathing, and then he spoke. "Sometimes it's the only answer."

She was chilled by his reply, frightened by the bleak tone of his voice. And then he lifted her from his lap, stood and walked to the window. He was a shadow against the starlight, a tall, gaunt reminder that there are hidden depths in every man that don't bear revealing, and Jenny hugged her knees to her chest, mourning the loss of his embrace.

She hadn't looked him in the eye, had blushed beneath his scrutiny at the breakfast table. Shay's hands gripped the handles of the cultivator and held it against the earth. Ahead of him, the mule leaned forward in her traces, and the combined force of his weight and her strength dug the three curved prongs into the ground, turning the hard dirt to tillable soil. His muscles bulged as he held the big implement steady, veering neither right nor left, staying between the rows of corn.

Behind him, Joseph followed, rake in hand, hilling the stalks, leaving the furrows deeper than the ridged rows. It was a hard job, and an hour at a time was enough to make a man rue the need for it. Noah stood at the far end of the row, waiting his turn behind the mule, and Shay was willing to give it up to him.

"I don't know how you managed it by yourself before your sons were big enough to help with this," he muttered, drawing his gloves off and tucking them into his back pocket.

"We all do what we have to," Noah told him, his grin wide and white. "Can't say it's my favorite way to spend a morning." He nodded at the broad haunches of the mule. "Not much to look at, the way I see it." Shay caught his meaning. It brought a laugh from his depths and he rejoiced at the moment of amusement. There hadn't been much to smile about thus far today.

Jenny had left the loft, silently and without his notice, as he stood at the window last night. Her slender form had caught his eye, her feet flying as she ran to the house, and he'd turned away from his dark thoughts, disgusted that he'd allowed her to flee, unheeded. The mattress had been hard and unyielding beneath his body throughout the long night, as he thought of the words she had spoken, the tears she'd shed against his chest. And most of all he remembered the feel of her curves, the warmth of her slender form as she clung to him, curled against his eager flesh, secure in his arms.

Breakfast had been brief, Jenny leaving the table to work

with a bread pan full of risen dough at the buffet. She'd refused to look up when he bid her good day, only mumbled a reply. Marshall, oblivious to his mother's mood, had followed Shay to the barn, and then to the cornfield.

Now he sat beneath tall bushes in the hedgerow, in charge of the water jars and carefully tending his collection of tin soldiers. On his stomach, smack dab in the center of a quilt Shay had spread for him, he kicked his feet in the air, laughing to himself as his miniature army marched across the corduroy patches. His golden hair was dark with perspiration at the temples, and sweat glistened on his nose as he looked up at Shay's approach.

"Mr. Shay," he called out. "Come see my soldiers." Rising to his knees, he motioned to the area beside him. "You wanta sit with me for a while?" His smile was bright and he reached to find a jar of water. "It's still pretty cool. Mama said to cover it with part of the quilt, and I thought it would make it warmer, but she said it would help keep it cool." His brow furrowed as his small hands enclosed the jar, offering it to Shay. "That doesn't make sense to me."

Shay unscrewed the lid and tilted the jar to his mouth, swallowing the sweet spring water, making no attempt to halt the cooling drops that seeped down his chin. They stained his shirt, dark blots penetrating the fabric, and he looked down, reminded of the hot tears Jenny had shed on this selfsame shirt last night.

"Your mama knows more than we do, I think," he told the boy. "Women have a knack of picking up on things. Now, we men," he said wisely, exaggerating the words for Marshall's benefit, "we just have to do the best we can, and pay attention to what we're told."

"You, too, Mr. Shay? Do you have to listen to my mama?" Marshall cocked his head to one side and frowned at the idea.

"Yeah," Shay said. "I listen to whatever your mama tells me, son." It seemed the boy had forgotten the moments from the evening before, his qualms buried beneath the ready smile and generous spirit he exhibited.

"I sure like you," Marshall offered offhandedly. "I bet my mama does, too."

Shay slanted him a grin, uncaring that his scar drew up, twisting his mouth. "You think so?" He thought a minute. "Maybe so, Marsh. Maybe so." Noah was at the end of the row, Joseph close behind. Another two swipes through the cornfield and he'd be switching places again. Just about time for a nap, he figured.

His sharp gaze scanned the fields surrounding them, searched the hedgerow briefly, and then settled again on the boy. "You be sure to wake me if anyone comes along, Marsh. I'm gonna close my eyes for a few minutes."

Marshall looked up, already absorbed in his soldiers, and nodded distractedly. "I'll keep an eye out, Mr. Shay." He bent to pick up a figure, adjusted the angle of its weapon, and sent Shay another look. "Even if my mama comes, should I wake you up?"

Shay watched him from beneath his hat brim, and chuckled, a low sound that seemed to please the boy. "Especially if your mama comes by, son. You be sure and wake me."

"Ess-pesh-ly," Marshall repeated, emphasizing the sounds, enjoying the flavor of the word. "Ess-pesh-ly."

"Our Caleb's got him a woman," Isabelle said, her air nonchalant, her words prideful.

Jenny looked up from her sewing, holding the needle in midair. "Someone from close by? Do I know her?" If Caleb had found a bride, it would mean allotting him land of his own to till and work. And one less hand to tend the fields here, she thought.

"Remember Sarah and Eli? The pair of them got married

soon as they could, after—'' Isabelle halted, weighing her words. "I still don't feel good about how some of our people left here, Jen. Like they didn't have it pretty good with you and Mr. Carl."

"They weren't free, Isabelle. I can't blame them for leaving. I might have done the same." She looked out the window to where the corn was almost as high as the pasture fencing. "Working your own land is different than sweating over someone else's crop."

"Well, if they'd hung around, you'd have give 'em a piece to work for theirselves," Isabelle told her. "Now they're doing shares with Doc Gibson, over south of here. And not likin' it much."

"Get back to Caleb's woman," Jenny said impatiently. "Is she kin to Sarah and Eli?"

"Their daughter. More girl than woman, I guess. Almost seventeen years old. She's been showin' up here every few days, makin' eyes at my boy like he's the cock of the walk." Isabelle's smile was tender as she ceased the rise and fall of the dasher. Churning was tedious work and talking made it palatable, but Isabelle tended to break her regular rhythm when she got caught up in storytelling.

"Caleb's a handsome man," Jenny agreed readily. "Tall and strong, and probably more than ready for a place of his own."

Isabelle slanted a glance across the kitchen, to where Jenny sat near the window. Taking advantage of sunlight was a double delight, she figured. It made the task of sewing more enjoyable to gaze from the window between times. Catching a glimpse of Marshall now and then as he followed Shay's tall figure around the place gave her a feeling of contentment that rested easy on her mind.

"Jen?" Isabelle sounded edgy now, and Jenny looked up quickly, aware that her mind had wandered. "Caleb's thinking that maybe he could build a cabin here, the far side of the pasture and maybe just work together with his pa. Maybe we could do shares, and put in more cotton, now that we got an extra hand.''

Jenny's thoughts traveled the convoluted path Isabelle had traced. It led to Shay. There was no mistaking her theory. Evidently Noah thought Shay was a permanent addition to the place, and Isabelle shared his notion. ''Shay hasn't promised to stay beyond the harvest,'' Jenny said quietly. She lifted the garment she was working on and bit at the thread, then spread her work across her lap.

''I surely hope these pants will fit Marshall for a while. He's growing like a bad weed.'' Carl's old homespun trousers would provide two pairs of pants for the five-year-old, she'd decided. Sewing was not a skill she'd ever pursued in her earlier years. There'd always been a house servant to do the mending and making of clothes. Now there was just Jenny, and her fingers had borne numerous sore spots from the needle before she'd discovered the knack of using a thimble.

''Mama used to tell me that ladies must learn to sew a fine seam, and I didn't know what she meant,'' Jenny mused, holding up her finished garment. ''I'm beginning to get the idea now.''

''You do fine, Jen,'' Isabelle assured her. The dasher thumped inside the churn as Isabelle resumed the rhythm. ''Noah don't seem to think that Mr. Shay's got intentions of movin' on.'' Her eyes were narrowed as she awaited Jenny's reaction to her words. And then she spoke more softly. ''What did you tell him the other night? When he carted you out to the barn and hauled you up in the loft, Noah was sure things were comin' to a head between the two of you.''

''Marshall told him that a big man had hurt me and made me cry.'' Her head was bowed as Jenny folded the small trousers she'd created. "Shay asked me what had happened."

"You told him?"

The room was silent as Jenny stood, carrying her sewing basket to the doorway. "I'll just put this away, and check on Marshall," she said quietly.

"The man's still here," Isabelle said from behind her. "You didn't scare him off, no matter what you told him."

"He looks at me differently," Jenny said softly, poised in the doorway, unwilling to recall the moments when she'd clung to him like moss to a tree, sobbing until her eyes were red and her nose was running, dampening Shay's shirt with her sorrow.

"He's still lookin' at you like he'd like to climb in your bed," Isabelle said. "Just like he has since the day he got here."

"I doubt that," Jenny told her, walking from the room and across the wide hallway to the parlor. Behind her the dasher thumped again and Isabelle's voice lifted, following Jenny's retreating figure.

"You're blind then, girl. Blind in one eye and can't see outta the other, you ask me."

The cabin went up, with all four men taking hours and days from their work to share in the building. Logs were notched, fitted in place and caulked with mud from the swamp. Finally, at sunset on the final day, the hammers still pounded, nailing the roof in place and Isabelle prepared a basket of food to carry to the men. Unwilling to forgo any shred of daylight, they toiled until Jenny forbade one more nail to be driven.

Taking turns, they sat for a few minutes at a time, eating and laughing together as if they had not worked unceasingly from dawn to dusk, days in a row. Caleb was the brunt of jokes uttered in male voices, and stilled when Marshall or one of the women was in earshot. Tomorrow, logs from the pile behind the barn would be taken to town to the sawmill, there to be cut into lengths of flooring.

Jenny decreed that no bride should have to sweep a dirt floor, and earned Caleb's thanks. His words earnest, his demeanor grateful, he pledged his loyalty to her. "I feel like a lord of the manor," she told Shay, sitting on a stump beside him.

The time shared in building had accomplished more than one result, in Shay's mind. Jenny was talking to him. That he had missed their time together of late was an understatement, he thought. As though the light had gone from his life, the lack of her presence had dimmed his soul, bringing him to his knees. And it was not a comfortable position to be in. Especially where a woman was concerned.

He'd never before found himself so enthralled by a female. Jenny was a danger to him, and he felt a sense of doom as he considered a way out of his dilemma. Leaving was out of the question, at least not until the cotton was baled and on its way to the gin. He'd given his word, perhaps not to Carl, back in Elmira, but to Jenny, here and now. A Devereaux never goes back on his word, his daddy had said, more than once. And beneath the skin of the man called Shay ran the blood of a man named Gaeton Devereaux.

The tools had been put up for the night, and Jenny picked up the basket of dishes and bits of food left over and carried it to the house. Shooing Isabelle and Noah on their way to the cabin they lived in, she looked after them, her expression wistful.

"Something wrong, Jenny?" Shay walked up behind her and she jolted at his voice, turning quickly to face him. The basket swung in an arc and caught him across his knee, eliciting an indrawn breath and a muttered word Jenny flinched at hearing.

"Well, hot damn," he said, his voice grating on the words. He bent from the waist and one hand cupped his knee.

"Oh, Shay!"

Jenny dropped the basket and crouched in front of him, her hands covering his fingers, rubbing the knuckles as though she would transfer her apology through his bones. "I'm so sorry. I didn't mean to hurt you."

He turned his hand, catching both of hers in his palm. "It's all right. I'm fine. Just took my breath for a minute there." And indeed the sharp pain had eased. Certainly, it was a far cry from the night a prison guard had deliberately cracked Shay's kneecap with a shotgun barrel. He'd learned to favor it through the years since, and unless the day called for unceasing walking, it managed to keep him upright.

Jenny looked up at him, and tears glistened in her eyes. "I didn't cause that sort of pain just whoppin' you with the basket, did I?"

He shook his head. "It's an old story, one you don't really want to hear."

She rose slowly, then bent to pick up the basket. "I told you something like that not long ago. Remember?"

"Yeah, I remember, sweetheart. But this story is better forgotten, and you've got enough bad memories of your own to add mine to the list." He turned her toward the house, his palm across her back.

"Oh, my word," she exclaimed softly. "I almost forgot Marshall. He's asleep on a quilt under the tree."

"I'll get him," Shay said. The boy weighed little and Shay lifted him into his arms, inhaling the sweet scent of childhood that arose from Marshall's hair. "You been using your soap on his head, haven't you?" he asked, walking beside her toward the house.

"Yes. In fact, he said he didn't want me to. Said it would make him smell like a girl." She lifted her free hand to smooth back a lock of hair, and glanced up at Shay. "He smells like a little boy to me," she told him.

"I was just thinking the same thing. I remember—"

"You remember what?" she asked, her eyes searching his face in the last dusky glow of twilight.

He shook his head. "Nothing. Nothing important anyway." The porch was before them and he stepped up, reaching for the screen door with one hand. Jenny walked into the kitchen ahead of him and reached for the lantern.

"Don't bother," he said softly. "I can make it to his room in the dark. I'll just take off his boots and peel his trousers down. Will that be all right?"

"Yes. Oh, and maybe undo his shirt, would you. He has it buttoned all the way up to the neck to keep the mosquitoes away."

The small task accomplished, Shay came out into the wide hallway. It ran the length of the house with two rooms off each side. A breeze flowed its length with doors to the outside open at either end. Jenny sat on the bottom step of the curved staircase, waiting for him, and he crossed to sit beside her.

"Will you talk to me about your knee?" she asked.

"Don't you need to put away the things from the basket?"

She groaned as she stood. "I forgot. They need to soak overnight, at least. The food won't spoil, standing out, but the plates should be rinsed."

"I'll help you." A candle on the buffet was lit and the basket emptied, Jenny pumping water into a big dishpan in the sink. With a clatter, she dumped silverware in first, then added the pile of plates.

"That'll do for now. I'll just put the basket in the pantry." Lifting it from the floor, she crossed to the narrow room that housed their foodstuffs and large pots and pans. Pickle crocks lined one shelf and baskets of various sizes sat at the far corner of the room. Jenny stepped into the darkness and Shay heard the sound of her movements, knew when she turned to face him again.

Deliberately, he blew out the candle and blocked the narrow doorway.

"Shay?" No fear marred her speaking of his name, only a curious note as she stood in the dark, just inches from him.

"Can we pretend, just for a minute, that we're not Shay and Jenny?" he asked. "Will you be angry with me if I touch you?"

"Who do you want to be, if not a man called Shay?" she asked.

"Someone else, maybe," he told her. "Someone who deserves a woman like you."

"And you don't?"

"No." The word was final, definite and though it was spoken softly, he knew she understood that it was irrefutable.

Her silence was long, and then she stepped closer, her skirt rustling against the shelves. He was immoveable, feet spread, hands at his sides. If she asked him to free her from the small prison he'd formed...he'd do it. And probably regret for all time his gentlemanly behavior. But it was not to be.

Her hand touched his chest, the palm outspread. His breath caught and he closed his eyes.

Her shoes nudged between his boots, and he felt the heat of her body, knew the scent of her woman's flesh.

Fingers crept up to his throat and then shifted, cupping the nape of his neck, exerting feminine strength to bow his head. He lowered his face, aware of her breath against his mouth.

Her lips brushed his, damp and wonderfully soft. Her

hands met behind his head and she funneled his hair between her fingers.

Bliss. Heavenly bliss. He reveled in the feel of her mouth moving against his, the weight of her breasts against his chest.

His groan was muffled as he surrounded her with his embrace. It wasn't enough. It could never be enough, and yet it might be all he would ever have of Jenny. She opened to his kiss, her head falling back as he scooped her from the floor, clasping her tightly against himself, her feet dangling.

She clung and he inhaled her essence, reveled in the warmth of finely textured skin and scented hair. She gasped and he released her mouth, only to utter one word.

"Again."

Chapter Five

Dark waves she had only dreamed of smoothing with her palm were in her grasp, and Jenny's fingertips savored them, testing the texture of silken strands. Shay's mouth was against her throat, then her cheek, lingering just beside her mouth, his breath warm, his voice murmuring words she'd thought never to hear from his lips.

"Again," he'd whispered, and she'd felt a thrill of desire settle deep in her belly, known the excitement of passion rising to swell within her breast. His kiss was more than she'd hoped for, less than her hungry body craved. And for this one moment, she gave herself over to the magic of knowing that Shay wanted her as she'd never been wanted before.

His body was hard, his arousal firm, pressing against her belly with an urgency she could not fail to recognize. And yet, with a deep intake of breath, he lowered her to the floor, held her as she gained her footing, and then pressed his mouth against her forehead.

"Come, Jenny," he said softly. "I'll take you to your bed."

Even as the words were spoken, she knew that they were meant in the literal sense. That he would lead her into her makeshift bedroom, and leave her there. The library door opened to his touch and they stepped inside the room that was her sanctuary. Flooded with moonlight from wide windows, it held little mystery. Only the corners were shadowed deeply. The bed itself was a pale rectangle against one wall, and white curtains moved softly as the summer breeze entered through the open window.

His voice was low, each word an aching reminder that these few moments in time would not be repeated. "Tomorrow, we'll be Shay and Jenny again," he told her. "I won't take advantage of you, sweetheart." Even the endearment held a sad note, and she shivered as he turned her away from him, his hands on her shoulders.

Broad palms swept the length of her arms, then his fingers enfolded hers and he lifted her hands, pressing them against her waist. His forearms lent support to her bosom, lifting and teasing the tender undersides of her breasts with gentle care. She groaned, a low, anguished sound, her head dropping back to lean on his chest. And mourned the love he would not share with her.

This was to be all of it, all she would have from Shay…this brief encounter under cover of night…these fleeting moments of pleasure at his hand. Hot tears slid from beneath her lashes and traced the lines of her cheeks, falling unheeded against the bodice of her dress.

"Don't cry, Jenny." His whisper was fierce. "I'm not the man for you, and we both know it."

You are. She fought the urge to shout her denial to the skies.

His hands dropped from her and he stepped back, leaving her bereft, chilled and more alone than she'd ever been. More abandoned than she'd felt the day Carl rode away to war. More saddened than the day she'd learned of his death.

The door closed behind her, Shay silent in his leaving. No footsteps told of his whereabouts and she bent her head, walking to the bed, silently removing her clothing, aware that he stood just beyond the wooden barrier. Perhaps he imagined her as she was now, bare but for the shift she wore, her dress and petticoats on the floor.

Reaching to pull her nightgown from beneath her pillow, she tossed the quilt aside, then stripped from the simple muslin shift. It fell from her hand, her fingers lax and cold. Her breasts ached, yearning for his hands to enclose them. Her mouth held the taste of his, her lips still damp from his kiss, and yet she craved more of the same. And deep inside, her womanhood wept for what would never be.

Her arms slid easily into the sleeves of her white gown, and she pulled it over her head, concealing her body, hiding her breasts, covering the length of her legs and the aching need that might never be fulfilled. Her pillow was soft, the feather tick comforting, and she shunned the covering of sheet and quilt, instead lying on her back, as if she awaited the lover who would never return.

It had been a grave error in judgment; he knew it, bone deep. And yet, he could not regret a single moment of the brief encounter. That he would forever pay penance for tasting her mouth, for stealing moments of pleasure in the dark, was a given. Jenny would ever remain in his mind as forbidden fruit, as the woman he could not have.

Standing at the edge of the cotton field, Shay shoved his hands deeply into his pockets, his hat pulled low over his forehead. The plants were nudging their way through the soil, fragile green shoots poking toward the sunlight. Once they gained ground, once their roots took hold, it would be time to chop out the weaker sprouts, guaranteeing the survival of the fittest plants.

Noah's measurements had ensured the proper planting, his forty-inch stick marking the rows, wide enough for the pickers to move between them come late summer, when the cotton burst from the bolls, ready to harvest. There was more to this than Shay had imagined, and he was struck with a moment of shame that his boyhood had been spent on a plantation, and yet, he knew little about the sowing and reaping of the crop. Only that an army of slaves tended the fields that ensured his family's well-being, their labor providing the funds that ran the Devereaux plantation.

And what was happening now, he wondered helplessly, on those acres where men and women had toiled with only food and housing as their reward for unstinting service? What were his parents doing, there in the plantation house that had once been filled with the luxuries of life that bales of cotton provided? Had they survived the rigors of war? Had Roan ever returned to the home he'd shunned for the North?

At the thought of his brother, he cast his eyes toward the horizon, north, to where Roan's journey had taken him. North, to where he'd joined the Union army and betrayed his roots, and the family he'd left behind. And what of Yvonne, the sister whose days consisted of parties and new frocks and tea on the veranda, the sister who had run off with a Yankee officer, leaving her parents to grieve?

He would probably never know. And that thought brought a strange sadness to dwell in his depths. Doomed to be a wanderer, he was a man without roots.

"Mr. Shay." Noah stood at his elbow and Shay jolted, shaken from his thoughts, stunned that he'd so escaped into memories that the man had come upon him unaware.

"It looks like a good crop, don't it?" Noah's voice was rich with satisfaction as his big-knuckled hand motioned toward the field.

"Yeah," Shay murmured. "How long before we need to thin it out?"

Noah pursed his lips. "Depends on the rain and the sun. We'll be choppin' in maybe a couple of weeks."

"How many acres will we plant, altogether?" Shay asked, thinking of Caleb and his bride-to-be.

"Maybe twenty. Along with the corn and the kitchen garden the women put in, that's about all we can handle."

"Twenty-five would be better," Shay said, glancing at the man beside him.

Noah shrugged. "More money, but we'd be bleedin' heavy by the time we got it harvested."

"Bleeding?"

"You ever picked cotton?" Noah's voice was soft, his look measuring. "You got any idea how them bolls cut up your fingers? You'll be wishin' for thicker calluses by the time September comes along."

"I'll manage," Shay said. And he would. If it meant that his hands wore bandages every day, he'd stick it out. For Jenny...for Marshall. And for the man he'd buried in Elmira.

The days flowed into weeks as the summer sun beat unmercifully against dark heads in the fields. Cotton had to be dusted with arsenic to keep the bugs away from the crop, and Shay was aghast at the thought of handling the lethal stuff. Yet it must be done, and they donned gloves, and then at his bidding, tied kerchiefs around their faces, covering nose and mouth in an effort to keep the dust from being inhaled.

Caleb's bride, Zora, joined them in the fields, and though Shay flinched at the idea of a young woman doing the work of a fieldhand, she would not be denied. And perhaps, Shay thought, it was for the best, for Caleb outdid himself for his young wife's approval. Zora went to the house at high noon daily, returning with the dinner basket, a task Jenny had allotted to her care. Shay ate with Noah at the edge of the field, speaking of the crop, the weather, everything but the woman he desired with every fiber of his being.

She ate with him at supper time, although not much chewing and swallowing took place. Already slender, she was becoming reedlike, her cheekbones more prominent. The joyous woman he'd known only weeks ago had become quiet and withdrawn, and he gathered the blame to himself for the change in her. His flesh ached for her touch, his heart mourned the loss of her ready smile, and he tossed and turned each night, knowing she lay in the room beneath his, a room he would not enter again.

Before long, after the cotton was picked, he'd be gone, and Jenny's life would be back on an even keel. There would be a man one day, a gentleman, fit for a lady, someone without death and nightmares haunting him.

Hands beneath his head, he stared at the ceiling, the heat oppressive, as thunder rolled in the distance. Rain threatened, with lightning low on the horizon, and he kicked the sheet from his legs, uncaring that his body was naked beneath it. From below, a whisper of movement caught his ear, and faint sounds told him that someone was in the central hallway. His door was open to catch any stray cross breeze, and he sat up, listening intently as the creak of the screen door at the front of the house caught his ear.

Perhaps Marshall was walking in his sleep. Shay stood quickly, stepping into his trousers, sliding his arms into his shirt. Picking up his boots, he walked into the hallway, then down the staircase. The library door stood open and he halted on the threshold. Waking Jenny was almost a necessity. He could only imagine her anger otherwise. Marshall wandering about in the middle of the night was a frightening thought.

He looked with misgiving at Jenny's bed. The thought of bending over her, watching her sleep, was almost too tempting to consider. His breath caught in his chest as he stepped closer, his gaze searching the bed. There was no temptation there to lure him, no graceful form to coax him near. Her sheets were rumpled, half on the floor, her pillow against the headboard and the bed was empty.

"Jen?" His whisper was incredulous. Where had the woman gone? Turning on his heel, he strode from the room and across the corridor to Marshall's room. The boy was a dark shadow against a white sheet, arms and legs sprawled in abandon.

The front door opened with the same creak of hinges he'd heard only moments ago, and he walked out onto the veranda. A double row of oak trees lined the rutted lane, their branches overhanging, forming a shaded approach to the house during the day. In the late-night hours, when only stars lit the sky, the area was in deep shadow, a dark tunnel leading toward the town road.

A pale form moved beneath the trees, barely visible, yet discernible to the man whose whole being was attuned to Jenny's presence. "Damn." His curse was low, a whisper that blended with the night sounds. A rustle of movement in the honeysuckle vines at the end of the veranda, the swift flight of a swallow across the yard and the croaking of frogs in the swamp surrounded him.

Where Jenny was going was a moot question. The chance of danger lurked beyond the boundaries of this place. Raiders were always a possibility, poor men who sought what they could find under cover of night. She might be as safe as a babe in his mother's arms, but even the slim possibility of harm coming to her was enough to send Shay after her. He tugged on his boots, then stepped down from the porch, moving quickly and silently in her wake. His steps were long, where hers were random and slow.

Unaware of his pursuit, she moved to stand beneath an oak, leaning against the trunk, her head bowed. He slowed his pace, his feet barely disturbing the grass where he stepped. If she heard his approach, she might cry out, possibly alerting Noah to trouble, and that would only serve to embarrass her, should she unduly sound an alarm.

He was behind her in moments, his hands reaching for her, one arm sliding around her waist, the other hand covering her mouth. She stiffened, gasping for breath, and he whispered against her ear.

"Shh! It's all right, Jenny. It's me." He felt the trembling begin, then knew the instant she recognized his touch. He took his hand from her mouth and she stiffened in his grasp.

"You frightened me," she said quietly.

His arm dropped from her and he stepped back a few inches. "I heard you leave the house. Thought at first Marshall might be sleepwalking."

"No, just me."

"I'm not sure it's safe out here for you, Jen."

Her hand rose to sweep broadly across the far horizon. "Nothing out there is a danger to me. The one person with the power to hurt me sleeps on the second floor of my home."

"I told you I'd never do that," he reminded her.

Her laugh was brittle, making him wince. "Too late, Shay Whoever-You-Are. You left your mark on me."

"My mark?" His tone was incredulous. "I bruised you?"

She shook her head. "No, it went deeper than that." Her voice trembled on the words she spoke. "I know what you feel like when you want a woman, when your body hardens and your scent speaks of loving."

She stepped back from him, an awkward movement, scraping her shoulders against the tree. Her head jerked and strands of hair caught in the rough bark. Lifting her hand, she clutched at the wayward tresses, attempting to pull her hair free.

"Wait," he said. "Let me help you."

"No." The refusal was sharp, and her other hand rose to block his approach.

"Don't be foolish, Jen. You're making a mess of it. You'll pull your hair that way."

"Don't touch me." Frantically, she tore at the strands that tangled more with each movement, and her sob of frustration tore at his heart. Her gown slipped low against her shoulder, and the pale shape of her upper breast was revealed, its slope tempting his gaze.

Touch her? He wanted to devour her, take her to his bed and keep her there, claim her as his own and then hold her in his arms throughout the long night hours. His much prized sense of honor fell by the wayside as his hands clutched her shoulders. Leaning against her, he held her immobile, his mouth seeking hers, his breathing strident as though he'd run a race he stood no chance of winning.

She bit at his lips, and he groaned, the rush of blood to his groin obliterating the pain she inflicted with her sharp teeth. Her lithe body wriggled against him, and his grip slid to her arms, taking the fabric of her gown with it.

The bodice gave way, shredding across her chest, exposing her left breast in its entirety, and she cried out. "Damn you, Shay." It was the sound of a woman in pain, and he cursed roundly. Pulling her roughly into his arms, his hands reached for her hair, holding it fast, then tugging it free from the bark.

"I'm sorry. I'm so sorry, Jen." His arms encircled her and he bent his head to speak against her ear. "Please, sweetheart, stop fighting me." Moisture fell from his mouth and his tongue reached for it, tasting the acrid flavor of blood. He drew back in surprise, feeling the warm drops on his lip.

"Hold still. I don't want to get blood on you."

She stiffened, leaning back, and her eyes sought his face, narrowing as she caught a glimpse of his mouth.

"I did that?" One slender hand lifted to press against his lips. "I bit you, didn't I?"

He searched in his pocket, whipping his handkerchief out and blotting his lips. Her hand held traces of blood and he wiped it, his movements clumsy. Against the pale skin of her breast, two dark stains bore mute testimony to the small wounds he bore, droplets that elongated as he watched. His handkerchief touched the crimson blemish, and Jenny looked down at the long fingers that pressed against her flesh, only that thin layer of fabric shielding her from his hand.

She was lost, her heart beating against his fingertips, a rapid cadence that must surely be pulsing loud enough for him to hear. Above her, the night birds sang their mournful song, and in the distance a dog howled his distress. Yet she heard only the frantic throbbing of her heart, betraying her with each beat, yearning for his touch.

"Let me give you my shirt," he said. "I tore your gown."

She laughed, pressing her lips together to hold back the sound. They'd done little else but cause hurt, one to the other. Biting his mouth was a hateful act, one she regretted to her very depths. Shay's hands had demolished her only nightgown, revealing her body in a way that should have shamed her. Yet, it hadn't.

Even now, as she waited for him to move his hand, his fingers pressed against the firm flesh. The handkerchief dropped to the ground as she watched. His hand clenched, then opened, fingers spread wide. The very tip of his index finger touched lightly, and the crest of her breast responded, tightening and hardening, aching for that errant fingertip to brush its surface.

Instead it circled, slowly, gently, carefully, and a cry of longing whispered from her lips. He bent, his mouth opening, there where her flesh longed for succor, and her hands flew to hold him against her. His arm held her upright, and she dropped her head, resting it against his shoulder.

"Jenny...I want you, Jenny." He lifted her, shifting her in his arms, gathering her high against his chest, and then bent his head again. She felt the laving of his tongue on her skin, the touch of teeth and lips, and the brush of his mouth as he whispered her name.

The grass was deep beneath the trees and he eased her to her feet, then spread his shirt before lowering her to the ground. He lifted the hem of her gown, his fingers smoothing the length of her legs beneath its fabric.

She shivered at his touch, knowing the decision she must make. If she allowed it, he would take her, here and now, and she would never be the same. Never be able to hold up her head, with the knowledge that her pride was intact.

She had given herself to a Yankee marauder, hated the man who took her with no trace of mercy, and lived to gain back her self-respect. It had been a choice she'd made, in full knowledge that it was a sacrifice worth the price she paid.

Taking Shay into her body was a different matter. Choosing to give herself, knowing that he would leave her, and never look back, brought her down to a level she could not live with.

"No." The word trembled in the air, and Shay stilled, his hands beneath her knees, his fingers tightening in response.

"Jenny?" Hoarse with desire, roughened with passion, he spoke her name with a voice that pled for relief.

She shook her head, knowing that the movement was visible. "I can't do this," she whispered. "I can't."

He shuddered, his shoulders seeming to bow in defeat, and then he turned to one side and rolled to his back, one hand lifting to cover his eyes. "Just give me a minute." Aching need coated his words, and Jenny sat up, folding her arms around her knees and hiding her face. She'd led him to this point, allowed his mouth to give her pleasure such as she'd never known. And then denied him fulfillment.

She knew in her heart that it was her right to refuse. As a gentleman he was obliged to bow to that refusal. But as a man, he was teetering on the brink. "I'm the one who's sorry," she said, her voice muffled against her knees. "I led you on, Shay."

He sat up, his breathing harsh. Lifting his shirt from the ground, he wrapped it around her shoulders. "You're a marrying woman, Jenny. I knew it from the beginning. It's why I've tried to stay away from you."

Standing, he lifted her to her feet. "Here, put your arms in the sleeves," he told her. His hands were gentle as he buttoned the shirt, careful not to touch the curves beneath.

"You can leave here if you want to," she said. "I won't blame you, and I'll explain to Noah." The words were like acid in her mouth, but the offer must be made.

"You know better. I told you I'd be here to harvest the cotton."

Relief flooded her, hot tears washing her eyes; and she bent her head, as if she must watch where she walked, turning from him. He followed her lead, close by her side, careful not to brush against her hand. "Thank you," she murmured as they approached the veranda.

"For what?" He offered his palm as she climbed the step and she accepted it, waiting as he opened the door. "I tore your gown, forced myself on you and behaved badly. I don't expect your thanks for that."

"You know what I mean." The door closed behind them and she crossed to the library door. So little time had passed since she walked across its threshold. So much had taken place, changing her forever.

"We'll talk in the morning," he told her, and she knew

he waited, watching as she left his side, and crossed the floor to her bed.

"Yes." It was a whisper, but he must have heard it, for he closed the door, leaving her alone. She listened for the sound of his boots on the staircase, then the muted steps down the hallway overhead. The floor creaked over her head and she imagined him lowering himself to the mattress.

Her feet were damp and she wiped them on the rag rug beside her bed, then curled on her side, facing the window. His shirt held his scent, and she lifted it to her face, inhaling deeply. Then, nestled within its covering, she slept.

The man was tall, powerfully built and black as ebony. Totally without a covering of hair, his head gleamed in the morning sunlight. Eyes dark as midnight held menace, directed at her and her household. Jenny had seen him a few times, early in her marriage, and recognized him as one of the people who'd wasted no time in leaving Pennington Plantation.

"Y'all got my girl here, and I want her back." He left no room for bargaining with his demand. Standing inside the kitchen, Jenny considered reaching for the shotgun hanging over the door. Whether she could pull the trigger or not was a question she had pondered before. Certainly, if it were a case of life or death, or Marshall's safety, she would sacrifice human life.

But if this man was Eli, Zora's father, there was a good chance she could reason with him. Perhaps his concern was for the girl's welfare. "Is Zora your daughter?" she asked, and then flinched as he climbed the step to the porch.

"Damn right she is, and you know it, Miz Pennington." His voice was a growl, his anger a palpable entity. "That sum bitch boy of Noah's snatched her up and brought her here, thinkin' we wouldn't do nuthin' about it. It takes ever livin' soul to bring in a crop, and I'm not doin' without my girl.''

"Caleb married the girl," Jenny said. "She wasn't taken from home against her will."

"*I* didn't say she could go—" his thumb jabbed his chest as the angry father drew closer to the screen door "—and that's all that counts."

"You're Eli, aren't you?" Jenny asked, aware of a presence behind her.

"Miss Jenny's got nothin' to do with your girl runnin' off," Isabelle said loudly from the kitchen doorway. Her bare feet moved swiftly across the wooden floor, her skirts swishing as she hastened to Jenny's side. "You go find Caleb and talk to him. This is a business 'tween menfolk."

Dark, thick fingers settled over the door handle and the door was jerked almost from its hinges. Face-to-face, Eli was an even greater threat, and Jenny backed from the doorway, wishing her hands held the shotgun.

"Is she in here?" Standing in the doorway, he peered over Jenny's shoulder, his gaze raking the corners of the kitchen, as though the two women had hidden his daughter from sight.

"No, she's not," Jenny said firmly. "And I forbid you to enter my home."

Surprise lifted Eli's brows as he looked down at the slender woman. "You think you could stop me, did I want to come in?"

"Maybe not," another voice said smoothly from behind Eli's back. "But the gun in my hand says you'd better back off."

Eli's big fists clenched in front of Jenny's face, and then his fingers splayed wide over his belly as Eli's bravado melted. With a last hateful look into her eyes, Eli backed onto the porch and turned to face Shay's long gun. It was a sight guaranteed to instill respect in the most angry of men, and Jenny knew Eli well understood the power of the rifle in Shay's hands.

"Step down off the porch," Shay told him, motioning with the barrel, and then his eyes found Jenny in the kitchen. "You ladies all right in there?"

"I never put a hand on them women," Eli told him quickly. "I come for my girl."

"If we're talking about Zora, she's with her husband."

"I never gave her leave to get married. I want her back home."

Shay shook his head. "I don't think she wants to go. She's doing just fine. No one's keeping her here against her will, Eli."

"You know me?" The man's surprise was quick.

"I've heard of you. Noah says you're sharing crops with Doc Gibson. You'd have done better to stay here. Miss Jenny would have given you your own land here."

"Maybe, maybe not. Fact is, I'm doin' fine where I am. All except for findin' my girl's snuck off and left home."

"I want you out of here," Shay said bluntly. "You come back and I'll get the law after you." Eli's head lowered, his hands fell to his sides and twitched, then formed ham-like fists again.

"You tell Zora her ma's wantin' her home."

Shay nodded gravely. "I'll do that. And you tell Zora's mama that she can come see her girl any time she takes a notion."

"You runnin' this place?" Eli asked, his words harsh.

"You might say that," Shay told him.

"You livin' in the big house?"

Shay's eyes narrowed. "You stick your nose in where it's not welcome and you're asking for trouble, Eli."

"You belong to the Devereaux bunch, don't you?" Eli asked, his head lifting a bit, his voice curious.

"I don't know what you're talking about."

"I made a trip to the big town," Eli said, "over in the next parish, and I seen a man there looks like you. Doc Gibson said he was Roan Devereaux."

"I don't know what you're talking about," Shay repeated. "Now, get on out of here. Go tell Zora's mama that her girl's fine, and she's not coming home."

Eli stepped down off the porch, eschewing the step and stalking across the grass to where a mule waited under a tree.

"Man ain't too bad off if he's got hisself a mule to ride," Isabelle said beneath her breath. "You mark my words, Jen, we ain't seen the last of him. He always had a powerful temper. Made your Mr. Carl mighty mad once or twice, bein' muley."

"Was Carl ever harsh with his people?" Jenny asked, appalled at her own lack of knowledge. Before the day Carl rode off to war, she'd had little to do with the folks who lived in the cabins beyond the barn.

"No," Isabelle said, her denial quick. "Eli never once took a lickin', at least not that I heard of. And I didn't miss much, not with Noah keepin' his hands on things the way he did."

"Eli's an angry man." Jenny watched as the mule set off at a fast clip, Eli's long legs hanging loosely on either side of the animal's wide barrel. His back was stiff, his shoulders hunched, and well they might be. Shay's hands were still filled with the gun, and his attention never wavered from the big man.

"Shay?" Jenny spoke his name quietly, then stepped down from the porch. He was rigid, the gun an extension of himself, and she thought he resembled a warrior, armed and ready to do battle for those he'd vowed to protect. She lifted her hand, reached for his arm, then hesitated, shoving her fingers deep into her apron pocket. Touching him might not be wise. In fact, after last night she wasn't sure where she stood with him.

"You keep that shotgun handy, you hear?" he said harshly. His head turned a bit and he glanced down at her. "The man's got a full plate keeping body and soul together, and losing a field hand's made him testy. Maybe I'll send Noah over to talk to Doc Gibson. Is he a reasonable man?"

"I don't know. Carl knew him pretty well, but I never met him. You won't go yourself?" she asked. He'd brushed aside Eli's reference, ignored the name Devereaux as if it was unknown to him. And now she waited as he turned to face her, his jaw set, his eyes dark and expressionless.

"I've got enough to do here," he told her. His look encompassed Isabelle in the doorway. "You women mind what I say. Keep that gun handy."

He strode from the porch to where his stallion waited, reins hanging loosely to the ground. He gathered them in one hand, speaking quietly to the stud. A single movement put him in the saddle, and Jenny marveled at the agile strength of the man. Rifle in his hand, he rode from the yard, his big horse leaping the pasture fence effortlessly. Man and horse seemed as one as the stallion cantered across the pasture, then cleared the far fence. Jenny walked back to the porch, then stepped into the kitchen. "What do you think?" she asked Isabelle.

"I think Caleb got him a handful of trouble, is what I think. And we're gonna get the overflow."

Chapter Six

What the hell Roan was doing in this neck of the woods was a question Shay would have given a whole lot to have answered. He'd figured that distance was his ally, and now, Roan was within arm's reach. Perhaps not today, he amended silently, but big Eli had certainly let the proverbial cat out of the bag with his remarks.

And Jenny had lapped up the information. He'd seen the light in her eye, felt the anticipation in her demeanor, and had been hard put to turn his back and walk away. The memory of her hand reaching out to him, then retreating with an awkward movement pierced his heart. Jenny should never have to restrain herself, never hold back the generous warmth that exuded from each gesture, each word she spoke.

That she'd retreated last night was to have been expected. He'd rushed her, tumbled her down into the lush grass and fallen on her like a man without control. Almost lost in the heat of her body, he'd been dragged from the edge by one simple word. Jenny's "no" had rung like a church bell inside his head, and the pain of her refusal was more than physical, although there'd been that to deal with, too.

He should have known better. His label for her was as true as the loyalty in her heart for the man she'd married over five years ago. *A marrying woman.* And he wasn't fit to be a husband to any female, let alone a lady like Jenny. His tongue found the sore on his lip and his grin threatened to split the small scab. Damn, the woman was wild. Maybe *lady* was the wrong label to pin on her. Anger and passion ran neck and neck sometimes in the race called desire, and Jenny promised to be a winner, should the right man claim her as his own.

Shay's horse halted at the edge of the cornfield, and he watched as Noah and his sons walked the long rows, checking for bugs, snapping them between their fingernails and dropping them to the dirt. It was a task they seldom had time for, but this week marked a layoff for all of them. The cotton was chopped and hilled, and the kitchen garden consisted of neat rows of beans and potatoes. Carrots from the thinning process were small and succulent, and they'd feasted on them yesterday. Isabelle predicted beans for Sunday dinner, and Jenny said they'd celebrate by using the last of the smokehouse bacon to flavor them.

Noah raised a hand to wave in his direction, and Shay turned his horse down the row to where the men worked. "We had company up at the house," he said quietly.

Noah's eyes met his and he straightened, glancing at his sons who worked several feet distant. "Anything I should know about?"

"Eli came looking for his girl. I told him to leave, but it took a look at my rifle to persuade him."

"Isabelle knows how to handle the shotgun," Noah said, "but I'd rather she didn't have to point it at anybody."

"Can Jenny shoot?"

Noah grinned. "She can make it look good, but whether or not she'd pull the trigger is another story. Be more likely to wag her finger in his face, maybe."

Shay couldn't resist the image and a grin tilted his mouth. "She's got spunk. More than I'd have thought." His memory turned back to their first encounter. "Though I expect she'd have lifted a gun on me if there'd been one handy, the day I rode up on her."

Noah sent him a knowing glance. "I wondered if she didn't give you that split lip." And then his head ducked, as if he'd stepped beyond a line.

"Not the way you think," Shay told him, fingering the sore spot.

"You makin' any plans, Mr. Shay?" Noah's words were low, almost muffled. "Miss Jenny's needin' a man around here, and this place'd make a good livin' for a family." He motioned toward his sons, and Zora, who'd joined them. "We ain't goin' nowhere, Mr. Shay. We got some land and a good life here."

"I'm not the kind to be tied down anywhere," Shay admitted. "My feet don't seem to stay planted long."

"That could change," Noah told him. "A woman like Miss Jenny could make a difference, did you decide it was time to settle down."

"The man will never stay put," Isabelle said firmly. "Don't you be hangin' your hopes on his coattails, Jen. He's not gonna last past harvest. Once that cotton's baled and weighed in town, he'll be ridin' out and you'll be left holdin' the bag."

"Not the way you're thinking," Jenny told her. "If he leaves, I'll be the same woman I was when he got here."

Isabelle laughed, her brow arched, and her hands flew in the air. "And ain't that a crock of you know what! You're never gonna be the same woman you was three months ago, Jen. That man's turned you upside down, like it or not. He's got you pinin' away like a girl lookin' to be…"

"Isabelle." Jenny spoke her friend's name sharply, then

felt her color mount with a rush of heat. Both palms pressed against her cheeks, as if she could cool her skin so easily. "What a way to talk," she said tartly. "Shay's a friend, and a big help to all of us. I'm sure he'll be on his way come September or October. That's all he said he'd do, just stay till the crop was in. And I'm not pining for anything," she said staunchly.

Isabelle's mouth turned down, her laughter gone. "I'll still be here, Jen. No matter what comes or goes, me and Noah will always be here." Her head tilted to one side and her dark eyes seemed to peer within Jenny's soul. "It wouldn't be all bad if you took what he's offerin', you know. The man's got eyes for you, and you know it. He'd be good for you, even if it's only for a while."

Jenny shook her head and leveled a look at Isabelle, holding her gaze. "I'll tell you the same thing I told him. I can't do that. All I could think of was my mama telling me that before I took a man into my bed, I'd better be sure I have a marriage certificate hanging over the headboard. I swear, she'd know. I can almost see her turning in her grave, should I take up with a man that way."

"You thought about it, then."

Jenny's mouth tightened. "I'm not too old to know what I'm missing. I'm neither blind nor dead, and I'd have to be both if I couldn't see what a prize package Shay Whatever-His-Name is." She covered the pan of bread dough she'd punched down to size and lifted it atop the warming oven.

"Did you hear Eli? Out there, when he mentioned the name *Devereaux?*"

Isabelle's knife slowed midway through the meat she was slicing. "What are you thinking? That Eli knew something?"

"Shay wouldn't look at me. He shut me out and rode off."

"You ever heard of the Devereaux family?" Isabelle asked. "Seems like the name's an old one hereabouts."

"No. But then, that doesn't mean anything. I never heard of much of anything till I married Carl. We lived right close to home, just went to town three or four times a year, and Papa didn't commune much with other folks."

"You miss your mama, don't you?"

Jenny's sigh was deep. "More than ever, now that Marshall's getting so big. There's things I'd like to ask her about."

"It's a shame you've never seen your pa since after the fightin' was all over with."

"I don't think it's over with, yet," Jenny said sadly. "There's still so much hard feelings and downright hatred among folks. I suspect my pa doesn't want to see me. He surely hasn't made any effort. He didn't even answer the letters I sent him. From what Doc Gibson said Pa just kinda pulled in his horns and let things go to hell in a handbasket. Most of his land's laying fallow and his people just tend to themselves, those that hung around. There's some that look out for him, but mostly he's barely getting along."

"Maybe you'd do well to take a trip there, while Shay's still here to go with you. See how the old man's doing. Might even ask him to come here and stay." Though her tone was casual, Isabelle's watchful gaze was anything but, and Jenny lifted her hands from the dishpan, letting the water drip where it might as she turned from the sink.

"You think that's a good idea?" she asked, dumbfounded at the suggestion. A small grain of hope took root in her heart as she considered Isabelle's words. "Wouldn't it be wonderful if Marshall could have a granddaddy? Carl's folks are long gone, and my pa's all there is left."

Isabelle shrugged idly, but her eyes were sharp with anticipation as she watched Jenny. "Wouldn't hurt to think about it anyway."

* * *

Supper was a bit of this and a bit of that, Jenny'd told him, but Shay managed to make a meal of the food she'd prepared. She'd watched him while he ate, barely pushing the food around on her own plate, her thoughts apparently on something that was making her tense and anxious. Marshall chattered on, oblivious to his elders, needing only an occasional nod or murmured word of approval to sustain his recital of the day's events.

"The tassels on the corn are gettin' all brown, Mama. Shay says we'll be eating it in the next couple of days, and I get to pick the first ears for the house." He drank from his cup, long swallows of cool milk, and then wiped the white residue from his upper lip onto his sleeve.

"Marshall…" She leaned toward him, using a napkin to complete the cleanup, and he grinned at her. "You must learn to use your napkin. Gentlemen eat neatly," she reminded him gently.

"Even Shay?" he asked boldly, gazing at his idol with childish admiration.

"Even Shay." The admonition was clear as Shay repeated the boy's query, answering him succinctly. "Young men should do as their mothers tell them," he added.

"Did you?" Marshall asked boldly. "Did you do everything your mama said?"

Shay's face held a faraway look as he considered Marshall's words. And then he shook his head. "Not lately, I haven't. But, when I was little, about your age, I did everything I was told and then some. I did my sums every day and learned my letters and helped in the garden."

"Did you watch the water jars and keep the flies away from the dinner basket, like I do?" Marshall slid from his chair and approached Shay. "Did your pa take you out to the field to help pick up weeds and kill the bugs?"

"Has he been killing bugs?" Jenny asked quickly.

Shay looked patiently at her. "All boys kill bugs, Jen. Wait till I show him how to get rid of the tomato worms."

She shivered. "I can't bear the things. Isabelle does that job."

"And does she turn them loose?" Shay asked with a grin.

"You know she doesn't." She sniffed delicately and turned her head. "I don't know what she does with them, and I don't want to know, either."

"Then Marsh and I won't tell you," Shay said. "We'll just let Isabelle do something else in the garden when the worms start chewing on the leaves."

"Marshall, go on out and call the chickens in for the night," Jenny said, having heard enough of worms and bugs to last for a good long time. "The pan for their feed is in the barrel. I think you can reach it if you stand on a stump."

"All right, Mama," he said agreeably. "But if they peck at my feet, I'm gonna whop 'em with the feed pan."

"Don't kill any of them," she said with a laugh. "I'll be canning the young roosters next week. Give them another few days to put on some weight."

Marshall left the kitchen and headed out the screen door, the spring slamming it shut in his wake.

"I want to talk to you," Jenny said, rising to pick up the plates and silverware. She leaned to gather his from in front of him, and he grasped her arm.

"Are you all right?" he asked quietly, demanding she look at him.

"I'm fine." His hand was warm against her skin, wrapping entirely around the narrow expanse of her wrist, his fingers overlapping. The urge to lift that hand to her mouth was a fire within her, and she gritted her teeth against the pain of denying herself that small pleasure. To brush her lips against his tanned skin, to feel the strength of those fingers gripping her own.

She closed her eyes, and his hand did the unthinkable, lifting hers to complete the very act she'd only yearned to do. His mouth was damp against her fingers, his lips warm and gentle. And then he released her, and she rescued herself from the warmth, lest it envelop her and consume her in its heat. She picked up his plate, stacked it atop her own and walked to the sink, settling the dishes in the pan.

"Jenny? I think we need to make a decision here."

Whirling to face him, she spoke quickly. "I do, too. I need someone to go with me to see my father, Shay. If I take Noah along, it leaves them shorthanded here, and I don't want to leave Isabelle in charge with Eli on the rampage."

"I'm sending Noah to talk to Doc Gibson sometime in the next couple of days," Shay said. "I don't know if it will do any good, but I'm willing to give it a try, and Noah said he didn't mind riding over there." His grin was wide as he spoke. "I offered my stud for him to ride, but he turned me down flat. Said a mule was just fine, and he wasn't going to climb up on a big devil like my stallion."

"Is he a devil?" she asked.

"Not with me. Maybe with someone who didn't know how to handle him."

"I've ridden bareback, when I was younger, but Carl didn't cotton to women riding astride a horse."

Shay's brow tilted. "Did he expect you to ride sidesaddle?" The words carried an unpalatable connotation as he drawled them out.

Jenny felt a blush, springing to Carl's defense. "It's the only way for a lady to ride, he said. And I didn't own a riding habit, so I just sat in the buggy and let the mare haul me around the place when I needed to go somewhere."

"You'd have done better to learn how to handle a horse,

just in case the time ever came when you had to get somewhere in a hurry and there wasn't anyone around to harness the mare.''

"I harness my own animals," she said quickly. And then she halted her words, regretting the harsh sound of her rebuttal. "I want to ask you a favor here, and I'm not going about it the right way, am I?"

"Yes, I'll go with you to see your father. How far is it? Will we need to take a dinner basket of food along for noontime?"

"It's two hours and better to get there. And when we get to his place, there's no guarantee he'll even be there. Last I knew, he was all alone in the house, the part that wasn't burned out, and eating whatever folks brought to the door for him.''

Shay frowned. "Why didn't you make him come here?"

Jenny shook her head. "There's never been any way of making my pa do anything he doesn't want to. Since my mama died, I've heard he's turned into a hermit of sorts. I wrote to him, several times in fact, but he wouldn't read my letters. He used to be so easy to deal with, and so full of common sense, and now, he's a different man. I want to go to him, but I'm not sure what I'll find when I get there. It sort of scares me.''

"Grief does some folks that way," Shay said. "Other people work it out and put their energy into day-to-day living, and then there's those like your father who just crawl in a hole. You're one of the strong ones, Jenny."

At his words of praise, she looked up quickly. Eyes dark as midnight took her measure and his mouth was soft, his lips relaxed. If she took just three steps, she could bend to him and place her lips just so against his, and then...

"When do you want to go?" he asked. The mood shattered as though it had never been.

"Let's wait and see what Doc Gibson says to Noah. Maybe we'll be able to get away before too long."

Shay nodded, and rose from the table. He was halfway to the door when the sound of chickens squawking and Marshall yelling at the top of his lungs sped up his steps. He cleared the porch step and his long legs covered ground with a rate of speed Jenny had never before seen. And then he pulled up short, as Marshall's actions halted Shay in his tracks.

In the middle of the chicken yard, the child spun like a top, the empty feed pan held at arm's length. Hens scuttled for cover, loudly voicing their displeasure with the boy. Shay's laughter rang out and he bent over double outside the gate, hands on his knees, gulping air. Jenny scurried past him and, dodging the metal pan, secured Marshall by the collar.

"Hold still, you're scaring the chickens half to death!" she scolded.

Marshall turned to her, dissolving in tears against her apron. "Mama, they was peckin' at my feet, and I was just chasin' them away."

"You shouldn't be in here barefoot anyway," she said, willing the humor of Marshall's predicament from her mind. "The hens won't lay if they get upset, Marshall."

Shay stood erect, one hand clinging to the chicken wire fence. His eyes were moist, his laughter still audible.

"It's not funny," Jenny told him. "I can't afford to lose my eggs because Marshall got mad at my hens."

"And you're not laughing?" Shay managed to whimper.

"I don't think Marshall's amused," she said hedging a bit. One young rooster stood next to the coop, shaking his head, then wobbling as he walked a few feet.

"I think I hit him with the pan," Marshall said between hiccups. "I shook the pan, and the chickens heard the noise, and they came inside the fence, and then I tried to get out the gate, but they kept chasin' me.'' He bent to point at the top of his left foot. ''See? That's where one of them got me.'' He bent low to inspect his dusty feet. ''Lookie there, Mama. On my other foot, too, in two different places. He made me bleed, Mama.'' His tone was mournful, and Jenny bent to pick him up.

His feet dangled to her knees, and he hung on for dear life as she carried him out the gate. Shay stood ready and fastened the latch quickly, even though the hens were busily pecking at the ground, searching out the prime bits of feed. Jenny's mouth twitched as she lowered Marshall to the ground.

''You should have tossed the feed away from you, sweetie. When you dumped it all around your feet, the chickens couldn't tell the difference between your toes and their supper.''

Marshall peered up at her doubtfully. ''Are you laughin' at me?'' he asked.

Shay scooped him up and lifted him high over his head, settling Marshall on his broad shoulders. He lifted one small foot and inspected it closely. ''Looks like you need a peck of soap on these feet, Marsh. And then we'll put some salve on your sore spots. How's that?''

''Can we go for a walk after that?'' Marshall asked hopefully. ''I could just ride on your shoulders so my feet won't hurt.''

''I suspect he's going to milk this for all it's worth,'' Jenny murmured, stepping closer to the two male creatures who'd so readily formed a bond during the hot summer days.

''How about if we all go for a walk?'' Shay asked, his gaze intent on Jenny.

''And I get to ride,'' Marshall chortled. His hands gripped Shay's collar as they set off for the back porch.

''After we clean up your feet,'' Shay reminded him.

* * *

"You know how to handle him," Jenny said quietly. The sun had set and the house was quiet. Marshall was asleep, sprawled across his bed with two narrow strips of cloth serving as bandages decorating his feet. "He's missed having a man here."

"Noah pays him some attention, doesn't he?" Shay asked, glancing up at her from his perch on the back porch.

"Some." Jenny sat in a cane rocker and looked down at Shay. Marshall wasn't the only one who'd become attached to this man, she thought bleakly. For all the good it did her. Her mind returned to the visitor Shay had sent on his way. Eli had seemed so sure, so ready to associate Shay with the man called Roan Devereaux. Should she mention the name, Shay would retreat, maybe even strike out down the lane, leaving her alone on the porch. And yet, if she ignored it, she might never know more about Shay than she did right now. Perhaps it was worth the risk.

"Whereabouts did you say your family lives?" she asked, counting the moments of silence as he picked up his hat from the porch. He'd put it on his head now, and set off by himself, she thought.

But his hands only turned the brim in a circle, touching the crown carefully to set a crease. "I didn't say," he said finally. The hat settled on his head then and he tilted it back as he turned to face her. "Some distance from here. They have a plantation, and I suspect my brother runs it."

"Roan?" She tasted the name, wondering if the man in question was as tall, as dark, as inscrutable as Shay. Not likely. Shay was one of a kind.

"His name was Valderone. My mother took a fancy to strange names."

"Valderone sounds French. Where'd she find Shay?" Her heart beat faster as he considered the question.

And then he stood, rolling down his sleeves, paying special attention to the buttoning process. "She didn't name me Shay." He walked past the end of the porch and around the side of the house.

Jenny closed her eyes. And wasn't that a strange one. His mother had not called him Shay. And yet, it was his name. He'd said so, and if she knew any truth in the world, it was that Shay would not lie over so trivial a matter. Perhaps over some major issue. He might quibble about his past, and avoid her probing. He had done just that, she admitted to herself, remembering his terse replies, his evasive tactics on more than one occasion.

She waited, listening for his return, hopeful that he would sit with her again, take up his talk of crops, maybe…

A sound inside the house caught her ear and she turned her head to the kitchen door. Marshall stood behind the screen door and rubbed at his eyes with both fists. "I'm scared, Mama. I saw a big chicken comin' to get me."

"It was a dream," she said, rising from the rocking chair and opening the door. Her hand rested on his shoulder as she turned him back to the main hallway, and then across to his room. "Come on. I'll sit with you for a bit," she told him.

He climbed into bed readily enough, and Jenny sat on the edge of the mattress, smoothing his golden hair and talking softly about the stray cat they'd found in the barn. "Would you like to take out a dish of food in the morning?" she asked. "In case the kitty is still around, maybe you could feed it and it would learn to like us."

"Could I keep it for my own?" he asked, and then smothered a yawn with one small hand. "We could give it some milk maybe."

"Maybe," she said agreeably. "You'll have to sleep now so you can check on it in the morning, Marshall."

"Why don't you call me Marsh all the time like Shay

does?'' he asked, his words slurring as he turned to his side.

''I will if you want me to.'' She transferred her attention to his back and her hand set up a smooth motion, patting softly, then running her fingers through his hair as he murmured beneath his breath.

She bent low to hear, and he breathed the words again. ''I love you, Mama.''

''I love you, too, Marsh.''

Shay appeared in the doorway and she glanced up at him. The dark visage was impenetrable, his gaze somber. ''Is he all right?''

Jenny nodded as she rose and walked past him, her skirts brushing his trousers. He followed her toward the front of the house, out onto the veranda, where she sought the support of a wide pillar. Her back pressed against its solid strength as she turned to face him.

''Marshall loves you, Shay. He's been a different boy these past months, following you around and learning to help with the chores.''

''I enjoy him, Jen.'' He turned his back to her, looking across the wide vista, where oak trees and long grass formed the neglected approach to the plantation house. ''I've tried not to let him get too attached, but he's hard to resist.''

''He's already attached,'' she said flatly. ''He needs a father, Shay.'' If he couldn't respond to that blatant invitation, she'd push even further, but her instincts shrank from the bold tactic.

''All boys need a father. Some of them have to make do without one.'' His words were bleak, his hands lifting to thrust deeply into his pockets as he spoke.

''Marshall's made do all of his life. I think he's pinned his hopes on you.''

Shay inhaled and his shoulders squared, forming a barrier

he reinforced with his reply. "Someone will come along one of these days. A man worthy of you and the boy. I won't be here much longer."

"I know that," she told him, feeling despair wash through her veins. And knew that she was not being fair to the man. "I figure you've given me a respite, and that's more than I'd hoped for when you arrived," she told him quietly. "I'd thought this would be the last crop, that I'd have to auction off the place this winter. I didn't see how I could afford another year. But, with the crops we're looking to harvest, the extra cotton we've planted and the good corn crop, we might be able to make it a little longer."

"Have you thought about putting your profit in cattle?" he asked. "Raising beef cattle is a hell of a lot easier work than chopping cotton. A man can tend to a good-size herd if he's got pasture and a decent hayfield."

"I wouldn't know where to begin," she said, frustration rising within her. "To tell you the truth, I'm sick of being in charge of this place, tired of being responsible for all of us." Hot tears rushed to the surface and she bowed her head, clenching her jaw to keep them at bay.

He took a step toward her and she lifted a hand, shaking her head. "No, don't touch me. I can't do this anymore, Shay. I want you to leave before I make a fool of myself."

He was like a statue before her. "All right, if that's what you want. I won't stay if you really mean that."

She took in great gulps of air, her lungs aching as she suppressed the tears, her heart rent with the pain of loving this man. "What I want doesn't have much to do with it, I'm afraid."

"What do you want, Jenny?" She looked up at him, her eyes feasting on the taut line of his jaw, the straight blade of his nose and the dark secrets hidden in the depths of his eyes.

"I want you to stay here, Shay. Not just for now, or the

next two months, but for the rest of my life. I want to go to bed with you and wake up with you and see you across the supper table every day. I want—'' Her voice broke and she repressed the urge to bow her head, uncaring now that her tears streamed, that her mouth quivered.

''I want you to marry me and be Marshall's father. And I know I can't have that. I know I'll live the rest of my life wondering what it would have been like…'' Her arm swept toward the shaded, grassy lawn. ''I almost wish I hadn't stopped you,'' she whispered.

''Would you stop me now?'' So softly she could barely hear the words, he whispered temptation in her ear. Leaning forward, ignoring the hand she thrust against his chest, he bent to her, his breath warm against her face.

She shivered, beguiled by the thought of his hands against her skin, lured by the dark splendor of his scarred face, enticed by the image of their coming together. And then she thought of the emptiness she would face, once she'd known the joy of loving Shay, only to have him walk away. It stretched before her and she closed her eyes against the pain.

''Could you do that? Take everything I've offered you, and then walk away from me?''

''Would you stop me now?'' he repeated, ignoring her words. His hands gripped her shoulders. ''Look at me.''

His face was a blurred image, and she stood no chance of reading the expression he wore. ''My mama will roll over in her grave if I do this. But no, I won't stop you.''

''I'm not worth your guilt. And I'm sure as hell not worth shedding tears over, Jenny. And I won't haul you out there in the grass and lift your skirts like the damn Yankee who put that look of shame in your eyes.''

As though her bones had lost their strength, she sagged, leaning against him. ''Then what will you do?'' she asked, her words muffled against his chest.

"I'll marry you." His grip tightened as he lifted her to her toes. "Look at me. Look at what you're getting, Jenny. I'm a man with blood on his hands and no love to give you. I left my soul in Elmira, buried in the mud of that damnable prison camp. And if I can't stick it out, if the demons find me here, I'll probably move on anyway. Is that what you want?"

She lifted her head, tilting her chin upward, the better to see his face. Harsh lines drew his mouth downward, emphasizing the scar, pulling at the corner of his eye. He might have frightened another woman, had she not known the essence of the man living behind that ruined face. But to Jenny, he was all that was beautiful in her world, where hope had become a lost commodity.

"I'll take whatever you give me," she told him. 'For as long as you stay. And if you leave—" she swallowed and smiled, aware that her lips trembled, but unwilling to make him regret his offer "—if you leave, I'll let you go."

"Where can we find a preacher?" he asked. "I won't wait longer than tomorrow."

Chapter Seven

And yet, waiting was on the agenda. Noah set off the next morning for Doc Gibson's place, and Shay, reluctantly, recognized that he and Jenny could not leave before the issue of Zora and her family had been resolved. He spent the noontime hours, when the sun was high overhead, working in the barn, hammering and sawing with Marshall close at hand.

Jenny's curiosity pried her from the garden once, but she was waved away from the open barn door by Shay's uplifted hand, and Marshall's giggles followed her as she headed back for the weeding that must be done. Isabelle sat on the porch, shelling peas, offering idle conversation, and Jenny worked the hoe with impatient movements, her mind alive with memories.

Shay had said he would not wait, and she sensed he'd withdrawn from her today in order to keep his mind from their loosely formed plans. His gaze dark, he'd left the kitchen without so much as touching her hand. So easily he could turn his hand to something else. Shame swallowed her aggravation as she heard the laughter coming from the barn, where he worked now, spending precious hours with her son. Marshall's voice rose in excitement as he called to her from the open doorway.

"It's almost done, Mama. And you'll be so-o-o surprised." He drew out the word at great length, then retreated into the cool, dim interior.

Jenny lifted a hand to her brow, where perspiration ran into her eyebrows, burning her eyes with its salty flow. "It's too hot out there, Jen," Isabelle called from the porch. "Come set a while."

Jenny rose, brushing the garden soil from her apron. "I'm dry, right to the bone," she said, walking to where water sloshed over the sides of the watering trough. Bending low, she splashed her face, then used her sleeves to wipe the water from her cheeks. The dress would dry in no time and in the meanwhile the damp fabric felt cool against her skin. She reached for the tin cup that rested atop the pump and levered the handle twice, watching as cold water gushed forth from deep in the ground.

The cup caught the flow, running over onto her hand, and she lifted the metal vessel to her mouth, relishing the cool drink. From the corner of her eye she caught sight of Shay, silent and motionless, framed in the doorway of the barn. He drew her like a magnet and she shifted to meet his gaze, watching his lips part and his nostrils flare, as if he could catch her scent, even from this distance.

Deliberately, she lifted the cup, tilting her head back as she drained it, then wiped her mouth with the back of her hand. From beneath shuttered lashes, she sought him out, but the doorway was empty, and her lips formed a secret smile. She reached for the handle, pumping again to fill the cup anew. She carried it to the porch for Isabelle, then settled beside her.

Caleb's lanky form rounded the corner of the barn, and Jenny heard Shay call for him. Quickly, Caleb followed the summons, and within moments the three male figures made their way through the doorway into the sunlight. Carrying a wooden framework, with a five-foot-long seat within its upright structure between them, the two men walked toward the live oak trees at the side of the house.

"They made a swing," Isabelle said, a note of astonishment in her voice. "Right in the middle of tendin' crops, Mr. Shay made that boy of yours a swing."

Even as they halted beneath a sturdy tree, Noah came into sight, and headed his mule in their direction. He held a gunnysack in his hand, waving it high in the air. "I got what you wanted on my way back through town, Mr. Shay."

Shay bent to Marshall and the boy ran to Noah, reaching for the burlap bag. He flashed a grin at Jenny and turned back to where the men waited beneath the tree.

"They're gonna hang that swing, I'll bet you," Isabelle said. "There's rope in that sack." Her prediction was proved valid when Shay emptied the burlap and a length of golden rope fell to the ground. "I got to get these peas on to cook for dinner," Isabelle said, rising and casting a longing glance at the men. "Those men will be hungry before you know it."

"I'll come with you," Jenny said. "They're having a good time, aren't they?" Her words were wistful, and for a moment she lagged behind, but her conscience prodded her and she followed Isabelle.

They ate dinner on the porch, Joseph sitting on the step with Marshall, Jenny and Isabelle bringing plates out the door to the men who occupied the chairs. Tender ears of corn and fresh peas were the mainstay of the meal, with thick slices of side pork fried until the fat was rendered from it. Caleb took two pie tins with him and went to find Zora, who'd spent the morning sewing curtains for their cabin.

Noah ate steadily, then answered Shay's queries, relating

the news from Doc Gibson's place. "Old Eli's about as ornery as they come, stubborn as the day is long," Noah told them. "But Zora's mama just shook her head. She says her man's just frazzled with tryin' to do the field work, and missin' his girl." Noah leaned back in his chair. "I guess I can see where he'd be up to his neck, tryin' to do the work of two men. Doc Gibson's a hard man to please."

"Would Eli think about bringing his family and coming back here?" Jenny asked.

Noah looked at her sharply. "After he acted so hateful? You'd even *think* about lettin' him come back?"

Jenny's mind filled with the memory of Eli's savage demeanor and she hesitated. "Maybe. We'd have to talk about it. I guess I'm just thinking mostly about Zora and her mama."

Chores took precedence over trying out the swing properly, and Marshall curled up on the seat in the shade while Shay went to the cotton field with the other men. Jenny watched from the house, aware that the boy had gone to sleep beneath the big oak tree. "He's so pleased, isn't he?"

"I reckon so," Isabelle answered. "It wouldn't hurt you to go on out there with him for a while."

"He's asleep," Jenny told her. And then she lingered at the window. "Maybe I'll just sit beside him for a while." The sun was hot, but beneath the oak tree a breeze blew and the shade welcomed her. She slipped Marshall's head from the seat and lowered herself carefully, trying not to waken him.

His eyes opened and he smiled sleepily at her. "Are you gonna swing with me, Mama?" And then he was asleep again, a lazy slumber catching him up in its depths. Jenny pushed at the ground with her toes, then lifted her foot, allowing the swing to glide as it would. Her hand touched the seat beside her, where Shay's hands had used a plane to shape the board, and then sanded the rough finish to smooth it.

Leaning her head back against the rope, she looked upward to where the branches were thick and the narrow leaves spread a shelter from the sun. Marshall stirred and her fingers threaded his hair, soothing him. His sigh was replete with the pleasure of his day as he nestled his face against her dress.

Shay had made it so. His sharing of time and talent with Marshall, building the swing...she enumerated anew the difference Shay's presence made in their lives. And now he'd vowed to stay, to marry her. She hugged the knowledge to herself. Perhaps not today or the next, as he'd planned, but soon. Maybe...maybe even tomorrow.

"We'll go to see your father in the morning," Shay told her after supper. "I've thought about it all day, Jen." His hand reached to touch hers, and his fingers traced the narrow width of her palm. "I'm trying hard not to be selfish here," he said quietly. "What I want and what we need to do seem like two different things right now." He met her gaze and the flare of desire was between them, as if it required only a touch, a breath or the whisper of her name to bring him to the edge of passion.

Reluctantly, he released her hand and walked from the house.

Her bed held little comfort as she thought of Shay's words, and what the morning would bring. The man who'd been her beloved father was a recluse now, and his unspoken denial of her existence over the past few years stung, no matter how she tried to put aside the memory of unanswered letters. And Shay was willing to forgo admission to her bed for at least another day, in order to set things to rights with her father.

He and Isabelle were united on this one thing at least,

and between them, they made the arrangements for the visit. Marshall would stay at home, Shay determining that should things not go well, it would be painful for the child to meet his grandparent in the midst of conflict. And Jenny could only wish the night hours away, so that the morning would come quickly.

She was awakened by sounds in the kitchen, and her gaze flew to the window. The sun was up, already high in the eastern sky, and she dressed quickly, arriving in the kitchen with breakfast already in progress.

"You didn't wake me," she said accusingly. "I never oversleep." Even to her own ears, her words were petulant, and she caught a quick glimpse of Shay's grin as he rose to pour coffee for her from the big pot. "Are you fixing my plate, too?" she asked, out of sorts for some unknown reason.

He nodded. "I can do that." And to her amazement, he took the empty plate from before her to fill it at the stove. Bringing it to her, he bent low to place it on the table, and his whisper was soft against her ear. "Tomorrow for sure, sweetheart."

She turned her head quickly, and his mouth brushed her cheek. It was enough. For now, it was enough.

Shay's hands at her waist lifted her into the buggy seat, and Jenny looked over his shoulder for a fleeting second to smile at Marshall, standing on the porch. The basket sat at her feet, a quilt covering it, with a jug of water added at the last minute. Marshall, close by Isabelle's side, waved sadly as they left, and Jenny felt a moment's guilt at leaving him behind.

And yet it was an adventure she wanted to share only with Shay. It seemed almost clandestine, this journey they set out upon. Just a man and woman, driving from home, with no duties to dodge, no chores to evade in order to be alone. Just the sunlight, the blue sky, birds taking flight before them, their songs trailing behind in melodies she seldom took time to hear. She touched Shay's hand, and he glanced down at her, his mouth curving as if he caught the mood she'd allowed to permeate her whole being.

They drove quickly through the nearby town, and Jenny gave quiet instructions as they passed through several small communities, journeying beside fields of corn and cotton. Cabins dotted the countryside, and burned-out structures gave silent witness to the scars of warfare.

"I hate seeing this," she told Shay. "It was easier not knowing, I think."

"Maybe, but this is the way it is, Jen. Life's different than it used to be. People have had to make changes to survive."

"I don't have to like it though," she said stubbornly. "I guess we were fortunate, weren't we?"

"If you say so," Shay answered, his thoughts dark as he considered what Jenny had sacrificed to hold what she owned.

Her final instructions to him turned the buggy down a shaded avenue. It was neglected, the narrow tracks almost covered by weeds and grass. Overhanging trees, with moss dripping from their branches provided welcome shade to the travelers as the buggy rolled past.

Jenny fidgeted, becoming increasingly tense, and Shay took her hand. "No matter what happens," he said quietly, "you'll know you made the first move to make things right." She nodded distractedly, sitting on the edge of the seat, leaning forward as they rounded the final bend in the lane.

The charred framework of a house was before them, only a part of it remaining unharmed by fire. "It seemed bigger when I was a child," Jenny whispered.

"Probably was bigger," Shay said. "Most of it's been burned down, sweetheart."

She lifted her head, shaking it mournfully as she viewed the ruins of her childhood home. "It makes my heart ache, just looking at it. This was my folks' home place." Her hand dug deeply into her pocket, searching for her handkerchief.

"It's not just the house, Shay. Look beyond the chimney, where the barns used to be, and the chicken coops and the springhouse. There's hardly anything left."

"I can see chickens scratching around out past the outhouse," he said. "Maybe they lay eggs enough for what your father needs. But it looks like there's only half of the barn left. Hard to say. If the roof's still good, it might be usable."

"I'm glad my mama can't see this." Jenny slid from the buggy seat and picked her way through the weeds to where broken steps led to the front veranda. "Do you suppose my father is really here?"

Shay followed her, grasping her elbow as she climbed awkwardly onto the wide porch. "Open the door, Jen. We'll take a look."

Amazingly enough, the door swung wide, its hinges in working order, and Shay stepped past her to peer inside. A hallway met his gaze, two open doorways to his left, the other side boarded up with a slapdash assortment of planks and pieces of wood. From one room a low snarl promised the presence of a dog, and Shay halted.

Jenny pushed past him. "That must be Crowder. Pa's had him for years, since I was a girl." Her voice was eager as she spoke the dog's name, calling him with a coaxing lilt that Shay thought would have turned any intelligent creature to mush. It seemed Crowder was no exception. A brown-spotted hound, he bounded from the dim interior, only to grovel at Jenny's feet, whining piteously.

She bent low to pet him, whispering his name and speaking softly. "Where's my papa, Crowder? Is he in here?" The dog's tail beat a tattoo against the door frame, and his head tilted back, eyes closed. A mournful howl was the dog's immediate response, and Jenny pushed him aside to enter the room.

"Papa?" Jenny moved carefully past a large sofa, around an overstuffed chair and toward a second sofa, barely visible on the opposite wall.

Shay followed her through the doorway. Heavy draperies were drawn over the two windows in the far wall, and he picked his way through an assortment of furniture to reach them. A cloud of dust flew as he tugged one tapestry drape aside and he sneezed, shaking his head at the accumulation of cobwebs crisscrossing the glass panes.

"Papa?" Jenny called again, and then turned in a slow circle. A sob caught in her throat. "Oh, Shay. How can he live here like this?"

"Maybe he's living in the barn." And that might be an improvement, Shay decided.

From the front door, the dog barked sharply. "Sounds like someone's coming in," Shay said. "Let's take a look."

Jenny followed him back into the dimly lit corridor. On the veranda stood a tall gentleman, looking uneasily through the open doorway. "Is Mr. Harrison at home?"

"We just arrived ourselves," Shay said, tugging Jenny to his side. "This is his daughter, sir. We'll come outside and talk, if you don't mind."

On closer inspection, Shay decided the gentleman had about worn the bejabbers out of his black suit, but threadbare or not, it was neatly pressed, and the shirt beneath it snowy white. "I came to visit with Jonah," the gentleman said politely. "He doesn't get out to church anymore, so I try to pay him a call every so often. Is he at home?"

Shay fought to control a grin. If this wasn't about as neat

a package as he'd ever been offered. It looked like heaven had smiled on this trek, and delivered a preacher up, right to the front door of Jonah Harrison's house.

"We were about to go out and take a look around," Jenny said. "I don't think I remember you, sir."

The gentleman offered his hand to Shay. "I've only been at the church in town since the conflict was over. My name is George Potter." He nodded to Jenny. "I remember your mama. You favor her a bit."

"Thank you." Her voice was choked, and Shay hastened to speak.

"You're welcome to come along," he said, unwilling to allow the preacher out of his sight. "In fact, you might have come to the right place at the right time today."

The elderly man removed his hat, holding it against his chest. "I'll certainly be available if I'm needed here." He looked from Shay to Jenny, then back again. "Are either of you in need of comfort, perhaps? Has something happened to Jonah?"

"He's not in the house. We were just heading out back to look around." Shay shortened his steps as they set out, one hand on Jenny's back, the other by his side, and for a moment he wished for the security of his gun at hand.

Together, they walked toward the shed. It was a ramshackle building, leaning to one side, looking as if it had been constructed from various bits and pieces of other structures. The wide door hung open and Shay stepped inside. Tools hung from the wall, along with a bridle. Beneath them a well-worn saddle was tipped on end. Two stalls sat empty, but the straw showed evidence of manure droppings.

"He's still got animals," Shay said. "There's another dog by the back wall. Maybe some pups, too. Looks like he'd do better to live out here. It's in better shape than the house."

"I don't remember this building," Jenny told him. She stood in the doorway, her shoulders slumped, her face mournful. "Everything's gone, Shay. The barns, the people, the house. No wonder my father—" She caught her breath, plainly on the verge of tears.

"Come on, Jen. Let's go look out back," Shay said hastily. "You coming along?" he asked the preacher.

"Yes, certainly. There's a back door. Shall we walk on through?"

Behind the shed was an open field, where the fragrance of fresh cut hay gave mute evidence of men working. "Does Jonah have people living here?" Shay asked the preacher.

"Last I knew, there were a couple of families left. The womenfolk bring food to Jonah and the men work the fields with him." One hand lifted to shield his eyes from the sun, and the preacher pointed to the far end of the hayfield. "Look under those trees. There's a stream back there, I believe. I think someone's out there."

Two men rose from the ground as Shay scanned the area, and one of them bent over for a moment, his arm outstretched. A third figure sat up and then rose to stand beside the first two.

"Looks like Jonah to me, with the two men who stayed on here," George Potter said firmly. "They must have been taking a nap. It's a good idea when the sun gets overhead. Your father's not a young man anymore, ma'am."

The three men watched as Shay set out across the field, Jenny and the preacher at his heels. "Jonah?" George called out, waving his hand. "Somebody's here to see you."

"Is that you, George?" The smallest of the three, a white man with snowy hair, stepped forward, then made his way toward them.

Jenny stopped short, and Shay looked back. Tears ran

freely and one hand covered her mouth. Her face contorted as she watched the approach of her father, and Shay turned back to grasp her arm, walking beside her.

"Mattie? Mattie, is that you?" From fifty feet away, Jonah's voice seemed frail, yet his pace gained momentum as he neared.

"No, Papa. It's Jenny." Leaving Shay behind, she hurried to her father, then stopped short as he shook his head.

"Of course, you can't be Mattie, can you?" One trembling hand reached to touch her hair, his fingers tangling in the waves that hung loosely. "Is it really Jenny?" And then he slumped to the ground.

Shay was at his side in seconds, lifting Jonah's head to his knee, brushing back the white hair that hung overlong, touching his shoulders. "Has he been ill?" he asked the preacher, who'd hastened to his side.

"No, he's been pretty strong right along. Just sometimes his mind wanders a little." He leaned closer. "Jonah, can you hear me?" He looked up at Shay then, smiling sadly. "He won't talk to anyone, you know. Just stays here and works and keeps body and soul together. Never been the same since Miss Mattie died."

"Doc Gibson tried to see him a couple of times when he was over this way," Jenny said quietly. "I sent him letters, but he said Papa tore them up and wouldn't read them."

"Why didn't you come yourself?" Shay asked, knowing the cruelty of the words, yet curious to know Jenny's motives. For a woman so dedicated to her home and family, the neglect of her parent seemed cruel.

"He didn't want to see me. He wouldn't see anybody, Doc Gibson said. And I suppose I was hurt that he hadn't come to me. I didn't even know that Mama died until months afterward." She closed her eyes. "You weren't here, Shay. You can't imagine how it was, trying to scrape together enough to eat, once the Yankees moved on. It took all day, every day, just to take care of ourselves and the animals. And then, when I sent letters and never heard back, I just gave up.''

''Old Jonah didn't even come out of those two rooms he lives in for the first little while after Mattie died,'' George said. ''Folks around here didn't know him well. No one seemed to know where'd he even come from.''

''He was Jonah Harrison,'' Jenny whispered. ''Of the New Orleans Harrisons.''

Shay leaned over the man, providing shade from the hot sun. ''I think we need to take him to the house. Or at least out of the sun.''

The other two men approached, and one of them held out a canteen. ''There's water in here,'' he said. ''Mr. Jonah's been feeling poorly today. The heat's gettin' to him.''

Shay uncapped the flask and wet his handkerchief, wiping the older man's face, then lifted his head to pour a few drops of water against his lips. Jonah stirred, his eyelids fluttering, then opened his mouth to drink. Shay accommodated him, allowing several swallows before he brought Jonah's head higher.

''Papa?'' Jenny called to him, and he squinted his eyes, seeking her face.

''I didn't want you here, Jenny. I don't like you seeing the place this way,'' he said quietly. ''I couldn't bring myself to leave your mama here.''

''Why didn't you write to me?'' she asked, kneeling beside him.

He shook his head, a hopeless gesture. ''You're better off without me.''

''That's no way to talk,'' Shay told him harshly. ''Your daughter needs you. Do you even know that you have a grandson?''

His nod was brief. ''Doc Gibson told me.''

Shay lifted Jonah to his feet, his arm supporting the smaller man. "Let's get you into the shade," he said.

"I'll take him, sir. My name's Henry," said one of the workers. He motioned to the man beside him. "This here's Clay. We work the land with Mr. Jonah." His husky arms lifted Jonah with no visible effort, then carried him, halting beneath a tree to lower the old man, easing him to lean against the wide trunk.

He looked up at Jenny, who was fast behind him. "You gonna stay on here with your pa?"

Jenny shook her head. "No, but if he'll come home with me, I'll take him today."

Henry looked dubious. "He's pretty set in his ways. My woman can't hardly get him to take a bath these days. He just works and sleeps, don't even eat much."

"Shay?" Jenny looked up at him. "Can you make him come home with us?"

"Not unless he gets cleaned up first," Shay said bluntly. He turned to Henry. "Does he have any clean clothes?"

"You can direct your questions to me, young man," Jonah said tartly, sitting up straighter. "Don't be talking over my head."

"Your daughter wants you to live with her and the boy, sir," Shay said, pleased to hear the first signs of vitality from the man.

"I'm doing fine where I am," Jonah told him.

"Well, she's not," Shay answered. "She needs her father, and the boy needs a grandfather."

Jenny opened her mouth and Shay sent her a telling glance. She subsided, allowing him to continue.

"I'm marrying your girl today, Jonah, if the preacher here will do the honors. You gonna clean up for the ceremony?"

George Potter stood straighter, a smile wreathing his

face. "That sounds like a grand way to celebrate this re-union, Jonah. You can give the bride away."

"After he has a bath," Shay said firmly. And then offered a hand to Jenny's father. "Will you honor us, sir?"

"Give me a drink of that water," Jonah said grumpily. "And you, Henry, go tell Martha I need something clean to wear."

"I can do that, Mr. Jonah," the big man said with a laugh. "She'll be happy to oblige. She's got your clothes all washed up, just waitin' for you to use."

It took a horse trough full of water and a vast amount of determination on Shay's part to complete the task, but Jonah appeared at the front of the ruined house an hour later, where Jenny sat with George Potter in the shade. His clothing rumpled, but clean and neatly mended, Jonah climbed the steps to the veranda and stood before his daughter. From within the hallway, Crowder barked once, then nudged past the open door to sit at Jonah's side.

Jonah put his hand on the dog's head. "I won't come with you today, Jenny. But I'll think about it, long and hard. Your fella here is pretty persuasive. He seems to think you need me around." His eyes were clear now, his manner courteous.

"You look..." Jenny halted, as if lost for words. "This is the way I remember you, Papa. With Crowder at your side."

"Well, some days I do better than others, daughter. Me and Crowder are both gettin' on in years."

And the years had not dealt with him kindly, Shay thought.

"This is a good day for you, Jonah," George told him. "A very good day. You need to stand up here by your girl and watch her get married to this fine man."

Shay nudged Jonah closer to Jenny, then stood at her

right side. "We're ready, preacher, anytime you are." It took an effort to keep his elation from showing. Things had almost taken a bad turn, but it seemed the man was lucid and aware of the events about to take place now. All in all, it couldn't have turned out better if he'd had a hand in planning things, instead of having to sort through circumstances the way he had.

"Are you sure you want to marry this man, Jenny?" the Reverend Potter asked, apparently willing to perform the ceremony with only his Bible in hand. "I'm sure I can remember the words, even without my book of sacraments available."

Jenny looked up at Shay. "He'll have to be willing to give his full name, won't he, Reverend?" Her eyes held doubt, and Shay bristled momentarily. Caught, was what he was. She'd put off digging at him, after Eli's visit, and now he'd have to tell her, in plain words, what she wanted to know, or lie in the face of a man of God.

"Of course, I'll need it to fill out the marriage certificate. You'll have to come by the church in town to get it when we've finished here, though."

"We surely do need that piece of paper," Shay told him, thinking of Isabelle's scornful glance, should he try to convince her of the marriage without proof.

"I think we're ready then." George opened his Bible and read verses from the first few pages, about a man and woman being one flesh, words that rang a bell in Shay's memory. Then the pages turned until the preacher found the passage he sought, closer to the back of the book. His voice became more melodious, his phrasing almost musical as he spoke of a mystical union, ordained by God. Shay shifted from one foot to the other, more than ready for the essential parts of this ceremony, as George read on about faith, hope and charity. And then it was time.

"Your name, young man?"

Shay cleared his throat. "Shay Devereaux," he answered, refusing to look down at Jenny as he spoke.

"And you are Jenny..." He paused. "Not Harrison any longer, is it?"

She shook her head. "No, I'm Jenny Pennington."

"Ah, yes. Your father told me you're a widow." His voice lifted, developed a lilt unlikely for a man his age, Shay thought. "Well, no longer, ma'am. Not if you agree to marry this gentleman."

His hand reached out to them both. "Place your hands in mine, if you please, and repeat after me."

Jenny's slender fingers lay across the minister's narrow palm, and Shay placed his hand atop hers. As if in a dream, he heard Jenny repeat words he'd thought never to hear in reference to himself, listened as she promised to love him, honor him and stay with him forever. And then he was asked to repeat those same vows.

He'd try, he promised himself silently. He'd do his level best, for Jenny's benefit. Hell, for Jenny, he'd lay down and die. Now, if he could only manage to be a decent husband and honor the promises he was making. He'd shied from promises over the past years, but not this time. And he couldn't even tell himself it was because of Carl that he did this.

This was for himself.

"...pronounce you husband and wife. You can kiss your bride, Mr. Devereaux."

Shay bent his head, releasing his hold on Jenny's hand and turning her to face him, his palms against her waist. Her lips were warm, trembling just a bit, but the kiss she offered was sweet. He'd have lingered a bit, but for the men watching. *Later,* he promised her silently, aware of desire's hovering presence within himself.

"Congratulations, young man," the preacher said heartily. "And you, too, Jonah. You've got yourself a new son-in-law. Maybe you ought to think again about tagging along with them today.''

Jonah shook his head, looking across the veranda to where tall oak trees lined the neglected approach to his house. ''No, not now. Maybe later on.''

Henry stood at the edge of the veranda. ''We'll keep an eye on your pa, Miss Jenny. Maybe he'll be better now, since you've been here.''

''Please think about coming to us, Papa,'' Jenny pleaded quietly, turning from Shay to touch her father's arm. She looked into his eyes and Jonah nodded, then for the first time reached for her, his embrace almost reluctant.

''I'll ponder on it,'' he said, and Shay recognized that they would have to be content with that.

''We'll need to be moving on,'' he told Jenny. ''We'll follow the Reverend to town to get the certificate from him.''

Jenny looked at him beseechingly. ''Can we share our dinner with them first?''

He'd forgotten the basket of food Isabelle had readied for them, and at Jenny's words, he nodded. Retrieving it from the buggy, he returned to sit on the edge of the veranda with the men and Jenny, watching with pleasure as she doled out the bread and sliced ham Isabelle had sent along. Half of a pound cake completed the simple meal, and Shay blessed Isabelle for her generous hand.

''Haven't had such good ham in a long while,'' Jonah said, wiping his mouth with his clean handkerchief.

''There'll be more where that came from. Noah hung two hams in the smokehouse from the hog we butchered,'' Shay said. ''It was about empty, but we'll be raising hogs for ourselves next year. We could use an extra hand to help, Jonah.''

''We will?'' Jenny asked, latching on to his first statement. ''And we're going to get a sow and raise our own?''

"Sounds like a good idea to me," Shay told her, delighted with her response. "Our cotton looks good. We can afford to get a couple of pigs to breed, besides another one to butcher, if we want to. We'll have to think about getting a boar, maybe, now that I think about it."

Jenny's cheeks flushed at his remark and she cast him a quelling glance. "We'll talk about it later, Mr. *Devereaux.*" It was a pointed reminder that they had more than one item to discuss, and Shay began to realize that the ride back home might hold some uncomfortable moments on his part.

There was no point in putting it off longer. The sun was well on its way down the western sky as he loaded Jenny aboard the buggy and stowed the basket beneath the seat. "Wave at your father, and don't cry, you hear?" he told her sternly. "I don't want him to think you're not looking forward to traveling home with me."

She looked past him, dutifully waving at Jonah and Henry. "I won't cry. I'm bright enough to know I might never see him again, but for now, it's all right." Jonah's form had shrunk, it seemed, and he leaned against a pillar, Henry tall beside him. "He's not quite right in his mind, is he?" Jenny asked, and then answered her own question. "It's like something in him died along with Mama, don't you think? He was with us there for a while, but now, it's like he's retreated again."

"I'm afraid you're right, sweetheart," Shay agreed. "There's a spark missing, and I'm not sure anybody can do anything about it." He cracked the reins over the mare's back, setting her into a faster pace. "Don't give up, Jen. He may change his mind. But we can't do it for him. You did what was right, coming here and mending the breach. Now it's up to him."

The stop at the parsonage was short, and Jenny rolled the certificate carefully, lest it wrinkle. She was quiet, weary from the long day, yet anticipation for the night ahead filled her mind. They halted in a small town, where only a general store told of any degree of prosperity, and Shay stopped for a few minutes to water the mare at a trough in front of the building. A woman inside the store watched him through the window, her eyes fearful, and Jenny wondered if he'd faced such lack of welcome in other places.

So used to his appearance, she seldom took note of his scarred cheek, but now her heart ached for the man who would carry the blemish for the rest of his life. Who would, one day, face his parents with the marks of his past apparent. He'd been a handsome youth. No, she corrected herself, he was still handsome, just tainted by the cruelty of a man somewhere who'd marred his perfect features.

Shay climbed back into the buggy and she reached to place her hand on his knee. He looked up quickly, surprise lighting his gaze, and she could not resist sliding closer, as though she must label him as her own, should the woman still be watching as they left.

"Why wouldn't you tell me before?" she asked. "You spoke of Roan, and you said he was your brother, but then you dithered when I asked you about your name. You said your mother had not named you Shay. So I thought you didn't want to lay claim to the family name, or else you were traveling under a different name."

"My brother fought for the North under that name," he said bitterly. "I think I hate him for it. I haven't claimed the name of Devereaux since…well, for a long time."

"You claimed it today," she reminded him gently.

"In order to marry you."

"Was it so great a sacrifice, then?" Her heart was saddened as she thought of family. He'd made a special effort to reunite her with her father, yet his own beginnings were pushed aside, with hatred marring his memories and with no intention of finding his family again.

His look was sharp, his eyes darkening with desire as he wrapped a long arm around her shoulders. Bending his head, he caught her mouth with his, and his kiss was possessive, deep and fervent. As if he must claim her, erase any thought of reluctance on his part, he imprinted her with his passion, and she was caught up against him, yielding to his touch.

He lifted his head and his eyes were hooded, his mouth damp. "I'm Shay Devereaux, sweetheart, your husband. And believe me, it will be no sacrifice on my part to make this whole thing official when we get home. That certificate is goin' over the headboard and you're goin' between the sheets."

He bent to her once more, offering a kiss that was softer, gentler, yet no less potent, and then he turned away, adjusting his hat and snapping the reins. "Now, behave yourself till we get home," he muttered. "No more squeezing my knee, or we may not make it back without stopping along the way somewhere."

"Seems like the man could've bought you a new dress to get married in," Isabelle grumbled. Her sharp eyes scanned Jenny, resting disapprovingly on the drab color of her best dress. "Didn't you drive past the store in town on your way?"

"It wasn't planned," Jenny told her. "It just happened. The preacher came by and my father was there." Enough said, she decided.

She filled her mouth with a bite of chicken. Isabelle had killed two of the young roosters and fried them up for supper, then fixed two plates of food to be held in the warming oven for the travelers. Pure ambrosia, Jenny thought, savoring each bite.

Her ear was tuned for the sounds of Shay's return from the barn. He'd dropped her off near the back porch and driven the buggy on. And Isabelle, grumpy with worry, had made Jenny sit down and eat without him.

Jenny's words announcing the impromptu wedding had brought silence for a moment, and then Isabelle's eyes flashed with indignation. "I could have made up something for you to wear to get married in," she said. "There's still some dresses in the attic from Mr. Carl's mama. Good material like that shouldn't lay there and moulder."

The thought of wearing one of the elder Mrs. Pennington's leftover gowns as a wedding dress, even cut and sewn into a different pattern, was not appealing to Jenny, but she wisely held her tongue.

"It would've only taken a minute to stop at the store and find something ready-made," Isabelle said.

"If there was anything available at all it would be something more expensive than I can afford," Jenny reminded her, slathering butter across a warm biscuit. "I'm just as married, no matter what I'm wearing. And the important thing is that my father was there to see it happen."

"Well, I wouldn't have minded standin' by, myself." Isabelle looked up as the door opened and Shay stood on the threshold. "If some folks weren't in such an all-fired hurry, you coulda done this thing up right. Your pa could have come here and we'd have celebrated together."

Shay laughed, and his gaze rested on Jenny. "I don't care if she's wearing a feed sack, so long as she's my wife." His hand rested for a moment on Jenny's shoulder as he rounded the table and pulled out a chair. "Besides, her father wouldn't come along, or things might have happened differently."

His glance held a warning as he spoke again. "We'll tend to buying her some clothes before long, Isabelle. We'll be selling off hay in a few weeks, and everybody will be getting new duds. Maybe even before then."

"Me, too?" Marshall stood in the kitchen doorway, his

eyes wide as he listened to Shay's announcement. "Do I get *duds,* too?"

Shay held out a hand to the boy and Marshall ran to him, climbing onto his lap. "What would you like, Marsh? Some new pants?"

Marshall shook his head. "No, Mama just made me two pairs. I need boots that fit me, sir. Mine make my toes all scrunch up."

Shay frowned, looking down at the boy's grimy toes. "Is that why you've been out in the field barefoot?"

"How can you tell?" Marshall asked innocently, holding up one foot for inspection.

"They need washing, that's why," Shay told him. "Don't you get into bed till you scrub 'em real good."

"Can I have new boots?" Marshall persisted. "And some stockings that don't have lumps from bein' mended? And a shirt without no holes?"

Jenny felt embarrassment wash over her. To think that her child should be so poorly clad was reason for shame in her book. And yet there'd been no help for it. The money had to go for necessities, and mended stockings were better than none at all.

Shay looked at her, his eyes softening. "Your mama needs some things, too, Marsh. We'll have to see if they have what we need at the store. Maybe Isabelle will take a trip to town for us next week."

"What's wrong with goin' yourself?" Isabelle asked sharply. "Miss Jenny should be pickin' out her own stuff, not dependin' on me to do it. That's somethin' a woman likes to do, and I'd think you'd know it."

"Isabelle." Jenny's voice was soft, but the message was clear. This was a matter better left alone.

"Yes, ma'am." Isabelle exaggerated the words, but the look she shot in Shay's direction diluted the apology. "If you don't need me anymore, I'm goin' home. Noah's about wore out tonight. I'm gonna rub him good with liniment.''

"I'll clean up," Jenny told her. "As soon as Shay eats his supper." Isabelle stalked to the screen door and let it slam behind her. With a muffled laugh, Jenny rose from the table and retrieved the second plate from the warming oven above the stove. Holding it with a towel, she placed it before Shay. "Watch out, it's pretty hot. But it sure is good chicken," she told him.

"Are you going to have enough roosters to put up in the pantry?"

"Enough for now. I need to get them out of the coop before they chase those hens half to death. And if I put them off by themselves, they'll fight each other."

"Will you have more hatching soon?"

"I've got three broody hens in the coop right now," Jenny told him. "We'll have another batch of fryers in a couple of months. It doesn't take long for them to get big enough when they have plenty to eat."

Shay shifted Marshall to his left knee, freeing his right hand, and picked up the chicken leg on his plate. He chewed and swallowed and reached for the cup of coffee Jenny had poured. "I take back all the ornery thoughts I had about Isabelle a few minutes ago. That woman can sure cook chicken, can't she?"

Jenny laughed. "She's just protective of us, Shay. She's been taking care of Marshall and me for four years longer than she had to. Noah could have moved on and taken Isabelle and the boys with him, but they stayed here, and I'm grateful."

"They're better off here than as if they'd sharecropped someplace else," he said. "Noah's had the run of things, with nobody telling him what to do or how to do it. That's important to him."

"Well, ignore what she had to say about new clothes,"

Jenny said quietly. "We'll be just fine until there's money enough coming in to cover it. And I truly don't mind if Isabelle picks out things for us. I know you don't want to go into town." She looked up at him, and he met her gaze, his eyes resting for a moment on her face. Then, with a gentle touch, he lifted Marshall to the floor and whispered in his ear, sending the boy out the door, Marshall stopping only to snatch at a towel from the sink as he passed.

"What did you tell him to do?" Jenny asked.

"I told him to wash his feet at the trough and dry them real good so he doesn't get muddy on his way back inside. It's time for him to be in bed." He picked up another piece of chicken, his eyes never faltering from hers.

"Where's the marriage certificate?"

"Where do you suppose?"

"It had better be the first thing I see when I get in your bedroom."

"I hung it as soon as I got in the house. Isabelle knew where there was a frame in the attic, and she got it down for me."

His teeth gnawed at the chicken bone and he chewed and swallowed slowly. A bite of potato followed, and still he was silent. And then he pushed his plate aside and leveled his index finger in her direction.

"It's almost full dark, sweetheart. Marshall's on his way in right now, and once he gets settled down for the night, you've got about ten minutes all to yourself. Don't make me wait."

Chapter Eight

"This is what I wanted. I asked Shay to marry me." Her words were fervent as Jenny slid from her clothing and into Shay's shirt. Her gown torn beyond redemption, she'd slept in this shirt for three nights. She tugged it down over her legs, conscious that the hem ended just above her knees. Trembling fingers tangled in her hair as she tugged at her braid, and then knotted the strings of her petticoat as she reached beneath the shirt to shimmy from the folds of her underwear.

A brief knock on her door, and then the turning of the knob, brought an end to her dithering, and she stepped from the circle of white at her feet. Bending, she picked up her dress and undergarments, aware of Shay standing in the doorway. Agonizingly aware of the bare length of her legs beneath the hem of his shirt.

"Should I go away and come back later?" he asked wryly, a knowing smile tugging at his lips, his eyes narrowing as he focused on knees and the curving line of her calves beneath the hem of his shirt. "I've checked on Marshall and put the cat outside and walked the length of the veranda three times."

Jenny's eyes widened at his words. "Did Marshall have that cat in his room? I told him she had to stay in the barn."

"She was tucked under his sheet. And only too willing to go outdoors, once I set her free." He closed the door behind himself, then leaned against it. "You didn't answer my question, Jen. Can I stay?"

Her hands made a hash of the petticoat, folding it loosely, then shoving it into a dresser drawer. "Of course, you can stay," she said shortly. "I don't know why you thought you had to wander around out on the veranda anyway." She turned from the dresser, clutching her dress to her bosom. "I'm just sorting things out. I think I'd better do some washing in the morning. I only have one clean dress left, and Isabelle says we're in for rain before long. Of course, that'll be good for the corn. It's been dry—"

"Hush." Shay's negligent posture vanished as he moved across the room, reaching Jenny's side in four long strides. "I don't want you worrying about anything. You hear me?" His hands took the dress she held and tossed it aside, then took possession of her trembling fingers.

"There's nothing to fret over, Jenny. I'm not going to pounce on you. We'll do this your way. If you're ready to be my wife, you know I'm more than willing. But if it's been too quick...if you want to wait, I can do that, too." His mouth twitched and his eyes softened, scanning her from the top of her head, where russet waves fell in a tangled mass across her shoulders and breasts, to the bare toes that curled against the floor.

"You look frightened." His hands lifted hers to his mouth and he blessed each fingertip with a brush of his lips. "The last thing in this world I want is to put fear in your heart, Jen. If your mind is hauling up memories that give you pain, I'll just be satisfied with some hugging and kissing for now." His gaze met hers over their joined hands and his eyes narrowed. "But I won't sleep upstairs. Don't ask for that."

"No." She shook her head. "I wouldn't do that. And my memories won't come between us, Shay. I promise you that. You've already put to rest the bad dreams I had before you got here." She lifted her chin and looked into his eyes. "You belong here, in my bed. It's just…different."

"Different?" His mouth brushed her knuckles, breathing the query softly. "How so, sweetheart?"

She took her hands from his, and he let her go, allowing her fingers to slide from his grasp, remaining where he stood as she walked to the window. For this small confession, she could not face him, not allow him to see the shame in her eyes. And so she looked from the open window, past the climbing roses he'd helped her train to the trellis. The memory of that day brought a warmth to her heart, and she cherished it, adding it to the wealth of memories Shay had already given her.

"I was a virgin when I married Carl," she began, her voice soft as she remembered that day, when life seemed so simple, when she'd been so young and untried.

"I would have expected that," he said. "And I'm sure Carl was good to you."

"Oh, yes," she said hastily. "He was always…kind. Sometimes he was in a hurry, but he always thanked me, and kissed me."

"Thanked you?" Shay's words were halting. "For what?"

Jenny twisted her hands at her waist and felt her cheeks grow crimson. "You know, for letting him…for accommodating him."

"You accommodated him?" Shay's voice was near at hand, and she felt his warmth behind her. His breath ruffled her hair as he bent to speak against her ear, his words carefully enunciated. "You *accommodated* him?"

Jenny's shoulders lifted in a shrug, and then were captured by Shay's hands, his grip firm as he turned her to face him. "Yes," she whispered. Tears filled her eyes as she lifted her chin and met his gaze. "I thought I loved Carl. I *did* love Carl," she corrected quickly. "But I didn't feel this way about him. Not the way..."

"Not the way you feel about me?" he asked.

Her nod was hesitant and her teeth bit into her lower lip. "Carl was good to me. He was. But he treated me like a china doll most of the time. I never knew what was going on outside of this house. He didn't talk about the crops or the people who worked here, or what things cost or how much money we had. He just was very kind to me and sometimes, I felt like the only time he really saw me was when we climbed the stairs to go to bed."

"He loved you, Jen. I'll swear to that on a stack of Bibles, if it will make you feel any better about him. I saw the man when he was dying, and his last thoughts were of you and the boy."

"I feel guilty, Shay."

"Why? Because you feel something for me that you didn't for Carl? Should I hang my head because you're the first woman I've been willing to give my name to, and yet I've..."

She shook her head quickly. "I don't want to hear about anyone else. Not tonight. Besides, that's part of my guilt. I almost forced you into this."

"Not on your life." His denial was firm. "I knew exactly what I was doing."

"I think I would have let you in here, even without the certificate," she admitted, looking up at the wall over the headboard.

"I think you'd have backed out, sweetheart. It's better this way, anyway. Now you won't be thinking that I'll leave you when the cotton's picked." His mouth was warm against her cheek and then his head turned as his gaze followed hers. "I'm just glad you had a frame up in the attic to fit that thing. I knew Isabelle wouldn't be happy till she saw it hangin' there."

"Well *I'm* just glad George Potter had a certificate left. He said he was saving it for a special couple, remember?" Jenny said. "I'm glad we were the ones he chose. My mama would be pleased."

"Where's the one from your first wedding?" Shay asked.

"On the wall upstairs," she told him. "I've kept it for Marshall. He'll need to know about his father. I have a picture of Carl in his uniform, and a small portrait of me I'm saving for him." She leaned her head against his shoulder, relaxing, as if a hurdle had been surmounted.

"Can I blow out the candle now?" he asked quietly. "Do we have things sorted out, or is there something else you need to talk about?"

"I need to tell you something else, but it will wait, I think." Jenny stepped to the side of her bed and bent to blow out the candle. Pulling back the quilt and sheet, she fluffed her pillows, then sat on the edge of the bed. Shay was a dark shadow against the window, where only stars lit the sky.

And then he moved across the floor, his footsteps silent. Jenny brushed her feet across the braided rug, lest they be dusty against the sheets, then turned, rolling to her side, facing the empty place that would be Shay's from now on. The rustle of fabric told her he was shedding his clothing, and then he was there, in one quick motion, occupying the space beside her. She saw him lift a bit, drawing his pillow beneath his head, watched as he leaned closer, and felt his hands guiding her to a spot on his shoulder.

She inhaled deeply, knowing the scent of him, recognizing the feel of male flesh against her belly, savoring the aroma of soap and skin, and the comfort of strong arms holding her. His mouth was warm and damp against her forehead and she lifted one palm to spread across his cheek, caressing his unflawed, clean-shaven jaw. The need to draw out this moment, to savor each breath was uppermost in her mind, and she sighed, willing Shay to be patient, to allow her these few seconds of pleasure.

And there was pleasure, bestowed by his mouth and his hands, his lips pressing soft caresses against her face and throat. She tilted her head, enjoying the warmth and comfort of his touch, sensing the harnessed power of his desire. He murmured against her skin, soft, broken phrases that pleased her, and she breathed in the heated scent of his arousal.

Beneath her touch, his body was firm and muscular as she slid her hand down from his hair, resting it against his bare shoulder, then to the sculpted lines of his back. He had come to her naked, and her palm swept the length of his spine, halting as she felt the rise of his hip.

"Jenny." His voice was soft, his mouth only inches from hers, and as he asked permission, he nudged her, brushing his nose against hers. "Can I touch you, too? Or am I only to hug and kiss you, then?" Amusement traced each syllable, and she shook her head, just the least bit.

"All right, sweetheart." The words smacked of satisfaction. "Now," he murmured, drawing out the word as his mouth tasted hers, "do we have to do this with my shirt all wrapped around you? Or will you let me take it off?" He waited for less than a heartbeat, then the hand that was resting against her hip slid between their bodies to where the buttons awaited his touch. He slid them from the buttonholes easily, slowly, familiar with the ease with which they gave way. One long finger sliding beneath the fabric to test the flesh between each button, he drew out the anticipation like a fine silken thread spun by a spider weaving a web.

Her hands were restless, and then one slid upward, reaching for purchase against his head, fingertips edging past his hairline, then circling the nape of his neck. Her fingers curled, tensing against the muscles there, then spread wide, gripping his hair.

He was slow, precise and thorough, releasing each button in turn. Then, smoothing one hand over her shoulder, he slid the garment along the length of her upper arm. "Sit up, Jen." he said, and her fingers tightened their grip, then relaxed, and she eased her arm from the sleeve. Sitting erect she dispensed easily with the other sleeve, then watched as he pulled the shirt free and tossed it to the floor.

"Put your head on the pillow," he told her, and she obeyed, aware that the soft light from the window exposed her to his view. She would have reached for the sheet, but his upraised hand caught her attention, and his soft murmur persuaded her to allow his touch and the appraisal he bestowed on her slender form. He knelt beside her and she held her breath, her skin tingling where his gaze rested.

Carl had never beheld her in this way, and she felt a twinge of guilt as she compared the husband she had loved as a girl to this man. This dark stranger, who summoned forth her deepest womanly desire, filling her with a yearning she could barely contain.

He was silent for a moment, his hands resting on his thighs, and then he reached to touch the curve of her breast, his fingers brushing delicately at her skin. The sigh of approval he uttered was vindication to her worry that he might find her lacking in some way, and she heard his words with a grateful heart.

"You're beautiful, Jenny." His voice was rough-edged, harsh, and yet his caress was gentle, his callused hands tender. His palms weighed her breasts, and he bent to taste the firm flesh he cradled. Reluctantly, his long fingers released their hold, only to drift from breast to waist, where he spanned her with outstretched hands. One palm spread wide across the gentle rounding of her belly, then brushed the dark wedge between her thighs.

His fingers caressed her hips, then measured the length of her thighs, his head bending low as if the progress of those big hands against her body was of utmost import. One hand lifted her knee, fingers tracing the line of her calf and circling her ankle. And when he spoke, the words were soft and intimate, feeding her woman's soul like manna direct from heaven.

"I've imagined you, here in your bed, Jen. I wondered how you would feel, how your legs were shaped, and how your breasts would taste." His chuckle was a whisper of praise. "My imagination didn't begin to show me all of you. I didn't think about your feet. They're so slim and straight. I like the way your toes curled when I came in the room." His words were musing and gentle, and his hands were careful against her skin.

She laughed softly and her foot twitched in his hand. "You make me feel ticklish in places that never bothered me before."

"Here?" he asked, running his palm up her leg, past her knee and to the inside of her thigh, the single word a teasing whisper.

She held her breath, wondering, wishing, waiting for those caressing fingers to ease the ache she'd lived with for the past days. He squeezed gently against the softness of her and she shivered, eliciting a low, rough sound from his chest. Deliberately, he lifted his other hand to join the first, making room for himself, there where she felt the heat of her woman's flesh yearn for his touch.

He knelt, lifting her legs, then, leaning forward, he was cradled in the embrace of eager limbs. Her arms circled his neck, her legs twining with his, and she drew him to her, her lips open for his kiss.

And here, too, he drove every thought of Carl from her mind.

His mouth took hers, as if he would possess each small increment of lips, teeth and tongue. He tasted her, sucked and probed, urging her compliance with coaxing murmurs, until she was breathless and giddy with the joy of being the object of his passion. He allowed her no refuge, his hands urgent against her body, cupping and measuring her breasts, then shaping them for his possession.

His tongue and teeth tasted and tested her flesh. His mouth and tongue suckled the rosy crests that peaked and hardened at his bidding. And she was lost in the tempest of loving he poured upon her hungry flesh. Like a river bursting over a dam, he surrounded her, his body heavy, yet welcome, his arms burrowing beneath her shoulders to hold her firmly in place.

And then the heavy probing of his arousal nudged her, seeking entrance, and she lifted her hips, offering herself to his pulsing manhood. His groan was deep, his body hard and rigid against her as he pushed within the narrow passage. She was ready for him, and yet her body rebelled, unused for long months and years.

He caught a deep breath, easing from her, and her protest rang out. "No, don't leave me."

He shook his head. "I don't want to hurt you, sweetheart." Breath shuddered from him as he forced himself to be still. Dark hair hung over his forehead as he held himself from her, his arms beneath her yet.

"It's all right. It is," she assured him, shifting and sliding her hips.

"Soften for me, sweetheart. I won't hurt you," he muttered, drawing another breath, and then eased himself within her heat, inhaling sharply as she tensed her muscles.

"Jenny..." He spoke her name with a reverence that humbled her, bent his head against hers in a submissive gesture that pleased her to her depths. "I can't wait for you, sweetheart," he whispered, his words a helpless groan.

"I'm here," she murmured, tilting her head back to kiss his face, her lips searching for his, stretching upward, yearning for the pressure of his body against hers.

He rose high above her, allowing her body to sink into the feather tick, his hands sliding to hold her hips fast. His movements were strong, his body thrusting against her, and she submitted to him, aching to speak aloud her love, yet breathless. She clutched at him, her very flesh crying out for his possession. And her tears flowed unchecked as her body accepted his seed.

The sheet was draped over her, covering her from waist to knees, Shay tugging it from her breasts insistently. "I want to look at you," he murmured against her ear, his hand curved beneath her full breast.

"I was worried that you might think I was—"

His hand moved quickly, stilling her words. "You're perfect, Jen. You're the most beautiful woman I've known."

Her voice was small, bemused. "I know better. But I'm glad you think so."

She fit against him wonderfully well, he decided, reaching to ease her leg over his thigh. Her body was warm and supple, blessed with a woman's full curves and the scent of their loving rose from her heated flesh.

A pang of regret touched his mind, that he had taken her without bringing her to release, and yet, she seemed not to hold the lapse against him. Instead, she curled closer to his long body, her breasts lush and soft, her arm twined around his neck. She'd asked for nothing, only given herself for his pleasure...*as if she expected nothing more.*

"Jen?" The urge to know was strong and he spoke her name again. "Jenny? Will you forgive me for leaving you behind? Next time…" He paused deliberately, willing her to respond.

Her face tilted upward and in the shadows he felt her tense in his embrace. "I don't know…forgive me, Shay. I thought I pleased you, and if there was something lacking in me, in what I did—"

"No." His denial was swift, and his hand slid to cup the curve of her bottom, pressing her against him. Already his manhood was firm, once more reaching arousal as his body responded to the scent and feel of the woman in his arms. "It wasn't you, Jen. It was me. I couldn't hold back, and I didn't satisfy you."

Her words were slow and puzzled, as if he mystified her in some oblique manner. "I don't know what you mean."

His hand slid lower against the curve he'd claimed, probing gently where he'd so recently emptied his essence within her body. She trembled, pressing against his fingers and a shiver traveled from that place, enveloping her in its sensual embrace. "This." He touched again, his fingers caressing carefully, and she moaned against his throat. "I left you wanting, sweetheart."

His mouth sought hers and he turned her to her back with an agile movement. His lips opened against hers, his tongue pressing inside her mouth, and she accepted it, responding to each thrust, each exploring movement, her breathing taking on an uneven pace. Beneath his touch, her hips rose in rapid response, her body trembling as he urged her, coaxed her, then pushed her beyond her own expectations.

She shivered, gasping for breath, and he gave her no leeway, allowed her no relief from the sensations that drove her. A cry of desperation rose from her lips and she buried her face against his shoulder as she convulsed against his agile touch. Shay held her thus for only a moment, then rolled to cover her, and she welcomed him, grasping him with eager arms, her body open for his possession.

He filled her, gritting his teeth against the pure pleasure. She was his. *His.*

Isabelle's silence was offset by Marshall's excitement. "Mama, Isabelle said you and Mr. Shay got married, and he's gonna stay here for always. And Noah said—"

"Isabelle's right, Marshall. We went to see your grandpa and—"

The boy's upraised hand and quick response halted Jenny's explanation. "What's a grandpa?" The childish query touched her heart and Jenny rose from her chair to round the table to where Marshall sat. His fork laden with cornmeal mush, he looked up at her with puzzlement alive in his expression.

Jenny knelt beside his chair and gathered him against her. His fork clattered against his plate and his brow furrowed as he kissed her with awkward enthusiasm. "I love you, Mama. Are you all right?"

She nodded. "Yes, I'm fine, Marsh. I just felt sad for a moment." She leaned back and brushed his hair from his forehead. "If things were as they should be in this world, you'd already know what a grandpa is, sweetheart. Shay and I went to see my father yesterday."

"I didn't know you had a father," Marshall said innocently. "I thought you was just goin' to town."

"You should've taken the boy with you," Isabelle said curtly. "At least one of us coulda been there for the wedding."

Jenny closed her eyes, ignoring the pointed remark. It would be a long time before Isabelle forgave her for getting married so abruptly, without due warning. It couldn't be helped. What was done, was done. She sighed and responded to Marshall's accusation.

"We did go to town, at least we drove past town. And everyone has a father, Marsh," she said, looking over the child's shoulder to see Shay in the doorway.

"Mine lives all by himself." She halted, unable to erase the memory of the shambles of her father's life. "His name is Jonah Harrison, and before I married your father, my name was Jenny Harrison."

"Can we go see him? Can I go this time?" Marshall's words were eager, his eyes alight with excitement. "Will he play with me, do you think?"

"He's..." How to tell this child that the man who was his grandsire was aged beyond his years, feeble with the pressure of grief and despair bowing him low? "Maybe he'd tell you stories and swing with you under the trees."

"Can we sit in my new swing today, Mama?" Marshall asked, distracted by the mention of Shay's latest project.

She nodded her head. "I don't know why not."

"There's room for all of us, if Mr. Shay holds me on his lap," Marshall announced. "Me and Isabelle sat out there while you were gone and shucked corn. Mr. Shay made it plenty big."

"We can go out now, if you like," Shay suggested. "I think we need to talk to Marsh, explain things a bit."

Jenny met his gaze, lost in the smouldering heat of dark eyes, her skin tingling at the remembrance of long hours spent in his arms. His mouth twitched and she recalled the magic of his kiss, the secret places those lips had touched. His hands spread wide against his hips and her own flesh burned as she brought to mind the small bruises his fingertips had left behind.

As if mesmerized, she watched Shay, aware only of the power he held over her.

"Mama? Can we do what Mr. Shay said?" Marshall

tugged at her collar, and she looked down at his inquiring gaze.

"Yes, certainly we can." She looked pointedly at his plate. "Just as soon as you eat your breakfast."

"How about you, Mama? Are you gonna finish yours?" Marshall asked, taking up his fork and filling it anew.

"Yes, of course," she said quickly, rising and returning to her chair. Shay moved from the doorway to stand behind her, one hand on her shoulder. She looked up at him, aware of the flush that colored her cheeks.

"I'll take my coffee along," Shay said, reaching for a cup, then pouring it from the pot on the stove.

"We're almost like a real family," Marshall said, his eyes alight, his head nodding vigorously as he spoke. "Ess-pesh-ly now. Ain't that right, Mr. Shay?"

Shay's tone smacked of satisfaction as he spoke his agreement. "You're right, Marsh. Especially now."

Chapter Nine

Lolling away an hour in the swing when he should have been sweating in the sun was a luxury Shay could not afford. But Marshall's delight in the lazy moments negated any sense of impatience Shay had carried with him from the house and out to the side yard. Sitting beside Jenny, he nudged the ground, sending the swing into motion, holding Marshall with one arm, lest the boy slide from his lap. Tugging the child's mother close to his side, he surrounded himself with the family he'd taken possession of.

Is this what you wanted, Carl? The query floated through his mind, surprising him with its potency. Carl had been a forgotten issue for the past days, only his dogged pursuit of Jenny filling Shay's mind. Perhaps this was what Carl had planned, with his talk of promises. For all Jenny's doubts where Carl's love was concerned, no man could have this woman and not recognize her value.

And if this was what Carl intended, if Shay had been chosen that day in Elmira to fill this place in Jenny's life, he could not fault the man's motives.

Shay's arm circled her shoulders, his fingers resting against her collarbone. It was fragile-seeming through the faded material of her dress, yet he knew her slender form held a strength capable of chopping cotton and harnessing mules to a plow. He knew her as Carl had not, and for a moment received a perverse joy from that truth.

In more than one way, she was a different woman than the girl Carl had married seven years ago. In her eyes this morning was a knowledge he recognized, a look of feminine awareness that spoke to his masculine being. She'd responded to him last night, withholding nothing, offering her body up for his pleasure. And yet, that surging delight dimmed beside his joy at discovering the unawakened woman he'd had the good sense to marry.

His selfish heart gloated, recalling her astonishment. And his hand was tempted, even now, to slide inside the front closure of her dress, to enclose her breast within his palm. As if Jenny sensed his thoughts, she glanced up at him, a small frown marring the smooth line of her forehead.

"Do you feel really married?" she asked, her eyes searching his face. "Are you sure this is what you wanted?" Her outstretched hand encompassed the three of them. "Getting a ready-made family isn't what you bargained for when you came here."

"Maybe not," he agreed, pushing his foot against the ground, keeping the swing in motion. "But it's what I got." His arm tightened around Marshall. "I don't know how good a father I'll be, but I can tell you right now, I'll give it my best shot."

"Are you gonna be my really papa?" Marshall asked, one hand lifting to touch Shay's cheek. His eyes squinted as he scrutinized the scar that caught his attention. "Will this go away, like the peckin' spots on my feet did?" He held his bare foot out for Shay's inspection, where only a tiny pale mark remained as a reminder of the last episode in the chicken yard.

"I'm afraid not, Marsh," Shay answered, allowing the

child's fingers to trace the long line of scar tissue that traveled the length of his cheek. "Does it bother you?"

"Naw," the boy answered quickly, disdaining the suggestion. "Noah said a scar like yours is a—" Marshall searched for the words that eluded him, and then his face brightened. "Oh, yeah. He said it was a badge of honor. And he told me that's something good."

"Did he now?" The remembrance of the man who'd died at his hands was anything but honorable, yet there'd been no choice. He'd killed again since that time, and the burden of those acts weighed heavily on his soul. "Sometimes, a scar is like a punishment, Marsh."

"I don't believe that," Jenny said quickly. "Maybe a reminder, so that we don't make the same mistakes again. But you'll never make me believe that you've ever done anything to deserve what happened to you."

His eyes devoured her glowing features, her eyes shiny with tears as if she defended his honor, her mouth still full and a bit swollen from the night past. "Every man should have so devout a champion, Miss Jenny," he said quietly. "I hope I never see your eyes turn cold when they look inside my soul."

She shook her head, a slight movement. "Will I ever be given that privilege?"

"Some things you're better off not knowing."

Marshall stirred restlessly. "We didn't talk about things, like you said."

Shay's gaze left Jenny, a reluctant smile drawing his mouth to one side. "No, we didn't. And there's really only one thing we need to clear up, Marsh. I want to know if it's all right for me to be your father from now on. I won't be your *really* papa, because you can only have one, and yours is the man your mama married before you were born. But I'll be here from now on."

He bent lower to peer intently into the child's eyes, waiting for the nod of understanding that seemed long in coming. Marshall looked worried for a moment, and then he grinned. "Can I call you Papa anyway?"

"I'd like that," Shay said, his voice thick with an emotion he was unused to. "There's just one more thing we need to talk about." He shot a quick look at Jenny, and then told Marshall of the other change that would take place. "I'll be sleeping in your mama's bedroom from now on."

"Will she let you?" Marshall asked innocently. "She told me I'm a big boy, and I can't sleep with her like I did when I was just a baby."

"Oh, yeah," Shay answered softly. "She'll let me. I'll guarantee it, son."

Jenny stood abruptly, the swing rocking wildly at her movement. "I've wasted half the morning already," she said, refusing to meet Shay's look of amusement. "I have vegetables to pick for dinner, and a kitchen to clean up."

Marshall slid to the ground, looking after his mother's retreating figure. "I don't like pickin' vegables. Can I go workin' with you today—" his hesitation was brief and then a grin curled his lips as he glanced back at Shay "—Papa," he said softly, tasting and testing the word, as he did all newly discovered additions to his youthful vocabulary.

Shay rose and offered his hand, pleased when the boy grasped hold and they set off toward the barn. From deep within, where only a cold vacuum had taken possession of his deepest emotions for the past years, a trickle of warmth penetrated the icy terrain. Woman and child alike had brought to life an aching breach in his defenses, and his first thought was to retreat from their advances. And yet, he could not bring himself to cause pain to either of them, especially not the child, whose disarming innocence even now was weaving tendrils of caring within Shay's breast.

Noah eyed the pair of them, his smile aimed at Marshall. "I'm headin' for the field with the wagon, boy. You want to ride along with Noah?"

Marshall glanced up at Shay, indecision alive in his face. Riding on the wagon was a treat. "Are you goin' along?" he asked.

"I don't know. Am I, Noah?" A challenge rang in his tone of voice, and Noah slanted him a measuring look.

"I reckon, if you're gonna ride up front with me. Marshall can look out from the back end."

Shay nodded, then followed Noah through the barn to the gated area beyond the back door. The wagon stood ready, with tools arranged on the bed. Shay hoisted Marshall on the rear and shot him a warning look.

"No jumping down, and no standing up," he said distinctly. "Understand?"

"Yessir," Marshall answered, his head nodding a quick accompaniment.

Shay opened the wide gate, allowing Noah to drive on through, then closed it behind them before he climbed onto the seat. "Is there a problem?" he asked, propping one foot on the front of the box.

Noah snapped the reins and the vehicle lumbered toward the acres of cotton, beyond the acreage where corn awaited harvest. "Now what makes you think anything's wrong, Mr. Shay?" Noah's voice was mild, his gaze trained on the track ahead.

"You're looking at me like I've made off with the family treasure," Shay said dryly. "And all I've done is make an honest woman out of Jenny."

"She was plenty honest before you got here."

"I thought you were encouraging me to marry her, not too long ago, if I remember right," Shay said, nudging Noah's memory.

"And that's all well and good, if you're plannin' on

stayin' here. My woman seems to think you married up with Miss Jenny just so's she'd—'' Noah looked over his shoulder to where Marshall was humming a tune and kicking his heels.

"I married Jenny because she asked me to," Shay said abruptly. The truth might not be welcome, but he suspected Noah would recognize it as such.

"You stayin' on?" Noah asked. "I need to tell you, if Miss Jenny gets hurt, there'll be hell to pay."

"Sounds like we're on the same side," Shay told him with a laugh.

"She know about you?" Noah's gaze was swift, his narrowed eyes piercing beyond Shay's swiftly erected wall of humor.

"Know what?"

"My boy, Caleb, tells me you got kin close at hand. Isabelle said Eli called you a *Devereaux.* If you go home to where your folks are, maybe you'll take Miss Jenny with you." His gaze returned to the narrow tracks that ran the length of the cornfield. "We'd be in a peck of trouble should that happen. Miss Jenny might need to sell off the place."

"I'm sure Jenny plans on keeping her land for the boy," Shay said firmly. "This is Marshall's heritage, from his father. I've got nothing to do with that."

"Miss Jenny gave us deeds to some of these acres, but we work 'em all, all of us together. I suspect it don't sound right to you, but we're as much a family here as any bunch of folks livin' under the same roof."

Shay nodded, grasping for assurances that Noah would accept. "All I can tell you is that everything will be as Jenny wants. This is her place, and her word goes."

Noah snorted in derisive laughter. "You know as well as me that once you married the woman you got the say-so over her property, Mr. Shay."

"Well, then," Shay said mildly, "I guess you'll just have to trust me, won't you?"

"Noah?" Marshall called loudly from the back of the wagon, looking over his shoulder, careful not to move from his chosen seat. "Noah? Did you know that my mama married Mr. Shay and he's gonna sleep in her bedroom now? And he said he's not my really papa, but I can still call him that if I want to."

"I reckon I knew most all that, Mr. Marshall," Noah said loudly. And then added under his breath, "all but the part about sleepin' in Miss Jenny's bed."

"You hadn't figured that out?" Shay asked with amusement coloring his words. "I'd have thought a smart man like you had figured out the most important part."

"Taking good care of her and the boy had better be on the top of your list," Noah told him, his hands flexing as he gripped the reins, shifting them in his grip. "And now I'll say no more, Mr. Shay. I already overstepped, I expect."

"No, I don't expect you did, Noah. Jenny would have been up the creek in a dry riverbed without you and Isabelle here to look after her and Marsh for the past few years. It's been a load on y'all. I'll do my share from now on. Jenny and Marsh are my responsibility." He looked out over the field where row upon row of sturdy cotton plants were hilled in neat array.

"I made a promise to Carl." That the promise had not been spoken until a matter of months ago was a fact Shay was not about to confess. He'd carried the shame and guilt from Elmira in his gut for years. And for the first time, he felt at peace with the memory of Carl Pennington.

"I figured as much," Noah said, drawing up on the reins, halting the mules beneath the trees at the edge of the field.

"Can I get down now, Papa?" Marshall called from his perch.

"Your mama and Isabelle are needing some nice young corn for dinner when we go back in a couple of hours," Noah told the boy. "You can pick a few at a time and bring them back to the wagon, boy. Do you know how many fingers you got?"

Marshall jumped down and ran to the front of the wagon, peering up at Noah. "I got four fingers and a thumb on each hand. See?" He held them up, his pudgy fingers spread wide so that Noah could inspect their number.

"Well, you get that many ears of corn, twice over, you hear?" Noah told him. "And then go back and get one hand more. That'll be twenty-five, all told. Can you do that?"

Marshall looked thoughtful. "I can remember if I lay them out on the wagon, and keep track of how many hands full I picked."

"Don't go too far," Shay warned him. "Just make sure you can see the wagon, no matter where you are, son. You can get all the corn you need from the first two rows. And make sure you feel the ears real good and get the biggest ones."

"All right," Marshall agreed, his shoulders squared and his steps long as he set off to accomplish his mission.

"I think we need to build a long table to use in the yard," Shay told Noah. They sat on the edge of the back porch, plates in their laps, as they gnawed at the rows of corn on the ears they held. Butter dripped from the golden kernels, splattering the potatoes on their plates, and running downhill to where the collard greens caught the flow. A plate of corn bread sat between them, more butter spread on each piece, and four pork chops edged that plate.

"You want to be sittin' at a table, go on inside and put your feet under Miss Jenny's," Noah said, tossing a barren ear into the yard, scattering a clutch of hens. They turned back to investigate the offering and pecked at the few remaining kernels, sidestepping and clucking their approval.

"It's hot in the kitchen, with the stove going," Shay said. "If we make a trestle table and a couple of benches, we can eat under a tree and catch a breeze most days."

"Where you gonna get long planks for that?" Noah asked. "We about used up all the big pieces of wood when we put the rest of the hayloft floor down last year. That stuff you made the swing out of was just bits and scraps. Not much of anything else left."

"There's a sawmill in town, isn't there?" Shay asked, sending his second stripped ear of corn toward the gathering of chickens. "I'll take the wagon in and see what I can find."

"You want me to do it?" Noah asked mildly. He picked up a pork chop and examined it. "Sure am glad we got us a young pig to butcher. I had Joseph fire up the smokehouse real good for the hams and sides of bacon."

"Jenny and I were talking about that yesterday. We'll need another one and a side of beef before long," Shay said. "I hate to hang a whole beef in this heat. Maybe I can find somebody to share one with us." He'd sent Noah to buy the pig and supervised the butchering, Jenny having a fit when he'd given Marshall the bladder to play with.

"We can go in together," Noah said. "Doc Gibson said Eli's done throwin' fits, and he's kinda gettin' used to the idea of Zora bein' gone. Maybe we won't have any more trouble from him."

Shay hesitated, his senses alert. The idea of leaving the women with only Caleb and Joseph for protection didn't sit well with him, and he wasn't sure why. "I still don't feel right about things. I'll go this time. Maybe tomorrow." Another idea struck him and he grinned. "I'll take Jenny and the boy along. We'll buy Marshall a new pair of boots, and get some clothes for my wife."

* * *

The general store had seen better days. A scant supply of clothing on the shelves gave little to choose from, but Jenny's smile was wide as she considered the selection available. "I can get along with one dress," she whispered, fingering the percale fabric of a simple gown.

"It looks too big for you," Shay said doubtfully, scanning the width of the waistline.

Jenny shrugged. "I can sew. I'll take it in a bit. By the time I tie an apron around my middle it won't matter anyway."

"Which dresses do you like?" he asked her, shifting from one foot to the other, glancing past her to where Marshall eyed a jar of hard candy.

"This will do," she said, picking up the simplest of the three dresses she'd dithered over before her. "I can get along just fine, Shay." She looked wistfully up at the shelf behind the counter. "But I'd really like a new nightgown."

His snort was subdued, and he bent low to whisper in her ear. "You don't need one for my benefit, sweet. You can just wear one of my shirts if you need something to cover up with. I kinda like the way it looked on you."

She felt a rush of warmth cover her cheeks, and her hands moved briskly, folding the dress she had chosen.

"What's the proprietor's name?" Shay asked, looking around the nearly empty store for a likely prospect.

"Herb Duncan," Jenny answered. "But I don't see him here. That's his wife, Tillie, coming out of the back room."

"Ma'am?" Shay held up his hand to gain the woman's attention. "My wife's going to take all three of these dresses. And she'll need to see a sleeping gown." He cleared his throat and patted Jenny's hand. "I'll go on over and help Marsh find a pair of boots while you take your pick," he said.

"Well, Jenny Pennington." Tillie Duncan said in a bemused voice, looking after Shay's retreating figure. "I hadn't heard that you remarried." Her gaze was admiring as she watched Shay's tall figure amble across the store, yet Jenny detected a hesitation as she spoke.

"Yes, I married Shay just recently," she said.

"Haven't seen him hereabouts before," Tillie said, turning to reach for a small stack of white gowns. "I'm afraid we don't have much of a selection. Things are still hard to come by. And the prices are awfully dear."

"I really don't need three dresses," Jennie said quickly. "I'll just take the one, and a plain gown." She looked to where bolts of fabric were stacked. "How about those bolts of material? Is any of that suitable for a nightgown? Perhaps I can just sew one up and save a bit on it."

Tillie pulled a bolt from the middle of the pile. "This here is real nice bleached muslin. It'd make up pretty. Kinda plain, but the material's soft, and you could sew a little lace around the neck to dress it up."

"Give me enough for two gowns then," Jenny said quickly, thinking of Isabelle. What the woman wore to bed these days was probably no better than the shredded gown she'd torn up for rags just today.

"Mama?" Marshall marched across the floor, leather boots sounding loudly against the wide planks. "Look what we found over there. Mr.—" He halted abruptly and a grin creased his face. "My new papa said I could have these." Pulling up his trouser legs, he stuck out one foot for inspection.

"Haven't been married very long, have you?" Tillie asked archly.

"No, not long," Jenny told her, then stepped closer to Marshall. "Are they plenty big, Marsh? I don't want you to outgrow them before winter's over."

He looked puzzled. "It's still summertime, Mama."

"I know, but they'll have to last for a good long time,"

she explained. She looked up as Shay approached. "Did you allow enough room for him to grow?" she asked.

"When they start pinching his toes, we'll buy new ones," he told her patiently. "I can afford them, Jen." Looking past her to the counter, he lifted a brow. "Where's the other two dresses?"

"I only need one," she said hastily. "I picked out enough muslin for nightgowns for myself and one for Isabelle, too."

Shay stepped up to the counter. "We'll take all three dresses and whatever else my wife needs." He turned to Jenny and she fell silent, recognizing the masculine arrogance in his tone and stance. His mouth formed a thin line and his jaw was set. "Did Isabelle tell you what we need for the kitchen?"

Jenny stuffed her hand deeply into her pocket, drawing forth a small bit of paper she'd written on. "Only a couple of things, Shay. Coffee and sugar, and a bag of flour." She peered at the list and glanced up at the waiting Tillie. "Maybe some lard."

"Let me see." He held out his hand and she nodded, giving over the list with scrawled notations filling each iota of space. His look was perplexed as he turned it over in his hand, and then he handed it back to Jenny. "Read me everything you wrote on there," he said politely. Pointing at one item, he bent low, his head beside hers. "Does that say *p-c-h*?"

Jenny blushed anew. "I didn't have room to write whole words, Shay. It means peaches, you know, the ones in cans. Sometimes Tillie has dented cans and she marks down the price for Noah to buy them a little cheaper."

"Do you have any?" he asked Tillie.

She nodded her head, her smile denoting her enjoyment of Shay's tactics.

"I want my wife to read her list aloud, since I'm having

some trouble deciphering her writing, and then you fill it for us, will you?''

"I surely will, sir.'' Tillie bustled back and forth, only shaking her head twice as Jenny read the list. "Things are hard to come by these days, but we get whatever we can.'' The stack grew, and Shay watched quietly as Tillie added up the total. The sum brought a gasp of dismay from Jenny and she placed her hand on Shay's arm.

"That's too much. Really, we can get along without all those things. I always write down more than I plan on having Noah bring home, and Tillie knows to send the most important things first.''

She turned to the storekeeper's wife, her eyes pleading. "Tell him, Tillie. I don't ever expect to buy everything, just the things you have in stock.''

"Well, today we're in pretty good shape,'' Tillie said expansively. "I had most everything.''

"Fine,'' Shay said. "Do you have a box to put the small things in?'' He hoisted the large sack of flour to his shoulder and picked up the five-pound pail of lard. "I'll take these out and come back for the rest.'' His look at Jenny was a warning. "Bring your dresses and have Tillie cut off the material you need. I'll be right back.''

The two women watched as Shay stalked to the door, Marsh ahead of him to open it wide. "That's quite a man you've got yourself,'' Tillie said emphatically. "My, oh my, he does have a way about him, doesn't he? And even with that nasty scar, he's quite a looker.''

"He's arrogant,'' Jenny said sharply. "You'd think I didn't know what we can afford.'' Her hands were reluctant as she picked up the three dresses, and yet her heart sang as she thought of putting her old ragtag clothing to better use. "I guess you'd better cut the muslin for me,'' she said. "I think about twelve yards will be fine.''

"I'll just get a big box for your husband and then get right at the yard goods," Tillie said, hurrying into the back room for an empty crate. Shay took little time loading it while the muslin was measured and folded, and then he pulled a black, leather purse from his back pocket. A gold piece touched the counter for only an instant before Tillie snatched it up.

"We don't get much hard cash like this these days," she said, weighing the coin in her hand. "I'll give you script in change, if that's all right."

"Why don't we just run an account, Miss Tillie," Shay said. "Put us down in your book and you can let me know when I need to pay more on the bill."

"That'll work just fine, sir," she said brightly, slipping the coin into her pocket. Her eyes were bright as she waved goodbye to the trio, and then she hurried to the door behind them. "You didn't introduce me to your new husband, Miss Jenny."

Shay turned back to her and slid his hat from his head. "I'm Shay Devereaux, ma'am. It's been a pleasure to do business with you."

The sawmill was next and Jenny waited on the wagon while Shay did his business. She caught the sidelong glance of several men, recognizing two of them as the elders in town. Too old to go to war, she thought sadly, and now, with so many not returning home, they were working to support large families.

The long planks fit easily on the back of the wagon, with only a couple of feet extending over the rear, and Marshall sat proudly atop the lumber. A small sack of candy clutched in his right hand, he was given the duty of holding down the load for the trip home. That his weight would be of little deterrent should the heavy boards need such help was a minor detail, Jenny thought. It was enough that Marshall felt important, and for that, she silently thanked Shay.

* * *

The boards were unloaded in the side yard and left for another day, Noah determining that work in the fields took precedence for the rest of the day. Marshall retired to the new swing after dinner, admiring his new boots, until his eyes grew heavy and sleep overtook him.

"He sure don't need those hot things on his feet, here by the house," Isabelle said, lifting her head from plucking carrots from the ground.

"I know, but he's getting so much enjoyment from them, I didn't have the heart to tell him that," Jenny answered. Her apron holding enough green beans for supper, she headed for the house. "I'll get a pan and wash these. Why don't you join me on the porch and we'll string them and snap them quick."

Isabelle got to her feet. "I wondered if you was gonna cut out your new sleeping gown today." Her dark eyes held amusement as she looked up at Jenny.

"I'll make yours first," Jenny told her.

"I 'spect that man of yours don't care if you never sleep in a gown, does he?" Isabelle cut through the rows of tomato plants and opened the gate, allowing Jenny to pass through ahead of her.

"I need one anyway," Jenny said, moving quickly toward the pump, flustered by Isabelle's teasing.

"Well, I can use one, that's sure enough," Isabelle called after her. "Haven't had anything besides a shift to wear to bed since I had to make Noah a shirt out of my last nightgown." She dropped the carrots on the porch and in seconds the screen door slammed behind her. "I reckon I better get you a pan to wash those beans in."

Jenny stood by the watering trough, holding the corners of her apron. Thinking about Shay simply sent her good sense into a whirlwind, she decided. Anticipation of the night to come lingered in the back of her mind. And from the look in Shay's eyes when he'd headed for the field after dinner, he was suffering from the same affliction.

Isabelle brought the bread pan from the kitchen, and Jenny dumped the contents of her apron into its depths. "I'll pump and you rinse them good," Isabelle said. "We can do the carrots, once we get these on the stove for supper."

Jenny sloshed the beans in the pan, dumping the water once and waiting as Isabelle refilled it. They walked to the porch together and Jenny's mind went back to the clothing issue. "There's still a few things left in the attic," she said. "Maybe Noah can use some of Carl's father's clothes. I never thought of him when I cut up some things for Marshall. Why don't we go up and look through them?"

"Later, maybe," Isabelle said. "It's too hot up there this time of day."

Within the hour, a kettle of beans was cooking, and Isabelle cut up a big onion and added a chunk of fatback for flavor. The carrots were put on the back of the stove, where they would cook slowly. Isabelle's eyes widened as she inspected the crate of food Shay had deposited in the pantry.

"Where'd you get enough money for all this?" she asked, peeking around the corner into the kitchen where Jenny was spreading muslin over the kitchen table.

"Shay bought it all," Jenny told her. "He made Tillie Duncan very happy. I don't think she's seen gold coins in a long time."

"Mr. Shay's got gold in his pocket?" Isabelle said, stepping into the kitchen.

Jenny nodded. "He did today. But I think he put it away somewhere when we got home."

"Well, the man's doin' right by you, Jen. I'll bide my time and keep my eyes open, but he ain't stingy, that's one sure thing." Her gaze swept the muslin fabric Jenny was eyeing, scissors in hand. "You cut that plenty wide in the skirt, you hear? My bottom ain't gettin' any smaller."

The scissors flashed as Jenny cut the length of fabric, then held it up for inspection. "Does this look long enough?"

Isabelle nodded. "Just sew up the seams, and gather it up around the neck. Don't worry about settin' in sleeves. I won't need them for this time of year, and old Noah knows how to keep me warm when the weather turns chilly." Her smile flashed. "I sure am happy we don't have to worry about scant supplies for the next little while. We got cornmeal enough to last till we get ours ground at the mill."

Chapter Ten

"You didn't make a nightgown, I see." Shay leaned against the bedroom door, watching as Jenny brushed her hair. Sitting on the edge of the bed, she'd managed to cover her knees with his shirt, but apparently the sewing she'd been doing before supper had been for someone else's benefit. He suspected Isabelle might be wearing the results of Jenny's swift needle plying the cream-colored fabric.

"Isabelle needed one more than I did," Jenny said, leaning forward to pull her brush through the length of her hair. It almost touched the floor in front of her, and she sat a bit higher, working at a snarl with both hands. The sunlight had brightened its hue, turning it a rich shade, more golden than chestnut, Shay thought. It would darken in the winter months when she spent less time out of doors, but for now, he could see the fire glisten throughout its heavy waves.

She was waiting for him, and he drew out his own anticipation, watching as she sat erect, the mass of waves settling over her shoulders and down her back. Her fingers gripped it at the nape of her neck, bringing it over her shoulder in a long tail, and he moved from his post to walk toward her, his steps silent in his stocking feet.

"Don't braid it," he said quietly. "I want it loose."

She looked up, watching as he rounded the footboard to kneel before her. "It gets all snarled. I had a hard time getting it brushed out this morning."

"I'll help you," he promised, touching a long tendril that hung across her breast. Beneath the shirt she wore, her breasts were full, rising abruptly with the quick breath she caught. "I want to take my shirt off you," he said, aware that his voice was gruff, yet unable to control the harsh sound of passion gripping his throat.

"Blow out the candle first," Jenny said, one hand clutching the front of her makeshift gown, as if she would ensure that the buttons stay in their proper places.

"I want to look at you, Jen."

Her glance shot to the open window, where the curtains caught the breeze. "Someone could see in," she reminded him.

"No one is out there, and they couldn't see past me anyhow, sweetheart. I'm between you and the window." His big hands covered hers, dwarfing her slender fingers as he enfolded them in his own. Placing her hands in her lap, he watched as she folded them together precisely. Then, carefully, he undid the first three buttons of the shirt she wore. A flush rose from her chest, bringing color to her throat and cheeks, and he wondered again at the relative innocence of his bride. Carl had missed much, it seemed. Beneath the shirt, her breasts were full, firm to his touch, the crests peaking before his gaze. Three more buttons fell prey to his agile fingers, then, spreading wide the garment above her waist, he allowed her to grasp it. She held it firmly over her lap, so that it concealed her skin below the small indentation of her belly button. Absorbed in the beauty of pale flesh that filled his palms, he bent closer, his mouth pressing kisses across the rise of her bosom, then touched the wrinkled, darkened peaks with the tip of his tongue.

She shivered and he smiled, uncaring that his face drew up with the gesture. Turning his head, he rested his cheek against her, as if her unblemished skin, there beneath his cruel scar, could somehow heal him.

Such foolishness. And yet, the heat of his face was cooled by her, the taut skin seemed more supple as his wounded flesh caressed the gentle curves, moving from one side to the other. He turned his head then, his mouth opening to capture her, hearing her small cry of pleasure as he suckled gently.

Her palms cupped his head, her fingers tugging at his hair, yet he clung stubbornly, unwilling to release the tender morsel from his lips. She moved toward him, leaning a bit, then turning to one side. Beneath his closed eyes, the room lost its glow, and he smelled the faint odor of the wick as it smoked.

Jenny had blown out the candle, and he lifted his head to search out her face in the dim light. She leaned to him, her mouth against his, her lips moving carefully as she kissed him, as though it were a novelty to be so bold. He opened his mouth, urging her to explore and she clasped his face, touching his lips with her tongue as he had taught her in the night hours. Beneath his fingers, the two remaining buttons gave way and he slid the shirt from her shoulders, then spread her legs to make a place for himself there. He leaned against her, gathering her to his chest, holding her closely for a moment before rising fully to his feet.

"Come lie with me," she whispered, her breath sweet in his mouth, and he groaned his reply.

"Don't move," he whispered, releasing her, stepping back bare inches as he stripped himself of his shirt. It fell on the floor, and he bent to shove his trousers down, easing his stockings off with them. Then he reached for her again, clasping her against himself as he turned and pulled her with him onto the bed. She clung tightly, lying atop him as he took his place against the sheet.

Her breasts were soft, nestling on his chest, her feet only reaching his shins, and he was wrapped in the length of russet waves as she lifted her head to peer into his face. Pushing his fingers through her hair, he lifted it from her face, the better to see her, and found her smiling in the glow of stars from the window.

"You're a fast learner, Mrs. Devereaux."

Inhaling sharply at his words, she whispered the name beneath her breath. "Mrs. Devereaux. I hadn't thought, until now," she said softly. "I'm Jenny Devereaux."

"You surely are, sweetheart." The ache began in his chest, spreading to his throat and he recognized once more his need of this woman. If ever he was given back his ability to love another human being, it would be Jenny who would receive the outpouring of that long-forgotten emotion. For now, there was the need, the wanting, the aching urge to possess her.

And he was filled to the brim with that yearning, aware of the burgeoning thrust of his arousal, even now causing him to shift beneath her slender form. "Hold on to me, Jen," he whispered, then turned with her, holding her tightly as he placed her beneath him.

She clung, her arms wrapped around his neck, her face buried in his throat, and he felt her legs part widely beneath him, ready to accept his possession. Shay's mouth softened as he smiled against her hair. There would be no rapid end to this night of loving. Jenny deserved more, and if it took every bit of patience and endurance he could muster, she would find pleasure in his arms before he lost himself in her sweet depths.

The days were long, the summer sun hot, and three weeks went by without rain. In the cornfield, the stalks were turning crisp and browning at the edges. The cotton fared better, but the kitchen garden required buckets of water, carried from the horse trough daily. Finding Jenny at the task, Shay had scolded her roundly, taking the buckets from her hands and tackling the chore himself. Twice he made the trek to the garden, then back to the pump, where he dipped the buckets into the horse trough to fill them.

"I toted water yesterday and the day before," she snapped. "Besides, who do you think did this before you got here?" she asked, standing in the shade of the house, while he carried his burden into the tomato patch.

He stood erect, wiping his forehead with his kerchief, then tucked it back into his pocket. "The point is, I'm here now. And while I'm here, you won't be lugging two buckets of water at a time, making who knows how many trips to this damn garden."

"This *damn garden* provides us with enough vegetables to get us through the winter," Jenny said forcefully. She sauntered from the shade into the glaring sun, then through the open gate to where Shay stood, watching her, his hands on his hips.

"You remind me of my sister," he said sharply. "She always had to have the last word."

"Your sister?" She blinked. "I don't think I knew you had one."

"Yeah, I come equipped with family, Jenny, including a sister who ran off with a Yankee officer. Yvonne has a lot to answer for, leaving my folks without a word of explanation."

"You left, too," she reminded him.

"I went back after the war," he said harshly. "It just didn't work."

He hadn't told her so much about himself since he'd arrived, Jenny thought. She ought to make him angry more often. "Then don't blame your sister for leaving. You weren't there, and you don't know—"

His hand sliced the air, cutting her off.

"You're pretty snippy for such a little woman," he said, his gaze sweeping her from the top of her gleaming head to the bare toes that showed beneath her old gown. "And where's the new dresses I bought for you?"

"I don't crawl around in the garden in my new things," she said, aware, that for the first time, they were exchanging words in a less than friendly manner. The thought brought a strange exhilaration to bloom in her breast, and she stood before Shay with rebellion boldly outlining her pouting mouth and lifted chin.

"When they wear out, I'll buy you more," he told her, his jaw clenched.

She was drawn to him, facing him almost toe to toe, and yet it wasn't enough. Her index finger poked at his chest and she spit defiance. "I didn't know you tied strings on gifts, Mr. Devereaux. I thought the dresses were mine to do with as I liked. And I *don't* like wearing them to crawl around in the dirt."

His palm circled her jabbing finger, capturing it firmly and she pulled at it, with no success. "Not so smart now, are you, missy?" he whispered, dark color ridging his cheeks. His eyes narrowed beneath the brim of his hat and his lips thinned. A look she had come to recognize turned his features into a hungry mask, and Jenny whimpered beneath her breath.

"Not now, Shay." Her whisper was pleading, but he ignored it, transferring his hold on her from the single finger to her wrist, and from there to her waist. One long arm snaked around her middle, the other hand gripped her chin, and she was drawn on tiptoes against him. His mouth found hers, and she moaned against his possession, a soft, yearning murmur that brought him to full arousal against her belly.

"I want to carry you in the house right now," he said, his voice harsh. His frame was long and woven with sinewy strength, his arms heavy with the muscles of a man who put in long hours of physical labor every day. And she was no match for the masculine power he could call into being with barely an effort.

Yet, there was no fear in her, no trepidation as she felt her breasts flattened against his chest, her feet lifted from the ground. Only the triumph of knowing that she was the target for the passion and desire he could barely contain. Her hands were free and she lifted them to his face, her fingers gentle as she traced the line of his temple, cheek and jaw. One side of his face so sharply drawn, so flawless, the other a blazing scar that felt ridged and thick beneath her fingertips.

"I love you, Shay." She whispered the phrase. Indeed, it was drawn from her as though the man who held her pulled the syllables from her depths. His eyes grew darker yet, his mouth twitching. Yet he was silent, and Jenny pressed her lips together.

"I'm sorry. I didn't mean to upset you," she said. "I can't help that I'm in love with you. I thought you already knew."

"I knew," he said shortly, lowering her to the ground, his hands gentle against her waist. Yet he held her firmly against himself, easing his manhood against her with a subtle thrust of his hips. "You're a loving woman, Jen. I'm a lucky man."

His eyes closed and she was swept by a wave of tenderness, of a different sort of loving, almost akin to that of a mother for a child, as she saw the bleak expression on his face. "You're good to me, Shay. I don't expect more than that from you. I almost begged you to marry me, and you did. Whatever else you feel for me, I know you care about me, and for Marshall. That's all I ask.''

His dark eyes opened and she caught a glimpse of pain there, quickly masked as he blinked. ''I told you I'm not good enough for you, Jen, and you wouldn't believe me. You deserve a better man.''

''I don't want anyone else,'' she admitted. ''I'll never love anyone else the way I love you. You've crept inside my soul, Shay. I'm filled with your presence, even when you're out in the field or in the barn.'' Her eyelids drooped and she smiled, her mind bringing forth vivid pictures. ''When I close my eyes, I can feel your hands on me, your mouth against my skin. I smell your scent on my pillow when I make the bed in the mornings, and I hug it to my face and pretend you're there with me.''

His arms caught her close again and his whisper was harsh. ''Whether I deserve you or not, you won't get rid of me, Jenny. I'm here for the long haul.''

''What're you doin', Mama?'' Marshall asked, tugging at her skirt.

She looked down quickly, her smile anxious. ''I didn't hear you, Marsh. Did you call for me?''

He shook his head. ''No, I just heard you talkin' out here and I came to see what you were doin'.''

''I'm hugging your mother,'' Shay said, turning Jenny so that her back fit against his chest. ''Did you come to help with the watering?''

Marshall's chest stuck out with the importance of having a task assigned, especially one he enjoyed so much. ''I like pourin' water on the plants,'' he said. ''Where's the dipper?''

''Run and get one from the kitchen,'' Shay told him. ''Your mother's been pouring it right from the bucket, but you'll do better with a dipper.''

The boy set off at a run, and Shay bent his head to

whisper in Jenny's ear. "Just stay where you are for a moment, and I'll be decent company by the time he gets back."

She smiled, aware of the problem she was keeping from Marshall's sight. "You're good with him, Shay. He likes helping you."

"He just rescued you from being ravished in the potato patch, you know," he said, his voice a teasing lilt.

"I know." She lifted her arm to wipe the beads of perspiration from her face, grasping for words that would take his mind from his problem. "Do you think it'll rain soon?" The sky was brilliantly blue, with only high, puffy, white clouds overhead, yet a haze covered the sun.

"I think so. Maybe by morning. The wind's coming up a bit, and the leaves are turning up to the sky."

"My father used to say they were looking for a shower when they did that."

"He was right," Shay said, releasing her as Marshall ran through the garden gate, waving the dipper in an upraised fist. "Let me set Marsh to work with his dipper now, sweetheart. I'll deal with you later."

The rain came late the next afternoon, while the men were still in the fields. The wagon pulled into the barn, Noah easing it through the wide doorway, and the four men jumped down, Marshall following suit. Caleb caught him in his arms and lowered him to the floor, teasing him with a burst of laughter.

From the kitchen door, Jenny watched, her apprehension eased, now that her son was in sight. The lightning and thunder had come on suddenly, with huge, dark clouds blowing in from the southwest, and she and Isabelle had kept watch, looking toward the fields for the past half hour.

"They don't want to get caught out there in a lightning

storm," Isabelle had muttered. "I've heard of men that got killed, standin' 'neath a tree mindin' their own business."

"They won't take any chances, not with Marshall out there," Jenny'd predicted cheerfully, even as her heart pounded a beat faster than was normal. And then, through the slanting rain, Zora had come running full tilt, jumping the pasture fence with an agile leap as she headed for the house.

"I'm just a fraidy-cat," she wept, huddling against Isabelle's shoulder. "I never did like bad storms."

"Well, we needed this one," Jenny said, willing to give comfort, even if it was halfhearted.

Zora was slender, looking even younger than her seventeen years as she shivered, soaking wet. The water dripped from her dress onto the floor and Isabelle drew her to the doorway, where a rug was placed. "Here, get the rug wet, girl," she said. "I'll get you a towel for your hair."

Jenny fetched a rag from the pantry and wiped up the wet floor, smiling quietly as Isabelle rolled her eyes at the younger woman's fears. And then they all watched as the wagon was emptied and the mules led from their harnesses into stalls where clean bedding awaited.

"They're gonna spoil those animals," Isabelle said. "Standin' out in the rain won't hurt them, not one little bit. No sense in messin' up that straw."

"Maybe Shay and Noah are afraid to expose them to lightning," Jenny offered, not sure of her ground.

"Huh!" Isabelle's grunted reply was neither agreement nor denial of that theory and Jenny stood framed in the screen door, watching the activity in the barn.

The rain began to lessen, settling into a heavy shower, the wind abating, so that the water no longer slanted across the porch, but poured from the eaves, curtaining the area. Jenny stepped out, her feet cooling when they touched the wet boards of the porch. She lifted a hand to brush a stray lock of hair from her eyes and drew in a deep breath, inhaling the fresh, rain-swept air. Behind her, Isabelle murmured to Zora, and Jenny heard a chair scrape against the floor, heard the movement of the coffeepot on the stove.

Coffee was good medicine, Isabelle firmly believed. It would comfort, warm and nourish the frightened soul. Jenny had sat at that same table over the years with Isabelle pouring dark cups of her brew for Jenny's benefit. Now she did the same for Caleb's wife.

From the barn door, Shay watched the rain, speaking over his shoulder to Noah behind him, then reached for Marshall. The boy wrapped his legs around Shay's waist and clung tightly to his neck. Bending low over the child, Shay ran toward the house, his long legs eating up the ground beneath him. Jenny moved back from the steps, and laughed as he bounded onto the porch, skidding on the slick surface.

She caught him, her embrace encircling Marshall and gripping Shay's belt. "You're soaked," she scolded. "You should have stayed out there a while, till the storm let up."

"It already let up, Jen," he answered. "Besides, we were soaked before we got to the barn. What a gully-washer this turned out to be." He lowered Marshall to the porch and held him against his legs, turning him to face the downpour. "Are you cold, Marsh?" he asked, and the boy shook his head vigorously.

"Naw, that was fun." He looked up at his mother. "We had to really hurry, Mama. The lightning was real bright, and a tree way out behind the field made a loud noise and then it fell right down on the ground."

"Lightning struck? That close?" Jenny asked, shivering as she realize how close the menfolk had been to danger.

"We were already on our way back," Shay told her. His arm was around her shoulders and her dress was wet from the two male bodies she'd hugged. "I think you need to change your clothes," he whispered, a grin curving his mouth.

Damp enough to cling, the worn fabric molded itself to each curve, and Jenny looked down at herself with dismay. "I didn't even think."

The porch was sheltered, almost cozy, she thought, and she nestled closer to Shay's side, her arm creeping around his waist. Marshall looked up over his shoulder and grinned. "This feels good, Mama. My new papa is big enough to keep us both warm, isn't he?"

"Yes." Shay's arm tightened its hold and she watched as his other hand stretched across Marshall's chest to clasp the boy even closer. It was almost too good to be true, too perfect, this small world they inhabited, and she shivered, remembering a phrase her mother had been wont to speak. *Nothing lasts forever.*

"We can't cut hay for a couple of days," Shay said the next morning as he forked straw into the stalls. "It would be a good time to find the extra stock we need. I've been thinking we should be on the lookout for a couple of heifers and a young bull." Shay leaned against his pitchfork and watched as Noah considered the idea for a moment and then nodded his head in a slow gesture.

"What kind of cattle you lookin' to buy?"

"Hereford maybe, or even Angus. They both do well without heavy feed."

"You think we're doin' well enough to afford buyin' more stock?" Noah's voice held a dubious note. "We'll have plenty of hay to feed," he granted, "once we get it cut and into the loft. More than enough," he amended. "But I thought you'd be sellin' some of it off, like Miss Jenny usually does, to put away for seed money."

"We're going to keep back the best of the cotton and

run it through the gin separately, so we have our own seed this year,'' Shay said. ''My father always said he wanted to know what seed he was planting, not just take whatever the fella at the gin kept aside to sell.''

''Will they let you do that?'' Noah asked. He took Shay's pitchfork and hung it between two nails, high on the wall. And then he looked back at Shay's arrogant grin. ''Yeah, I guess they will. Anybody who can ride off with a woman in the morning and come home at night married to her oughta be able to find his way around most any problem.''

''We'd already decided to get married,'' Shay said. ''It was just a matter of when and where.''

''It's been weeks, and Isabelle still hasn't forgiven you for leavin' her out of it.''

''She'll get over it,'' Shay told him. ''It was more important that Jen's daddy be there. Isabelle will feel better about things when we get Jonah Harrison to move here, bag and baggage.''

''Think you'll talk him into it? Miss Jenny says he's bound to that place. She's afraid she'll never see him again.''

''She told you that?'' Shay's voice was sharp.

''Told Isabelle. That's about the same as tellin' me, I guess.''

It wouldn't do for Jenny to be fretting over her father, Shay decided. Once the corn was in the crib and the stalks brought in for silage, they'd be ready to pick the cotton and get it off to market. Then he'd take Jenny for another trip to visit the old man.

In the meantime, there was the matter of buying cattle to be considered.

''I'm going to be leaving for a few days,'' Shay said abruptly. ''I want to look for some stock while we're in a lull.'' For long moments they'd sat together on the porch, watching the sun as it hovered on the horizon, as if it would linger just a while longer. With Shay's announcement, Jenny was wrested from her reverie.

''Where do you have to go?'' she asked, a feeling of panic seizing her as he spoke. She frowned, choosing her words carefully. ''Isn't there anywhere close by for you to buy what you're looking for?'' She straightened her shoulders, not wanting him to think she was a demanding wife. Yet, what did it matter? When he left, he was bright enough to know she'd be watching for his return every minute he was gone. As would Marshall, she thought, grateful that he was in bed sleeping soundly, not privy to this discussion.

Shay shook his head. ''Noah doesn't think so, and he's been here a lot longer than I have. There was an outfit raising cattle ten years ago, about seventy miles from here. The thing is, I'm not sure they've got anything left, what with the war.''

''Can you find out about it?'' Jenny asked, already sensing what his answer would be.

''There's only one way to do that. There's no one hereabouts to ask. Folks around here have milk cows, like we do, but no one does any breeding that Noah knows of. Most people are lucky to have one cow, Jen. I need to go looking, find a place where they have a decent-size herd of cattle, and breed them for a living. I can maybe find a couple of heifers in this area, but a good bull's something else.''

''But you know where to go, don't you?'' she asked, aware suddenly of her limited knowledge of the surrounding area. Her whole life had been spent within the boundaries circumscribed by the distance between this place and her childhood home. Shay, on the other hand, was familiar, not only with places in close proximity, but with towns and cities and territories far beyond this place.

''Yeah, there's one family I can check with, but traveling

seventy miles doesn't appeal to me,'' he said quietly, touching her cheek with his palm. ''Not with you here waiting for me.''

''Have you thought about finding your brother?'' she asked. ''Maybe he'd be willing to help.''

His gaze darkened and his mouth thinned as he looked deeply into her eyes. ''No. I won't do that. I know where to find him, Jen. But that's not where I'm heading.'' He looked out toward the barn and the fields beyond it. ''If I wanted to go back to my family, I'd have done it before now. This is where I'm staying. Call it hiding, if you like. I call it peaceful. And that's something I don't want to take any chance of losing.''

''I'll still be here when you come back,'' she told him. ''Although I'd rather go with you.''

He shook his head. ''I'll ride fast and hard. I'll get there quicker on my own, and if I find what I'm looking for, I'll bring it back with me.''

''When you talk about breeding cattle you don't sound like a man who grew up raising cotton,'' she told him. ''More like you spent some time on a ranch before you came here.''

''Yeah, I did. Several places, in fact. Across the northeast for a few months, then longer in Missouri, Texas and Kansas. Beau Jackson raised fine beef, but he was more into training horses and selling them.'' He drew up one leg to lean an elbow on his knee; and when he spoke, the words were chill and forbidding. ''Going back there isn't an option.''

Beau Jackson. Jenny stored the name in her head, then looked up to find Shay's gaze focused on her with interest. He'd slipped, mentioning that name, and now she'd warrant he was trying to decide whether or not she'd caught its importance to him. His whole being was concentrated on her, as if he calculated her interest in the words he'd spoken without due forethought.

In the shadows of twilight, she forced her face to register only a casual interest.

"Was that the last place you lived?" she asked innocently.

"I left there a year ago. I worked my way south and then east."

"Worked? On farms?"

"Mostly in saloons. Wore a deputy sheriff's badge for a few months."

"You worked in saloons?" she asked, unsure whether she'd understood his words.

He turned from her, facing the faint glow that marked the last rays of the sun. Around them the crickets chirped, the tree frogs peeped cheerfully, and the stray cat stalked toward the house from the barn, arrogance alive in her uplifted tail and haughty manner.

"She's thinking she'll jump through Marshall's bedroom window," Shay predicted, eyeing the feline creature as she detoured by the porch to head around the side of the house.

Let her. Jenny's edict concerning Marshall's pet held little import right now. Shay was deflecting her interest, but she pursued him, quietly, but with persistence.

"Did you barkeep?"

His features were hard, his jaw set. "You mean pour liquor for the customers?" he asked. And then before she could reply, he shrugged. "No. Not that I wouldn't, if I needed a job."

"You're determined not to tell me anything about yourself, aren't you?" she asked, and recognized the hurt she'd tried to conceal, in the tremor of her voice. She rose abruptly, unwilling to hear his roundabout tales that gave her nothing of his past, only wove a tangled web.

He reached up and grasped her wrist, his palm and fingers holding her fast. "Don't walk away from me, Jen. I told you I worked on ranches. I wore a badge and I earned my cash in a whole string of saloons."

"You're a gambler?" she prodded, visualizing him in a seamy saloon, where loose women and a steady flow of whiskey provided an atmosphere she could only imagine. Her gaze touched the long, lean fingers that gripped her, visualizing a deck of cards held between those strong hands. He was more than handy with those agile digits. She knew that from personal experience, and his harsh features were capable of concealing anything he was not willing to expose.

"Don't sound so shocked, honey. It's not dirty money. You didn't mind it when it bought food for your kitchen and clothes for your back." His words were an arrogant snarl. "Hell, gambling's a way of life for a lot of men."

His jibe stung, but she lifted her chin and tossed back a sharp retort, choosing to face him down rather than let him see the hurt he'd inflicted. "You gambled that I'd let you stay when you came here, didn't you?"

He was silent. And then he nodded, a barely perceptible movement of his head. "I guess you could say that," he allowed quietly.

"And you were right. I've been gullible more than once in my life."

His grip on her arm eased as he stood to face her. "You're not gullible, Jenny. Trusting, maybe." He drew her closer, one arm circling her waist, and his voice lowered, coaxing with its vibrant tones. "I've told you more about myself than anyone else knows. I've answered your questions, for the most part."

She would not be taken in by his assurances, and she stiffened in his embrace. "You talk in circles, Shay. I think I deserve more than that from you."

His shoulders lifted idly, and he loosened his hold.

"Maybe so. But remember, I let you know right off the bat that I wasn't much for talking about the past. I told you you'd be sorry you—"

Her hand rose swiftly to cover his mouth. "I'm not sorry," she murmured, looking up into eyes that hid beneath hooded lids. In the lengthening shadows she could find no softness there, only a bleak, forbidding darkness that offered nothing. And she was chilled with the knowledge that there were no guarantees where Shay was concerned.

Chapter Eleven

For the first time in their marriage she slept before he came to bed. Crawling between the sheets in the dark, she'd rued her words, and yet knew that she'd only spoken truthfully. Perhaps she hadn't been fair, expecting more than Shay was willing to give her. But life was seldom fair, she'd found to her dismay over the past years.

Jenny Pennington had married a man more than familiar with saloons—a gambler. Yet, there was more to Shay than that fact. Instinctively, she knew that he was a good man, that somewhere not far from here, his family mourned the empty place he'd left behind. Perhaps in Texas, or maybe Kansas, he'd received scars that marred his soul.

She loved him; probably more than was good for her, she decided. For certainly Shay was not willing to return her love. He'd said he had none to give, and she might have to be content with what she had, for he would share nothing else with her. With a troubled frown and a heavy heart, she tired of waiting for him, and lost herself in slumber.

The sun was high in the sky and the kitchen was empty when Jenny walked through the doorway in the morning. Isabelle was in the yard, filling a washtub with a bucket, trekking from the pump, and then back. Looking toward the house as she turned back to the pump on yet another circuit, she caught sight of Jenny, and waved. ''Coffee's on the back of the stove,'' she called and, turning, resumed her task.

The copper wash pan was atop the front of the big, iron stove, covering a large expanse, and the heat brought perspiration to Jenny's brow as she walked to the side, reaching for the coffeepot. Pouring a cup, she glanced again through the window, but no men were in sight, not even Marshall's small figure. The cream pitcher was on the buffet and she smelled it, judging it to be fresh, before she poured some in her cup. The remainder she poured into a small bowl by the door for Marshall's cat.

The cat waited patiently on the step and she let it inside. Then, allowing the screen door to close noisily behind her, Jenny sat down on the edge of the porch to nurse her coffee. Isabelle stood next to the watering trough, her right arm working the pump handle, forcing water from beneath the earth to fill the bucket, which she'd hung on the pitcher as it filled. She lifted it, dumping the contents into her washtub, and then turned to Jenny.

''I thought you'd sleep the morning away. Mr. Shay said not to wake you when he left.''

''Where's Marshall?'' Jenny asked, her mind working furiously. Shay had gone. But, where? Out to the fields with Noah?

''Noah and the boys took him along on the wagon,'' Isabelle said. She walked to the porch and grinned. ''You musta been sleepin' hard.''

Jenny shrugged, and bent her head to sip more of the hot brew. ''He didn't wake me.'' And wasn't that the truth, she thought ruefully. For all she knew, he might have slept with Marshall or on the sofa. Except for the fact that his pillow held the impression where his head had rested all night.

"Did he say when he'd be back?" she asked idly.

Isabelle was silent and Jenny felt a warmth creep up her throat, to settle on her cheeks. "Didn't he tell you?" Her words were sharp and probing, and Jenny could only shake her head in reply.

"You mad at him?" Isabelle asked.

"We had a few words before I went to bed. He talked about going somewhere to find a young bull. He seemed to think that he could find a couple of heifers around here maybe, but the bull would be more difficult to locate. I don't know which he's planning on doing first, though."

Isabelle nodded. "That's about what he told Noah while he saddled up that stallion of his. I sent him along some bread and meat from yesterday's dinner, and he left right at sunup."

"Well," Jenny said, rising and dumping the remains of her coffee on the ground. "I'd better get busy. Did you separate the milk yet?"

"No, I was just about to start the wash. You wanta help me carry out the copper tub?"

Within a few minutes, Isabelle was hard at work with the scrub board and a thick bar of lye soap, working on the men's shirts. "Zora's bringin' hers and Caleb's stuff up after a while. I think she's lonesome for her mama, now that she's got their place all fixed up. Sure would be nice if Eli'd let the woman come to visit."

Jenny lingered, her mind working at something she'd stewed over since the rainstorm the day before. There was no way to ask politely, she decided, and Isabelle was the one most likely to know. "Is Zora in the family way?" she asked. "It's hard to tell with the dresses she wears. They're in worse shape than mine. But when I saw her yesterday she was soaked to the skin, and she sure looked like I did when I was about halfway through carrying Marshall."

Isabelle nodded, her hands ceasing their movement

against the corrugated board. "Caleb told me about it when I asked him this morning." Her eyes were troubled as she met Jenny's gaze. "I don't know if Eli was mad about that, or if he'd just been throwing a general fit over the whole idea of her gettin' married." She bent her head and picked up the shirt she was working on. "I thought I'd talk to her while we're scrubbin' clothes. I'm about the closest thing to a mama she's got these days."

"Well, at least she'll have someone right at hand to deliver the baby when the time comes," Jenny said with a soft smile of remembrance. "I don't know what I'd have done without you when Marshall was born."

"I've done my share of birthin' babies," Isabelle allowed. Her smile glittered brightly and her words were lilting as she spoke softly. "This one'll be real special, Jen, even if they did sorta get the cart before the horse. My first grandchild. Noah's as proud as if he had something to do with it."

"I haven't had my monthly since before Shay and I…" Jenny halted, biting at her lip, wondering how those words had slid so easily from her mouth. She'd only just recognized the absence of her menses in the past several weeks, and decided that the changes in her life had somehow delayed her cycle. Now she began to think there might be a more logical reason for the lack.

"I wondered," Isabelle said. "You haven't done any woman laundry in pretty near two months or so, have you?"

Jenny shook her head, stunned as the thoughts swirled through her mind.

"No wonder you slept half the day away," Isabelle said archly. "I always dragged around for the first three months when I was carrying a baby under my apron." She rose from her knees in front of the washtub and walked to where Jenny stood. Her index finger touched gently at Jenny's eye and she drew down the lower lid, peering at the exposed membrane.

"Looks pretty white," Isabelle said, nodding her head. "That's a sure sign, girl." And then she frowned. "Here I went and let you help me tote that copper tub out here. Never should have done it. You don't be lifting anything heavy for the next couple of months, you hear?"

"I'm healthy," Jenny answered, the words an automatic response. "I worked hard the whole time I carried Marshall."

"Well, I'll be lugging the baskets out of the garden for the next little while," Isabelle said, turning back to the washing. "Won't Mr. Shay have a surprise when he comes back home." She laughed aloud, a triumphant sound. "Come next spring, we'll have all kinds of new things gettin' born around here. He told Noah we'd be ready to buy a couple of young sows from Doc Gibson the end of the week, and to go ahead and get us another shoat to butcher. We'll be eatin' high this winter, won't we?"

"I thought he was going to get a pair and breed them."

Isabelle shook her head. "Changed his mind, I guess. Noah said it's dangerous to have a boar around. It's just as easy to have Doc Gibson bring his over when the men get ready to breed the sows."

"Are Noah and the boys going to butcher right away?"

"No," Isabelle said, wringing out the last of the shirts she'd scrubbed. She turned to dump them in the rinse tub, then rose, walking to the porch to pick up a pile of work pants. "Mr. Shay said to wait till he comes back. He said they'll pen up the shoat and feed him good, fatten him up for a while first."

Jenny walked past her and went into the springhouse, thankful for the cool shade the interior provided. *A baby.* She should have recognized the signs, few as there were. There was no morning sickness to cope with yet, and her mind recoiled from that memory. She'd hung over a slop jar more than once before Marshall was born. For almost two months, in fact, regular as the sunrise, she could count on wakening with waves of nausea sending her to the covered pail in the corner of her bedroom.

Maybe this time would be different. Then, she'd been dealing with Carl's leaving and the fear of facing childbirth alone. Her days had been spent in hard work and her nights in mourning the loss of life as she'd known it for twenty years. Marshall's coming had not been cause for true celebration. Although his birth had given her new reason to put her heart and soul into this place, to preserve the land for his inheritance.

Now... She wiped her forehead with the back of her hand. Would Shay welcome the news? It could hardly come as a surprise, given the nights they'd spent in each other's arms.

He hadn't kissed her goodbye. That bit of painful knowledge came to the forefront of her mind, and she bowed her head. She'd angered him more than she'd realized, and he'd ridden away without allowing her to speak those words that prefaced every parting.

Be careful. Take care of yourself.

Spoken almost as a charm, as if they carried with them some sort of magic that would wrap the traveler in safety, she'd heard them all her life as folks came and went from her childhood home. They rang in her mind now, as she'd called them after Carl. She heard them anew as she remembered leaving home the day of her wedding, when her mother had whispered them in her ear. And now Shay had left, and she'd been prevented from wishing him well.

A chill passed over her. "Just a goose walking over my grave," she scoffed, inhaling deeply as she turned to the task of separating the cream and setting about with the job of churning butter. And yet, her heart yearned, wishing she could transport herself back twenty-four hours, recall the words she had spoken with such a harsh tongue.

She moped for the next two days, working, staying busy, but aching for Shay's return.

Joseph worked close to the house during the long days, building a pigpen for the sows and a smaller pen for the shoat. "Mr. Shay'll likely be back tomorrow," he predicted to Jenny as she watched him hammer in a final nail. With ease, he righted the feed trough he'd put together and set it in place next to the fence. "I'll fix up a lean-to and lay some straw in the morning."

"You'll be building a cabin for yourself to live in one of these days, won't you?" she asked. Her forearms rested on the fence he'd constructed, and her gaze swept the work he'd done with such ease and skill.

Joseph grinned up at her. "I got my eye on a pretty gal, Miss Jenny. I'm gettin' sick of sleepin' in the tack room. Pa says I'm old enough to have my own place."

"Are you planning to stay on here?" she asked, already confident of his reply.

He nodded. "Family's too hard to come by to throw them away and move off somewhere else. There's nobody who'll do for you like your own folks." He rose and gathered his tools, placing them in a denim bag. "And one of these days, it'll be my turn to take care of my ma and old Noah."

Jenny thought of the man she'd left behind, for the second time, only a few weeks ago. Jonah Harrison needed looking after, and her resolve built as she thought of bringing him home with her. Shay would agree. She knew, as surely as night followed day, he would back her in this. She turned toward the house, her gaze seeking the avenue, where surely Shay would appear today. If he'd found the heifers he looked for, he'd return soon.

Zora was at the house, peeling potatoes for dinner, and she looked up quickly as Jenny came in the door. "Isabelle told me to help inside," she said. "She don't want me in the fields when it's so hot."

"Isabelle's right," Jenny told her. "You'll be worn out when we all start picking cotton next week. Everyone has to pitch in then." She walked on through the kitchen and across the corridor to her room. The nightgown she'd begun last evening waited for her and she picked it up, gathering scissors and her spool of thread into her apron pocket. The window beckoned and she stood before the open expanse wishing for a cooling breeze, but the white curtains hung limply in the heat.

It would be cooler under the oak tree, she decided, and turned to seek out the comfort of the wooden swing Shay had built. The grass was deep under her feet and grasshoppers jumped from her path as she disturbed their hiding places. From the field beyond the pasture she could see the men moving about, and then Marshall's slight form jumped atop the wagon bed and he waved in her direction.

She lifted her hand in greeting. Isabelle had told the boy to find some corn for dinner, if there was any left fit for the table. It was time for him to carry them to the house, and Jenny wondered if he would be able to tote them all. Perhaps Noah would help. Even as she watched, Marshall jumped from the wagon and disappeared from sight, the tall cornstalks concealing his progress.

The swing moved at her nudging and she settled into one corner, opening the fabric she'd folded the night before. The gown was almost done, only the buttonholes to be stitched and the hems to be sewn. Isabelle had shown her how to circle the slits she'd cut for buttons to pass through, and now she bent her head to ply her needle with care, catching the thread and tugging it in place.

From the field a sharp cry caught her attention and she

glanced up, her needle piercing her finger as she moved quickly. Lest a drop of blood stain her gown, she pushed the material aside and sucked at her fingertip, rising to see what the men were about. Caleb shouted a command and Joseph answered him, pushing his way through the rows of corn, disappearing in the direction Marshall had gone only moments before.

Marshall. The sound of his name rang like a church bell in her mind, and Jenny heard it as through a mist. Whether by a mother's intuition or simply a sixth sense that served as a warning, she knew that her son was in danger. The gown tossed aside, she picked up her skirts and ran.

Across the grassy area beneath fruit trees to where the pasture fence blocked her path, she raced without thinking. Her lungs ached with the effort of breathing as she climbed the pasture fence, and she bent low for a moment, hands on her knees as she caught her breath. Then, as she lifted her head, Joseph appeared just beyond the expanse of grazing area where the horse and cow spent their days.

He carried a limp bundle in his arms, and Jenny's heart paused for an almost imperceptible moment, then resumed pounding with ferocious strength against her breastbone. Marshall's arm hung limply, his small form held tightly to Joseph's chest as the tall, long-legged man hurdled the fence and ran toward the house. Jenny turned in her tracks, seeing the direction Joseph took, and retraced her steps.

Isabelle was at the door, and she held it wide for Joseph's entrance. Jenny's mouth opened as her feet flew over the parched earth, and she heard the sound of her son's name cried into the wind, only dimly aware that it was her own throat that sounded the wailing agony aloud.

And then she was there, bursting through the doorway, into her kitchen. Marshall lay on the floor, Joseph on his knees beside him, bending over the boy's leg. Joseph lifted his head and spat on the floor, then bent again and took Marshall's flesh into his mouth.

"Snakebite." Isabelle spoke the single word, her hand holding a small knife, its blade stained red, and Jenny recognized it as the one Zora had been using to peel vegetables.

"What kind?" she asked, her heart pounding in a relentless rhythm. She clutched at her chest with one hand, as if she could cease its rapid beat, and felt the heavy weight of despair fall upon her shoulders.

Joseph spat again. "Not a cottonmouth," he muttered, then bent to his task.

Marshall's eyes were open, his lips pressed tightly together. A trembling seized him, even as Jenny watched, and he shivered violently.

"Watch he don't have a fit," Zora said quickly. "My least-size brother got snakebit and went into fits, right off."

"Hush!" Isabelle said, her voice sharp as she glared at the girl. "Marshall's just scared, is all. He's gonna be fine. Probably just a garden snake bit him. Joseph's just makin' sure." Yet, her eyes were dark with fear as she looked up at Jenny. "Y'all better be prayin', just in case," she said. "He's not but a little mite."

Noah stood in the doorway behind her and Jenny moved from his path. His big hand rested on her shoulder, as if he would lend strength. "I'm sorry, Miss Jenny. I just sent him off to pick the corn for dinner before we headed back up to the barn. Just like always. I told him watch for snakes and don't go too far." He wiped sweat from his forehead with his shirtsleeve and dealt her a look fraught with sorrow. "I heard it rattle, Miss Jenny."

"It's not your fault, Noah," she said quickly, astounded that her voice was so calm, so steady. Joseph backed away, still kneeling, but giving Jenny room beside him. She sat on the floor, her hands touching her son, registering the chill of his skin, the pallor of his face. Bending low, she kissed his cheek, then his forehead, a calm settling over her. And her heart sent a petition to heaven as she held Marshall's hand in hers.

Isabelle came with a quilt and covered him, and the boy nodded, a mere whisper escaping his lips. "Where's my new papa?"

So forlorn a plea, Jenny thought, as she tried in vain to form a reply. Where indeed was his papa?

Caleb's feet resounded on the porch as he leaped there from the ground. "Man comin' on horseback," he said through the open door. "Looks like it might be Mr. Shay. There's a couple animals followin' him."

"Run on down and fetch him," Noah told him. "The boy wants him here."

And so do I. The thought was fervent, and she sent another entreaty after the first, with a note of thanksgiving for Shay's return. As if he'd been sent by a heavenly messenger, and that thought didn't seem too preposterous right now, she decided.

In moments, Shay was in the kitchen, tossing his hat in the corner. He knelt by Marshall, and met Jenny's gaze, his own eyes dark and forbidding. "What happened?" Even as he spoke the query, he reached for the boy, touching him as had Jenny, his forehead, his hands and then leaning closer to peer at the bite on his shin.

"Get it all out?" he asked, scanning the men, seeking the one who'd suctioned the wound with his mouth, even though he might have risked his own life for the child.

"Yessir, Mr. Shay," Joseph answered. "I drew blood three times." He glanced toward the spot where he'd emptied his mouth over and over, where even now Isabelle was scrubbing with a rag and lye soap. "I don't know what got him. Sounded like a rattler, but it looked like a pine snake to me. They rattle, too. Anyway, I wasn't takin' any chances. A fella as little as Marshall can get sick from less.''

Shay's look was level, and he nodded. "You have my thanks, Joseph." He bent over Marshall again. "I'm sorry I wasn't here, Marsh. Something told me to hurry home this morning, but I should have run the legs off those cows, and gotten here sooner."

Marshall attempted a grin, but his mouth was rigid with fear and his voice was a whimper. Shay placed his face beside the boy's, turning to kiss the downy cheek. His big hands gripped the narrow shoulders, and he spoke quietly. "I'm going to move you, Marsh. Just into your room, and on your own bed. Then your mother and Isabelle are going to put drawing poultices on your leg and make sure we get every bit of that snake's spit out of you. If it was a real bad snake, you'd be sick by now, son. I think Joseph's right and it was a pine snake. You should be right as rain by morning."

"I've got the water hot already," Isabelle said. "By the time you get him settled, I'll have it ready, Mr. Shay." She stood by the stove, pouring a small amount of hot water into a pan, then stirring the contents into a thick paste. Jenny's hands left Marshall then, and she watched as Shay lifted him, careful not to shift him with rash movements.

"You're being brave, Marsh," he murmured. "You can't cry, son. We don't want your blood to pump any faster than it is right now. And I'm telling you, boy, there's nothing to be afraid of. Do you believe me?"

To his credit, Marshall whispered a single word of assent, then lay inert in Shay's arms as he carried him across the wide hall. Jenny was there before him, pulling back the quilt and sheet, plumping Marshall's pillow.

"Get cool water from the pump," Shay told Joseph, who watched from the doorway. "Have Isabelle fill a basin and bring in a couple of towels. We'll want to keep him cool."

Jenny watched as Shay cut Marsh's shirt with a single, long slash of the knife he drew from his boot. "It wasn't worth saving," Shay decreed, and then slit the boy's remaining trouser leg from waist to hem. The pants were old ones, coming only just below his knees. Jenny took them from Shay's hands as he lifted Marshall's slight form to slide the garments from place.

"Now we wait," Shay said, watching as Jenny tended her son, settled the poultice against the swollen area. "I think we're safe, Jen. It wasn't a rattler, or he'd be—" He halted, and Jenny nodded her understanding.

Standing outside the house, Caleb bent to look in the open window. "I put the heifers in the pasture," he said. "Do they need any extra feed, Mr. Shay?"

"No, there's plenty of good grass left out there," Shay told him. "Make sure the big tub has water in it, though."

"Joseph did that already," Caleb said. "Looks like we'll get rain yet tonight." He lowered his voice. "Everything all right in there?"

Shay nodded. "Looks like a bad scare, maybe enough to make him sick."

"That'll happen," Caleb agreed, backing from his vantage point.

"Shay, did you eat anything today?" Jenny asked.

"Not since breakfast." He reached to wipe Marshall's forehead, then left the cool cloth there. "I'll get something later on." He bent to tug at his boots, sliding them from his feet. "I asked Herb Duncan at the store and he directed me to a farm about forty miles west of here. Spent the night there in the hayloft and ate breakfast with the farmer and his family. I brought home two dandy Hereford heifers, pretty little red things. One of them is already bred. Checked a couple of other places for a bull."

"I'm glad you're home," she said.

"Yeah." The single word carried a wealth of meaning, she thought, and yet he did not look at her.

"Shay?" Jenny spoke his name with a note of pleading, and he lifted his head, his gaze wary.

Without waiting for him to reply, she rose and walked around the footboard, kneeling before him as he sat on the edge of Marshall's bed. Her hand reached to smooth the boy's hair, but her words were for Shay, an apology she'd formed during the day, waiting for the opportunity to offer the simple phrases.

"I was wrong to nag at you the night before you left."

He was silent and she ventured a glance upward. His eyes held worry as he looked from her to Marshall and then back. "We'll talk about it later, Jen. I left you sleeping, and then worried the whole time I was gone that you'd be angry at me for it." One warm hand touched hers and she bent to lay her cheek against his skin.

"I'm dirty from traveling," he said quickly, drawing back.

"Do you think I care?" Her heart ached from the rift between them and she bowed her head.

Marshall stirred restlessly, reaching for her. "Mama, I feel better. My new papa fixed me, didn't he?"

Shay leaned closer. "Joseph was the one who carried you to the house and helped you, Marsh. We're just thankful that it was probably a pine snake you scared up. He bit you, but mostly you were frightened, son. You'll be fine."

Jenny lifted the poultice. "The red is almost gone, Shay."

Marshall sat up, peering down at his leg. "Let me see, Mama." He inspected the site of his injury and grinned. "Did you know that Joseph cut my leg a little bit with the paring knife? I'm gonna have a scar."

"Not a very big one," Shay assured him. "Joseph only cut a tiny bit, so he could suck out the bad stuff."

Marshall looked disappointed and flopped back on the mattress. "I thought I'd have a scar, Papa. And then I could have a badge of honor, too."

Shay leaned closer to look at the small incision, the reddened area already returning to its normal color. "Well, I'd say that might qualify, son." He offered a nod of consideration. "Yeah, I'd say that might be called a badge of honor."

Shay filled the largest tub with hot water, and claimed the privacy of the kitchen after supper. "I smell like a horse and I've got hay sticking to my neck," he told Jenny. "I almost went out to the stream, but I'm too tired. I'm thinking the hot water will feel good."

She found a book of children's stories on the library shelf and settled herself beside Marshall. His injured leg propped on a pillow, he reigned supreme, a small bandage covering his wound, and a length of cloth holding it in place. "Sit by me, Mama," he demanded, patting the bed beside him.

"Just for one story, Marsh," she told him, leaning against the headboard, so that he could look at the pages with her. With one ear tuned to the kitchen, she read a favorite of his, and watched as his head tipped to rest against her shoulder. By the time the story was finished he was sleeping, and she laid the book aside to scoot him down on his pillow. Her hand brushed against his forehead and she kissed his cheek, her heart thankful that the fright had proved to be just that. Snakes were a fact of life, and the outcome could have been...

She shivered, thinking of what might have happened. From the doorway, Shay's deep voice spoke her name and she looked up. Wrapped in a towel that barely met at his waist, and only reached the middle of his thighs, he watched her. His dark hair was damp, his long body pale against the bronzed hue of his arms, and she welcomed the sight.

Picking up the lamp, she left the room, Shay stepping to one side as she drew the door shut behind herself. In the glow of lamplight, his eyes were dark and mysterious, and his jaw wore a two-day beard. An aura of menace surrounded him, and her eyes swept his length, noting the widespread feet, the broad shoulders and the grim line of his mouth. Dangerous. The word flew into her mind, and lodged there.

Dangerous. Yet she felt no trace of fear as she met his gaze, only a warmth that swept through her with the force of a whirlwind.

"I'm glad you're home, Mr. Devereaux," she whispered.

His hand rose to examine his jaw. "I've washed away the dirt, lady. Do I need to shave?"

"Not for my sake." She blew out the lamp, placing it on a table in the wide corridor before she reached for him, her hands touching his chest, her fingers buried in the triangle of curls. Burrowing her face against his shoulder, she inhaled his scent, recognizing the masculine aroma of male flesh brought to arousal.

"Take me to bed." It was as brazen an invitation as she'd ever dreamed of. One she would not have issued to Carl, lest he think her bold. Whether or not Shay shared that opinion signified little. Only his compliance with her request mattered right now.

He left her no doubt, lifting her in his arms, as easily as he'd carried Marshall hours earlier. His stride was long as he crossed the hallway, leaning to turn the knob on her door. Twining her arms around his neck, she clung to him, feeling herself lowered, the mattress at her back. And still she held him fast, unwilling to release her grasp, lest he move from her.

There was no chance of that, she found, for his fingers

were between them, working at the buttons on her dress, shoving it from her shoulders. "Help me, Jen," he muttered, his voice rasping and harsh. She complied, lifting her body, relaxing her hold on his, easing his way as he stripped her clothing in a small series of economical movements.

She was naked beneath him when he tossed the bundle to the floor and turned back to her. His hands found her in the darkness, his fingers exploring each curve and valley, his mouth and lips tasting and touching, as though he had been long without the scent and feel of her skin.

Only three days, she thought. It's only been three days. *An eternity.*

He was not patient, as was his wont. Like a man starved for nourishment, he came to her, seeking the replenishment she provided, his hungry body moving against hers. Heat swept through her from the skin of her breasts, where his growth of beard abraded the surface, bringing her to a yearning awakening, to the place where her woman's flesh opened for his taking.

He knelt between her knees, lifting them to circle his hips, and she moved to his bidding. She trembled beneath him as he took possession, his strokes long, his breathing harsh. Against her throat, his mouth was warm and damp, and then he slid upward, until, imbedded fully, he covered her, his weight pressing her into the mattress.

Jenny welcomed him, turning her face, angling it into the curve of his shoulder, where her teeth touched firm muscle, and the salty flavor of his skin met her tongue. A cry rose from her lips as he drew away, and her fingers clutched at the smooth flesh of his back, seeking purchase.

He murmured assurance, whispering his need aloud, moving carefully, slowly, within her until she surged fretfully beneath him, seeking ease for her aching flesh, searching for the fulfillment his possession promised.

It was what he'd waited for it seemed, for his voice became ragged, urgent and coaxing, and he met her rhythm with long, sure strokes.

She cried aloud again, and his head bent, his words guttural and harsh, his movements heavy and forceful. "Jenny..." As from afar, she heard him groan her name, his mouth against her hair, his voice straining to sound the syllables. She was battered, tossed about, flailing for an anchor, and only the solid strength of his body offered a haven, as she clung with all her strength.

Her breath caught in her throat as the splinters of delight shattered her into a thousand pieces, and she was convulsed by the pounding, fierce pleasure he brought into being. Gasping for breath, she shivered, trembling in his embrace, and once more he whispered her name, his jaw taut, his teeth clenched, as if he held on to his passion with one fragile shred of control.

Then, sliding his arms beneath her, he lifted her hips, taking possession anew with a driving, primitive force, and she was filled. Achingly, abundantly filled.

Chapter Twelve

"It's my cotton," Jenny'd said stubbornly.

Picking cotton was hard work, he'd told her. Shay'd kept her from the field as long as he could. Citing meals to be prepared and carried to the men at noontime, Shay had persuaded Jenny to stay in the house during the morning hours for three days. The four men worked unceasingly during the daylight hours, once Noah deemed the crop ready to begin harvesting. And then Zora joined them, telling Shay that she was tired of being lazy. With a glance at Caleb, he'd nodded assent. Caleb could keep an eye on her.

The thought that they would pick cotton for the next several weeks, filling the bags, then emptying them to begin anew, gave Shay new insight into the life he'd known little about as a boy growing up on the Devereaux plantation, a place named River Bend. His fingers had never bled from multiple sticks and stabs. His back had never before ached beyond description. Now, he ached and bled, muttering heartfelt curses as he bent over miserable cotton plants all the livelong day.

The tough calluses on Noah's fingers took on new meaning. Yet even those patches of thickened skin gave way to the brutal bloodletting that was a result of picking cotton,

wresting the dirty white fruit from the bolls holding it captive. Their fingers wrapped in thick layers of rags to contain
the seeping blood—lest it damage the crop—the pickers
made their way down seemingly endless rows of small,
sturdy plants, finally kneeling when the pain of bending
became intolerable.

And then Zora succumbed to the heat, stumbling and
finally sitting with bowed head, unable to bear up under
the brutal sun. It was at that point that Jenny made her
move, decreeing that Zora would work in the house. The
young woman gratefully took Jenny's place in the kitchen.

And Jenny joined the pickers in the field. Shay had protested, but at the subtle shake of Noah's head, he'd backed
off. There was apparently going to be no stopping the
woman for now, and he would not fight her, not when it
was her lifeblood at stake. The plantation was her inheritance, and in turn would be Marshall's. She would not be
deterred from joining in the harvest that might provide a
turning point in her battle to keep her head above water.

Now, Shay watched as Jenny bent, mere feet from where
he worked, her hands agile as she plucked the cotton from
the bolls that held it captive. Only the wince of pain and
the occasional grumble gave proof of her injuries, and he
forced himself to back away, feeling her misery, but unwilling to mar the serenity he'd found in her presence.

Marshall flitted the length of the rows, his youthful ex-
uberance bringing smiles to all of them. He lugged heavy
sacks of cotton to the wagon, where each of the men took
their turn at emptying bags, then carried back the empty
sacks. They were long, narrow containers, hanging from
the left shoulder by a wide strap, trailing on the ground,
growing heavier as they filled.

"I can take my turn on the wagon," Jenny decreed after
dinner. "I've emptied bags before."

"Not this year," Isabelle said bluntly, shooting a look

of warning at her, and Shay took note of the undercurrent between the two women.

He followed Jenny from the shade as she sought privacy in the nearby grove of trees, and she turned as a branch broke beneath his foot. Stealth had not been his object. Indeed, he'd walked behind her carelessly, surprised that she hadn't sensed his presence there.

"I'll be right back," she told him. "I'm only going to—" Her hand moved restlessly as she hesitated over the reason for her stroll through the trees.

He grinned at her, strangely pleased by her reluctance to speak boldly. She was such a lady, his Jenny. He'd have told her he needed to take a leak, and watched the blush color her cheeks. Now, he took one step and circled her in his embrace.

"I know where you're going, sweetheart. I promise I won't watch," he teased, watching as her mouth primmed, then twitched into a reluctant smile. "You're trottin' off into the woods on a regular basis these days, aren't you?" he asked.

Her shrug was negligent. "Maybe. I'm drinking a lot of water. The sun just bakes it out of you, doesn't it?"

She hedged, he thought. "I'll wait here. You go on ahead," he said. "Watch for snakes."

Her nod was sober, and the memory of Marshall's frightful experience was alive between them for a moment. Shay leaned against a tree, grateful for the shade, his keen hearing catching a bit of melody as Noah sang the beginning notes of a song. The men and Isabelle took turns, in an unspoken agreement, it seemed, choosing ballads and mournful songs, one voice lifting softly, then another joining it. At times the harmonies were sad, with minor notes and chords that gripped Shay's heart.

But always, they sang, and he'd begun joining them, beneath his breath, humming, sometimes picking up the words from his memory. Jenny knew all the songs they sang, and her soft, melodic voice lent a lighter tone to their harmony.

Shay closed his eyes, inhaling deeply of the humid air, aware suddenly of the scent of Jenny's soap, and the warmth of her body before him. His lashes lifted and he beheld her lifted face, mere inches from his own. There was no self-protective instinct when it came to this woman. He'd recognized that fact for weeks, months in fact. So aware of danger in the long years he'd traveled alone, he'd become attuned to the presence of another human, even in slumber, awakening quickly should a stranger approach.

But Jenny was no stranger. She was a part of him, the other half of his soul. *And isn't that an odd idea?* His mouth twitched as he pursued the thought. And his hands moved rapidly, clasping her lest she move away. But it seemed there was no danger of that, for she leaned against him, fitting herself between his legs as he used the tree as support for their combined weight. His hands moved to enclose her hips, curving beneath the rounding of her bottom, pressing her against the rising length of his manhood.

She smiled, a tempting, sloe-eyed expression urging his mouth to touch hers. Damp lips met his kiss, and her tongue touched his with the speed of a hummingbird seeking nectar on the honeysuckle vines. "I love you," she whispered, and the words vibrated in his head, spoken into his open mouth, accompanied by the taste and scent of sweet tea and spearmint. It was a treat she favored, floating the leaves from her small patch of herbs on the cool glasses of tea she preferred.

Now, he was pleased by the cool flavor, by the warmth of her body against his, and the soul-nourishing words she spoke. Her whisper was soft, tempting him, luring him to her, and in truth he could not be closer to her supple body without stripping away the layers of clothing that separated them.

"I love you, Shay," she repeated softly, as if she must speak aloud the words that radiated silently from her eyes. It was a declaration that expected no reply. She'd made it clear that he need not respond in like manner, only that he hear her words when they burst from her in a spontaneous fashion.

If only... The thought of losing himself in the love of a woman had long lured him, and he'd had the good sense to keep his soul inviolate from such a commitment. Yet, with Jenny, he felt the surge of affection swell within his breast each time she spoke the avowal of her love.

Almost, he was able to repeat the words. Almost.

"We need to go back to work," she whispered against his throat, her head against his shoulder, her body relaxed in his embrace. She'd become limp, and he wondered at her ability to take these short moments as a gift, as if she fed her inmost being on his touch, on the strength she drew from his caress. Now, she sighed and pushed away from him. He allowed it, dropping his arms, and standing upright.

"You're all done playing hooky?" he asked, his gaze hungry as she lifted her arms to smooth her hair into place. Her bonnet hung down her back, removed while she ate, and now she pulled it into place, tying the strings with a practiced movement. She was feminine in all that she did, with an innate quality of womanhood, of graceful movements of hands and fingers.

Her body swayed when she walked, her hips moving in rhythm, drawing his eye. The color of her hair was lighter with exposure to the sun, glistening with copper streaks when she took her bonnet off and shook out the simple snood she wore. He savored the moment each day when she brushed the fiery length, bending forward, allowing it to fall unimpeded to touch the floor.

Now, his manhood gave him no rest as he watched her turn away, walking back toward the scattered workers bent low over the cotton plants, and he deliberately turned his mind from her.

Rags bound his fingers and he pulled at them, tearing them from his hands and stuffing them in his pockets. Noah said it would come to this. That he would grin and bear it, growing the calluses, allowing his hands to become hard and rough. It was time.

Barely an hour passed before Jenny left the field again, stopping for a moment to tip a water jar to her mouth, before she disappeared into the thicket. His frown noted the frequence, and a thought nudged at his mind. She wasn't acting her normal self these days.

This morning, she'd reached for a dry crust of bread on the table beside the bed before she'd put her feet on the floor, and coming back into the room to get his gloves, he'd found her chewing slowly. She'd glanced in his direction and her eyes had widened at the sight of him in the doorway.

"What are you doing?" He'd been puzzled by her actions, and the stealth in her movements as she rose from the bed.

"I'm hungry." Her words were abrupt and, turning her back, she'd shed her gown and slipped into her dress. Leaving off her petticoat, she'd stepped into drawers and tied them at her waist, then picked up her shoes.

Now the incident took on new significance. His mind searched the past weeks, seeking a clue, some small evidence to support his suspicions. A smile nudged as he dredged up memories, hours and nights spent in Jenny's arms, surely enough to ensure the creation of life within her woman's body.

And if anything guaranteed his presence here, that fact alone would tilt the scale. A child, his child. His and Jenny's. Exhilaration such as he'd never known transformed him, his heart pumping rapidly, a thrill of discovery bringing him to full alert.

He watched for Jenny's return, glancing up from his task each time he stuffed cotton into the sack, careless with the bolls that stabbed and tore at his flesh, uncaring of anything but the woman he awaited. She walked from the stand of trees to where he worked and his gaze scanned her slender form.

"Are you all right?" Even to his own ears his voice was gruff, and she looked up at him quickly.

"Yes, of course." She bent to pick up her sack and slung it over her left shoulder, lifting it easily. "Why wouldn't I be?" Her gaze was on the plant before her, her fingers careful as she grasped the white fibers and tugged them from the boll. Then she flinched as the razor-sharp, dried edge sliced into her finger.

The injured digit went into her mouth, and she closed her eyes for a moment. Shay felt a twinge at the base of his spine, knowing, recognizing the quick sting of pain. "Jen, I don't want you out here." The words were angry sounding and he watched as her eyes opened wide, then focused on him.

"This is my cotton field, Shay Devereaux. You don't have the right to forbid..."

"Love, honor and obey," he quoted softly, his words reminding her of vows she'd made only weeks ago.

"This is *my* cotton field," she repeated stubbornly.

"You married me." He prodded her quietly, nudging her memory. "Legally, Jenny..." The words were unsaid, but her stunned expression told him she'd understood the implicit warning. He could claim the property, should he choose. A woman's right expended only as far as the marriage certificate. Beyond that piece of paper, she was owned, bag and baggage, by the man she married.

Tears filled her eyes, and he was overcome by the pain shimmering in them. That he had purposely hurt her did not set well, and yet, if his suspicions were on target, she had no business toiling beneath a hot sun.

"I thought better of you," she said, her voice trembling. Yet she stood her ground, facing him across a row of cotton plants, her fingers stained with dried blood, the newest cut still oozing, her face pale beneath the brim of her bonnet.

He slid from the bag he had come to think of as a permanent appendage, allowing it to lay in the dirt at his feet. Marshall's voice called out from fifty feet away, and Shay was aware of the boy's constant observance.

"I'll get your bag, Papa." Moving carefully between the plants, Marshall was there in moments, picking up the sack, weighing it with a perplexed frown. "There's not much in it."

"I'm going for a walk with your mother," Shay told him. "Empty both of our bags, Marsh. I'll be back in just a little while." From several rows over, Isabelle caught his eye, nodded briefly, then returned to work, and Shay's mouth thinned at the unspoken message.

"Come with me," he told Jenny.

She dropped her bag, as he had, and walked to the end of the row, a short distance separating them as he followed her apace. She halted there, beneath the shade, stripping her bonnet from her head, and inspecting the latest scratch on her finger.

Shay stood beside her, and his hand enveloped hers, lifting it to his mouth, touching the sore spot with his tongue. He met her gaze, watching as fresh tears filled her eyes, and his voice was tender. "I'm sorry, Jen. I'd never do anything to hurt you. I'll never try to take your property from you."

"That's not what I heard coming from your mouth." Her eyes accused him and he nodded.

"I know. I just had to get your attention." He kept her hand in his grasp and led her toward the wagon. "I want you to go back to the house, and stay there."

"Why?" The single word was a challenge, even as she eyed him warily.

"Do you want to tell me? Or shall I tell you?" he asked curtly.

"Tell you?" Her cheeks burned as his meaning penetrated, and she looked away from his gaze. "I only just figured it out myself," she murmured.

"Then why didn't you say something?" He'd had to solve the puzzle alone, and he ached that she had not confided in him. "Why didn't you tell me?"

She lifted one shoulder in a silent reply.

"You knew I'd keep you from the fields, didn't you?" The tone was gentle, his eyes filling with the rare beauty of this woman. She carried his child. As surely as he knew his name, he recognized that the fullness of her breasts was even more pronounced, and her skin bloomed with a radiance beyond its former beauty. Most telling of all, she'd missed more than one monthly, and he cursed himself silently for not recognizing that most prominent sign. A need to protect her rose within him, a dual need, one that included his child. But most of all, Jenny. If something should happen to her... He brushed the thought aside, unwilling to consider that possibility.

"I'm fine, Shay, really I am." Tilting her head back, she looked up at him with a faint smile curving her lips. "You're worried, aren't you?"

"I didn't mean to scold you in front of the others," he said, his apology not coming easy. "I was angry for a moment, that you would work so hard when you knew you should be taking it easy." His mouth tightened. "You sent

Zora to the house, remember? Do you think I would care less about you? That I would let you risk yourself for a field of cotton?''

"Isabelle said the same thing," she confessed, glancing to the field where her friend stood watching.

With a quick wave of her hand, Isabelle went back to work, and Shay lifted Jenny to the wagon seat. "Take the wagon back and help Zora. We'll need more water soon. Maybe she'd like to bring it back to us while you rest." His hands gripped her thigh through the fabric of her dress, sliding restlessly against her skin. "I want you to stretch out on the bed for a half hour."

"A half hour?" she asked, her words teasing.

"There's no point in asking for more than that," he admitted. "And eat something, you hear?"

"Yessir," she said politely, bending to touch his mouth with hers. "For today, I'll do as you say. At least we're making Isabelle happy."

He stepped back from the wagon and nodded, watching as she turned the mules around and started the trek back toward the house. "Me, too," he murmured beneath his breath. It had been easier than expected, and that thought bothered him. She'd given in almost too easily.

He threatened her independence. He was bossy and overprotective. On top of that, he'd reminded her of her vow to obey. And vows were important, not to be taken lightly. Jenny stood at the stove and cut an onion into the kettle of green beans. Sweating in the kitchen was easier than bending over cotton plants in the hot sun, she decided. All in all, she could not fault the man.

The long spoon turned the beans in the pot, and she inhaled the seductive aroma of bacon, onions and fresh beans from the garden. It wouldn't have been nearly so tempting upon awakening this morning, she decided, remembering the quick surge of nausea she'd suffered. The crust of bread on her table solved the problem neatly. And then Shay's appearance in the doorway, watching as she subdued her early-morning problem, had been the first of small circumstances throughout the morning.

He knew. Whether he was pleased with the news or not was still a moot question. He was for sure not pleased with his wife's dithering.

Jenny turned from the stove, lifting plates from the shelf as she set about preparing for supper. With dinner consisting of leftover meat and bread, the men would be ready for a hot meal when the day was over. If things were laid out in the kitchen, they could all lend a hand and carry the entire meal to the side yard, where the big table waited for use.

Zora had carried water out and not returned. She was probably still in the field with the others, watching, maybe helping empty bags. It was good to be alone, a circumstance Jenny had not found herself in for days. Always with the workers, or caring for Marshall, she hugged these hours close.

The sound of a wagon alerted her. "It must be Zora coming back," she murmured, pumping water to cover the peeled potatoes. But it wasn't.

A tall form blocked the sunlight, filling the open doorway, and Eli stood just outside the screen door, his hat held before him. His face in the shade, he was an unknown situation, ready-made for disaster, Jenny thought. Wiping her hands on a towel, she approached him, glancing up at the gun over the door. She shook her head. It would not do to approach a visitor with her finger on the trigger. Although Shay might dispute that idea.

"Hello, Eli." No tremor marred the even tone of her voice. "I didn't expect to see you here today."

"No, ma'am, I don't 'spect you did. I come to talk."

Stepping back from the door, he waited, and Jenny hesitated only a moment before she walked out onto the porch.

"Won't you sit down?" she asked, waving a hand at the two chairs where she and Isabelle usually perched on while they peeled or shucked or sorted.

"I'll sit on the step," Eli said, and lowered his long form, his feet on the ground.

Jenny recognized his attitude, one she'd taken for granted in the years before the conflict, during which men like Eli had gained a freedom they'd only dreamed of. And for a lot of them it amounted to naught. Eli had thought to be free of Pennington Plantation, and she'd watched him leave with his family. Only to find that the freedom he sought meant little when he still was beholden to another man for every bite of food he put into his children's mouths.

"Did you come to see Zora?"

"Kinda, ma'am." His long fingers clutched his knees and he bent his head. "My woman's missin' her girl."

"Zora's married now, Eli. Caleb built her a cabin and she's worked hard to fix it up. I think she's happy with him."

"My woman's not." His tone was quiet and the eyes he turned in her direction were dull, as if he'd fought a good fight but was willing to admit defeat. "I got three fine boys, Miss Jenny, but Zora's mama's real partial to her girl."

"I remember your boys, Eli. They were just little tads when you left here."

"They're growin' good," he said, a note of pride lifting his voice. "They been a big help with the crops." He stood and turned to face her, his hat held protectively against his stomach, his long fingers rolling the brim in a nervous gesture. "Ma'am, Miss Jenny...I'm wonderin' if you'd like for us to come back here to live. We could fix up the old cabin we used to have, and maybe work shares with you, like you offered before."

Jenny frowned, her mind sorting out the reasons Eli would have for such a request. "Is Doc Gibson not treating you well?" she asked quietly, and then bit at her lip. It was not seemly to suggest that her neighbor was being unfair to the people who worked his land.

"He don't measure out shares real well, ma'am," Eli said hesitantly. "Seems like I always come out on the short end of the stick. I can't afford to work for less than what's right."

"Have you talked to him about it?" she ventured.

Eli nodded his head. "He seems to think we don't have any choice. He said you wouldn't let me come back here, what with the way I left." He lifted his head and looked at her squarely. "I was wrong to come carrying on the way I did about Zora. Caleb's a good man, and he married her for good reason."

Jenny looked out toward the cotton fields, wondering how long it would be until the men quit for the day. "I can't say one way or the other," she told him. "Not until I talk to Shay." She met Eli's gaze, unwilling to make a promise she could not keep.

"Is he still ready to skin me?" Eli asked. "I made him mighty mad, that day I showed up here."

"I don't think he's angry with you," Jenny reassured him, hoping she was right in her assessment of Shay's feelings. "Why don't you ride your mule on down to the field and talk to him?"

"You think it would go over better, if you spoke first?" Eli asked. He looked toward the kitchen door. "Is my girl here? Maybe she'd talk to me?"

Jenny shook her head. "No, she went to the field with water. I think she stayed on for a while to bring the load of cotton back to the shed. It's almost time for them to quit anyway."

Eli tugged his trousers up around his waist, and clapped

his hat on his head. "I'll go take a look. Maybe give a hand if they let me." He walked to the hitching post and untied his mule's bridle, then mounted with an easy movement. Jenny watched him go, staying on the porch until his figure was swallowed by the shady lane leading back to the cotton fields. Beneath the overhanging trees, he was but a shadow as the mule turned the bend and disappeared from sight.

"Be kind, Shay," she murmured, turning back to the kitchen. Eli seemed contrite, and she tried to recall the man from the early years she'd been here. She could only recall a big man, whose smaller wife was soft-spoken and pretty, seeming too young to have four half-grown children. If they should return, she would deed them a five-acre piece, and let Eli work shares.

One of the old cabins could be repaired and made livable easily enough, she supposed. With everyone pitching in, it wouldn't take long, perhaps a day or so. And Zora would be delighted to have her mother close by. Jenny's mind worked rapidly as she sliced tomatoes and cucumbers for supper. The oven held a smoked ham, the meat almost falling from the bone, and she lifted it carefully to the stove top.

She ended up cutting chunks, the ham being too done to slice neatly, and she filled a platter with the tender meat. The pan of potatoes cooked down until there was only a bit of water left in the bottom, and she added cream with a generous hand, and then a chunk of butter and a heaping tablespoon of flour to thicken it. A dish of leftover peas from the garden was tossed in and she stirred it gently, then put the kettle on the back of the stove.

Silverware was next, and she scooped up the knives and forks, putting them into a loaf pan. Everything was about ready, she decided, and then as she picked up the plates to carry them into the yard, she heard voices from the barn.

The wagon, pulled in from the big back door, stood in the middle of the wide aisle. Men swarmed around it, two of them unhitching the mules, another putting tools up on the wall. Shay was on his way to the house, Marshall still exuberant, running beside him.

"Shay?" Jenny stepped onto the porch. "Did Eli find you?"

He nodded curtly. "Yeah. I talked to him. I sent him on home for now."

Her hopes sank. Shay was more than tired, his clothing damp with sweat, and he halted at the watering trough, gesturing at Marshall to pump fresh water. The boy pumped with a will and Shay bent his head, catching water in both hands and dousing himself liberally. Behind him, Joseph led the team to the water, and they dipped their noses deeply into the trough, then tossed their heads, spraying Marshall.

He laughed and bent his head to wash his face, following Shay's every move. "I'll bring out a pan of warm water and soap," Jenny told them, hurrying to the sink for the basin, then to the stove for warm water. A towel over her arm, she went back out to the porch, lowering the pan for Shay's use.

"Thanks," he said. "We're all pretty grimy."

Within ten minutes, the men had all washed and waited beneath the trees, where the long benches offered a welcome seat in the shade. Jenny and Zora carried out bowls of food, Isabelle toting the heavier plates and kettles. Bread sliced fresh from yesterday's baking filled a basket, and Shay's eyes lit as he surveyed the meal Jenny had prepared.

"I believe I'll keep you in the kitchen from now on," he murmured as she brought him a glass of buttermilk.

"If you take Eli on, you won't need me in the field," she reminded him quietly.

"I'm considering it." He chewed on a bite of ham and

filled his fork with creamed potatoes. "You didn't tell him he could stay?" His look was searching as she sat beside him on the bench.

"I told him he'd have to ask you," Jenny said, reaching for a slice of bread.

"That's what he said." Shay ate steadily, halting only long enough to butter a slice of bread. "If you want him back here, it's all right with me. We can use the help, and you're right. It'll free you up from field work." He slanted her a glance. "You know him better than I do. What do you think?"

"Noah's the one to ask," Jenny told him, raising her voice a bit. "He'd be better able to judge."

Noah looked up from across the table, nodding slowly. "Eli's a good man, just blessed with a fiery temper. His woman can hold him in line pretty good."

Shay nodded. "It's settled then. I'll send Caleb over to tell him."

Chapter Thirteen

Heat surrounded her, stifling heat that made her gasp for air, as if her lungs could not inflate properly. Jenny sat up, aware that she was tangled in the sheet, conscious of Shay beside her, yet enmeshed in the dream. Her hand reached to touch him, needing to know for sure he was there, that his presence was not just a part of the dream.

Rock-hard and solid, his chest beneath her fingers was her security in the dark, and she spread her palm wide across the broad expanse. It warmed her chilled flesh, and she closed her eyes, steeping herself in the reassurance he gave so unknowingly.

She turned to him, curling against his side, her face against the rounding of his shoulder, and then sat upright, her heart beating wildly in her chest.

He was hot. Not just the natural warmth he exuded, as if his internal workings were set at a higher pace than most other human beings. This was different, she thought, moving her head upward, so her cheek lay against his forehead. Heat, pervasive and intense, rose from him and she absorbed it. Her hands framed his face and she brushed his mouth with her own, receiving the expected response. His lips opened. He released a breath, a sound preceding it that could only be called a moan. Sweetness, heavy with the scent of fever met her nose, and she rolled from the bed.

He reached for her, grunting a phrase that demanded her return, but she ignored it, concentrating on the lamp beside the bed. Fingers trembling, she lit a match, irritated by the globe that clinked against metal, the round knob that resisted her touch. And then the wick was glowing, flaring into flame, and she lowered the globe back into place.

Shay was silent, and she rounded the foot of the bed, lamp in hand, placing it on the table beside his head. Its glow cast a circle of light, and he was caught in its midst, eyes shut, mouth barely open, a red flush across his cheeks proving her worry to be valid. He was fevered, taken by some rapidly advancing illness, and her thoughts circled frantically, sorting out all the remedies she could bring to mind.

Cool water first. Then tea, elderberry tea, mixed with boneset to bring down the fever. She bent low over him, her mouth against his brow, her whisper soft against his skin. "I'll be right back, Shay. I won't leave you for long."

The lamp in her hand, she crossed the hallway to the kitchen and went into the pantry. Her box of supplies was in its usual place and she brought it back to the table, the better to search out what she needed. Small envelopes, folded bits of paper, held dried blossoms from the elderberry plants in the hedgerows and she poured the contents of one into a pan on the stove. Water from the heavy teakettle was still warm and she poured the pan half full. Boneset leaves would help, she decided, and added a pinch from the cloth bag that held her supply.

The fire was banked for the night, but with the addition of kindling and three well-placed chunks of wood, it blazed in moments, the heat rising to the pan she'd put in place. The back door opened soundlessly and she picked up the water bucket beneath the sink, heading for the pump in the yard. The water was cool there, not passing through the pipe that led to the kitchen, and speed was of the essence.

Only three smooth movements of the handle were needed to send forth water that felt cold to her hand and she filled the bucket halfway, then started back to the house.

"Miss Jenny?" Joseph appeared out of the darkness. "Are you all right?" His voice was as soft as the night air, and she turned to him gratefully.

"Shay is feverish," she said quietly. "Will you come in the house with me and watch the tea I'm brewing?" Her steps were rapid as she retraced her path, climbing to the porch and reaching for the door.

Joseph was there ahead of her, holding the screen door open, and she passed him, heading for the table. His dark face held concern as he took the bucket from her hand and waited. "I'll do whatever you say, Miss Jenny."

She snatched up a towel from the buffet and nodded at the doorway. "Take it to my room, please. I'll be right there." Peering within the pan, where tiny bubbles rose to the surface of the water, she pressed her lips together. "Hurry..." The single word was fervent, and she followed Joseph from the kitchen, carrying the lamp with her.

"You'll have to find a candle in the kitchen for light," she told him, entering her room. He was bending over the bed, his broad hand rising from Shay's forehead as she neared.

"He's awful hot." His eyes widened and she sensed his fear. "You 'spose he's got summer fever?"

"No." She dipped the towel into the water, then, wringing it almost dry, sat down on the edge of the bed. "There was fever in the camp he was in during the war. This could be left over from that time, I suppose." The towel soaked up the heat from his skin and she lifted it, dousing it again and replacing it. "Find me another towel, Joseph. You'd better get a lamp from the parlor, I think. And check to see if the tea is boiling. It will need to be strong, but don't let it boil over. I don't want to waste any of it.''

Joseph hurried from the room and Jenny stripped down the sheet, leaving only a narrow band across Shay's hips. He was naked, as was usual, and for that she was thankful. Removing his clothing, even drawers and undershirt, would have been a heavy task for her. Instead she beheld his wide chest, the narrow waist and hips and long, muscular legs, the form of a strong, solid man. That knowledge sat well with her.

No matter how high the fever, whatever ill beset him, he could overcome this sickness. A man who had come from Elmira, who had traveled the countryside and made his way across hundreds of miles of rough terrain in order to fulfill a promise made to a dying man, would not be laid low by fever. Carl had trusted well in his friend.

She took the towel in hand and swung it through the air, cooling it rapidly, impatient with the wringing-out process. Opened wide, it covered his chest and belly and she sat back, picking up his hand, holding it between her palms as if she could pour strength through the callused skin from her own reserves.

Joseph appeared in the doorway with two more towels in his hand. She reached for them, wringing them out in the bucket and spreading them over Shay's legs. And then repeated the process, one at a time, beginning with the cloth covering his chest. She swung them through the air, creating a breeze over his heated flesh, then placed them alternately upon his head, chest, arms…only to remove them moments later when they soaked up the heat from his massive frame.

The scent of elderberry tea reached her as Joseph carried a large cup between both hands, protecting his skin by several layers of toweling. "It's mighty hot, ma'am," he whispered. "And there's more in the pan."

"Push it to the back of the stove, Joseph." She glanced up at his retreating back. "You can go on to bed now. I'll be fine."

"I'll just lay down on the porch," he told her. "If you need anything, you'll know where to find me."

She nodded, her attention already drawn back to Shay. His mouth was dry, his lips shiny in the lamplight, and she took a corner of the towel, dampening it in the tea, then dripped it slowly against his mouth. His tongue touched it, and he moaned, an audible plea. "Hot. I'm burning. Mama? Where are you?"

Jenny repeated the ritual, squeezing the tea from the towel into his mouth and he swallowed it quickly. Joseph had placed a spoon in the cup and she blew against its contents, cooling the small amount, then allowed it to flow against the corner of his lips. His tongue welcomed it and his murmur was appreciative.

"Shay, can you hear me?" she whispered. But there was no response, nor had she expected one. Still, she fought the disappointment as he merely murmured incoherent words, names she had never heard.

"Maggie?" His eyes flew open, glazed and wild and then they focused on her. "I won't let him touch you," he said, his teeth clenched, his lips drawn back in a feral snarl.

Well, that was a new one, Jenny thought. He hadn't mentioned a woman before. She returned to the ritual with the towels, and Shay pushed her hands aside. "I need to—" He closed his eyes, his hands flexing, then reaching for her again. "Don't..."

"Shh...I'm only trying to get you cooled off," she said quietly. "Shay, listen to me." And for a moment, it seemed he did, quieting as her words demanded his attention. "Drink this for me," she said firmly, lifting his head to spoon the tea into his mouth.

"Thanks," he said, the word coherent. He swallowed,

then shivered, and she saw his jaw clench. His body trembled, as if caught in a chill so potent, he could not contain his trembling. "I'm cold, Mama," he whispered. "Tell Roan I..." His words trailed off.

Jenny took the towels from him, and covered him, drawing the quilt up from the foot of the bed. Still he shook, as did the slender, small pines when the rain and wind swept through the forest. His mouth trembled and his arms jerked, hugging himself in an involuntary movement. There was no help for it, she decided, pulling aside the covers and sliding beneath them. Her arms encircled him, her face against his chest, as she lent her body heat to his. He was cold, drawing the warmth from her, and she lifted her legs to surround his, situating herself atop him.

His arms slid from beneath her and circled her, holding her fast against his body, and his mouth trembled against her ear. "I told him..." The pause was long, his words guttural as if wrenched from his lungs with great effort. "No love in Gaeton..."

Gaeton. Another name she'd never heard before. From somewhere in his past, Shay was dredging up memories, and she gathered each word, each priceless thought he uttered, storing them to be pondered over.

How long she held him, until the shuddering ceased and he lay lax beneath her, she could not tell. Minutes perhaps, certainly not more than half an hour. She relaxed against him, only to feel the pervasive heat once more emanate from his skin. Restless now, he pushed at her and she dragged herself from the bed, watching as he kicked off the covers, uncaring of his unclothed condition, lost in the fevered netherworld where his demons pursued.

"Carl!" The single word rose from his lips in long drawn-out agony. "I'm sorry," he whispered after a moment, and then a single tear slid from beneath his closed eyelid.

Jenny placed a cool towel against his chest, bending to retrieve another from the bucket, wringing it almost dry and draping it over his thighs. His hand snaked to his side and snatched at her wrist, squeezing the slender bones in his grip.

"You're a dead man, Rad Bennett." As clearly as if he spoke from a rational mind, Shay muttered the promise, and Jenny shivered at the menace contained in the simple phrase. "You touched her." His voice was cold, deadly, and his eyes opened for a moment, their dark depths radiating hatred such as Jenny had never known.

"Who?" she whispered, the query meant only for her own ears, and yet Shay turned his head, watching her from beneath hooded lids.

"I won't shame her," he whispered sadly. "I'm sorry, Beau."

Beau. Another name, but this time one she'd heard him speak. Beau Jackson, a man he'd worked for in... She thought, concentrating fiercely. Had he said Kansas?

She bent to her task, changing the towels again, swinging them through the air to cool both man and heavy fabric. He was silent now, breathing heavily, his face and chest ruddy with the heat his body shed.

In the kitchen, she heard movement, and Isabelle appeared in the doorway.

"Fever?" she asked, a towel gripping the pan. The scent of herbs rose in the air and Jenny motioned her close, nodding at the empty cup.

Isabelle filled it, carefully keeping the leaves within the confines of the pan, then leaned over the bed. "How long's he been this way?"

Jenny shook her head. "I don't know for sure. Several hours. He woke me, and then Joseph heard me out at the pump and he came in and helped." Her words ran together,

her head pounding with a headache she'd only just recognized.

"You look puny," Isabelle said bluntly. "Go get yourself some coffee and something to eat. I'll tend him."

Jenny felt a surge of nausea, and it propelled her to the slop jar in the corner. Kneeling before it, she slid the lid out of the way just in time, retching horribly as bile filled her mouth.

Isabelle was beside her, handing her a damp towel. "Wipe your face," she said quietly. "You don't want to get sick, Jen. Eat something, even if you don't feel like it, you hear?"

Jenny nodded, compliant as she recognized Isabelle's words as truth. Staggering to her feet, she made her way to the kitchen, thankful for the coffeepot that sent out a fragrant aroma. She swallowed hard and poured it, filling a cup halfway, then added cream and a spoonful of sugar, stirring it briefly. A loaf of bread lay beneath a kitchen towel, and Jenny snatched at it, tearing off a bit and easing it past her rigid lips. She chewed stoically and swallowed, washing it down with a small sip of coffee.

Sliding into a chair, she inclined her head, inhaling the steam from the cup, then, eyes closed, she lifted it to her mouth. Heavy with cream and sugar, it settled in her empty stomach and she breathed deeply. Another bite of bread followed the first, and she chewed and swallowed in a rhythmic fashion until a goodly portion had settled her nausea.

Shay. She must get back to him. What if he'd worsened while she dawdled at the kitchen table. She rose quickly, staggering as her nightgown tripped her up, then lifted the skirt and hastened across the hall.

"Mama?" Marshall's voice beckoned her and she hardened her heart to his summons.

"Get up and get dressed, Marsh," she called hastily. "Isabelle will get you breakfast."

"Mama!" His voice demanded her presence and she hesitated.

"I'll tend to him. Your man needs you now," Isabelle told her, rising from her knees beside the bed. "He's restless since you left the room."

"Been that way all night," Jenny said, her breath short as she hurried to his side.

"Not like this," Isabelle said. "It's like he needs to know you're here."

And her words were proven true as Shay reached wildly, his hand groping, until Jenny clasped it within her own, drawing it to her breast. He murmured, a petulant sound, then sighed as he turned his head to face her. "I'm here," she whispered, leaning close, her nose scenting out the smell of his fever again.

"He's buried deep," Shay whispered, his tone confidential. "Bastard cut me pretty bad, didn't he?"

"Your face?" Jenny asked quietly, holding her breath lest he realize the import of his words.

His eyes opened, a faraway look dulling the dark surface and his teeth gritted, the sound harsh and grating. "He killed Gerald." The whispered sound tore at her heart, as a sob wrenched Shay's chest. "Carl, watch—" His grip on her hand turned cruel and she swallowed the cry of pain, wriggling against his greater strength. And then he relaxed his hold, his head tossing from side to side.

"Don't touch her." It was a primitive growl, the words almost incoherent, so smothered with hatred. "Damn you, Rad...Maggie!" It was a cry from his heart, a painful blending of the woman's name and a phrase that cursed a man to hell. Shay's arm swung wide and Jenny ducked the blow.

She sprawled across him, holding him to the bed, her

whispers in his ear a mixture of pleading and prayer. He clasped her tightly, rolling with her to the opposite side of the bed, holding her against himself with masculine force, and she was held captive by the strength of a madman. He struggled to rise above her, straddling her slender form and one powerful arm drew back, the fist clenched.

"Shay! No!" Her voice was sharp, the words penetrating the feverish demons that drove him, and he shook his head, dropping the weapon he'd threatened to use on her fragile bones. "Shay, look at me," she begged, her hands reaching to frame his face.

And he did. For one long moment, his eyes were lucid, his lips drawn tightly against his teeth. "Jenny...merciful God, Jenny." He rolled to the side, shivering, whether from the fright of threatening her or with a resurgence of the chills, she did not know. It was enough that she was free from his weight, that she was able to slide from the bed and round the footboard to where the tea sat on the table.

Again, she leaned over him, coaxing him to open his mouth, lifting his head to receive the cup at his lips. He responded, quiet and almost withdrawn, drinking the cooling tea with great gulps. She set the cup aside and pulled the sheet to his waist, then wrung out a towel for his forehead.

He watched her, one hand lifting to touch her cheek. "Carl? I killed the bastard for you, for Gerald...maybe for Maggie, too." And then his head wagged slowly from side to side. "No, that was Rad, wasn't it?" His eyes narrowed and a furtive look crossed his face as he looked over her shoulder. "He's buried deep, Beau."

"Beau's not here," Jenny said soothingly. "Just me, Shay. It's all over."

"All over." He repeated the words with satisfaction, nodding, his eyes closing.

By noon, he'd passed through another bout of chills and

the fever returned full force. Jenny brewed tea again while Isabelle sat with him, and then as he rested once more, Jenny crawled up on the bed beside him, her arms holding him fast, his dark hair nestled against her breast.

She awoke to find him looking into her eyes. His face was drawn, his jaw set in a rigid, controlled pose. "How long?" he asked, his voice raw, as if his throat were abraded from the force of his illness.

"Just since the middle of the night," she answered, knowing he resented losing track of time. "It's afternoon now."

He lifted her hand, kissed the palm and focused on the bruises he'd inflicted on her wrist. "Did I do that?"

She tore it from his grasp. "It's nothing." But he would not have it. With a gentleness she was familiar with, he drew it to his mouth.

"I'm sorry, Jen. I never wanted you to see me that way. I thought—" He drew in a deep breath. "I thought I was done with the fever. I was wrong."

"It's all right. You're better now," she said, her body weary, her eyes heavy with fatigue. There was much to be done, and she rose reluctantly from the bed. "I'll get clean water and wash you," she said. "You need to drink a lot of water, and some soup wouldn't be amiss."

"Jenny." He called her back as she forced her legs to move toward that doorway.

"I'll be right back," she told him, her mind racing with the disjointed words and phrases he'd spilled forth over the past hours.

Isabelle was on the porch, and Jenny gave quick instructions. Warm water, soup and coffee, the latter for herself. "Marshall?" she asked, aware suddenly that the boy had gone without his mother's attention for the whole day.

"He's with Noah, Jen. Don't worry about him. The men are all helpin' get a cabin in decent shape for Eli. Noah went over there first thing this morning, just like Mr. Shay told him to yesterday.''

The day before had been a blur of excitement, with the first bales of cotton going to town to be weighed. Shay had come back with a bundle of clothing for the men and a new dress for Isabelle. For the coming baby, he'd brought the best part of a bolt of outing flannel and handed it to Zora. Now the hours of enjoyment seemed an eon away, Jenny thought. Her memory so taken with the events of the night and the long hours of illness throughout this day, she'd lost track of time and happenings.

''Did Eli bring Zora's mama along? And the boys?''

Isabelle nodded vigorously. ''They're workin', gettin' the roof tight. The floor's not too bad, and they put a lean-to on the back for the boys to sleep.''

''See if there's anything upstairs they need,'' Jenny told her, and caught a glimpse of anger in Isabelle's gaze.

''They can make do for a while, Jen. Old Eli ain't comin' back here like the prodigal son. It's enough you took him back without makin' a big fuss. Let him earn his way.''

She would not argue, not now, while her bones ached and her head was too heavy for her neck to hold it upright. ''I'll go start washing Shay, and get my bed changed,'' she told Isabelle, dragging herself into the house and through the kitchen.

Shay was on the side of the bed, head in hands, when she came through the doorway. He looked up at her, his eyes wary. ''Did I have a lot to say?'' he asked.

Jenny hesitated and smiled, torn between honesty and the need to harbor his words to herself, until she could sort out the meaning of all he'd told her. ''Not a lot. Mostly just gibberish.'' She tilted her head, and thinking to make him smile she asked one query. ''I didn't know I was up against another woman, Shay. Who is Maggie?''

His already pale skin turned ashen and he staggered to his feet. "What did I say?"

Jenny hurried to his side, clutching at his waist. "Sit down, you foolish man. You've been sicker than a dog all day and half the night, and now you're trying to fall flat on your face. You didn't say anything, Shay. Just called her name." She forced another smile. "I was trying to decide if I should be jealous."

He shook his head. "No, never of Maggie." Slumping down on the bed, he stretched out again. "You're right. I'm not ready to get up yet." His eyes closed and Jenny recognized his method of escape.

"Not yet," she told him. "I'm going to help you wash up and then I'll change the bed." She bent to untangle the sheet from his hips. "Lift up, Shay. I can't get this undone by myself."

"I can wash," he told her. "Just bring in some water and I'll sit on the chair while you make up the bed." His eyes were lowered as he spoke, his voice subdued.

"You won't tell me who Maggie is?" she asked, sorry now that the name had been spoken aloud between them. Aware that he would not supply any answers to her curiosity.

"Not now, Jen." He moved to the chair, holding the sheet like a shield between them, then slumped against the wooden surface.

Isabelle knocked against the open door, announcing her arrival, and brought a basin of warm water to place beside him. "Can you reach it?" she asked, and at his nod, she turned and left the room.

"I'll get clean sheets," Jenny told him, handing him a clean washrag and towel from beside the basin. "Be careful you don't fall off the chair."

Shay slept the rest of the afternoon away, until twilight darkened the sky outdoors and the sounds of men in the yard faded to echoes from the cabins beyond the barn. He lay sprawled on the fresh-smelling sheets, his mind churning with the faint memories he'd managed to put together. Somewhere in his delirium he'd seen Carl, and Gerald, the two men who'd been abused by the guard. He lifted his hand, fingering the scar he wore as a constant reminder of that day. Both of his friends were dead, and the guard had found his final resting place behind the prison huts, in a hastily dug grave. Several men had joined him, working with frantic haste to complete the task before they could be found out.

He remembered the nightmare of killing Radley Bennett, of dragging him into the woods, only to find him choking his final breath between blue lips. He'd meant to shoot the man. Attacking a small woman had gained Rad the death penalty, no matter that he'd been halted in his attempt to rape her. Shay Devereaux was capable of murder. He'd known that for years, had lived with the memory of men who had died by his hand during the war, and a couple who had found justice where they least expected it.

And now Jenny knew. From the bleak look in her eyes and the drawn expression on her face, she was well aware of the dark side of the man she'd married. On top of that, he'd hurt her, bruised her wrists, and perhaps worse. He'd look her over, come morning.

And for what? he asked himself, one arm covering his eyes. The damage was done. He'd shown himself at his worst. If Jenny couldn't love him enough to accept all that he'd done, all he'd become in the past four years, his days here were surely numbered.

Chapter Fourteen

"There's plenty of credit available on our account at the store, Jenny." Shay waited at the door until she turned to face him. There remained a strain between them, and he was at a loss as to how to solve the problem.

Her face was composed as she met his gaze. "You paid ahead on the bill?"

"I gave Herb Duncan scrip when we sold the cotton the other day. He made a page in his account book for us, so you can buy what you need." He felt his jaw tense as he remembered the event. "Damn paper money doesn't fit well in my pocket," he said roughly. "I've decided to hang on to my gold and we'll do things this way for a while."

She nodded. "That makes sense to me."

She was, on the surface, as obliging as ever. He could not fault her in the bedroom, for she turned to him eagerly at night, and responded in increasing measure. Almost as though she feared the rift that threatened to dissolve the close companionship they had shared. Yet, when morning came, she was silent, a slender wraith, with only the small rounding of her form to remind him of the child she carried.

He'd refused her request, had turned thumbs down on confiding in her, and now he paid for his stubborn pride.

And the longer the wall remained in place, the worse he felt. There was no joy in him, he realized. Only the fleeting pleasure he sought in Jenny's arms in the dark hours of the night.

Reaching for a towel, she dried her hands, her eyes scanning his features. "You haven't had more fever, have you?" she asked. One slender palm touched his forehead and he circled her wrist as she stepped away.

"I'm fine. Let me see your hand." For the first time, she'd approached him, and he was loath to allow her retreat. The bruising he'd caused was long gone, not even a dark trace to remind him of the harsh treatment he'd dealt her. And yet, he kept her hand captive, at a loss to put an end to the tension simmering between them like summer heat.

Her eyes were clear, searching his, as if for a sign, and he allowed the scrutiny, pushing aside the hateful memory of his feverish hours and the harm he'd done to her.

"I love you, Shay." Her words were simple, a reassurance, and he allowed his smile to give a silent reply. Her lips were sweet beneath his, soft and receptive to his gentle assault. He tasted the tender, inner flesh of her lower lip, traced the line of even teeth and explored the length of her tongue with his own.

A ritual of sorts, he supposed, this kiss that demanded nothing, but expressed as well as words his feelings for her. It was their coming together at the end of the day, their parting when he left her in the morning, a gentle mating of mouth, lips and tongue. And he cherished each moment she gave him, each touch she bestowed upon his person, hoarding his memories should a bleak, lonesome road ahead be his future.

Now he took his ease for a moment before he headed back out to the field, holding her against himself. "There's no chores you need to do this afternoon. Go to town with

Isabelle and get what you need for the kitchen, and clothes, too, if there's anything you want," he told her.

"Take the gun with you. I'll have Zora come to the house and keep an eye on supper."

Jenny stepped away from him, glancing at the stove where a big kettle simmered on the back burner. "It's cooking slow, just beans and potatoes with the ham left from yesterday. She can take them off the stove in an hour or so."

He nodded. "I'll tell her." Gently now, he circled her waist, his fingers stretched wide, both front and back, noting the thickness she'd gained. His heart beat heavily as he thought of the child she carried beneath her skin, where even now her belly curved against his palm.

"I'm getting fat," she whispered.

"You're getting more beautiful every day," he said, then felt a flush rise to his face with the speaking of such flowery words. And yet, her smile told him she was willing to linger here, and he searched his mind, seeking words that would bind her more closely.

"You make me feel beautiful," she admitted, leaning her head against him, inhaling deeply. "I like the way you smell, Shay. All clean and fresh and…" She lifted her face. "I can't smell it now, but when you come to me at night, there's a scent on your skin…." She closed her eyes, and he wondered anew at the honesty of this woman, that she would tell him such things, giving her very thoughts into his keeping.

And she seemed to hold no grudge against him, no anger that he did not give her what she asked for; the words that would fill in the empty places of his past. She only waited, silently, patiently, and the effect was like water on a stone, wearing away his shield.

"Go on to town," he said abruptly, his tone gruff. "I'll see you later on, if you're home in time for supper."

"I'll be here," she promised.

* * *

The store was busy this afternoon, and Jenny waited her turn, walking past the meager displays, fingering the few bolts of fabric offered for sale. The barrel of pickles was filled to the brim, but she had enough of those to last for the whole winter, right in her pantry. A fifty-pound sack of flour sat on the floor in front of the counter and she cast greedy eyes in its direction. If it were not already bought and paid for, she would haul it home in the wagon.

"Mrs. Devereaux, I believe you're next," Tillie Duncan said cheerfully. "Are you needing some more dresses?" Her eye scanned Jenny's waist and her expression brightened. "Maybe something a bit larger?"

Jenny felt the flush rise to paint her cheeks. "Perhaps," she murmured. "But for now, I'd like to have someone carry this sack of flour to my wagon, if it isn't spoken for. Isabelle's out there waiting for me."

"No, I just haven't had Mr. Herbert put it up yet. He'll be happy to tote it on out," Tillie said, waving her hand in the air to catch her husband's eye. "What else can I get for you?"

Jenny consulted her list. "Lard, five pounds, I think. We'll be butchering soon and I'll render out more then. And coffee, as much as you can spare." Her finger moved on down the list. "Do you have vanilla?"

At Tillie's nod, Jenny breathed a sigh. "I'm so pleased. Cake just doesn't taste the same without it." She turned to look at the crockery in the far corner of the store and pointed at a large bowl. "How much is the biggest mixing bowl over there?"

"They come in a set, usually," Tillie said, "but I can break it up if you only want the one. The big one is twenty cents."

"Do you have a big bean pot?" Jenny asked.

"Just fifteen cents, with the lid and all," Tillie told her. "I've only got one left. There's not much call for them. It's kind of a luxury."

"I'm feeling sort of extravagant today," Jenny said. "I'll take some tinned fruit if you have any."

"Peaches, just in yesterday, and apricots, too."

Jenny nodded, glancing at her list again. "A bag of hard candy for Marshall, then. And I might as well have material for a couple of dresses. The nightgowns I made turned out pretty well. I think I'll try my hand at a dress."

Tillie bustled around, lifting the bolts of fabric Jenny chose and measuring out seven yards of each. "Go pick out the candy for yourself," she told Jenny, waving at the big jars on the end of the shiny counter.

"All right." Small paper sacks were piled beside the jars, and Jenny chose one, opening it as she made up her mind. Marshall liked the red cherry flavor, but Shay favored the root beer. Maybe some of each.

"You're pickin' those out for your husband, you might want to get root beer, ma'am." The voice was low, vibrant and somehow familiar. Its owner was behind her and Jenny froze where she stood, one hand on the lid of the jar, the other holding the sack in midair.

She closed her eyes. "Who are you?" Fearful of what she would see, she held her breath, waiting his reply.

It was not long in coming. "Turn around. Take a look for yourself."

Pride rode each word, and Jenny sensed he would not be denied. She turned, opening her eyes, her gaze falling upon a dark shirt, a wide belt holding a gun and long legs that ended in dusty boots. "Ma'am?" The single word prompted her to look upward and she did so, reluctantly and fearfully.

A sharp blade of a nose with a heavy moustache beneath it was centered between two dark eyes. They bore a startling resemblance to those she looked into every morning upon awakening, and she blinked as she recognized the man who could only be Roan Devereaux. His mouth was twisted into a half smile, and his hands rode his hips with an arrogance she was familiar with.

"You're his brother, aren't you?"

His nod was slow and deliberate, and his gaze moved over her. A narrowing of his eyes alerted her as he took note of her waist, of the thickening she could no longer conceal beneath her gathered skirt.

"You're carrying," he said, bluntly and forcefully. His gaze swept upward then and met hers. "You're Gaeton's wife."

"Shay," she corrected him quietly. "I'm married to Shay Devereaux."

The quick movement of his hand brushed away her rebuttal. "He might call himself that. His name's Gaeton. It's registered in the parish church. My mama named him after her grandfather."

"He calls himself Shay," Jenny said with a jerk of her chin.

"Damn if you don't look like Katherine when you do that," Roan said, his eyes lighting with pleasure.

Jenny stood stock-still. "Katherine?" Not Maggie. That name she'd heard. But *Katherine?* "Who is that?" she asked slowly.

Roan's mouth twitched. "My wife. Gaeton doesn't know about her, you wouldn't recognize her name." He stepped back, his hands tucked neatly into his pockets. "You bring her to mind when you tip your chin that way. I can always tell when she's gettin' ready to put her foot down, just by the way she squints her eyes and jabs that chin at me."

"You're Shay's brother," she repeated slowly. "I guess I'd have known, just looking at you. Eli told me he'd seen you, weeks ago."

"I traced Gaeton this far, once I heard he was in these parts," Roan said. "Just by luck I rode over here yesterday to look at some horses. I came in here to see if I could get directions to where he's living, and a fella over in the corner told me who you were, when you came in the store."

"I'm not sure he'll be happy to see you," Jenny told him. "He still hasn't sorted out all his feelings about..." Her hesitation was long, and he waited until she gathered her thoughts. "I don't even know everything he's done in the past few years, or all the places he's been. I guess if he wanted to see y'all, he'd have gone to visit."

"Well, that put me in my place, didn't it?" His brow tilted, and Jenny was taken aback at the similarity to Shay, the dark eyes hooded as Roan snapped out a reply.

She lifted her shoulder and released a sigh. "I can't stop you from seeing him, Mr. Devereaux, but don't be surprised if he's not welcoming. He spent time in Elmira, and it sticks in his craw that you fought the war wearing a blue coat on your back."

"That's in the past, and he'll have to learn to leave it there." Harsh words with no hint of compromise made her shudder, and she turned away from him. "Look at me," he said, his voice low and demanding.

She shook her head, stiffening her spine. "No man tells me what to do," she told him. "I've been on my own for a long time, Roan Devereaux, and until Shay came along, I wouldn't have given you two bits for the best man in the world. Now, I'm telling you I don't need to hear what you have to say." She reached for the candy jar again, making her selection with fingers that trembled.

As though the words came hard, he sighed. "I'm sorry, ma'am. I'd like to offer my apology. Katherine would have my head on a pole if she heard me talking to you that way."

"Well, good for her," Jenny said sharply, thinking that

the absent Katherine was someone she wouldn't mind meeting.

"I want to see my brother." The words hung in the air as Jenny replaced the lid and folded down the top of the paper sack. "Please, ma'am."

"My name's Jenny." She turned to face him. "Jenny Devereaux, sir. And my husband's name is Shay. It's what he wants to be called, and it's what he's known as hereabouts. If he wants to see you, that's fine with me. But don't blame me if he runs you off the place."

A grin curved his mouth as Roan offered his hand. Jenny looked down at it with a frown. He twitched his fingers. "I'm only asking you to shake it, Miss Jenny. Not spit on it."

Her grin answered his. "I wasn't intending to."

"It sure looked like it there for a minute."

Tillie called from behind them. "Your things are ready, Miss Jenny. I'll have Herbert carry them out to the wagon."

"I'll tend to that, ma'am," Roan said quickly, striding to the counter where a box waited, a wrapped bundle beside it. He slid the box to his shoulder, holding it in place with ease, then picked up the bundle. "Lead the way," he told Jenny, nodding at the door.

Isabelle's eyes widened as they approached the wagon, and she bent low to whisper against Jenny's ear. "Damn, where'd you get that one? He's kin to Mr. Shay, ain't he?" Her head lifted and, turning in the seat, she shot a challenge at Roan. "You comin' to make trouble, mister?"

Roan's eyes focused on the stalwart woman who held the reins, and she met his gaze unflinchingly. His grin was spontaneous. "I reckon I see why my brother was smart to find himself a home with you, Miss Jenny. You've got yourself a ready-made guardian angel, don't you?"

There was no softening to Isabelle's demeanor as she

offered a hand to Jenny. "He comin' along?" she asked, ignoring Roan's presence.

"He can follow if he wants to," Jenny told her, climbing atop the wagon seat. "We can't stop him from tagging behind."

Isabelle picked up the shotgun, holding it across her lap. "He'd do well to behave himself, is all I got to say."

"Yes ma'am," Roan said meekly, lowering his burdens onto the back of the wagon. He strode to the hitching rail and untied his horse, mounting in a motion that again brought Shay to Jenny's mind.

Two men so alike, yet so different. No wonder Eli had recognized Shay as a Devereaux. And now, for the first time in years, a lot of years, she amended silently, the two would meet. And either sparks would fly, or they would be accepting of their differences and be brothers once more.

"Where the hell'd you find *him?*" Shay's voice was a low growl, dark with anger as he slid from his stallion. The last one in from the field, he'd ridden the length and breadth of the acres they'd planted to cotton, estimating the remaining crop, sending the men back on foot. Now, he held the reins of his horse, looking down at Jenny as if she had somehow betrayed him.

"He was in town. He said he wanted to see you, and there wasn't much I could do about it, Shay. He followed behind the wagon when we came home." Glancing at the porch, where Roan was stretched out, his booted feet crossed at the ankles, she felt apprehension settle between her shoulder blades.

"Sure looks comfortable, don't he?" Shay said, leading his stud into the barn. Joseph held out a hand, and Shay delivered up the reins with a mumbled thanks.

"Shay, please." Not knowing what she begged for, Jenny stood beside him. "Don't have a big fuss with Marshall looking on," she said finally. Speaking of the child might deter his harshness, she thought, and a sigh escaped as Marshall came out the kitchen door to squat beside the visitor.

"This your boy?" Roan called out. "Don't look much like you, brother."

"Ah...*hell.*" Shay's curse made Jenny wince and she stepped ahead of him, only to be drawn back by his hand on her waist, holding her fast, tugging her to his side. "Wait for me, lady," he said quietly. "You may find yourself in the middle of this."

"I already figured that out." Neither of them frightened her, she decided. Only appealed to her, on a different level, of course, with Shay holding her heart. But Roan was quick-witted, with a smile that was capturing Marshall even now.

"He's my new papa," Marshall said, his voice carrying clearly across the yard.

"Yeah? And how do you feel about that?" Roan asked the boy. "Is he mean to you, making you work all day pickin' cotton?"

Marshall laughed, as though he saw through the droll question and appreciated the humor therein. "Naw, I just tote the bags back and forth. But I helped with the planting. And sometimes I watch the water jars and keep the flies off the food." He jumped from the porch and ran to where Shay and Jenny stood, his grin wide.

"That man looks like you, Papa, only he doesn't have a badge of honor." Reaching for Shay, Marshall clasped his hand around two long fingers and tugged him closer to the porch.

Roan's eyes darkened as he swung his feet to the ground and stood, facing his brother. His gaze swept Shay's long frame, then focused on the side of his face. "Did he pay?" he asked, his voice deceptively gentle.

"You better believe it."

And that was more than she'd been able to have him admit in almost six months, Jenny thought, a spark of anger lighting her fuse. "Can we go inside?" she asked, her words crisp.

"Yeah, we can go inside," Shay agreed, climbing the step and opening the screen door. His hand touched Jenny's back and she moved ahead of him, Marshall close on her heels. "After you, *brother*," her husband said, and she shivered at the note of derision he made no attempt to stifle.

Isabelle had plates on the table, and watched their entrance with silverware in her hand. "I didn't know if y'all were ready to eat or not," she said to Jenny. "I'll dish up quick, and then take what's left to the men."

"You won't join us?" Roan asked, shooting a glance at Isabelle.

She shook her head. "My menfolk will be hungry. They're comin' in from the field." Her look was long and searching as she took measure of the two brothers. "I think there's things to be settled here. I believe I'll take Marshall along with me, Miss Jenny, if that's all right."

So easily she assumed the servant role, Jenny thought, aggravation running rampant as she watched Isabelle dish up a serving bowl full of the savory stew. The green beans were limp from long, slow cooking and the potatoes, whole and still firm, nestled among them. Chunks of ham and thick broth completed the meal, along with a plate of sliced bread Zora had set aside, covered with a clean towel.

Isabelle lifted the kettle from the stove, a double layer of towels protecting her hand from the handle, and walked to the door. "Come along, Marshall."

He ran to hold the door for her, looking back longingly at the two men who faced each other across the table. But, obviously aware that Isabelle's word was as valid as his mother's, he made no complaint, leaving with a small wave of his hand.

Roan returned the gesture, then looked at his brother. "New papa? How long you been here?"

"Long enough," Shay said, reaching to pull Jenny's chair from beneath the table. She sat down and watched as the two men took their places. They ate, their forks moving almost in unison, silent, yet watchful. Until both plates were wiped clean with bread and pushed aside. "Why'd you come looking for me? What do you want?" Shay asked his brother. His gaze searched out the coffeepot, then sent a silent message to Jenny.

She obliged him, unwilling to make a fuss over his high-handed gesture, rising to find cups and pour the strong brew.

Roan's words were soft-spoken, as if he offered a casual invitation. "Thought it was about time you came to see your family."

"I saw *them* four years ago." Shay's reply was clipped and precise.

"So I heard," Roan said, leaning back in his chair. "I take it you don't consider me a relation?"

"You're a traitor."

Well, he couldn't be much more blunt than that, Jenny decided, casting a glance at the visitor, gauging his response. From Roan's stoic expression and nonchalant shrug, Shay had not hit home with the pointed accusation.

"I couldn't abide the idea of owning slaves any longer."

"Because of Jethro?" Shay asked. "He ran off, Roan. He knew Pa wouldn't let him get away. Anybody else would have whipped a runaway. Pa just gave him what-for and made a lot of noise."

Roan nodded. "I know all that now, but when Pa turned loose the dogs and scoured the swamp to find the best friend I'd ever had, I decided River Bend was the last place

I wanted to be. When I saw Jethro in chains, I headed north, wishing I could take him with me. I carried that scene in my mind for a long time." His eyes held memories, Jenny thought, and not all of them good.

And then he blinked and shrugged. "Might not have been the best move I ever made, but it turned out all right." Roan looked directly at Jenny. "I met and married Katherine in Illinois, right after the war."

"You brought her home with you?" Jenny asked, feeling a kinship to the woman who'd married a Devereaux.

Roan grinned suddenly, a beguiling expression that probably would lure most any woman into his web, Jenny decided. "Katherine, and a string of horses besides," Roan said. "She trains them."

"I'm surprised Pa didn't meet you with a shotgun," Shay said. "They'd all but written you off when they found out you were wearin' a blue uniform."

"They weren't overjoyed, I suppose. But then, I had Katherine with me, and she was carrying their first grandson." And as if that explained everything, he leaned back in his chair. "I heard you were in Elmira."

Shay stood abruptly, his face white with anger, the scar prominent against his cheek and jaw. "You'd do better if we didn't talk about that."

"I reckon we'll have to, one of these days," Roan said quietly. "Either that, or have a private war of our own."

"That can be arranged." Shay's words were bitter, spat from his mouth as if he detested their flavor.

"Won't do any good," Roan said pragmatically. "Only mess up your pretty face."

The table flew across the kitchen, dishes shattering against the black stove, silverware flying through the air. Roan was on his feet, his arms at his sides, hands fisted, and yet there was a relaxed air about him, as if he would only do battle if pushed to the wall.

"I'll bet Jenny won't appreciate cleanin' up that mess," he said, shaking his head at his brother.

Shay took two long steps, coming up against Roan's stalwart frame, their faces only inches apart. "If you're a smart man, you'll leave right now," he said in a deadly murmur. "If you stick around any longer, there'll be blood shed between us, and your mama and papa won't like that even a little bit."

"They're your mama and papa, too," Roan reminded him gently.

"Shay!" Jenny moved, her hands outstretched, reaching to come between the brothers.

Without sparing her a glance, Shay shook his head. "This doesn't concern you, Jen. Stay out of it."

"If it concerns you, then it's my business, too," she cried. "I won't be a party to bloodshed between brothers. There's been enough of that already." Her voice broke as tears gave way to sobs and she lifted trembling fingers to grip their shoulders. "Can't either of you see how useless this whole thing is? The war is over. We can't change anything that happened, only pick up and move ahead."

"Listen to her, Gaeton." Roan stepped back, as if he would pacify the angry man facing him.

"You weren't there," Shay said bitterly. "I suffered the insults and the beatings. I saw my friends dying around me."

"Yeah," Roan agreed. "You did. And I saw the men released from Andersonville, the ones that lived through it. Their blood ran just as red as the Rebels' in Elmira." He lifted his head and his eyes glittered with tears. "I can't change any of that. And neither can you. But if you don't bury it pretty soon, it's gonna eat you alive." He walked to the doorway, looking out on the yard.

"You walked in and out of River Bend and left our folks holding the bag. They didn't know where you'd gone or if you were dead or alive." His voice was tired, as weary as if he'd traveled a thousand miles to get to this place. And perhaps he had, Jenny thought.

"They're getting old, and they need to see you." He turned to look at Shay. "I'm not much for begging. You know that. But I'm asking you, as nicely as I can, to come home and let them know you're all right."

"I went home, and Mama cried every time she looked at the scar I'm wearing," Shay said. "Pa started in giving orders, just like always, and I found out I'd had my fill of it. There wasn't any peace to be found there."

"Did you find peace anywhere?" Roan asked, and then his eyes touched Jenny. "Before you got here?"

There was no answer for a moment, and Jenny held her breath as Shay looked at her, his eyes searching her face. "Jenny's my anchor," he said simply. "I'm not leaving her." His long arm reached for her and he swept her against his side, his grip almost bruising in its force. "I don't want to stir up the past. If you've made your peace with the folks, that's sufficient. Tell them…"

He paused and his fingers pressed with almost cruel force into Jenny's flesh. "Tell them I'm fine. I'm married and I'm working Jenny's place."

"That's it then?"

"Yeah, that's it." Shay stood his ground.

"You're my brother," Roan reminded him. "Nothing can change that. All you have to do is look at me, and you'll see yourself. And every time Pa looks in my eyes, I know he's wondering about you, Gaeton. You're his oldest son, his…" His hesitation was long as if he groped for words.

"You're his heart. And that's painful for me to admit. Mama misses you, too, but it's different with Pa. He's getting old, and he needs to see you."

Shay shuddered. His body trembled against her and

Jenny ached for the pain coursing through him. "Maybe. I'll see," he said finally.

"There's a room upstairs you can stay in," Jenny told Roan. "Nothing fancy, just a mattress on the floor."

"It'll beat the tree I slept under last night." His mouth twisted in a sad smile. "I left in a hurry yesterday. Pa had a bad spell, and Katherine told me to find my brother."

"How'd you know where to look?" Jenny asked.

"A big fella from around here somewhere saw me when I went to the city a while back. The man kept starin' at me until he made me downright upset." His grin was subdued now, but potent, nonetheless, Jenny thought. "I asked him about it, real nicely."

At those words Shay loosed a snort of derision and Jenny caught a glimpse of satisfaction in his eyes. "I'll bet you scared old Eli out of his wits."

Roan's eyes narrowed. "You knew about it?"

Shay nodded. "He came here, and announced that I must be one of the Devereaux fellas. Said he'd seen a man that looked like me."

"You knew I was looking for you, then."

"I had a good idea."

The two men, so evenly matched, so alike, yet such opposites in demeanor, shared a silence, and Jenny wished fervently for some way to bring them together. Neither must be forced to lose his dignity, or be made to lay aside that cocksure arrogance that marked them as the men they were.

"Can we talk about it in the morning?" she asked Shay. "Let Roan get some rest and we'll see what tomorrow brings."

Shay nodded and Roan echoed the gesture. "Point me in the right direction, Jenny," he said, "and I'll be out of your way."

She walked into the hallway and looked upward to where

the wide staircase opened into a hallway. "Third door on the right," she told him. "I'll fetch a bucket of water for you."

He shook his head. "I can get it, once I take care of my horse and get my saddlebags." He looked beyond her to where Shay stood in front of the kitchen window, and then bent low to brush a kiss across her forehead. "Thank you, new sister of mine. It'll work out. I wouldn't dare go home to Katherine if I didn't think things would be well."

Jenny managed a smile, but her heart was bleeding for Shay, for the decision he must make and the path they must trod. Together, she thought. They'd be together, no matter what happened.

"He'll..." She closed her eyes, finding tears blinding her once again. "He's a good man, Roan. It just might take time."

"Hell, that's the problem, Jenny. Pa didn't look good yesterday. We may not have much time left."

Chapter Fifteen

His anger had been defused, whether by Roan's own unwillingness to be involved in a fight, or by Jenny's tears. Whichever the cause, Shay felt empty, drained, as if the plug in the watering trough had been pulled, leaving the container dry and without substance. The night air refreshed him, and he drank it in, unwilling to face Jenny across the expanse of their bed. Sitting on the back porch was a poor substitute for tucking his wife against his side, but he lingered.

Marshall cried out softly, and he heard the quiet movement of Jenny's feet across the hall as she answered the boy's summons. Hearing made acute by months spent waiting while guards passed by, was attuned now to the woman and child he'd taken under his protection.

She barely breathed without his notice, seldom made a move without catching his eye. Only when he was away from her, working in the fields or gone from the house for one reason or another, did he lose track of her movements. And in those hours and minutes, he was intensely aware that she was not near at hand.

Her words were not discernible in the stillness of the night, but the sounds were soothing. And then she was at the door, her scent reaching him through the screen, her voice speaking his name. "Shay? Are you coming to bed?"

"You don't want me in there right now, Jen," he muttered beneath his breath. "I'm just past being angry. I'm afraid I'm not good company."

"I don't mind," she whispered.

He rose, reluctant but unwilling to hurt her, and opened the door. She stepped back, a slender shadow in the dark kitchen. Her hand touched his arm and she slid it to his wrist, then to clasp his fingers, leading him across the hall to her room. The door closed behind them and she turned to lean against it, her white gown visible in the darkness. She looked like a ghost standing there, he thought, although the specters that haunted his dreams over the past years had not been nearly so appealing as Jenny.

"Get undressed," she told him, and he bristled, unexpectedly.

"I've been listening to my brother tell me what to do for the past hour. I don't need you to take up where he left off."

She left her post and walked to the bed, rounding the footboard to sit on the opposite side. "All right. Have it your way. I'm not going to argue with you, Shay."

And for some odd reason, he wished she would. Wished fervently that he could vent his buried anger. "You argue enough any other time."

She turned her head and he was struck by the beauty of her profile. "If you want to talk so badly, tell me the things I want to know." Her chin tilted as she looked toward him. "It's dark in here. You can't seem to talk to me face-to-face. This way I won't even be able to see you."

"I've talked to you," he snarled. "Too much, if I remember right, while I was lyin' in that bed and you were gettin' your head filled with my crazy talk. And that's all it was, lady. Crazy talk. Not a word of truth in it."

"You're a liar, Shay Devereaux." She rose and walked back around the bed, uncaring that the moonlight made a mockery of her nightgown, that he could see every curve and valley of her body through the soft material.

She faced him, and he wondered at her courage, that she would face down a man twice her size. "That's the wrong thing to call me," he said softly.

"Then tell me you never knew a woman named Maggie, or a man named Gerald. Tell me you don't recognize the name of Beau or Rad Bennett." She drew in a deep breath, and then her voice rose. "Tell me how you buried the man who cut your face. The man who killed Gerald."

"I didn't tell you that," he said harshly.

"No? Then how did I know?"

He was silent and she lifted her hand, forming a fist. It pounded against his chest and she repeated the query. "How did I know, *Gaeton Devereaux?*"

"Damn, you've got a mouth on you," he growled, his voice a rasping snarl. The woman was determined to dig deep, and he wouldn't have it. He might have poured out a lot of claptrap while he was filled with the fever, but she had no right to throw it back in his face.

He pulled her against himself, then bent to scoop her into his arms, lifting her from the floor. As though she weighed less than nothing, he carried her to the bed and tossed her against the sheets. Then followed her down. He was heavy on her and he knew it, only lifting enough to ensure that she could catch her breath.

"I think you've lost your manners," she taunted, pushing at his chest.

"I'm not sure I ever had any," he said, bowing his head to take her mouth in a punishing kiss. She whimpered against his teeth and tongue, but the fight was gone out of her, and he felt the welcome pressure of her arms creeping around his neck. "Don't tell me you don't want me, Jen," he whispered. "I know better."

"Damn you, Shay. I hate being the one who loves, wishing for what I can't have."

"What do you want?" he asked, his tongue tasting the sweet flavor of her throat, then trespassing where her buttons gave way beneath his touch. "If you want a man to love you, Jenny, I'm the best fella available."

"You don't mean the same thing I do when you speak that word," she sighed. "I want you to—"

His mouth took her breath as she would have spoken the cry of her heart, and she moaned her surrender. Her fingers slid through his hair and she opened her legs to his silent urging, allowing him the place he demanded. One hand groped to gather her nightgown, and he drew it up over her legs. "Lift up," he muttered, and slid the garment from beneath her. It lay gathered around her waist and he rose from the bed, his movements swift as he stripped the clothing from his body.

She felt like a pagan sacrifice before him, her body pale in the moonlight. He stood naked beside the bed and she thought again of their wedding night, of the new and wondrous knowledge he'd brought to her in the darkness. He'd only ever been gentle with her. Even when his passion was at its peak, he'd not harmed her. Rushed her, perhaps, she thought, smiling as she remembered his fierce taking of her flesh on more than one occasion.

"You find something to smile about?" he asked, nudging her legs farther apart as he settled between them.

She refused to answer. Let him wonder at her mood, since she'd been pondering his for the whole evening.

He lifted her knees and bent to fit their bodies together. She was dry and tight and he grunted a word beneath his breath, an irate sound, then found her with his fingers. Unerringly, he pressed against a sensitive spot, and she whimpered beneath her breath.

"If I tell you no, will you stop?" she asked.

His fingers stilled their motion and she lifted her hips, an involuntary response as she felt the hot wash of desire his touch brought to her female flesh.

"You won't," he muttered.

"If I did?" she prodded.

"You know I'll stop. If you don't want me, I won't force you. I'd like to kill the man who did."

"You killed another man for that reason," she said quietly.

"He tried." Shay was unmoving as he gave her that small bit of knowledge.

"Was it Maggie?"

"Are you gonna ask me questions all night?"

"Just one for now." She surged against his touch and he shuddered as his hand found slick dampness.

"Yeah, it was Maggie. But he didn't do more than this. I dragged him off her."

"Did you kill him?"

"I said just one answer for now," he told her, adjusting his body against her, silencing her with the force of his entry.

She gasped and his big body was immobile.

"Jenny? Tell me I didn't hurt you."

"No, never," she whispered, glorying in the power of his possession.

He rocked with her, rode her with long, smooth strokes and took his satisfaction in moments, sounding her name with harsh, gasping groans against her throat.

She held him close, unwilling to allow a hairbreadth between them, her hands clasping the muscled strength of his shoulders and back. "If you never say the words, I'll still love you, Shay." It was a confession from her heart, and although she'd said as much before, tonight was a time of reassurance, of comfort given and passion received.

"I've never told a woman that," he said, his voice muffled. "Not even when my mother rocked me in the big rocking chair and sang me to sleep."

His pause was long, and she waited for what might come. "My mother loved me the way you do," he said after a moment. "Oh, not with the same kind of love, but the same way, without expecting anything in return. Unconditional love."

He lifted his head and looked at her, his eyes hooded, his expression barely visible in the dim light. "I don't deserve that from you, but you give it anyway, Jen. This isn't easy for me, but I need to tell you what I feel." He whispered the words softly, tenderly, gently.

"I love you, sweetheart. I love you." And then his mouth took hers in that same easy, undemanding kiss she had come to welcome from him. And again the words spilled from his lips, as if once said, he could not cease the message they brought to her needy heart.

He rolled with her, until they were twined in the middle of the big bed, facing each other. His voice was ragged as he began. "I think you know most all of it already—but I'll tell you what you want to know about Radley Bennett and Maggie, and about Beau Jackson." He recalled the day when Maggie had been set upon by Beau's cowhand, how he'd heard her puppy barking outside the springhouse and how he'd dragged Radley from her unconscious form.

"I pounded him into the ground," he said with a vicious growl, "And then I lifted him by the collar and dragged him into the woods. I was going to shoot him dead, Jen. If ever a man deserved to die, it was Radley Bennett. I don't remember how long it took or where we ended up. I only know that when I looked down at him, his lips were blue and he'd stopped breathing. Whether he choked on the collar around his neck, or I beat the life out of him, I can't tell you.''

''What did the sheriff say?'' she asked, unwilling to prod for details, but aching to know if a sign was up in a jail anywhere, with Shay's name on it.

''We didn't tell the sheriff. Beau doesn't even know where I buried the man. And I left before morning.''

She drew in a deep breath. ''What about Gerald?''

''I didn't kill Gerald, Jen. He was my friend in the prison camp in Elmira. A guard kicked him to death and was starting in on Carl when I put a stop to it.''

''You killed the guard? How?''

He shook his head. ''You don't need to know, sweetheart. Some of the other men helped me dig a hole in the mud and we buried him, deep as we could go.''

''They didn't miss him?''

He shrugged. ''Yeah, they missed him, but he was the meanest man I ever knew, and I don't think the army figured he was any great loss.''

She was silent, filled to overflowing with sorrow for the pain he'd borne, for the scars he still bore. ''Did he cut your face?''

He nodded. ''That's all, Jen. No more.''

''All right.'' It was enough. And if he thought that the knowledge of his past, of the men he'd buried would mar her love for him, she would spend the rest of her life proving otherwise.

''All right?'' His hand cupped her chin and he tilted her head back, the better to see the expression on her face. ''You can still love me, with all you know about me?''

''I'll always love you, Shay,'' she whispered. ''I love the man you are right now. And your past is a part of you.''

And then, so easily, so softly she could scarcely believe her ears, he surrendered the final barrier he'd erected.

''Will you go with me to see my folks?''

* * *

Roan was gone. A scrawled note on the kitchen table and a long look from Isabelle told the tale. He'd done all he could, he wrote. The rest was up to Shay, but he'd deliberately printed his name in bold letters. *Gaeton.*

"He said not to rouse you," Isabelle told them. "He was up before dawn, and snatched a bite to eat. His horse was saddled and he was gone before I had the coffee boilin'."

"I'm not surprised," Shay said. "He was determined not to fight with me."

"And how do you feel now?" Jenny asked, turning bacon in the pan as Isabelle went out to milk.

"You know how I feel," Shay said, lifting a brow as he slanted a long look in her direction.

"Tell me, too," Marshall asked, standing in the doorway, his nightshirt sagging from one shoulder, the cat in his arms.

"You're supposed to button that shirt, and don't bring that cat in the kitchen," Jenny said absently.

"Yes, ma'am," he replied obediently, grinning at Shay.

"Why don't you just take off your nightshirt and get dressed?" Shay suggested. "We're going for a long ride after breakfast."

Jenny turned quickly, her eyes alight. "Today? We're going today?"

"I don't see any reason to wait," Shay said. "But we can't go anywhere till that bacon gets done."

Marshall scampered from the room, the cat at his heels. Jenny watched him go, then turned back to the stove, lifting the bacon from the pan with careful deliberation. "Do you think your mother will welcome you?" she asked.

Shay shrugged his shoulders. "Roan seems to think so, and that's about all I've got to go on right now." He cleared his throat. "If you're worried about this, I can go alone, Jen."

"Oh, no!" Her mouth twisted as if she fought tears, and the bacon was dumped on the tabletop with little ceremony. "I'm going with you, Shay. No matter what, we'll face this together. If your father is as ill as Roan seemed to think, you need to be there. You'll never get over it if you don't make things right with him."

He reached for her, drawing her to sit on his lap. One hand brushed a lock of hair from her cheek, the other held her firmly in place. "Is that how you feel?" he asked. "Have you made things right with your father?"

She frowned, her lips compressed tightly for a moment. "I don't think I felt the same way you do. I tried to keep in touch, but he turned me away."

"And you didn't feel any guilt?"

"I could have visited him, I suppose. I think my pride was hurt, Shay, that he didn't answer my letters, that he didn't care about my being alone here."

"He's an old man, Jen. An old, feeble man who's given up on life."

"Whose side are you on?" she asked sharply. "I thought you understood."

"I do." He kissed her lightly and she withdrew from his touch. "Don't be mad at me, sweetheart," he whispered. "I think we need to give it another shot, see if he'll come here with us."

"And if he won't?" Her lips trembled now, and he ached for the stubborn pride she wore like a coat of armor.

"Then we go there whenever we can, and make sure that Marshall gets to know his grandfather."

"Why can't you be so forgiving of your folks as you are of my father?" she asked quietly.

He mulled her words over for a moment and grinned at her petulant look. "I'm not the one he hurt," he told her gently. "I can ache for you, but still see him as a tired, old man who doesn't know how much life still has to offer.

Our job is to give him Marshall, let him get a taste of being a grandfather and then wait for him to come to us.''

''And what will our job be when we go to River Bend?'' she asked soberly. ''Have you got that all figured out, too?''

He shook his head. ''Not quite. Making peace is my first aim. Letting my folks know I regret walking away from them four years ago comes next, I guess.''

''You won't want to go there, will you?'' she asked. ''I mean, not to stay?''

He shook his head. ''Roan's there, running things. They don't need me. And you do. I've got all I can handle right here, Jen. This is my home, if you'll have me.''

Her head nestled against his shoulder and her body relaxed against him. ''I told you a long time ago I'd let you go if you wanted to walk away, but I think I've changed my mind. I could live through it if you left me, but I'd never have any joy in my life without you.'' She lifted her head to meet his gaze. ''I love you.''

''Mama, are we gonna eat pretty soon?'' Marshall stood at the doorway, a pout drawing his lips down at the corners. ''We can't go for our ride till we eat, and you're not sitting in your chair.'' He walked to the table, eyeing the bacon, then reached to pick up a piece. ''How come you threw the bacon on the table?''

Jenny slid from Shay's lap and rapped Marshall smartly on the head with her knuckles. ''You haven't washed your hands. Breakfast will be ready in a minute.''

Shay shrugged at the boy, sharing a quick grin. ''Better listen to your mother, son. She's runnin' the show this morning.''

It was near noon before they headed down the avenue of oak trees, the mare pulling the buggy, their lone piece of baggage strapped on the back. A basket of food tucked beneath the buggy seat promised supper, and Shay estimated they would be near a hotel by late evening, in the small town not far from River Bend.

Lush grass formed a carpet beneath them as they stopped by the side of the road to eat, and the mare dipped her head gratefully as Shay removed the bit, allowing her to graze. A quilt thrown on the ground provided a table, and Jenny dug into the basket for the meal Isabelle had prepared.

Slabs of ham, a bowl of pickled beets and onions and thick slices of bread provided nourishment, and Marshall crowed with delight as he found tarts made of fresh pumpkins from the garden. "I didn't know Isabelle baked these," he said, biting into the flaky pastry.

"Save one for me," Shay told him sternly, and the boy turned twinkling eyes to his mother.

"Isabelle always bakes stuff for me, doesn't she, Mama? I'll bet these are my treat." The remaining bits of the tart clung to his lips as he cast a triumphant look at Shay, and then he laughed wholeheartedly as he was rolled across the quilt beneath Shay's marauding hands.

"I'll teach you to eat my dessert," Shay growled, his mock ferocity causing Marshall to giggle and squirm beneath long fingers that sought ticklish spots.

"You make him throw up his supper, and you get to clean it up," Jenny said firmly. "You're acting like a pair of scamps."

Shay drew Marshall to his lap and whispered loudly in his ear. "She means it, boy. We'd better watch out, or she'll be after us." And then his whisper turned to a soft declaration of intent. "Us men have to stick together, don't we?"

"Yessir," Marshall said quickly, with a triumphant look at his mother. "We sure do."

Jenny rose from the quilt and pursed her lips, looking down at the pair of them. "Well, the men around here have to pick up the remains and pack the basket while I tend to some private business. We need to be on the road.'' She turned from them, hearing their soft laughter as they agreeably did as instructed, her own mouth wide with a satisfied smile. Shay was so good for Marshall, so generous with his attention, so ready to be a father.

Her hand touched the rise of her belly, where even now another child grew. She'd been blessed to have good men in her life, doubly blessed to be given a second chance at happiness. Carl's memory was still there, his kindness to her a reality, his care of her but a faded remembrance. And he'd sent Shay, she reminded herself. And for that she would be forever grateful.

Shay stood by the side of the buggy when she returned, short moments later. "Marsh went for a walk in the bushes. He'll be right back,'' he told her. "Did you get enough to eat?'' His hand curved against her cheek and she was drawn to his warmth.

"I'm fine. Just tired. I'm not used to long rides in the buggy. I'll be glad to get to the hotel.''

"I'm ready now,'' Marshall announced, running from a stand of trees to where they waited. He climbed agilely into the buggy and reached for Jenny's hand. "I'll help you up, Mama. We need to find the town where the beds are.''

Shay grinned at the boy's descriptive phrase. "You told him we'd be sleeping in a hotel,'' he said. "And sure enough, that's where the beds are.''

It was full dark by the time the buggy rolled up to the facade of Riverside's only hotel. A light glowed from the ceiling, illuminating the lobby, and a man with stiffly starched collar and cuffs stood behind the big desk. Shay stepped into the ornate foyer and looked around.

"Hasn't changed any,'' he said quietly.

"You've been here?'' Jenny asked, impressed by the

high ceiling and the curving stairway that led to the second floor.

"Yeah. Years ago. My pa brought us here for dinner once when we came to town for Sunday church. It was a long way from home, and we didn't go real often, and that one time was a special occasion." His eyes were shadowed as he scanned the carpet and heavy draperies. "They let the boys in blue stay here. Saved the place from being burned."

"Can I help you, sir?" the desk clerk asked, clearly searching Shay's face. "Seems like I've seen you before."

"Probably," Shay said, then pulled money from his pocket. "We need a large room for the night, with a cot for the boy."

"You belong to the Devereaux family?" the clerk asked, watching as Shay wrote his name in bold script across the page of the register. "Yep, I guess you do," he concluded, turning the large book around. "Never heard of your name, though. There was just the two boys, I thought. Roan and Gaeton. And then the girl. Pity about her, runnin' off the way she did."

Jenny's hand stayed Shay's involuntary movement, as he would have reached for the hapless clerk. "May we have the key to our room?" she asked politely.

"Sounds like everybody in the parish is gonna be talking about Yvonne." His growl was low and frustrated as he turned Jenny toward the staircase.

"Probably not," she said quietly. "I'd have thought it happened long enough ago for folks to have forgotten it."

"Gossip hangs around a long time," he grumbled, his feet heavy on the stairs as they climbed the steps in unison.

"Did that man know Mr. Roan?" Marshall asked. He skipped down the hallway before them, turning to walk backward as he queried Shay.

"Turn around before you trip and fall," Jenny said

sharply. "Look for the room with fourteen on the door," she told him.

He stopped stock-still. "I don't know what a fourteen is, Mama. I only know to number ten."

"Look for a four, then," Shay said. "It'll have a one in front of it." The room was next and he slowed Jenny's progress, giving the boy a chance to use his knowledge. In less than a moment, Marshall pointed his index finger in triumph, standing squarely in front of the designated place.

"He'll be up all night," Jenny said quietly. "He's never been so far from home before."

"I'm plannin' on him sleepin' real sound," Shay whispered next to her ear. And then laughed aloud as she batted at him with her reticule.

The sound of laughter beneath their window woke Jenny with a start. Voices called back and forth and a horse neighed loudly. So this was life in town, she thought, looking up at the ceiling, where a border of cherubs rimmed the top of the walls. A strong arm tightened around her middle and she tilted her head back to look into dark eyes that glittered with intent.

"Oh, no you don't," she whispered, catching hold of his hand before it could move upward.

"Just one little squeeze." He breathed the words in her ear and she shivered as his warm breath and the impudence of his plea coaxed her to compliance. Her hold relaxed and his fingers circled her breast, cupping the weight in his palm. His groan was heartfelt, and she inhaled sharply.

"Marshall's looking out the window," she said quietly, noting the empty cot beside the bed, her quick glance spotting the boy across the room. He turned, as if he'd heard her words, his eyes alight.

"Mama, there's men out there, and ladies and horses. Everybody's in town, aren't they?" He turned back, apparently not needing a reply, leaning on the sill, his head leaning from the open window.

"Don't fall out," Jenny said quickly, sitting upright as she watched her son's actions. She looked down at the man beside her, his face relaxed, his mouth turning up in a teasing grin. That the side of his face responded to the movement of his mouth by drawing up in a grimace no longer seemed to bother him, and she was pleased that he smiled so readily.

"Are you ready to get up?" she asked, sliding her feet from the bed.

"No, but I don't think I have a choice," he grumbled from behind her. His hand slid from her body as she moved from him, and then patted carefully at her bottom as she stood.

She stiffened, looking over her shoulder, and again his grin was for her benefit. "I can wait," he said. "Just barely, but I can wait."

Chapter Sixteen

The avenue leading to the house was narrower than she'd expected, but it spoke of faded elegance. Overhanging branches of oaks on both sides provided a shady path, gray moss hanging in fragile-seeming tendrils to touch the roof of the buggy. A bend in the road ahead drew her, and Jenny leaned forward in the seat, as if those few inches could improve her view.

"Don't fall on your nose," Shay's voice was gruff, and she glanced at him quickly.

"Are you all right?"

His nod was slight. "About as right as you'd expect."

And wasn't that a cryptic answer, she thought. His mouth was drawn into a thin line, his scar showing clearly against dark skin, and his eyes seemed flat and lifeless, as if he expected little from this venture. White knuckles told the tale, she decided, looking down at his hands. They held the reins firmly, drawing the horse to a trot as she would have broken into a canter. From ahead, a whinny announced the mare's reason for excitement, and Shay cast a knowing look at Jenny.

"She hears a stallion," he said, then looked ahead to

where the mare's ears twitched and her tail flagged high. "She didn't pay this much mind to my stud."

"Maybe she wasn't ready," Jennie told him smartly. "Females are allowed to make a choice, you know."

"Yeah, I know," he said, a grin touching his lips.

The bend was taken at a faster clip than Jenny had expected and she gripped the buggy seat, leaning toward Marshall, whose attention was attuned to the view before them. His sounds of appreciation were fervent as the journey ended, and Jenny's thoughts echoed those of her son.

"Just look at that," Marshall said. "They got a whole lot of horses, Papa."

"They sure do," Shay agreed. "Roan said Katherine had a string of them. Looks like they've got yearlings, too." Shay drew back on the reins and the mare halted at the hitching rack.

The corral was large, extending from the side of the barn, and beyond it a verdant pasture drew Jenny's eye. "There must be twenty horses out there. Do you suppose they're willing to sell any?"

Shay slid from the seat. "Hard to say. But I'm probably thinking the same thing you are, Jen. We couldn't go wrong buying stock here. That sure is a dandy bunch of horseflesh all in one place."

"Pa's been keepin' them there all morning, just for your benefit," Roan said, from his perch on the porch. So intent was she on the display in the corral and pasture, Jenny had missed his long form, leaning against an upright post. Now he stepped to the ground and approached the buggy. "Thought you'd come in the front way," he said. "Pa's been lookin' from the parlor windows for the past hour."

"What made you so sure we'd be here?" Shay asked, tying the reins to the long rack. And even as he spoke, Jenny saw his eyes glance toward the screen door behind his brother.

Roan looked at Jenny, his smile welcoming and warm. "I knew." Simple and to the point, he offered his thanks to her with a nod, walking to the buggy where Marshall was eagerly climbing in Shay's wake. Roan's arm snaked around the boy's waist and he lifted him against his side. "Hey, there, young'un. There's some folks inside wantin' to meet you."

Marshall's head turned to the side, his grin flashing. "Me? They wanna meet me, Mr. Roan?"

Roan turned him upright, allowing him to slide to the ground, then gripped his shoulders and squatted before him. "Let's get this straight, boy. I'm your uncle now, and I want you to remember that. I'm Uncle Roan and here comes your aunt Katherine."

From the doorway, a woman with chestnut-colored hair stepped onto the porch. Small boned, yet rounded with an advanced pregnancy, she smiled a welcome, her blue eyes brilliant in a tanned face. "Somebody get my new sister off that buggy," she said.

I'm going to love her. The thought spun in Jenny's mind, flashing like sunshine, bringing a warmth to her heart that was almost overwhelming. Shay turned back to her, holding up his hands and she bent to him, confident of his strength as he lifted her to the ground. Her footsteps never faltered as she climbed to the porch, ignoring the curious look cast in her direction by Roan, oblivious to Shay's hands as they released her.

She faced Katherine, only a foot separating them, and held out her hands. With a grin of delight, Katherine grasped her tightly, sliding her arms around Jenny's slender form, until a sturdy thump against her belly told Jenny that Roan's son or daughter was protesting close quarters. She laughed aloud, pleased at her welcome, and whispered in Katherine's ear.

"I hope our babies will be friends."

"You, too?" Katherine asked, her face wreathed in a wide smile. She leaned back, the better to look down Jenny's length. "Roan didn't tell me," she muttered, a long look of accusation tossed in her husband's direction.

"I just got back last night," he complained, "and I've been busy."

Katherine's mouth firmed. "You're going to be a new uncle, and you were too busy to tell me?"

"You were busy, too," he reminded her, his mouth twitching, his eyes glittering with mischief.

She flushed, then turned to Jenny. "Ignore him. He's hopeless anyway."

Jenny lifted a brow. "I'm married to his brother. Remember?"

Behind them a woman stood at the screen door, silent and watchful. Jenny met her gaze through the screen and looked long at the wistful expression. "You're Shay's mama, aren't you?" she asked quietly. "He has a look about him…" Her pause was long and then she stepped closer, her fingers gripping the door handle.

"And you're Jenny." The woman opened the door wide, holding out a hand to her newest daughter-in-law. "I'm Letitia. Won't you come in?" A fragile smile touched her lips, and she looked beyond Jenny to where Shay watched from the yard. "I named him Gaeton," she said softly. "He must have taken Shay from his godfather's name. Jack Shay was black Irish, and LeRoy's best friend…years ago," she said, a note of sadness tinging her words.

Well, that answered one question. Jenny stepped closer, and Letitia touched her face with slender fingers. "You're a pretty one, aren't you? I'm so glad our boy found you." Her gaze swept Jenny's length and rested on the rounding of her belly. "Four months?" she asked, her eyes bright with hope.

Jenny nodded. "Just about." And then she bent closer. "He's worried, you know."

Letitia smiled eagerly. "No need for that. I'm his mother, after all." She stepped past Jenny and onto the porch. "Gaeton?" Hesitantly, she halted, her outstretched hand dropping to her side.

"Mother." Shay's steps were long, his eyes fastened on the small woman, and he picked her up from the porch, lifting her to eye level. She protested with a squeal, but her lips curved with pleasure. "You haven't grown any, have you?" he asked, leaning forward to kiss her on either cheek. Lowering her to the ground, he held her steady for a moment, then released her, offering a hand to Jenny. "You met my bride."

"She's lovely," Letitia said, her eyes overflowing with tears. "Your father's inside, son."

"You've got your mother crying already, I see." The man at the door growled the words almost in Jenny's ear and she turned to face him. He aimed dark eyes in her direction. "You're the woman fool enough to marry him, I suppose."

Shay muttered a single word and, setting his mother aside, bounded up the step, pulling Jenny against himself. "This is my wife, yes, and you'll treat her with respect.

"This man is my father, Jenny. His name is LeRoy, and his manners are not fit for pigs." Nostrils flaring, Shay faced his sire and Jenny drew in a breath, tossed between two men who seemed capable of physical violence. That LeRoy was older and white-haired mattered little. And yet, she saw a tremor in his hand, noted a flicker of unease in his dark eyes, and found her sympathy surging in his direction.

She reached for his hand, holding the gnarled fist between her palms, gaining his attention as she eased between the two men. "I'm glad to meet you, sir," she said, not allowing him to retrieve his fist. And then he stilled his attempt and met her gaze, his eyes sharp and searching.

"You're kinda feisty for such a little girl, ain't you?" he asked. "Sure you're not related to Katherine?"

Jenny felt a smile bloom on her lips. "Yes, as a matter of fact, I am," she said politely. "She's my new sister."

"Cut from the same cloth, if you ask me," LeRoy muttered, opening his fingers to clasp Jenny's hand. His other arm touched her shoulder, urging her closer, and he bent to press his lips against her forehead. "Welcome, daughter. I'll let you bring the boy inside. We'll talk later." He released her and turned away, his shoulders seemingly held in place by strength of will as he crossed the wide kitchen floor.

At the doorway, he touched the jamb for balance and she resisted the urge to go to him. "Let him be," Shay whispered in her ear. "I'll see him in a while."

Letitia and Katherine followed them into the kitchen, Roan at their heels. "I think Susanna has dinner almost ready," Letitia said. "We were lookin' for y'all to come in the front door. I hate havin' you to walk through my kitchen this way." She bustled past them and led the way into the central corridor of the house, down toward the front door and into the parlor.

"Have a seat and I'll call Susanna. She must be out in the back somewhere, or maybe upstairs." Letitia turned to leave the room, looking to Katherine in a seeking fashion.

"She's setting the spare room to rights, Mama," Katherine told her. "I'll go get a pot of tea. You stay and talk to Gaeton."

"I'll help," Jenny said, shooting a glance at Shay. "You've got a lot of catching up to do," she told him pointedly, then followed Katherine from the room.

In the hallway, Katherine stood leaning against the wall,

one hand over her mouth, tears filling her eyes. Jenny touched her shoulder. "Are you all right?"

Katherine nodded quickly. "Roan told me about his face," she whispered. "But seeing it for myself just wasn't the same. It makes me ache for him."

Jenny was astounded. That the scar should so deeply affect the other woman was beyond her comprehension. "You'll get used to it," she said softly, her arm around Katherine's waist as she turned her toward the kitchen. "I hardly notice it anymore."

"That's not it," Katherine said, once the kitchen was gained. "He reminded me of my brother, Lawson. The last time I saw him, he had a scar like that. Not as long, maybe, but all I could think of…" She gulped back her tears. "No wonder Roan took it so hard, that his brother was scarred. He said I'd understand, better than anyone else."

"Where's your brother now?" Jenny asked.

"Dead and buried." Katherine's eyes filled with new tears. "I'm just weepy these days," she said with a choked laugh surfacing. "It was a long time ago, but seeing Gaeton brought it back."

"I think you're allowed to be…." Jenny held out her hands with a helpless gesture. "I know how you feel. I've shed tears for no reason lately. And I'm a long way from birthing this baby." She looked at Katherine closely. "Any time now?" she asked.

Katherine nodded, one hand clutching at her back. "I can hardly wait. I can't even hold Jeremy on my lap anymore."

"Jeremy?" Jenny looked around.

"He's napping, upstairs. In fact, I wouldn't be surprised that Susanna went up to get him." She turned to the stove, lifting the big teakettle with both hands. "Take the cover from the teapot, would you, Jenny?" The hot water splashed on tea leaves and steam rose as the pot was filled. "By the way, you can call me Kate if you've a mind to."

"All right," Jenny said agreeably. "Where are the cups?" She looked around the tidy kitchen, spotting a tray set out on the buffet. "Here we go," she murmured, lifting the tray to the table. "How old is Jeremy?"

"Almost three," Kate said. "He was born after Roan and I came home."

"Here?" Jenny asked, lifting the teapot to the tray.

"We've been here three years now." Her smile revealed a dimple as Kate turned from the stove. "Three wonderful years."

"You're happy here, then."

"I'm with Roan," Katherine said simply. "You want to carry the tray?" She turned to the buffet. "There's a plate of cookies here someplace. Susanna baked yesterday." Retrieving the heaping plate, she followed Jenny back to the parlor.

Shay stood up as they crossed the threshold, his eyes seeking his wife, his hands reaching for the tray. Relief apparent in his faint smile, he carried the tea tray toward the sofa. "Mama just said she wondered if the two of you had decided to drink yours in the kitchen," he teased.

"We've got a lot to talk about," Jenny told him, settling beside Letitia. From the doorway behind her a small voice announced the presence of Jeremy, his tones demanding his mother's attention.

"Mama!" He stood erect, his dark brows beetled, his mouth looking so like Shay's, Jenny wanted to laugh aloud. "I dint find you." His lips puckered into a pout, and he ran to Katherine. She held him against her side, then sat on the sofa, one arm surrounding his shoulders, her mouth touching his forehead.

"I'm right here, sweetie," she murmured, but the boy would not be pacified.

"I need hugs," he said, one leg attempting to scale the sofa, seeking a place on her lap.

From the doorway, LeRoy's dry announcement caught Jeremy's attention. "Look here, boy. I've found you a cousin." Hand tightly clasped by the white-haired gentleman, Marshall looked eagerly at the younger boy.

"He's kinda little, isn't he, Grandpa?" As an aside, it almost got past Jeremy's hearing, but his head came up and he slid to the floor.

"I'm bigger," he stated, rising to his full height. He strutted across the floor, looking up at Marshall. A half-head shorter than the other boy, he nevertheless tilted his chin and squinted his eyes. "I'm Jeremy," he said firmly.

Marshall laughed with delight. "Come show me your dog," he said, holding out his hand, which Jeremy promptly took. And then Marsh looked up at Roan. "I'll look after him, Uncle Roan. I'm dependable. My papa says so." And as if that were the final word on the subject, the two small boys left the room.

"He's a handful, I'll warrant," Letitia said warmly, her smile a delight to see. Jenny nodded. Children seemed to pull things together, she thought. Now if only they could work a miracle of sorts between LeRoy and Shay.

The feather bed was soft beneath them, and the light from the window outlined Shay's broad shoulders as he leaned over her. Jenny touched his face, her fingers traveling the familiar route from temple to jaw, as though by mere touch she could erase the scar he lived with.

"Your mama said it wasn't as bad now as four years ago."

"It was pretty fresh then, all red and angry. It's not nearly so ugly now," he said. He lowered his head to the pillow next to hers. "But Katherine was upset, I think."

"She cried," Jenny whispered. "She hurt for you, Shay.

Not because of how it looks. Not that. Just that you'd been so wounded."

"Sisters under the skin, aren't you?" His voice held a trace of humor, the words dry, as if he accepted the alliance the two women had formed so quickly.

"She's wonderful," Jenny said simply. "And we resemble each other, don't we? With just about the same color hair and all."

"Yours is prettier, redder," Shay said, "and your eyes are softer."

"I think you're prejudiced," Jenny said, laughing beneath her breath. "I'll bet Roan is telling her the exact opposite, right now."

"And I'll bet the two boys are still gigglin' and wrasslin' around in that big bed."

"No," Jenny said. "I just checked before I came in. They're sideways across the bed, both of them sound asleep." Her sigh was deep. "And I'll bet they'll be up long before breakfast. Marshall wants to show Jeremy how to gather the eggs. And they're going to look for a new litter of kittens in the barn."

Shay stirred, turning to face her. "Sounds like I've got my work cut out for me. They'd better wait till Roan or I get there. They can't be turned loose out there all by themselves. There's more trouble they can get into than you can shake a stick at."

"Your father said he'd go out with them, and Jethro will keep an eye out." She took his hand and kissed the back, rubbing it against her cheek. "You need to spend a while with your mama. Just talk to her and tell her about..." Her pause was long. "About things, Shay. Not everything, but enough to let her know why you couldn't stay here.

"Tell her about Elmira. Not about the guard and all of that, but the rest. About Carl, and the men who died and

the men who lived,'' she whispered. ''It scarred you, Shay.
Not just your face, but deep inside. Let her see the scars.''

''I can't do that,'' he protested quickly, his voice harsh.
''She's my mother. She can't understand how a man feels.''

''I do. Because I love you,'' Jenny told him. ''And she
loves you, too.''

''I know. Funny, isn't it? It used to bother me that Roan
was always her favorite.''

''And you were LeRoy's. Roan told us that. But you're
still her son, and she doesn't understand why you came
home, only to vanish without a trace. How do you think
I'd feel if Marshall were to grow up and go from home and
not let me know where he was, or if he were alive or
dead?''

''I'd go after him and...'' He paused. ''I couldn't stand
to see you hurt that way, Jen.'' The silence was long, and
then he rolled atop her, his knees making a place for himself. She moved agreeably to his silent bidding, her hands
lifting to embrace him.

''I'll do it,'' he agreed softly. ''I'll spend time with her
and talk to her. And then I'll go for a long walk with Pa,
as long a hike as he can handle, anyway. Maybe we'll sit
under a tree for a while.

''He looks older, Jen. But Roan said he'd improved
while he was gone, has more color in his face.''

He bent, his kiss deliberate, enticing her response, and
her lips opened to his, answering his caress. He groaned
beneath his breath. ''You don't know how I've waited for
this, all day.''

''Sure beats last night, doesn't it?'' she whispered.
''Marshall's three rooms away, and our door is shut tight.''

''I locked it,'' he murmured against her ear.

''You did?'' She turned to look through the darkness, as
if her eyes could see the latch. ''I didn't see a key.''

''There isn't one, just a bolt, up at the top. This used to

be my room when I was a boy—I'd put the bolt on to keep Yvonne out." His grin shone white in the moonlight. "There wasn't any keepin' Roan out. He just climbed the tree and came in the window if he wanted to."

"Are you friends again?" she asked. "Have you put aside your differences?"

Shay considered the thought. "Pretty much," he said finally. "He's like my other half sometimes, and I don't understand how our minds work in such different ways. I suppose I'll just have to accept that they do, and leave it at that."

"Are we going to talk all night?" she asked plaintively, wriggling beneath him.

"Not when you make that kind of an offer," he said, bending to nuzzle her neck. "Am I too heavy for you?" He lifted onto his forearms and rose over her a bit.

"Never. At least not for now. Ask me again in three months or so."

"Now, that's a woman for you," he muttered. "Three answers to the same question." And then he stilled her sputter with the movement of his lips against hers, the nestling of his manhood against her belly and the touch of two hands that held her face, cradling her tenderly between his palms.

"Let me love you, sweetheart," he whispered. His mouth was gentle, then possessive, as her hands clutched the muscles of his back, and her legs drew up to clasp his hips. He groaned softly, adjusting his position, rocking against her. "Are your breasts touchy?" he asked, lifting to look down at the swollen mounds he yearned to caress.

"I like it when you touch them," she whispered.

"Me, too," he muttered, shifting lower in the bed, his cheek brushing against her bosom. He turned his head, catching the dark crest in his lips and nuzzled it, murmuring beneath his breath. Her indrawn breath alerted him and he halted.

"Feels good," she told him, the words breathed against his head.

"Well, by all means, sweetheart, I want to make you feel good," he told her, his lips capturing the scrap of flesh once more, suckling it gently, feeling the hard, pebbled surface draw against his tongue.

She lifted her hips against him and he looked up, frowning. "Now, don't start that, lady. I'm going to be busy here for a good long time, and then I'm going to see what else you've got under this sheet that I need to tend to."

"Shay?" Her voice was plaintive, her hands moving to clasp his hips, her fingers digging into the firm muscles of his backside. With an urgency she could not hide, she tugged him closer. "We can mess around later on. I need you right now."

"Later on?" He lifted over her, his manhood throbbing with renewed life at her words. "More than once? I won't hurt you? It'll be all right?"

"We need to make up for lost time. And I'm tough, Shay. I'm pregnant, not sick. You can't hurt me."

He found her with searching, seeking fingers, recognizing her readiness, and with a smooth, easy movement, slid into paradise.

Early morning found LeRoy behind the barn, leaning on the pasture fence. Shay sought him out there, lifting one foot to the bottom rail and clearing his throat. "You still angry with me?" he asked abruptly, wishing there were some easy way to mend these particular fences.

"Nope, I guess not. That'd be like holding a grudge against myself," LeRoy said, rubbing the nose of a black mare that approached with a toss of her head.

"How's that?" Shay asked. His hand itched to touch the sassy mare, but he refrained, willing LeRoy to continue.

The older man glanced at him, and his mouth quirked in a sad smile. "I used to look at you when you were comin' up, and wish I could protect you from the pain life deals out. Now, Roan was different," he said slowly. "He didn't let things eat away at him. When he didn't like the way we did things here, he just up and rode away. And when he came back, he recognized that we all do the best we can."

"You make it sound easy, Pa," Shay said. "It's not that simple for me."

"I figured that. You never could accept the changes, could you?" LeRoy asked. "When you came home, you were so filled with pain, it stuck out all over you." He offered his palm to another mare, the two horses jostling for position.

"I knew things would never be the same again. I was changed, our whole way of life was turned upside down, and I just didn't fit here anymore."

"I guess I understood that. I hurt for your mother, mostly, that you walked away, just when we thought you'd come home to stay."

"It won't do any good to say I'm sorry, Pa. You were better off without me then. I wasn't fit company."

LeRoy nodded. "Like I said. We all do what we have to, boy. At least you've come back. We've never heard from Yvonne. When Roan showed up, it solved a lot of our problems. Gave your mother hope for the future."

Shay took a carrot from his pocket, placing it on his palm. The fickle bay nosed it politely and accepted the offering. "You got these animals spoiled rotten," he said with a chuckle.

"These two are Katherine's," LeRoy told him. "They're both breedin', from Roan's stud. The black's Kate's favorite. She gave me the first foal the mare dropped."

"Would y'all be open to selling a couple of yearlings, come spring?"

"You can ask Kate. You comin' back?" LeRoy asked, his gaze fixed on the horses.

"Am I invited?" Shay held his breath.

"You're our son. I guess that oughta answer your question." His voice was gruff, and Shay gritted his teeth against the tears that threatened.

"I'll be back," Shay said. "Soon as Jenny has the baby, we'll make a trip here."

"That'll make your mother happy," LeRoy said, glancing to meet Shay's gaze. "Me, too, as a matter of fact."

Tears fell and hugs were exchanged among the women, while the men clasped hands in the accepted male bonding ritual. And then Letitia turned to Shay and held him in a tight embrace, whispering words of affection in his ear. He climbed blindly into the buggy where Jenny held Marshall close to her side. If his vision was blurred, no one paid attention, for the watching eyes were filled with tears of their own as the vehicle rolled from River Bend.

"Will we come back?" Jenny asked after long moments had passed.

"How about after you have the baby?" Shay's gaze focused on the horizon, his words curt. Knowing his dignity was at stake, she only nodded and patted his knee, not at all surprised when he clutched at her hand and drew it to his mouth. His lips were damp, his kiss tender, and she clasped his fingers tightly.

"I like havin' a grandma and grandpa," Marshall announced, leaning heavily on Jenny's arm. His yawn was wide and Shay glanced at him.

"You're about worn-out, son. That dog led you around like a monkey on a string, didn't he?"

"I wish I had a dog like Jeremy does, Papa." Marshall's

small voice was wistful. "He was lotsa fun, and he likes to sleep by Jeremy and me when we're playin' on the porch."

"We'll see about it," Shay told him.

Marshall sighed blissfully, settling his head on Jenny's lap, his eyes closing.

"A dog?" Jenny asked softly. "Where would we get one?"

"Your father had a litter of pups in the back of the barn when we were there," Shay told her. "Why don't we stop by and take a look. It's been months, but he may still have one left. We can ask anyway."

"Is it much out of the way?"

He shook his head. "Not far. Just a short jog south, then due west."

The short jog south took them into farm country, with no nearby towns to spend the night. Shay stopped at a farm, where the barn was larger than the house, and inquired about renting a place to sleep. The farmer took scrip, and gladly, Shay thought. His wife provided quilts, and the hay-loft offered a cushion for their comfort. Jenny decided one night of such primitive facilities was enough for her as they started out the next morning.

"I'm still picking hay from my hair," she complained, scratching the back of her neck. "If it had been my house, I'd have offered a spare bedroom."

"You didn't want to sleep in their house," Shay said with a grin. "I wouldn't have accepted the offer of breakfast, except I figured we were beyond hungry, and hot food might be welcome. The stuff Susanna sent along will have to do for dinner, I think."

Jenny looked at him, her curiosity alive. "Do I want to know what the house was like inside?" she asked finally.

He shook his head. "The barn was the best choice, sweetheart. Trust me on this."

The morning was long, and the basket of food beneath

the seat was empty of cheese and bread by the time they approached the familiar lane leading to Jonah Harrison's place.

Marshall bounced on the seat. "Is this where my other new grandpa lives?" he asked. "The one who has puppies?"

"I thought he was asleep," Shay murmured, and Jenny shrugged her shoulders.

"You'd better hope he's still got one of them left."

Jonah stood in front of the barn as the buggy wheeled into the yard, and lifted a hand to shade his eyes. "Is that you, Jenny?" he called. "Is that fella treatin' you right?" he asked, peering up at her face as Shay drew the vehicle within a few feet of the older man.

"I'm happy, Papa. Shay's good to me," she said joyously, pleased at being recognized. "I brought someone to meet you."

Marshall scooted back in the seat, suddenly shy as he became the center of attention. Jonah leaned to look past Jenny, his bushy brows lowering as he surveyed his grandson for the first time. "Looks like a Harrison to me," he said gruffly. "Puts me in mind of myself when I was about his size."

Marshall looked closer at his grandfather and his brow furrowed. "Is my hair gonna be white like that?"

"Not for a long time," Jenny assured him, lifting him to her lap. "Do you want to get down and talk to your grandfather?"

Marshall nodded, sliding from the buggy. Jonah reached to grasp Marshall's hand and it was swallowed up by the bent, gnarled fingers. "I got some half-grown dogs runnin' around out back of the barn. I'll bet you'd like to look at them, wouldn't you?"

"That answered that question," Shay said under his breath.

"You got more than one dog?" Marshall asked, eyes wide in wonder.

"You want one?" Jonah offered. "There's a couple of them goin' beggin'. Crowder's the daddy, and the mother's a stray that stuck around. One of the litter belongs to Henry, but the other two need some young fella to take care of them."

"*Two* dogs?" Jenny asked, watching as Marshall skipped beside his grandfather around the corner of the barn.

"Better than none at all." Shay stepped down from the buggy and held his hands up for Jenny. She gripped his shoulders and he lifted her, snatching a kiss as she stood before him. "I'm going to ask him to come home with us," he said quietly. "The winter will be hard on him, Jen. It'll be cold enough to light a fire some days, and he needs someone to look out for him. What do you think?"

"I'll love you forever, Shay, if you can talk him into it. We can probably get enough furniture from here to take along, and I'll bet Henry and Clay would drive him in the wagon—"

"Whoa! Back up a little there, ma'am." Shay's arms circled her waist and drew her against him. "If I *don't* talk him into it, you're not gonna love me forever? Is that the way it goes?"

She shook her head impatiently. "No, silly man. You know better than that. I'll just make it worth your while if you're very persuasive." And then she blushed, her cheeks flaming as she spoke the provocative challenge.

"Damn. An offer I can't turn down," Shay said with a hoot of laughter. "That's a promise if I ever heard one." His mouth formed against hers and his words were a seductive whisper against her lips.

"Just watch me, Jenny Devereaux. For you, I can talk the birds out of the trees."

Epilogue

March, 1870

The sign hung between two posts, white sentinels gracing the end of the long drive. Shay had made it from a piece of oak, burning the letters deep, then sanding it smooth before he varnished the finish to a rich burnished hue. They'd thought long and hard about a new name for the place, Shay being agreeable to keeping the old, but Jenny determined to make a beginning that would include the whole family.

So it became The Oaks. On this spring morning Shay and Noah worked at the momentous task of putting up the sign at the end of the avenue, with Jonah looking on. Posts finally in place, they lifted the board, then stepped back to view their work, all of them recognizing the unspoken bond forged through the past months. "This deserves a celebration," Jonah said. "It's kinda like a christening."

The sound of a bell echoed through the trees, clanging in a continuous rhythm, and Shay looked toward the house. "Something's going on," he said, bending to pick up the tools. "We'd better hightail it back to the house and see who's pulling the bejabbers out of that rope."

"You don't suppose…" Jonah's eyes lit with excitement. "Maybe Jenny's taken to her bed."

"Isabelle's there," Noah said placidly. "She'll tend to things till we get there. Ain't no place for a man anyway."

"Well, they'd better wait for me," Shay said firmly, climbing into the wagon. "If y'all want a ride, you'd better get on." He offered a hand to Jonah, hauling him onto the seat, and listened to Noah's chuckles as he eased his way onto the wagon bed.

"Don't you worry, Mr. Shay, it takes a good long time to birth a baby. You'll probably still be walkin' the hallway when the sun goes down."

"Do you suppose she'll have a girl?" Jonah mused. "Maybe she'll name her after her mother. *Mattie*. Wouldn't that be grand?"

"Katherine's hoping we'll have a girl," Shay said. "She wants her daughter to have a cousin to play with." Shay cracked the reins over the backs of the mules and the wagon rolled into motion.

Birth was at the forefront of his mind, with new life appearing on every hand. He'd helped deliver two litters of piglets, and a calf, and watched as four kittens made their appearance in the past month. Even the chickens were producing, with three hens sheltering chicks beneath their wings in the broody house. Zora's babe had made an appearance before Christmas, a son for Caleb.

The new mare was ready to foal any day now, and before long they'd be making a trip to River Bend to pick up two yearlings from Katherine's stock. Not to mention showing off the new grandchild. And at that thought, Shay felt a surge of impatience. Pulling the wagon to a stop by the back door, he jumped from the seat.

"Take this on out to the barn, Jonah," he said, his long strides carrying him onto the porch and through the door.

Isabelle stood by the stove, the big teakettle steaming in front of her, towels draped over her arm.

"About time you showed up," she said shortly, lifting the kettle and turning toward the doorway. "We're havin' us a baby right quick, and you don't want to miss all the fun." She looked at him sternly. "Miss Jenny wants you with her, and you gotta promise not to cause me any trouble."

He washed quickly, anxious to be with Jenny. Surely bearing a child was the hardest task a woman could be called upon to face. And now he would stand by her side, able only to watch and wait. It might well be the most difficult position he'd ever experience, he thought, crossing the hallway to the bedroom door.

He turned the doorknob.

The March winds brought the scent of roses, and Jenny inhaled deeply of the aroma, recalling the day, almost a year ago, when Shay had put the trellises in place on either side of her bedroom window. Shay...this was his doing, she thought, gritting her teeth. They'd rung the bell for him. Surely he'd be on his way.

Sweat beaded her brow as she allowed the pain to take her again. It had begun, as with Marshall's birth, across her back, then swept to clench beneath her belly. But this time with unexpected speed, and ferocious intensity.

"Won't be long now, Jen." Isabelle scrubbed in a basin near the door, finally satisfied that bed and bedding, and especially Jenny herself, were as clean as soap and warm water could make them. "You've got this thing down pat."

"Shay?" He stood in the doorway and she closed her eyes. "Come hold my hand." The words erupted on the heels of a groan, and Shay crossed the room to kneel beside the bed. His hands gripped hers, and he bent his head to brush his cheek against her hair. "You don't have to stay if you don't want to," she told him. "I can do this."

Her hands clutched at him and her nails dug into his skin. "Hang on, baby," he crooned, easing to sit on the edge of the bed and holding her firmly. "You didn't tell me when I went to hang the sign that you were gonna do this today."

"She didn't know it herself till about half an hour ago," Isabelle told him. She reached to strip off the top sheet, her hands efficient as she slid towels beneath Jenny's body. "You better get behind her, Mr. Shay. You made it just about in time. That red-headed child is gonna be born before you know it."

Shay moved quickly, climbing on the bed, and Jenny leaned back against his chest, gasping for breath as the pain abated, then cried aloud as it returned with renewed force.

"Push that young'un right into my hands, girl." Isabelle leaned forward, her fingers probing, stretching and easing the way. "Don't waste your breath complainin', Jen. Just get to it and give me my baby."

The pain engulfed her, wrapped her in tentacles of agony and, for the first time, brought tears to her eyes. Jenny bent her head, bearing down against its fury, her hands wrapped now in the ropes Isabelle had tied to the bedposts, as she fought a silent fight for the end to this struggle. Her head tilted back against Shay's shoulder and her teeth clenched tightly as the muscles she bid to obey brought forth her child.

Isabelle lifted the infant high, its lifeline still intact and pulsing, and her cry was joyous. "You got you a girl, honey. Prettiest hair I ever seen on a baby." Her laughter rang out and Jenny smiled, the pain almost forgotten as Isabelle turned the tiny form to be inspected. The delicately formed lips opened and a piercing shriek erupted, bringing a shout of laughter from Shay.

"Damn, that girl can holler," he said.

"You won't be half so thrilled about her carryin' on when she gets goin' in the middle of the night," Isabelle promised him, grinning widely. "Come hold your baby, Mr. Shay, whilst I cut the cord."

He slid from behind Jenny, propping her with two pillows, and delivering a quick kiss against her cheek, then grasped his daughter, holding her firmly while Isabelle busied herself with string and scissors.

Then with a clean, warm cloth, she wiped the small face and head, laughing as the tiny mouth opened eagerly to suckle her finger. Tossing a square of flannel across Jenny's stomach, she nodded at Shay. "Wrap her up good and give her to her mama. They need to get acquainted."

His hands were clumsy, but wrap her he did, and Jenny watched through tears of happiness as he nestled their child in her arms. She grinned at him, tired but triumphant. "We'll have a boy for you the next time, Shay."

He was thunderstruck, his amazement obvious. "You'd willingly go through this again? I was afraid you might be mad at me forever for making you suffer so."

"It wasn't that bad," she said, her hand gentle against the cap of flaming curls. "She's really going to have red hair, isn't she?"

"What do you mean? Not that bad?" Shay pulled the sheet up to cover her, then sat down on the edge of the bed. "I was here, Jen." His big hand reached toward the baby, and miniature fingers curled around his thumb.

"She's strong," he whispered. "Look at how pretty she is."

And indeed, she was, with slate-blue eyes that promised to darken over time. Her mouth formed a tiny O, and she turned to nuzzle against Jenny's breast. Easing her gown aside, Jenny offered sustenance and the rosy mouth sought its source. "Her eyes will be like yours, Shay."

"She looks like you, though. What shall we name her?"

"Do you mind if we call her Mattie, for my mother? I think Papa would like that." Tears threatened as she spoke and she swallowed the lump that formed in her throat.

"Just watch. Jonah will never want to leave," he told her. "He was pretty well settled in already. And this will cinch it, honey."

"Do you mind?" Her fingers cupped the tiny head, and she bent to inhale the scent of newborn flesh. Then she looked up as Shay shook his head.

He bent to press his lips against her cheek, and his whisper was low, meant for her ears alone. "I knew I'd never be able to resist you, sweetheart. Not from the first minute I saw you."

"Really?" she searched his face, leaning wearily back against the pillows. "I've wondered sometimes if I didn't..." She hesitated, biting at her lip. "I seduced you, Shay. I wanted you to marry me, and I..."

"Yeah." His smile drew at the scar he wore, and he grinned uncaringly. "You did, at that. I'd never been seduced before. I kinda like it." Passion blazed from dark eyes as he bent to kiss her. "Matter of fact, I can hardly wait to give you another chance at it."

Isabelle picked up a bundle of bedding from the floor and chuckled, opening the door. "I told you a long time ago to watch out for that man, Jen. He'll keep you hoppin'."

"Mama?" Marshall stood outside the doorway, clutching his grandfather's hand.

"Come on in, son," Shay told him, "and bring your grandpa with you. Tell him Mattie's here."

* * * * *

*Please turn the page
for an introduction to James Kincaid,
Carolyn's swaggering, gambling,
utterly irresistible hero
from her short story,
THE GAMBLE.*

THE GAMBLE is part of the

**MONTANA MAVERICKS:
BIG SKY GROOMS**

*historical collection, on sale August 2001,
which also features beloved authors
Susan Mallery and Bronwyn Williams.
Don't miss this rare opportunity
to discover how the famous Kincaids began!*

Chapter One

The man behind the bar poured a shot of whiskey into the glass, then spun it across the slick, wooden surface toward his customer. "It's still morning," he said, with a measuring look at the man who eyed the amber liquid.

"It's never too early in the day for some things." James lifted his drink, twisting his lips in a sardonic grin. His gaze swept the interior of the dusty saloon, lingering for just a moment on a red-haired woman with a satin dress stretched over her voluptuous form. Not what he had in mind, he decided easily. His head tilted back as the whiskey slid easily down his throat, and he winced at the impact of it on his empty stomach.

"Hair of the dog, Kincaid?" the barkeep asked with sympathy and amusement. His bushy eyebrows lifted as James thumped the heavy glass on the bar.

"One more should do it," James said, his blue eyes narrowing as he focused on the four men slouched around a table at the far side of the room. "That game been going on long?" he asked in an undertone.

"All night," the barkeep told him. "They just keep movin' those little piles of money back and forth between them. I've been waitin' for one or the other to go to sleep over there.''

James lifted his glass and sniffed at its contents, then replaced it on the bar. ''Maybe I need to help them out, sorta relieve them of their *dilemma*.'' His voice slurred on the word, the only sign of inebriation he allowed to blur his image. The mirror behind the bar reflected his likeness and he cocked his hat at a jauntier angle, bending forward to peer into his own blue eyes, straightening his string tie with a hand that barely trembled.

''Why don't you walk up them stairs and take a nap, Kincaid?'' the barkeep asked mildly. ''There's an empty room at the end of the hall. You look like you've had a long night.''

James grinned, knowing that his smile was his best friend. He'd coaxed more than one woman into his arms with its seductive gleam, hoodwinked more poker players than he could count with an innocent flash of teeth and curving lips. ''Naw, I'll just amble over and clear that table for the gents. Give them a chance to fold their cards in an honorable manner.'' He spoke concisely, each word slowly formed and enunciated.

A commotion outside caught his attention, and he turned from the bar and looked askance at the swinging doors, then back at the poker game. Boots thumped on the wide wooden walk, and skirts swished as women hurried past. A shout from farther down the street warned of danger, and then the sound of jangling harnesses and shrieking horses penetrated his whiskey-soaked mind.

''Sounds like trouble,'' the barkeep said, pulling his gun from beneath the bar. He held it at his side, his gaze fastened on the swinging doors.

''I'd say so,'' James said flatly, his stance altered as if by magic. The grin was gone, the eyes alert beneath the wide brim of his hat. He stalked to the entrance and looked over the top of the double doors, then eased one of them open. The sidewalk was clear, as if a giant broom had swept it clean of humanity. Except for two men who stood hesitantly in front of the bank across the street.

With red bandanas tied around their faces and saddlebags flung over their shoulders, they sure as hell looked like a couple of fools who'd robbed the damn place. Where their horses had disappeared to was any man's guess, and the pair of them were waving guns in the air and cursing up a blue streak.

The morning stage still vibrating from its sudden stop in front of the hotel next to the bank seemed to offer them the next best exit and, ignoring the rearing horses who'd reacted badly to the gunfire, the men leapt from the sidewalk and ran to the coach, shouting instructions to the hapless driver.

From within the vehicle, a woman's shrill voice called upon heaven to help her, and James felt a twitch at the corner of his mouth, even as his hand lifted the gun from his holster. Fool creature needed to learn that God helps those who have enough sense to run from danger, he thought wryly. Bending low, he left the dubious shelter of the swinging doors and crouched behind the even more uncertain refuge of a four by four post that held up the porch.

The two men glanced quickly at the stage driver who was making a hasty exit, leaping to the ground and then running full tilt toward the hotel doorway. One of the bank robbers climbed atop the stage, the other pulled open the door and dragged the shrieking female from its depths, casting her like a bit of rubbish to the ground.

"Now, that wasn't the least bit polite of you," James said, lifting his gun to take careful aim. The slight tremble in his hand was gone, the barrel shone dully in the morning sunlight and his aim was true. As the stagecoach rumbled into motion, the horses rearing and plunging forward at the command of the second robber, James pulled the trigger. The would-be driver fell to the ground, motionless in the dirt.

The second man turned toward his cohort, then looked frantically across the street, lifting his gun to level its barrel at James.

"Well, damn," James said, firing a second shot.

The bank robber's finger twitched on the trigger as his body jolted. The gun fell to the dusty road, and the man fell in a heap, holding his arm and cursing with a steady stream of cuss words that made James shake his head in disbelief.

From the ground only feet away from the wounded man, a wail of protest erupted, and James looked again at the female who'd made such an inelegant exit from the stagecoach. Her eyes were scrunched up behind wire-rimmed glasses, and her mouth was pursed in a way that gave him pause. She looked about ready to shed a bucket of tears, and if there was anything in this world James could not endure, it was a crying female.

He left the shelter of the post, jamming his gun back where it belonged, and strode across the street. She didn't look much better up close, he decided, all dusty and teary-eyed, her skirts hiked up above her knees.

Her knees. His glance swept the length of her legs and returned swiftly to those pink, rounded, dimpled knees. Beneath them, garters held plain, lisle stockings in place, and he allowed a swift appraisal to bathe his aching eyes with pleasure. Damn, she did have a fine pair of legs. Calves rounded and curvaceous, just right for a man's palm, he decided judiciously. And slim little ankles that barely showed above the tops of half-boots.

But those knees. He shook his head. A man could examine those pretty little legs for half a night, and still find something to look at....

CAROLYN DAVIDSON

Reading, writing and research: Carolyn Davidson's life in three simple words. At least, that area of her life having to do with her career as a Harlequin Historical author. The rest of her time is divided among husband, family and travel—her husband, of course, holding top priority in her busy schedule. Then there is their church and the church choir in which they participate. Their sons, daughter and assorted spouses are spread across the eastern half of the country, along with numerous grandchildren.

Last, but certainly not least, is the group of women who share Carolyn's love of writing—the Lowcountry Romance Writers of America. She is a charter member, and holds her fellow members, due to their encouragement, partly responsible for whatever success she has achieved in the pursuit of her career.

The Seduction of Shay Devereaux is her twelfth book for Harlequin Historical, the sequel to her January 2001 release, *Maggie's Beau*. Carolyn welcomes mail at her post office box: P.O. Box 2757, Goose Creek, SC 29445.

HHIBC556